WILLIAM PALMER

THE GOOD
REPUBLIC

Minerva

A Minerva Paperback
THE GOOD REPUBLIC

First published in Great Britain 1990
by Martin Secker & Warburg Limited
This Minerva edition published 1991
by Mandarin Paperbacks
Michelin House, 81 Fulham Road, London SW3 6RB

Minerva is an imprint of the Octopus Publishing Group,
a division of Reed International Books Limited

Copyright © William Palmer 1990

Acknowledgement is made to following for permission
to reproduce extracts from copyright material:
Penguin Books Ltd for 'The Hour' from *Selected Poems :
Vladimir Holan*, translated by Jarmila and Ian Milner,
copyright © Vladimir Holan, 1971, translation
copyright © Jarmila and Ian Milner, 1971;
and for *The Republic* by Plato, translated by Desmond Lee,
copyright © H.D.P. Lee, 1955, 1974. Faber and Faber Ltd
for 'Sonnets from China, X' by W.H. Auden, from
Collected Poems by W.H. Auden. The Peters Fraser & Dunlop
Group Ltd for *Black Lamb and Grey Falcon* by Rebecca West.

A CIP catalogue record for this title
is available from the British Library
ISBN 0 7493 9117 0

The Random House Group Limited supports The Forest Stewardship
Council® (FSC®), the leading international forest-certification organisation.
Our books carrying the FSC label are printed on FSC®-certified paper.
FSC is the only forest-certification scheme supported by the leading
environmental organisations, including Greenpeace. Our
paper procurement policy can be found at
www.randomhouse.co.uk/environment

MIX
Paper from
responsible sources
FSC® C016897

Printed and bound in Great Britain by Clays Ltd, St Ives PLC

I

So an age ended, and its last deliverer died
In bed, grown idle and unhappy; they were safe:
The sudden shadow of a giant's enormous calf
Would fall no more at dusk across their lawns outside.

W. H. Auden, *Sonnets From China*

envelope glowed white, furry-edged, promising, or threatening, something.

3

The work room had been divided precisely into two halves.

Ella held the other end of the tape measure when he first demarcated their zones. Twelve feet – what the hell was that? He worked it out in metres from a pocket diary, marking the half-way point on the newly painted wall. On either side of the mark two quite different rooms had grown.

He gained the window, pleading his poor eyesight, giving in lieu an extra alcove in his part of the wall. Now, standing in the doorway he looked with irritation at her side of the big north-facing room.

The bookcases went up to the ceiling, giving to that already gloomy end a hemmed-in, claustrophobic air. Her roll-top desk was quite unclosable, with papers and books heaped on top and wedged into every slot and compartment. On the floor magazines and journals were piled in chronologically mouldering stacks: the fossil remains of the Fifties; the Sixties yellow and tatty beneath the slightly ragged, dull Seventies; the still bright Eighties. It was just possible to get to the desk by following a narrow maze.

In contrast to her clutter, his part of the room was severe. There were only two long shelves, running from side wall to window. Leather-bound Minute Books marched along the top shelf; each one bore a gilt-stamped year: 1945, 1946, 1947 . . . all the way to 1979. Thirty-five years of arguments, motions, decisions. Feuds. Excommunications. Trials in absentia. Copies of letters to Kings, Presidents, Prime Ministers. To Embassies. Newspapers. Their briefer replies. These records, made by Jacob as Secretary to the Congress of Exiles of his homeland, recorded from time to time hope revived. Berlin. Hungary. Prague . . . And now there was the new reform and nationalist movement springing up back home. Not that that could mean anything to those whose words were recorded here. They were all dead now, or decrepit. From being their secretary he had become their curator; this room a mausoleum, the only record of their memories – the inside of each emptied or emptying skull.

On the lower shelf were the files of his book-dealing business; bibliographies; a few fat volumes of auction records. Most of his correspondence was done from home – he visited the shop most days but left the running of it to Miss Vacik. Miss Vacik had been chosen for her knowledge of Slavonic languages. He had picked her after his experiences with several younger and more attractive women assistants. Sooner or later, he had fallen in love with all of them. The affairs, where not inconclusive, had sometimes proved rather humiliating. He was sure that Ella suspected at least one of them. The last had been, what – five, six years ago? There was no danger of anything like that with Miss Vacik.

The room was cold. Outside, the sky was grey. In the gardens the few, thinly leaved trees swayed restlessly. He took out his cigarettes and counted how many were left in the packet. The first of the day. He looked at the white envelope on his desk. He had delayed as long as he could, but still hesitated.

The postmark was of the capital of a country that no longer existed; the Soviets had subsumed the little republic into their empire in 1944. The Russian stamp was a bland recurring insult. He turned the envelope in his long thin hands. It had been opened and then resealed. The new openness? Name and address typed on a good machine; the envelope surprisingly fresh and of good quality. But – it came from a land of ghosts, and he was afraid of any claims, long delayed, that might come from them. He opened the letter.

The cigarette had made him lightheaded. At first he could not concentrate. What was this? The Committee for Patriotic Democracy. A properly printed letterhead, with an address in the national capital and a telephone number. Had things moved this far? It seemed barely credible.

The letter greeted him by name. Its writer – Velta Ruksans,

he glanced at the signature – said that the name Balthus was still green in their country:

> . . . your father's martyrdom shines as a beacon to our hopes . . .

It praised his own work for the Congress of Exiles. It seemed, said the letter, that at last an end might be in sight. A new beginning. A new age. A conference was to be held in the capital to form a new national consensus. To press for freedom and an autonomy, which, however limited at first, would lead inevitably to the full restitution of their democracy as, once again, an independent state. By your presence . . . your name . . . your father's example . . .

They invited him to return. The Russians had given their blessing and safe passage in and out of the country to all invited exiles. Generous funds have been allocated from our friends overseas in America and Britain. Obviously the writer could not discuss all the details of travel and accommodation – but the conference was only a month away, at Easter. So his early answer was most urgently required. His UK contact was Miss Julia Wallace. Her telephone number and address in London were given. If he could contact her as soon as possible . . .

He could go back. His hands shook. Of course there were dangers. Of course. But, tremendous . . . incredible . . . he was young once again. The dreadful things . . . well, they had all shared in them. Long years had at last dragged themselves to some sort of hope.

'Ella! Ella!' he shouted. 'Come up. Come up here.'

'What is it?' The muffled voice was irritable.

'Please. Now.'

He sat, waiting for her, remembering with aching fondness the large, thickly furnished rooms of childhood; the smaller ones, lit by love and friendship; the bitter wanderings . . .

Ella, grumbling, mounted the stairs. She loomed in the doorway.

'What, your legs have gone?' She looked round the room as she always did when he was in here, as if expecting to find someone else with him. They never worked in here at the same time.

9

'News . . . news from my country.' He stood up and held the letter out.

She came laboriously across the room and took it, holding it at arm's length. 'This type is too small without my glasses.' She waved the letter, a white flag in the dim room. 'What does it say?'

Proudly he read it through, pausing over and repeating the mention of his father. 'You remember that? You remember him, Ella? Such a man!'

'You are going?' she asked.

To his disappointment, she did not seem as surprised or excited as he had expected. Well, well, it was not her country, but . . .

'I don't know,' he said, thrown into indecision by her dull response. Then he revived. 'Yes, I think so. Yes.'

'Is it safe?'

'Safe? Again, I don't know – but the letter says so. These people have had to live with it. They should know. Why shouldn't it be? Things have changed. What *could* they do? My father . . . People go to and fro nowadays. And to Poland. You should go back too, Ella. Friends, family – you are not even a political like me. You would have nothing to worry about.'

'No,' she said.

But he hardly noticed. 'Perhaps it's as Campion says,' he said. 'Our dreams *do* presage the future. Nonsense of course, but last night I dreamed of the old days again. You know – me, you . . .'

'And the others,' she said. 'But they've all gone, haven't they?'

'Yes – and here is a chance to do something. For their memory. Something real – after all this.' His gesturing hand dismissed his life's work on the shelves above. '*Real* work.'

'This Wallace woman – you are going to ring her?'

'I shall ring her from the shop.'

'You're going in this morning?'

'Yes. There'll be things to arrange before the trip. And you – your affairs, you must put them in order too.'

'You want me to come?'

'Of course Ella. Of course.' He looked again at the letter. 'Yes. Yes. I'll ring from the shop.' He stuck the letter in his pocket. 'It will be more secure.' He lived already in a world of action and decision. 'I'll go now,' he said, looking at her again.

'Don't forget your overcoat then. It's cold out.'

'Oh, Ella.' He laughed. 'You women. You'd wrap the world up if you could. And of course you must come – you've worked so hard for us too.'

4

Outside the window large drops of rain had begun to fall, like a doleful syrup. Ella could not go to her desk yet. She acknowledged – still – that the house was hers to look after, to clean, to keep as a nest for Balthus to come home to. The fact that the work was mindless and demeaning sometimes must be accepted. As must the fact that Balthus's work in the 'Congress' had been pointless, almost manically redundant. He was one of those who have spent their lives refusing the evidence this century offers them; believing they live their lives by an effort of their will – not that the world twists and grinds them into its shapes. But she could not renounce her part in the farce. Life was not like that, not at the little level where they inhabited these rooms, ate this food, received letters . . .

'Women are the niggers of the white world.' Who said that? She repeated it to herself. She saw its truth. By any reckoning she was cleverer than Balthus. She could easily out-argue Balthus. She was even physically stronger than Balthus. Years ago, she could hug him in bed until the wind came out of him in a gasp and he would not dare, for his own pride, to complain. But he had that fat little wand between his legs and whiskers thicker than hers; he could be made to suffer and she must comfort him. She wanted him to be happy. Above all, she knew, that is the difference; women want men to be happy; men want their women to be as unhappy as they are. She headed towards the cupboard under the stairs where the vacuum cleaner was kept.

For Balthus and she were tied; by whatever ties everything together in a seamless whole: wars, death, love; interesting times. The Chinese say it as a curse: 'May you live in interesting times.' After two thousand years the fall of Jerusalem becomes a dry series of words in a fat, thin-papered, many-paged book; the screams of the dying, at first unbearable, are thinned by time to a set of dreary statistics. The same would happen to the fall of the Warsaw Ghetto. Even now people look on that famous picture of the little boy with his arms raised in surrender, the German soldier behind him leering at the future – they look at that with an eye to its composition as a work of art . . . How powerful . . . Such compassion . . . The image would not work in colour . . . Number 93 in your catalogue. The progression is from pain, to aesthetic, to statistic.

The lopped triangle of the stairs door stood open. Ella dragged out the huge cylinder of the ancient vacuum cleaner. She screwed on its wrinkled grey elephant's trunk and unspooled the lead to the plug.

The work obliterated thought. It was only when she had finished the hall, dining-room and front room and sat down for coffee and a cigarette that she permitted herself to think of Balthus again.

He had worked for years for that bunch of émigré romantics. What had he thought he was up to? And she had helped, hiding her scorn. Hiding other things . . . This was typical of them. He had had a right to a pension after serving them for so many years. Somehow though the last of their gold had gone with Moldau, the Finance Minister, when he died. *Finance Minister* – for God's sake. He had, Balthus told her, confessed to rash speculations, to trusting a compatriot whom he refused to name. They visited him in hospital. He wheezed, yellow and thin, hardly raising the blankets of his bed, telling a wandering, confused story of treachery and theft by comrades who should have been trustworthy but were rampantly not. 'Thieves, thieves,' muttered Moldau, dying.

It was her money, saved, that set Balthus up in his

12

bookselling business. He made a living of a sort. They had their state pensions, and a little from Ella's translations.

They rubbed along.

She had her faith. He had his remote, absurd, dreams. With all that had happened to them, she had thought that they had a few comfortable years ahead, at least. Then she and Balthus would be dead and no one would ever know . . .

'Pishhh . . .' She leaned over the table and turned on the radio to drown her thoughts.

'. . . evidence of a cause. But this is certainly no excuse for taking to the streets. For riot. Damage to property. This is not a symptom, ah, a consequence even of some imagined cause, such as unemployment – which I may say is declining at an unprecedented rate. Rather, I would strongly suggest, it is, once again, one of the fruits of the decline in personal morality, in family discipline, in educational standards that we have suffered since the 1960s and perhaps before . . .'

'Yes, but the Minister . . .' A thin, rather whiny voice, like a fly trapped in the ear, broke in. The previous, plump voice listened to the mad insect's protests before cutting smoothly back in.

'I take Mr Broccoli's point. But I would ask him to consider . . .'

She switched them off. This nonsense went on for hours. The voice of the people. God, and what people these English were! Supine, craven, docile, greedy, uncultured . . . She extinguished her cigarette with a savage twist.

He had gone out bearing his letter so proudly.

Perhaps she should have shown more surprise. Pleasure? But the letter had not been a shock. Not after the telephone call. When she had stood in the hallway, whispering because Balthus was upstairs – whispering, 'No, no – I cannot get involved. Not now. I'm sorry. What is it you want? No, I'm sorry.' She had put the telephone down on the voice.

But she knew it would ring again.

5

In the packed, dizzying streets the taxi seemed to start and stop again every few seconds. Pedestrians, dreamy, floating, wild-eyed, feinted bullfighter fashion away from the car that spurted on towards them from its last obstacle. The city seemed too huge, too richly stuffed for the figures scurrying in it. Balthus had taken the taxi as a luxury after his news. It turned into the wide clinical boulevard of Euston Road. Used to being borne underground to Leicester Square tube station, nose buried in a book, it was a shock to see the changes being made in the city. It was as if some great, heterogeneous monster was raising itself up, trampling its bed beneath it. The blocks along here seemed to be forever in the process of being torn down and rebuilt. Enormous cranes beaked the sky. A tower of bronze glass reflected a warped quilt of the March sky. Another, solid stone, like the wall of a medieval castle, was pierced with the long narrow slits of black windows. A hoarding announced the coming of satellite television. On another, a mad-eyed Prime Minister attempted to smile.

He slumped back in the seat, watching the legs of the girls on the wide pavements; the back of the driver's neck – his head covered with a thick grey helmet of hair; a single thin gold ear-ring; a copy of *The Sun* wedged against the windscreen.

'Just up here, squire?'

'Thank you. That will do perfectly.'

He had asked the man to halt a little short of the clump of bookshops in Charing Cross Road. It would not do at all for other dealers to see him descending from a taxi. Their prices to him would rise just that little more. The world of second-hand book dealing is characterized by an air of ostentatious indigence. As if to say, you see my poor premises, my ten-year-old suit – I don't do this for the money, good God, no . . .

He walked on, past their dingy windows, into Cecil Court.

An Egyptian eye was painted in the centre of the name board above the window of the Psyclops Bookshop. A small plate at the side of the door announced 'J. Balthus – Slavonica, Bought and Sold – Upstairs'.

He could not afford to take a whole shop so he rented the room above John Campion's Psyclops shop. The two together were an odd match – but then incongruity is another mark of the trade.

Not that Campion did not complement his stock in every way. A white door blind advertised the shop's specialities. Alchemy, Astrology, Atlantis – a reversed swastika – then, Cabbala, I-Ching – another swastika – Magic, Mystery, Myths – and then a huddled rag-bag in small letters, Lost Tribes of Israel, Numerology, Palmistry, Supernatural, Tarot, UFOs, Witchcraft. Anything Occult!!! Inside, the shop could have done with being two or three times bigger. The shelves along the walls and between the walls had been squeezed so that you had to sidle between them. At the back of the shop was what looked like an old telephone kiosk. This was Campion's office and behind the glass his enormous head, bald on top, grey-red bearded, was bent forward, reading in an appallingly dim light. As the shop door sang, he got slowly up, still reading, turned and emerged.

He was tremendously fat and tall and dressed in a black tent that fell to the floor and dragged along behind him. The tent was embroidered with faded gold crescent moons and silver stars. Jacob wondered how Campion could contain his bulk in that tiny compartment. If it was perhaps a conjurer's illusion. Perhaps a black curtain at the back of the tent gave way and a little man climbed timidly out each night.

'Oh, it's you Mr Balthus,' Campion said disapppointedly. 'I thought it was a customer.'

A tall thin young man squeezed past Balthus and disappeared behind a bank of shelves.

'I'm sorry. No,' said Jacob.

A girl, rustling in shiny brown leather, came in and went down the same way as the young man.

'Excuse me,' Campion whispered to Balthus. He produced

from some inner fold of his robe a long bamboo cane to the end of which was fixed a small mirror. He drew in the robe and glided silently between the shelves. At the end of the first bank he stopped and extended the cane, waggling it slightly to gain a reflected view of the hidden aisles. He considered the view for a moment. The cane disappeared again into his robe and he made his way, waddling sideways, back to Balthus.

'You cannot be too careful,' he whispered. 'I get such a lot of thieves in here. One day – did I tell you? – I surprised a couple indulging in an act of sexual congress. Would you like some tea? I have just put the kettle on.'

Behind the office-kiosk was the greasiest, dirtiest sink in London, as far as Balthus knew. And a rickety little card-table with a kettle and a few assorted cups and mugs, some still harbouring at their bottoms the mouldering solidified remains of Campion's previous offers.

'The tea is camomile today. It is very good for the nerves.'

'Perhaps later,' said Jacob, as pleasantly as possible.

'I will give you a shout then.'

Jacob passed on, leaving Campion hovering anxiously by his shelves, trying to catch a view of his customers. Past the office, the sink, was a short dark corridor from which a wooden staircase led steeply upwards into Balthus's shop. At the top, as his head emerged, Miss Vacik looked down on him from behind her typewriter. It was possible, he thought, that there could be on Earth one member of the male sex whom she did not think of with the utmost contempt – but then she probably had not met him. Still, he paid her hardly anything at all. She was someone for whom work is all – worth even putting up with the likes of Balthus.

'Good morning,' he said with the hearty intensity he used every morning to try to win her over. It worked no better today.

She had sorted the meagre post into three piles: cheques, bills and orders. God knows what she did the rest of the day – but she did take the occasional order over the telephone, and had even been known to sell a book in person to a customer sufficiently hardy to stand her sniffing, disapproving presence behind them as they looked over the shelves. The business brought him a small erratic living, with an occasional coup as a bonus. Ella looked after the accounts.

He looked through the post without much interest. He pushed it aside and took the letter from his pocket again. At first he had been flattered by it, now he wondered if it was a hoax. He would ring this woman, Julia Wallace. But not yet. Not yet. It was Miss Vacik's half day off. Although she never wished to take it, he would insist today, jangle his keys, say that he wanted to lock up. Please Miss Vacik. He would ring when she – eventually – had gone. The past crowded in on him, making work impossible. In his head he began to compose a speech to the conference. A compelling, bitter-sweet homage to the past . . . Though an old man now myself. Wait for denials. There is the future to be faced . . . A long exile . . . Katerina . . . My father. The Island. The forest. He could not. And Katerina. To want someone still, after fifty years – a miracle.

Miracle.

At her desk, Miss Vacik continued to slowly repair, with whatever love drove her, a page in Virobouva's *Memories of the Russian Court*.

6

Ella lit another cigarette. She adjusted the desk lamp to shine on the book that lay beside her ancient Underwood typewriter. The novel was Polish and she had a commission to translate it by the end of the month. She was behind with the work because the novel irritated her more and more as she got into it. Sincere; misguided; mistaken. The revolution was more important than this man's worries about it; about himself. *His* love; *his* mind; *his* class. History would not pardon those who walked away from it – or tried to. Who made themselves

17

a rickety, leaky shelter from its winds, calling it Conscience. Or Love.

She drew on her cigarette, and the smoke flared from her nostrils, ascending to darken a little more the orange-stained ceiling above her desk. Still it must be done. Work. It kept her in touch with the language, if nothing else. The ideas – and of this she was most proud – *they* could not contaminate her.

A pure spark glowed in her, a spark of the sort that can only be sustained after long absence from its parent fire by being blown on continually and carefully. Fostered in the dark, the brand glowed more intensely for being secret. She – and others she did not and would never know – they were the true martyrs. Oh, she slid back every now and then – more than that, Ella, she chided herself – into what she derided as bourgeois sentimentalities. Only the lost comrades had the pure, cold flame in their hearts.

Erich had been one. He had shown her the way. Ella had rage in her heart when she met Erich. He showed her why. When she had been a girl in Warsaw in the Twenties she had always had shoes to wear and fire to warm her and food to eat. Then the whispering began between her parents. Something out in the world came and took away her father's small fortune. He still had the money, the bonds, the great, beautifully engraved share certificates. It was simply that some mad arithmetic rendered them worth less and less day by day. They moved from the house to an apartment, then to a tenement building. She looked down into the well of the courtyard and saw children with no shoes and took off her own and went down and joined them because she thought it was a game. Bread with potato, that was what they ate. In the tenement rooms light died at the windows. In the greyness things began to disappear. Vases, statuettes in porcelain and bronze, of animals and Greek heroes. Watercolours left pale oblong ghosts on the darker wallpaper. She used to love to look into her mother's jewel box. She lifted the lid one day, and – as if by a conjuring trick – stared only at the black lacquer bottom. But they at least had something to sell. Their neighbours . . . the woman dying of starvation on a bed in the flat below, her children standing in the doorway, looking in. Then the food parcels began to arrive from America. Later, when he re-taught her the history of her country, Erich explained those too. They were the *quid pro quo* to reward Pilsudski for driving the Bolsheviks back from Warsaw after the Revolution. Her father had hung up Pilsudski's portrait and toasted it every evening before their meal. And, as a child, she too regarded Pilsudski as a great hero. That was before Erich explained such men to her. Erich could explain everything.

She met him at one of the picnics they had as students and to which they sometimes invited members of the University staff. Erich was a physics lecturer, a German exile – about thirty, she guessed, with a long lean body and wide bony shoulders; he smoked incessantly and fed himself aspirin, transferring the little white tablets from coat-jacket pocket to mouth like a fastidious animal. They made love in his lodgings; but after, when she said, nuzzling against him, 'I love you', he was already in the process of twisting his long back to her and reaching for the packet of cigarettes beside the bed. She told him all about herself and her family. Her father's collapse. The poor people. The poor people, she repeated. How angry she felt at them sometimes. They were picked up, cast down, and were forever puzzled at their predicament. It was as if they were dice in the hand of God.

Sitting hunched forward, arms clasped round his knees, Erich talked quickly but calmly, explaining to her why she felt this way. In what way she was right, more fundamentally how she was wrong. Without knowing the works of Marx, of Engels, of Lenin, of Stalin, it was impossible to make sense out of the situation, other than to indulge in useless bourgeois pity. The Social Democrats, the Socialists, all wished to ameliorate the situation, but their efforts were doomed because the very structures of their organizations, their theories, were underpinned by the system they strove to change. In the end all such people reverted to their most basic class loyalty and proved to be reactionaries.

It was the first time she had heard this word 'bourgeois' delivered with such a vicious sneer – and painful to know that she herself was a member of the class he despised. She devoured the books he gave her. *What Is To Be Done? The Eighteenth Brumaire. The Communist Manifesto* . . . It was as if she had been living all her life in a small shabby warm room, and suddenly the walls dissolved. She saw the world for the first time. She could see through all the walls and how the wretched of the world worked and lived and died. She saw also who lives off the poor – their own well-being directly dependent on the sufferings of others. She saw how the shams of parliaments and religions and reforms are merely velvet masks on faces of iron.

Teaching her, Erich was coolly sarcastic when she displayed any naivety. How she longed though for his approbation when she hit the correct line, offered the only possible interpretation. The only time she saw the almost supernaturally calm Erich angry, angry almost beyond control, was when he came back to their room and found her reading from an anthology of socialist writing she had had from the University library. She started to tell him how deeply moved she was by the writings of the handsome young revolutionary – there was a picture – by his description of his exile, with wife and young family in their little house surrounded by snow while he wrote by lamplight and snowlight. Erich took the book from her. 'Trotsky. You're reading Trotsky!' His face had become distorted by uncontrolled anger. Trotsky was a spy, he said. A traitor. A Social Fascist. He lived in luxury in Mexico in a house given to him by American capitalists. He had betrayed the Revolution. It was unforgivable – he lapsed into German. For one terrible moment she thought he was going to throw her out. But no, it was he who stormed out of the room. The offending book lay on the bed where he had thrown it – Ella was afraid to touch it. The book contained demons that threatened her love for Erich. When he came back he was calm, his annoyance suppressed in the tight downdrag of his mouth. He questioned her on why and how she had got hold of the book. When he was satisfied that she was telling the truth he said she must burn the book and tell the library she had lost it, offering to pay. 'That way there will at least be one less copy in the world.' This was not offered as a joke.

Even at the time of the worst purges in Moscow and Leningrad, he had not shared any of their cell's doubts. When messages from Poland to comrades in the East went unanswered; if news came of Polish friends arrested and disappearing – Erich had answers. The evidence was overwhelming. In a country whose constitution outlawed the death penalty and torture – where else in the world would such traitors be put on *public* trial? And they all confessed. For only the second time she saw him angry. Someone returned from Kiev sardonically told them the '4 a.m.' joke. This was evidently the favourite time for the NKVD to call. In the apartment block the roomers are woken by loud thumps on their doors, the sound of running footsteps. The Ivanovs wait trembling in night attire. In a moment a soft knock on their door. A whisper. They put their ears to the door. 'Don't be afraid, comrades,' says the whisper. 'It's only me, Davidovitch. Just to tell you that the building is on fire.' Erich was not amused.

All through that time together, while Ella dreaded the coming of the war, Erich seemed to glow in anticipation. These were the last days before the Fascists over-reached themselves, he said. History awaited its inevitable outcome. Out of the blue Erich announced that he had been offered a post at the University of Kalnins. 'Kalnins?' Where was Kalnins, for God's sake? In one of the small bourgeois Baltic states, he said. That is not important, he said impatiently. Will you come with me? I want you with me, he had added, turning away.

'Is it a Party thing?' she asked quietly.

'I can't tell you,' he said. Then he was back in control of himself. 'I have asked for you. Permission has been given.'

She would have a job assisting in a news agency in the capital. They would leave immediately. They would join a local cell, but take no part in local politics, nor appear as anything but apolitical professionals. The Party was illegal in that country. She would be mixing among businessmen and politicians and would report back to him whatever was said of any importance. They would not be able to live together. She should cultivate her own friends. He would go on ahead and contact her.

She travelled north with a purpose, looking with contempt on her fellow passengers, on the people in the busy station, on the streets of the smug capital.

She found her room, her job. But when she was contacted, it was not by Erich. He had been summoned 'home', she was

told. She had never seen him again. 'Home' meant Moscow –
a promise and a warning. So Erich had disappeared into the
century – with so many million others.

Once, in Poland, he had lit a match and held it up for the
group to see. They watched as it flared, flamed, dwindled,
bent, and went out. That, said Erich, is the life of an ordinary
man. A spurt; a little, waxing age – then ashes. Who cares?
But in your lives, your lives, he repeated, you pass down a
torch through the ages. It thrilled her then – this evidence
of use, of worth, of service . . .

But to ask her *now*. It was too late. She was too old. They
were too old. Past was past.

From downstairs there came a loud knocking on the
front door.

7

A large shadow on the door's frosted glass. She rested at the
bottom of the stairs a moment, then went forward.

'Mrs Balthus?' The young man leaned over her, smiling.
His face was large featured, coarsely handsome.

'Yes.'

'Have a message for you, Mrs Balthus. Well, really for Mr
Balthus.' He overflowed the space between the jamb and the
door she was trying unsuccessfully to keep half-closed. 'I'll
come in,' he said. Then he was inside, a huge warm hand
covered hers on the lock and pushed the door shut.

'I must ask – whoever you are – to leave.' Her voice seemed
to come from far away.

He advanced down the hallway. Over six foot, his brown
leather jacket stretched tight over wide shoulders. 'This the
living-room, is it?' He went in.

She opened the front door and looked out. The street was
empty. She could not run.

'You can shut that, you know. Draught.' The large good-looking head poked into the hall, advising her in his bland cockney accent.

He stood waiting for her in the centre of the room.

'You must leave,' she said. 'I do not know who you are. If it is money you are after I must tell you we have none.'

'Now.' He looked calmly and patiently round the room. 'I don't want you to think there's anything personal in this. I don't know you. You don't know me. Right? It's just a job.' He continued his survey.

'Get started then.' He crossed to the fireplace. On the mantel were two porcelain figures: a Staffordshire shepherd and country girl at a stile; a French Europa and the Bull, carefully mended. His hand swept them off. The English piece shattered on the copper fender in front of the gas fire. The French thudded on the carpet, intact. He picked up a dining chair and began to smash it against the table. It was solid and took time to break. Then he used one of the legs to score deep scratches in the polished surface of the table. The chair-leg, used as a club, broke the front of the china cabinet, rooted among the plates and figures, dispersing and smashing them. He took a vase of daffodils from the windowsill and emptied flowers and water onto the floor, grinding the flowers into the carpet in a slow, swaying dance, grinning at her.

He took a craft knife from his pocket and knelt down at the bookcase. Now she felt sick. I do not have to watch this. He will not harm me. It is his job.

She went unsteadily back to the kitchen. Her hands trembling, she managed to light a cigarette. From the front room there was an appalling silence. Then the sounds of tearing and banging came again. Surely he must stop soon. Then would he come in here? It was as if all the years of her life had been compressed together and made worthless in this one moment of time. The noise stopped.

His frame lumbered into the doorway. He was breathing a little harder. He straightened the jacket across his shoulders with a little shrugging motion, like a builder just finished work.

'That's it,' he said. 'I must say you've taken it okay. None of this screaming or carrying on. It doesn't do any good.'

23

She stared at the fresh cigarette that magic had put between her fingers. Her hand shook. She would vomit as soon as . . . As soon as what?

'It's just that they want these houses emptied,' he went on. 'They're too old, see. Not fit for human habitation. It's just a taste – one room. Much better to pack up and go. I was just told to tell you – go. All right? Have a good day.'

She heard the front door bang behind him. Her nausea had diminished. She felt sure she could contain it now. She must simply sit here and keep a toe-hold on this little bit of the universe. Under the floorboards was the earth. And this earth was spinning with her and the ruined room and she must not go in there. It was full of small animals dripping with blood. Of children, mutilated by some insane bestiality, their tender faces smashed. Of purple. Of blood. Of green. Of blood. Her hand shook. The smoke wobbled up but she was rooted to this little piece, this square foot of earth.

8

After dithering at her desk, pulling drawers in and out, hesitating, finger on lips, over some paper or other, Miss Vacik had gone at last.

He hung the rope with the closed sign at the top of the stairs and sat down at her desk where the telephone was. He dialled the number in the letter. A youngish woman's voice, cool and competent, answered.

Yes, yes, she was Julia Wallace. The voice brightened when he told her his name. Why, it's Mr Balthus, isn't it?

She had been told to expect his call; they had better meet soon she thought, to iron out all the details. 'Isn't it very exciting?' she said. 'Will you be going yourself?' he asked. He wondered what mental picture she had of him. Oh yes, she hoped to. She would love to. And how many others were going – it must be quite a job to organize it all . . . ? Oh, only you, Mr Balthus, I think, from England, and one other. My father.

Then you are my nationality yourself?

Only a half, unfortunately. Now, where could they meet? Where was he? Had he a car? She could pick him up, if he wished.

No, no, he would not dream of it. He had the address of her flat. Why did he not come over and see her? If it was, of course, convenient . . .

She was going out for an hour now, but by all means come over this afternoon, Mr Balthus. I shall look forward to it.

He put the phone down, enchanted. The warmth with which she had greeted him, the engaging, bubbling quality of her responses . . . What would she look like? In his mind he constructed a long-legged, fair-haired, slim, tall woman with that quintessentially English thin-boned face, the long pale lips. He had intended working in the shop this afternoon, there was much correspondence to write replies to (he never dared to dictate to Miss Vacik). But, no, he was too excited now to think of work. He looked at his watch. In half an hour he would be able to make his way across London to her flat in, where was it? He reached for his *A to Z of London*. North Kensington – Notting Hill. What to do till then? He had refused politely Campion's first summons to tea, the voice fluting up the stairs. Now he could smell again the sickly, flowery odour.

When he came down, he locked the stairs door and proceeded along the corridor and past the sink. On the little card-table a mug steamed, the string of one of Campion's herbal tea-bags hanging over the side. Campion was haggling with someone at the counter, or, rather, remonstrating, with an elderly, bearded man.

'No, no,' Campion was saying, 'I do assure you, my dear sir, Theology is a drug, a positive drug on the market. I can sell books on spirits, on ghosts, on poltergeists, on pyramids – oh, on any of the hundreds of things on these shelves.' His sleeve waved like a sail as he pointed up at his shelves. 'But not *God*. It's unfortunate, but no.' He beamed.

The man gathered a large plastic carrier bag to his chest

and lifted it from the counter. 'Where do you think I might sell them, then?' he pleaded.

'Try anywhere among the *general* shops. You may be lucky.'

The man headed for the door, and Campion sailed back down.

'I swear I shall give up, Mr Balthus. Give up. I've hardly sold a thing all day. There seem to be more people selling books than buying them in this trade sometimes. That man then – bag full of theology. A few odd people may collect it, I suppose.' He stirred his cup. 'Can I tempt you to one of these *now*, Mr Balthus? Oh, good. I'll just boil up again.' He pushed the plug into the ancient electric kettle. 'As I was saying – he won't sell them. He won't. Any book except a Christian one. Good heavens, people don't come here to find books on worship or high-flown metaphysics. They come for answers, Mr Balthus. I deal in answers. How's trade with you?'

'I have other things on my mind, more important than trade.'

'More important?' said Campion rather sniffily.

'I may be resuming my political career.'

'Oh yes?'

'Not in the House of Commons, I hasten to add. Emigré politics. A rather recherché subject for the outsider, I'm afraid.'

'I suppose it must be.' Campion had cooled towards him; Jacob hoped he had not upset him. 'Excuse me.' Campion sailed towards a man who had come into the shop. 'Can I help you?'

Jacob watched them. He laid down the mug and realized he had had no lunch. It could wait. In a little while he could go and see Miss Wallace. Julia. How should he address her? Miss Wallace. He was a gentleman. Campion wrapped a book in brown paper for his customer. Balthus, the man of destiny, the *invited* man, watched. For years he had served his country in exile. Now perhaps would come some recognition. And now the thought of returning to his home city, to whatever and whoever was left from the war, caused the first tremor of fear to run through his body.

9

This time he went by tube. Getting off at Notting Hill Gate, he was grateful to turn away from the seedy vivacity of the main road into the squares and crescents to the north. The rain fell thinly and steadily. Dilapidation and wealth mixed on the faces of the stuccoed terraces, black bin-bags full of their refuse leaned against the railings.

He came to her address. She had told him on the telephone that she was in the basement flat. He hesitated a moment then descended the steps.

He rang the bell and waited. He stroked back his hair and adjusted his dark blue overcoat. Then the door opened, her voice said, 'Mr Balthus?' and he went in.

She was not as he had imagined. Older. Her face was pale, surrounded by a halo of frizzy, red-gold hair. She was quite tall, her body concealed in a thick, lumpy sweater.

'You found it okay then?'

Her legs too looked rather heavy in faded blue jeans, as he followed her down the narrow hallway into a back room. Lightly furnished, the end wall was panelled in wood and glass. Outside the heavy glass-paned door was a tiny paved area from which stone steps ascended to a lawn.

'I have brought the letter.' He reached into his pocket. 'The details, it says – to see you, Miss Wallace.'

'Please – Julia.'

'Julia.'

She read the letter without a great deal of interest, he felt, and passed it back to him with an overly bright smile.

'Well, I'm afraid there's not a lot more I can tell you, Mr Balthus. You see from the letter I'm just a sort of contact person. My father is the one you want to see. Please sit down. Would you like a drink? Scotch? Gin?'

'Scotch would be fine. A little water too if you wouldn't mind.'

The tumbler she handed him was more than half-full. There was not a lot of water in it.

He sipped. She turned one of the dining chairs round and leaned over the back, her legs straddling it. She smiled down at him. She was not as young as he had first thought. As he had heard her on the telephone. There were small lines at the corners of her eyes; her mouth thin, the upper lip a little crimped.

'I do not quite understand,' he began. 'What precise connection does your father have with the patriotic movement – the Committee?'

'Sort of behind the scenes. Fixing up finance, contacts – that sort of thing. He's quite disgustingly wealthy. I'm not. That accounts for the lumpy sofa. And the flat.'

The flat looked fine to Jacob.

'But he really is *tremendously* busy. That accounts for you getting me, I suppose. Sorry about that.' She gave a mock sigh, as if to sympathize with him in his misfortune. 'He does come from your country. Originally.'

'Wallace?' Wallace?

'And I think he has some business tie-ins he's trying to improve with your people. Isn't it marvellous that things are opening up so much over there – that you have a chance now to go back?'

'There has not been much opportunity to do that for a man in my position. I think they would have had a prison cell reserved in my honour a few years ago.'

He wondered if she was married. He took another pull at the glass. The whisky went straight from his empty stomach to his head.

'Yes – it must have been awful. And the war and everything. Tell me about it – if you want to. About your country – when it was *your* country. I'd love to hear about it. Let me fill you up.'

She did sound genuinely interested. The whisky was making him want to impress her. She *was* attractive. As he began to speak, he realized that the land he had left nearly fifty years ago had grown more than a little fantastic and fabulous in his head. A phrase kept repeating itself, and he used it to her: The Good Republic. That's what it was – a good republic. A kind, small place, suspended almost out of time, ruled by the good, leading a charmed life – looking back – between mad giants. Did it exist now anywhere but in his head? When we are gone – it will be gone. Was it a dream that they could create a just society in those times? It had its drawbacks – what didn't? But our economy, our arts, our justice, our great men – of whom no one now would ever know . . .

'You can remind them,' she said softly.

How much they had had – how quickly it was taken away. The awful things . . . It was best to remember the good things – and talk about them to someone so, so young . . . Who could not know how much of it he made up, how much he wished was true. How much – heartrendingly – was true. Our lakes, our forests, our wonderful silver beaches. Oh, you could never know . . . He spurred himself on. My father . . . My friends . . .

'Excuse me.'

The telephone was ringing in the hallway. She was already heading out of the room. He went to drink, and was surprised to see the glass was empty. The benign whisky haze that had encircled them had dissolved. The room was gloomy, the afternoon darkening down. He got up, his legs stiff. He felt tipsy.

He could hear her muffled voice. She came back in smiling.

'That was Daddy. I rang him earlier to say you were coming here. He wonders if you could meet him. He suggested this evening.'

'I would be delighted.' He hovered. He didn't quite know whether to sit down again. He realized he had not thought of Ella once today. She would be cooking dinner for six o'clock. He was starving. If he kept on drinking whisky he would be drunk when he met Wallace.

'It's a little way out of London,' she said. 'I suggest I drive you over later on – unless you have other plans.'

'My wife. I shall have to . . .' He looked round him for somewhere to put down his empty glass.

'Of course. I am sorry – I didn't think. Would you like to phone her?'

She guided him to the telephone. Irritatingly he could not get through. There seemed to be no connection. He dialled the operator. No, he answered the bright voice, there was no accounts problem, he simply could not get through. She would check the line.

'Oh dear,' said Julia. 'Will she be worried?' Her concern made him sound like a hen-pecked newly-wed.

'No . . . no.'

'Where is it you live?'

He told her.

'Well then, there's no problem. It's roughly in the same direction. You can pop in on the way.' She looked at her watch. 'It's half past four – we could go now.'

'It's no trouble to you . . . ?'

'It's our party, isn't it. I'll just get my coat.'

She came back in a few moments dressed in a worn but expensive-looking long leather coat. It suited her auburn hair.

'Shall we go?' she said.

10

The great blocks of flats that surrounded the ghetto of older streets loomed ahead. He saw another newspaper poster of the Prime Minister; huge, truncated at the waist, high on the wall of a half-demolished building. The mouth was tight-lipped as she gazed towards the flats, as if she saw unwelcome guests arriving in the distance. The portrait had disappeared, appeared again and then again from different angles as the little car darted into side streets. Approaching from a direction that was not his usual one, Jacob was lost. The few people they passed bent into the wind. They looked poor and ill-dressed, as if they lived a thousand miles and twenty years away from the bright streets the car had come from.

'Ah – perhaps here.' By some bump of direction Julia had taken over from Jacob's dithering, dwindling instructions and steered them at last into the correct street.

'I should have left it to you all along,' he said.

'Yes.' She smiled, and drew carefully up outside the house.

'Perhaps now I may repay a little of your hospitality,' he said. She looked at her watch.

She followed him up the steps and waited till he fumbled his key out, turning to smile apologetically at her. The door swung open.

In the hallway he gave a deep sigh and carefully hung up his coat. 'May I?' – and then Julia's beside it.

'Please,' he said. 'This way. Ella? Ella?' he shouted.

The kitchen door opened a little.

The woman was, and was not, what Julia had expected. Large, her big, folded face was earth coloured, her body suggestive of great strength – but she seemed to cling to the door jamb with a raised hand.

'It's you, Balthus,' she said dully. She did not seem to notice Julia.

'And a friend, Ella. This is Miss Wallace. Of the letter? Please – do make yourself at home.' He gestured to the door on Julia's left.

'Not there.' Ella almost screeched.

Julia felt herself smiling involuntarily, the way people do at funerals.

'Nonsense. A guest, Ella,' he said and he opened the door, half-bowing her in to the room.

Julia entered.

'. . . The living-room,' Balthus announced.

There must be some mistake, Julia thought, some awful misplacement in the house. It was the room of a mad person. On the big dining-table, in almost the centre of the room, a sheaf of daffodils sprawled out of a broken-necked vase, their yellow mouths bugling on the brown varnish, the water lying in a raised pool and in deep freshly gouged scratches.

Everything that could be smashed had been. Books slashed and ripped apart; ornaments shattered. The table was surrounded by chaos and violence. There was not a safe place in

31

the room. Even strips of wallpaper had been torn off, dangling drunkenly from the wall.

She did not want to look any more. She was conscious of a wide-eyed, grinning idiocy once more seizing her face, and a nervous laugh escaped from her before she could smother it. He looked in bewilderment at the room, then at Julia, then back at the room.

'Ella,' he said. Then more loudly, 'Ella.'

'I do not know . . .' he said to Julia.

'Please . . . Is it – burglars . . . ?' A tentative, quiz-game question.

'Burglars?'

By repetition the word seemed to become ridiculous, to take on a floating, balloon-like existence.

'Burglars sometimes . . .'

'Yes. Yes. Please excuse me. Do sit down.'

He went hurrying out of the room, throwing back this last absurd social injunction. But she might as well sit down. She picked up an unbroken chair, lying on its side.

Her eyes wandered round the violated room. She wished she had her cigarettes. They were in the car.

Before she could get up, however, Jacob reappeared in the doorway.

'Please . . .' He beckoned her to follow him.

As she got up she glanced out of the window to check the car. Across the street a tall, well-built young man stared up at the sky.

11

When Ella had finished telling them what had happened it was as if she had gained strength from her recital.

'But how extraordinary,' said Julia. 'He did not take anything?'

'We have nothing worth taking,' said Jacob.

'Oh, you'd be surprised nowadays.' Julia was about to deliver a lecture on just how surprised they would be to discover how much even quite ordinary things were worth, when Jacob broke in.

'Then it was political.'

'*Political*? But no . . .' said Ella.

'I have many political enemies.'

'He was not like that,' she insisted. 'He was young. A hooligan.'

'They could hire anyone.'

'Was there only the one?' Julia asked.

'One. Only.'

'Would you recognize him again?'

'I do not want to recognize him again.'

'No – of course not.'

Silence fell around the kitchen table. Ella snatched at another cigarette.

'What about the police?' Julia said.

'No.' Ella sounded very decisive.

'No,' said Jacob.

'What could they do?' said Ella.

'Well.' Julia had come to a decision. They couldn't sit around all night like characters in a play. 'I was going to take Mr Balthus to see my father. Now you both must come. This place obviously isn't safe for you.'

'But the front room?'

'We can see about that later.' And against all their arguments, rapidly weakening as they were, Julia prevailed. Ella went upstairs and packed a small suitcase for herself and Balthus. After all, thought Julia, these people are used to being refugees of one sort or another. It was astonishing how resigned they looked, standing in the hallway as she opened the door to check the street.

'It's okay,' said Julia. 'Let's go, shall we?'

'That's funny,' she said as she led them down the steps.

'Pardon, my dear?' Ella was got up in a huge fur coat which made her look as if the bear had got back into his skin.

'That chap running up the street. I'm sure he was standing outside your house when I came.'

'Where? Where?' Ella said eagerly, squinting round.

Julia pointed at the figure loping towards the bend in the road, towards the flats.

'Come. Let's go,' Balthus hurried them on.

'Have you locked the door?'

'Yes, yes. Get in.'

He was jolted awake by the sudden slowing of the car. To his shame he must have drifted off. The warmth of the car. The whisky this afternoon. He looked out of the window.

'We are in the country,' he said.

'Surrey, actually,' said Julia. 'What's left of it. We're just coming up to Guildford.'

They passed through a city that held, like most of the towns he had seen in England, a central cancer of glass and stone eating its way outwards into an older body. 'That's the Cathedral over there,' Julia called out. He looked for St Paul's or Chartres and saw only a huge, vaguely gothicized grain elevator.

'Horrible, isn't it?' said Julia brightly. 'Best we can do, I'm afraid.'

He straightened up, brushing a grey caterpillar of cigarette ash from his knee.

They came out of the city along a wide road raised above the surrounding country.

'They call this the Hog's Back,' said Julia.

He gazed out over a plain that was beginning to fall into evening. Thin roads led from one village, starting to glitter, to another, or from one farm to the next. Then his view was blocked by a row of suburban houses. The red sign of a large modern hotel glowed against the enormous, rolling grey sky. The car slowed again and Julia turned off down one of the narrow roads.

'My father's house is just down here,' she said.

High hedges and trees rushed past as Julia, too fast for Jacob, drove through a labyrinth of darkening lanes.

Then the road straightened. The hedges drifted lower. They turned into a driveway, between two square brick columns topped by stone globes.

The driveway was bordered on both sides by tall larches.

Between their trunks stretched parkland with sheep grazing in the dying light. Ahead, the trees thickened to a wood through which the road pierced a tunnel. As the trees thinned out again Jacob began to catch glimpses of a large house. It showed no lights. The car swept onto gravel that circled a dry fountain, under the facade.

Jacob and Ella climbed stiffly out. They followed Julia to the house.

Above the porch, obscured by stray tendrils of ivy, a coat of arms was cut in a stone panel; the weather of some hundreds of years had eroded its outlines, rendering the beasts supporting the shield unrecognizable. Julia ran up the steps and turned the round iron handle on the door.

From the narrow hallway a doorless stone arch gave into the entrance hall proper. Julia strode in; Jacob and Ella stood under the arch with the reluctance of strangers, then at last moved forward.

In a great fireplace gas flames leapt and flickered among indestructible logs. There were fresh daffodils on an ancient sideboard.

'Hello,' Julia shouted. 'Daddy?'

There was no reply.

'Excuse me,' she said. 'I'll go and stir him up.' She patted the back of the sofa as she went out.

'Please, do not mind us,' said Jacob looking up at a tapestry. Leda, in eighteenth-century costume, appeared to be conferring amiably with the Swan, who was actually more like a goose with an impossibly elongated neck; at his back, in the distance, another swan, abandoned by her fickle mate, swam on a pond with ducks.

Ella sank with a great sigh into the sofa. 'Balthus – come and sit down.'

He felt suddenly nervous. He took off his glasses and polished them. The tapestry seemed to swell, its colours glowed, the sharp outlines dissolved as if they too were behind glass and someone had blown on it.

There was the sound of footsteps on the wooden tiles. Jacob turned and peered myopically in their direction. A large man stood just inside the arch.

'Ah Jacob – then you did get away?' The voice drawled

across the room, almost a parody of a rich, rolling, educated Englishman's accent. Jacob felt as if a cold wave had been pushed forward by the warm voice and washed about his heart.

His hands trembling, he replaced his spectacles.

Larger, as if inflated, plumped out in the face as if heavily made-up by the years – as if it could be *him*. Yet there was no disguising the line of the triumphantly smiling mouth, the extraordinary eyes.

'Max?' he said. 'Max Sawallisch?'

'Wallace now actually, old boy.' He stepped forward.

'But I thought . . .' That you were dead. Safely dead.

'I understand we are to be travelling companions, Jacob. Back to the old country. Who would have thought it? What memories it will bring back, eh Jacob?'

And Jacob looked at him with all the fear we have when a ghost confronts us.

What memories, eh? What memories . . .

II

It might have been that the eye of the future should see Europe for some space of time as a pale West, like a fading fresco painted by genius, a troubled and writhing German people, a barricaded and pre-occupied Russia, and a chaplet of shining small countries, delighting in life . . .

Rebecca West, *Black Lamb and Grey Falcon*

I

His first memory was of glass. And then of glass growing out of water. A square of glass with squares of red and blue glass at each corner. Of the water broken by trees, then reeds, then revealed as a lake; as a sea; as the curved water at the top of a glass.

Thunder far off. Tepid water in the bathtub. A dead daddy-longlegs on the top of the bath water, the water raised in long limpid blades along each side of each limb. His mother a blue cloud descending to roughly, gently scrub him, roughly towel him; a kind blue elephant to be followed to the table below the window that was raised on a stick with notches so you could look out to the trees and tiny piece of sea with no glass between.

The window was repeated, crescent shaped, on the shoulder of the white porcelain jug that held the white-blue milk and had blue and red five-petalled flowers and lime green leaves on its white belly. And the first noise the chatter of birds in the morning from where the light came and the calls of other children, at the water's edge, or broken in half by the water. His father naked, emerged from the water, glittering. The immeasurable day; the evenings that lasted and lasted, refusing to grow dark; but at last folding imperceptibly around, they delivered him to sleep . . .

And in the mornings again the white cloth, the coffee pot, the hot milk in its white jug, the blotched wooden sill, the raised glass. His father bending to kiss him good morning, goodbye, before going out, brown leather satchel in hand, to the black English car that took him to the city each day.

Goodbye Jacob.

Goodbye.

Until tonight.

2

Jacob sat at the window.

What was it – one, two in the morning? The other villas, discreetly distanced among the seaside pines, had finally silenced their gramophones, their voices, barking dogs. His cigarette glowed in the dark wooden room. In the clearing a deck chair left out emerged in the starlight, a crouching, watching figure with two ears pricked above its dark, striped belly.

He opened the window to the last notch on the bar. With the dark, the smell of the sea came stronger. He would stay here all night. But it grew cold and he got up and put on one of his thick sweaters. He sat at the window again, leaning his arms on the sill, breathing in the sweet night. How could he sleep?

Earlier tonight, he had lingered on the tiny landing outside her apartment door, waiting for the last of the theatre people to leave. They emerged agonizingly slowly, jabbering over their shoulders to those left behind; one or two nodded at Jacob. That tall German with excessively blond hair swept out, ignoring Jacob, blowing a kiss from the stairs back to Katerina, who now had come out. And Jacob was left with that divine girl, under the lamp at the top of the stairs.

'I thought you'd gone, Jacob.' The room behind her was empty.

He wanted to say all the things he had rehearsed over and over in his head. She had spent so much time with him, talking to him – but she was so close to him that all he could do was step forward and – astonishing himself – kiss her. Her mouth met his without resistance. After a moment or two she pushed him gently away, stepping back into the apartment.

'Can I see you again?'

'Of course.' She was smiling all the time she was shutting the apartment door on him.

'When?'

'Lunchtime. One lunchtime.'

'Monday? Monday, for lunch?'

'I'll try,' her voice murmured from the closing door.

'The Café Stieckus?'

'Fine.'

'The Café Stieckus,' he said to the door. He ran down the twisting flights of stairs and into the narrow street. He crossed and stood against a yard wall and looked up. A pale curtained rectangle showed her window. He made his way slowly to the corner, drunk with the music they had danced to, her eyes, the lips that time – looping back – pressed time after time on his. From the alley beside the Synagogue a whore called to him. He hurried on. Tonight he was a white and shining courtier.

He came down the hill from the Old Town, and into Palace Square. The Opera House was closed. The three horses pulling an empty chariot reared above a dead fountain. Across the great square, two sentries marched heavily in and out of the light above the gates to the President's Palace. He passed under the moon shadows of the cathedral spires, and into a long street of expensive shops, with some of their displays still brilliantly lit. Into another street, of smaller shops and cafés, with the baroque facades of apartments above them.

It was near the end of summer. The city, spacious, low and airy between its two rivers, seemed to be floating out to sea. Most families were still on holiday in the villas and hotels and guest houses along the coast, with only the men commuting in each day to work in the city. Even furniture and pictures and bookcases were shipped away from town houses to furnish the summer dwellings. The city in the late afternoon and evening was a dwindling, quietened place; at this time of night it appeared empty. Only in the Old Town did any sort of life still go on. Especially at Katerina's. And the café.

There was no one in the Square of the Republic, except the statue of the President. The far side of the square dropped clean down to the estuary; the masts and funnels of fishing boats and small steamers stood darkly along the low walled edge.

A last empty tram gonged dreamily past, accelerating up the wide, newly macadamed street that shone like blue-black leather.

41

Now he was at the end of the South Bridge, the Bridge of the Harvest. Its long double row of gas-lit moons stretched across the river. As he mounted the bridge a ghost passed in front of him, reeling drunkenly through one of the lamp standards, the stone bridge wall, falling silently onto the water below and twisting away towards the sea . . . Panicking, Jacob delved in his pocket for his glasses. The moons shrank back into rigid globes, the white-grey road, which had soared ahead of him into the night, gleamed flatly and ironically between the bridge's supports. The phantom being carried away on the water was revealed as a large paper sack, blown from some estuary barge.

He struck out across the bridge, turning his face seawards so that the fresh salt wind pushed back his hair.

On the far side he walked through the village that had grown in the last few years into a prosperous suburb around the new Hydro and the Thalassotherapic Clinic. A policeman standing in the Clinic gateway gazed steadily at him as he passed.

At last the suburb dwindled away. Dark fields stretched into the night on either side of the road. The moon, a huge white medal, hung high. Ahead, the forest into which the pale road led was a gently flickering dark line under the plum-blue sky.

He had gone perhaps a couple of kilometres when a car passed and came slowly to a halt just ahead. The passenger door opened.

He did not hurry his pace. He did not want a lift, or any company except the thought of Katerina. As he drew level a loud, jolly voice shouted in German.

'Going to the Poltava Woods? Hop in.'

Jacob still hesitated.

'What – you don't recognize me, young Balthus? It is young Balthus, isn't it? You know me – Herr Schwarzwald. Get in.'

A reluctant Jacob climbed into the passenger seat. The car picked up speed. There was a mingled smell of beer, cigar smoke, leather and sweat. Jacob looked at the driver.

The man's face was a large, amiable potato with bumps in place of cheekbones, chin and nose.

'Counsellor Balthus's son, eh? Know you anywhere. *Senior*

Counsellor, I should say. Dad's a fine man, eh? Yes – of course he is.'

Had the man picked him up to flatter his father?

'Help me to a light, would you?' A box of matches was thrust at him. Half a cigar stuck out of the potato. In the matchlight, held under the probing, snuffling cigar, Jacob saw that Schwarzwald was dressed in the blue shirt and black breeches of the Auxiliary Police. The smell of leather and sweat drowned the last memory of Katerina's scent.

He wished again he had not got in the car.

'Thought you'd been nicked, eh?' Schwarzwald laughed. 'Just a hobby. Duty as well, of course.'

They entered the forest. At intervals, between dark blocks of trees, the sea would appear for a second or so, unmoving, but shimmering in row on row of knives under the moon.

'Do a lot of business with your father. A gentleman. And now he's got his son in the Ministry with him, eh? Balthus et Fils. No stopping you now, eh?'

'I would not put it exactly like that.'

'Course you wouldn't. Very important to this country, the Foreign Ministry. Trade. Oh yes. But . . .'

Jacob was surprised by the pain in his leg. The fat man had jabbed a finger down once, twice, just above the knee.

'. . . any time you get bored there, or want a change – youth must have its fling, eh – come and see me. You know my yards in the docks. Offices. Warehouses. Come and see me. I'm serious, mind. Could do with a smart young fellow like you.'

The potato face lost itself in a potato smile again. He stopped the car just before a junction in the thick of the woods.

'Now, look – my house is here. Can run you on, if you like.'

'No, no, please don't bother. I like to walk.'

'Drop you with pleasure . . .'

'No – please.'

'Creeping back in, eh? Young devil. Before you go . . .' This time the plump fingers closed on Jacob's knee, unmistakably detaining him. 'A word of advice. From an older man. I know you. I know your father. There's not a lot I don't know in this little city of ours, eh?' His voice rumbled jocosely, but the fingers continued to grip. 'But – hope you don't mind if I speak frankly – Jacob. When you're young it's nice to ramble, eh? But – for the sake of your career – all these *people* in the Old Town – Jews, artists, God knows what. Have your fill, but don't bring them home. You understand? Not for us, eh?' The fingers relaxed their grip and patted his knee.

'I don't quite see, Herr Schwarzwald . . .'

'You will, Jacob. Ask your father. There are two sides to every river, and you can't walk on both.' The fat man leaned across Jacob and undid the door. He settled back, smiling in an entirely pleasant way. 'Don't mind my frankness? I am your father's friend – and yours. Don't mind? No, of course not.'

Jacob found himself at the edge of the road, the car turning away between the trees.

How dare he! How dare that fat awful German-Balt – whatever the hell he was – meddle in his affairs. How monstrous that he should know of them, taint them with his beery, sweaty presence. It was as if he had been watched all night.

He walked. The wood had long ago swallowed the noise of the car. In a small city you are bound to get spying and meddling. Especially these days. Some of the café crowd belonged to the banned Communists. What was he supposed to do – report them?

As he trudged on a few lights flickered through the trees from the cottages. A sound of laughter. But the forest swallowed everything. The sound of his footsteps fell into softly giving pine needles.

Silent, the forest was a magical place; the tent made by two fallen trees was a satin-black, endlessly deep well. The white sand path unwound in front, almost a ghost of the path his eyes remembered. His breath hovered before him. Above, caught in the vertiginously spiring trees, each square and parallelogram of branches held one, two, or at the most, three stars. He forgot the German. The conventions of night – stars, strange entanglements of branches, the scuffling of tiny animals, his own breathing – restored him to the thought of Katerina. To the knowledge that he loved her. Was in love. He stopped walking, and was gripped in an ecstasy that was both sexual and spiritual, that glowed through body and mind like the slow release of some great energy, the thrill of orgasm slowed down, as if all the veins were pinched and slowly released their blood again. This was a feeling that once gained he must never lose.

Now the path curved consistently to the right, towards the sea. There were no big tides; the sea rocked gently and the waves were pushed by the wind, breaking softly on the long beach. The shingle made a shush-shushing as he came from between the trees and followed the path at the top of the dunes. Back along the coast he could see the lights of the capital; the glow of the empty squares fanned up to the sky like lanterns turned on their backs. Off the harbour a dark ship triangled her riding lights against the sky.

Then the path plunged back down into the trees and he was at the villa.

He had told his parents he would be back late from the city this Saturday night.

He walked as quietly as he could up the three wooden steps onto the verandah and let the door off its latch. He tiptoed past his parents' bedroom off the passageway, and into his own room . . .

Turning at last from the window, he lay down on the bed, pressing out his cigarette on a plate beside the bed. He drew the counterpane over him and settled his hands behind his head, thinking of Katerina, how he would love her, how his father would smile gravely, his mother looking tearfully on, and welcome the beautiful girl to the Balthus family . . . He fell asleep.

When he woke he was warm. The ceiling had grown light. There was something he just had to do.

Under the window was his wind-up gramophone. He knelt beside it and opened the album of records he had brought from their apartment in the capital. Yes, here it was. Miraculously the same version as the one played as he danced with Katerina at the party.

He wound the machine and lowered the needle. He waited through the hissing introduction for his eyes to prickle with pleasurably sentimental tears. Ah, here it came. The swaying, rather off-pitch violins; the suddenly darting, light American voice of Fred Astaire:

Dar-ling – never, never change
Keep that breathless charm
Won't you please a-rrange
It – 'cause I love you
Just the way you look tonight . . .

La, la; la-la. Oh but you're lovely With your smile so . . .
It *was* the party. His eyes filled.

In the corridor between bed and gramophone he swayed.
The record revolved too fast away; a pleasure that had to be
renewed. He put it on again. He twisted and danced, stretching
out his arms to an invisible, infinitely desirable Katerina.

As the needle knocked in the last grooves, a voice spoke from
behind him.

'A little early for that, Jacob?'

His father stood in the doorway in his dressing-gown.

'A little early,' he repeated.

Jacob's face burned.

'We did hope you were not going to play a concert.'

The needle continued to hiss and clack in the last closed
groove, slowing as the machine wound down.

'No – no. I'm sorry I woke you.' Jacob hurried the disc
back into its card sleeve. He could feel his father's affectionate,
sardonic stare on his back. He heard him take a step into the
room. Jacob fussed with the heavy black discs, pretending to
be busy. He knew that his father was inspecting the room.

'I would have got up soon anyhow – it's not worth going
back to bed. Care for a dip?'

'Yes. Of course.' Confident once more, Jacob stood and
faced his father. 'Let me get ready.'

'Have you slept yet?'

'Sort of.'

They smiled at each other. His father went out, closing the
door softly.

Jacob stripped off the clothes he had worn since yesterday
with an odd mixture of gratitude and regret, as if he was
stepping out of the night he had loved. The growing light
left pockets of darkness in the corners of the room. The cheval
glass reflected milky shadows in his pillow, in the rivers of the
disordered counterpane. His body looked paler in this light

than the summer sun had left it, his face yellower and more melancholy. His black hair, cropped short for the summer, was starting to sprout again. The body was still adolescent, the shoulders broad but the chest not yet filled out, the pale tube . . . He turned decisively away from the mirror. He did not want to involve *that*. To defile his love for Katerina. The chasteness of first desire gripped him. He hurried into his dressing-gown and cold leather slippers.

His father was waiting on the verandah. In silence they walked across the grass and into the misty dampness between the pines. Looking up, Jacob saw that the tops were already a pale yellow, though the thick forest that stretched behind them still held the sun that rose out of Russia every morning. They came out onto the hummocky sand-dunes, and through them to the silver beach.

His father's dressing-gown collapsed behind him. Scissoring his legs he prised off each sandal with the toes of the other foot. Jacob admired the hefty maturity of the thick short body, the shoulders with their pelt of hair. He folded his dressing-gown neatly on top of his father's, letting him go on ahead. Then he followed him down to the lapping water's edge, his flesh creeping a little at the expectation of its coldness, feeling terribly small and naked under the vast, lightening sky.

'To our island,' his father called, wading out. 'Race you to our island.'

They called it their island, although it was only a sandbar a few hundred metres off their beach. And *their* beach because his father got up earlier than anyone and woke Jacob to join him.

God, the water was *cold*. Jacob struck out after the confidently plunging body ahead.

The world tilted and lapped about him. Gulls commented ironically on his progress. He caught water in his mouth and arrived, spluttering, into the tiny bay of the sandbar. His father stood, a brown pillar, hands on hips, his legs grotesquely foreshortened by the clear water. Jacob dipped and wallowed, avoiding looking at his father's nakedness.

'All right?' shouted his father jovially.

'And back,' Jacob shouted, and began to swim ferociously back, without giving his father time to rest. He just made it

47

to the beach ahead, staggering up from the water and running to the dressing-gowns, his father's shout pursuing him, 'Sly, Jacob. Sly. I'll beat you next time.'

He went on up through the dunes, rubbing his gown against himself to towel off the water; his father followed in a leisurely way, tying his belt as he came.

A small terrier dashed down the path between the trees. The first of their neighbours up. He clutched his gown decently around him.

As he mounted the verandah he smelt the coffee roasting. His mother moved about in the living-room at the end of the hall.

'Tomas? Jacob? Breakfast is ready,' she called. His father's steps mounted heavily behind him. 'It is going to be a lovely day,' he shouted back.

Jacob slipped into his room. The holiday season was over for another year. Tomorrow he would go into the city again with his father, leaving mother to close up the villa. He kicked off the damp slippers and tossed the dressing-gown into the corner. Then he dressed in white trousers and white shirt. He stood in front of the mirror. He smiled at himself.

He felt marvellously clean and quite unreasonably happy.

3

The apartment looked strange and denuded after their long absence at the sea. The taps rattled and knocked before spurting water. The maid was new and did not know where anything was kept. Jacob's father told her not to worry. They would breakfast in the city.

The capital was coming back to life. Trams rumbled purposefully into the squares, disgorged office workers and stenographers, and rattled lightly off, relieved of their loads. The stout women who hosed down the pavements each morning

had finished work and stood chattering among the flower sell-
ers under the statues of great men. Spires and domes gleamed,
bronze and green. The sky was a pure blue, with only a hint of
autumn – like the decay which is called 'character' in a face.

In the restaurant near the Ministry, civil servants and
businessmen were already breakfasting. Everyone looked
tanned and relaxed. There were loud, jolly 'Hellos', hand-
shakes and bows. The capital took great pride in its jovial
formality. There was much business to be done in a pleasant
way in places like this, and the breakfasters could be forgiven
for feeling satisfied with themselves.

Ever since the Kubin coup of a few years ago had disposed
of a fractious democracy, the country had prospered and
fattened. Someone once said that a man is seldom more
innocently employed than when he is making money – the
people got on with their innocent lives. Of course, old enmities
bubbled under the surface. The Soviets infiltrated spies and
agitators across one border; the German-speaking *Volksdeutsche*
cast their eyes southwards to where the Führer ʳ ːamed
promises to *Ostland*, and kept alive their dreams ot a German colony. But the trains rattled through from one enemy
to another, doing business.

The threat of war was assiduously discussed, but you can't
worry all the time, can you? Many said, 'Why should they
bother with us? Kubin will keep us out of it.'

The people made love, read books, went to the cinema,
put up shelves, cooked, ate, shook hands and made deals.
The beaches had been full every weekend this summer, the
towns and cities dozing under the sun. Who would want to
harm them? They carried fear secretly like a weight under the
clothes, a stone in the stomach.

'You see,' said Balthus's father, tapping the folded newspaper by the side of his plate, 'how extraordinarily magnani-
mous and gentle we are, assuring these two giants that we will
not stamp on their toes. Take those away please, will you?' He
pointed to the vase of chrysanthemums in the centre of the
table. The waiter lifted them away. 'They bring my son out
in a rash.'

Jacob blushed. A quite gratuitous piece of cruelty, he
thought angrily. It seemed that his father liked to say these

things every now and then simply to reassert his dominance. He wanted to reply but could think of nothing.

He concentrated on buttering his hot roll, the butter melting to a rich gold.

'Have you met our Herr Schwarzwald?' His father was looking straight at him over his raised coffee cup.

'Man, a man . . .' he coughed to clear his throat. 'Chap of that name gave me lift back to the villa on Saturday night. First time that I've met him. I thought that he . . .'

'Yes. Yes. Please keep your voice down,' said his father in his cool civil servant's tone. 'We don't say what we think of someone outside our home. It is not good manners – and may be quite dangerous politically or commercially. I only say these things for your own good. If you are to get on in the Ministry . . . Well, things are changing so rapidly, aren't they? Perhaps for the better, almost certainly for the worse. It's our job to keep things ticking over, keep the machine going. These are very difficult times.'

How difficult, Jacob had almost forgotten. Katerina had eased all that from Jacob. He could think of nothing but her. Sometimes, when his father recalled Red atrocities years ago, he wanted hotly to defend his friends, who were all on the Left. Only his heart was not really in it. They were artists, after all.

'Anyway . . .' His father tidied a few flakes of bread crust on the tablecloth, shepherding them with one plump, little finger under the table mat. 'These English Theatre people – all right, are they? I've seen them once or twice – when old McCulloch ran things.'

'I'm afraid he's dead. They're a bit different now. And they're not all English. Gerald Stillinghurst runs it now.'

'Of course, there are so many of these theatres. The National. The Folk. The German. The Jewish . . .'

'If you are going to warn me against my friends . . .'

'My dear Jacob – I have no intention of doing anything so crass. Rightly or wrongly, you would do quite the opposite of whatever I said. It is the ancient law of parents and children.'

The pale blue eyes looked across the table. Was he making fun of him? Once again, as he had started to lately, Jacob felt envious of his father's sleek, well-fed good looks. There had been rumours in the Ministry of affairs. Quiet – or rather, subdued – rows through the wall of his parents' bedroom in the apartment. With the sudden courage of the timid Jacob said:

'I've already had to put up with a lecture from your informant Herr Schwarzwald.'

'Schwarzwald is an irritant,' said his father quietly, 'but not stupid. It would not do to run him down in public. Have you a cigarette?'

Jacob fumbled out his case and held it over the table. His father tapped the cigarette on his thumbnail and waited.

'And a light?'

The waiter circled their table. 'Anything else, gentlemen?'

'No, no thank you.' He looked round the emptying restaurant and said, 'No one is trying to restrict your friendships, dear Jacob. Just consider before you make commitments that could affect your life. Times may get difficult. In what ways we don't know yet – your new friends may even do you good if matters fall one way – or harm you if they fall another.'

'I cannot be that calculating, I'm afraid, about where I bestow my friendship.' The speech was pompous, but he would not give in.

'No.' His father stubbed out his cigarette. 'Come on. I want to show you something.' He got up and carefully put on his trilby hat, adjusting it in a mirror to a slight angle.

Instead of crossing the square to the Foreign Ministry, his father led him along a row of shops whose big plate windows reflected the lime trees and the trams in the square. They halted in front of Klein's, the patissserie.

'You see that – no, I'm not going to point. In the centre of the window.'

Jacob looked.

In the middle of the rich display of ornamented loaves, tarts, flans and cakes was placed a vase, from which two black, white and red swastika flags leaned on their sticks.

'Walk on,' said his father. 'We'll turn for the Ministry. You look in most of the German shops now – you'll see something like that. Or a picture of the Führer. There's a lot of pressure in the community to display these things – but most of it is genuine. All right, as far as it goes. I understand it – we've German blood in the family ourselves. There was little of this, though, as long as *his* eyes were turned southwards, on the Czechs. Now the man is talking about the Corridor and Poland. And us.'

'The Russians would not stand by for that?'

'Who knows. But either way, it does not make for a nice feeling, being the filling in the sandwich, does it? Ah, that's your Mr Stillinghurst.'

They halted by one of the round kiosks on which posters and handbills were pasted.

This one announced that, as part of the annual Independence Day celebrations, the English Theatre Troupe would be giving a special charity performance at the Presidential Palace of Shakespeare's *A Midsummer Night's Dream*. On Wednesday, August the 23rd, 1939.

'Are you taking part?' said his father, looking at him keenly.

'I may take a small part.' Jacob knew his face was burning red.

'Good. Good.'

They walked on, the grey-colonnaded facade of the Ministry looming up.

'Where are you lunching?' asked his father as they mounted the steps.

'With my friends.' Did his voice sound so defiant?

'Have a good time,' said his father equably.

The doorman saluted as they entered.

4

The café lay half-way up one of the remaining cobbled streets that led into the Old Town. Across its square, rather dirty window the single word STIECKUS was painted in thick white capital letters. In contrast to the neat, be-flowered cafés of the Oswald chain scattered across the newer parts of the city, Stieckus's had almost the air of a backstreet French bar; the heavy dark wood, the deep, dimly lit interior making the passer-by on the street uncertain whether the café was open or shut.

Jacob had first heard of Stieckus's at university; and about its artists and poets and revolutionaries. But he was a serious student, and it never occurred to him to visit the place on his vacations home.

It was after visiting an old university friend who had a room in the Old Town, that he happened to pass the café. His reunion with his friend had not been a success.

Jacob cut the tedious evening short, half afraid that he had been as boring as the other man. He came down through the Old Town and saw the name across the café window. Should he go in? He had all the proud loneliness – and desire for company – of those whose adolescence has been unduly prolonged. Scenting excitement, he pushed the door open.

It was a long room. Cigarette smoke hung dying under the lights. Half-way down, past a newspaper rack and a hatstand, the bar, copper topped, lay like an enormous coffin. At the very end of the room a few wide steps led up to two wooden, glass-pannelled doors. Behind these, he learned later, the mysterious, rarely seen Madame Stieckus kept rooms for 'respectable' guests. They were sometimes seen, looking down through the glass, with amusement or slight disgust, at the people in the bar. The two sides of the house rarely met.

Nearly all the tables were full; most of those sitting at them were young. Conversation was intense and noisy. At one end of the bar counter a little knot of working men were gathered. A checkers board lay on the bar. On the business side a huge man with a yellow Austro-Hungarian Empire moustache – it was that impressive – moved a piece towards the workers.

Heading for the bar, going between the tables, Jacob's sleeve was suddenly caught. He looked down into a young man's face. Brown, absurdly widened eyes, gazed up at him.

'Excuse me.' The hand detained Jacob. 'But, your head – did anyone ever tell you your head was *remarkable*?'

The other young man and two girls at the table were it

seemed on the verge of collapsing with laughter. With a confused smile, Jacob tugged himself away.

He stood at the bar feeling an intense embarrassment. Every eye must be on his back. The enormous *patron* went on playing checkers, completing a victorious, hopping move with a great burst of laughter before he at last glanced down the bar. He folded a towel with great deliberation and laid it neatly by the game board; only when this task had been completed to his satisfaction did he amble down the bar to Jacob.

'Yes, my young sir?' The face was knowingly insolent, the eyes set in pouched, wrinkled saucers, the eyebrows raised in mocking inquiry. This was Stieckus.

Jacob ordered coffee. Stieckus retired to the end of the counter and produced it from an ancient copper. He pushed the cup across the counter, took Jacob's money and went back to his checkers game.

Jacob drank standing at the bar, trying to – and trying not to – look at himself in the gaps of the bottle-filled mirror. His head – remarkable? What was remarkable about it . . . ?

Perhaps a certain distinction?

'Excuse me. Pardon me.' Someone was tapping him on the elbow.

He turned. It was the other man from the table.

'*Pozhalsta . . . Bitte . . .* Do you speak English?'

'Why yes,' said Jacob.

'Sorry about that – one never knows quite what language anyone's going to speak in this place.' He seemed relieved and looked into Jacob's face with such a look of genuine concern that Jacob dropped his eyes.

'I felt I just had to come over and apologize for Frank back there,' the young man went on. 'He is outrageous sometimes. I hope you weren't offended.'

'No . . . no.'

'My name's Stillinghurst.' He thrust out his hand. 'Gerald Stillinghurst.'

They shook hands.

'I *hoped* you wouldn't mind. Come and have a drink with us.'

'Well . . .'

It had been three hours later that Jacob had risen unsteadily to his feet and been pointed in the direction of home.

The outrageous Frank had welcomed them back to the table. He was a Cambridge chum, Gerald explained, staying with him at his mother's house just outside the city.

'I'm on a European tour, my dear,' said Frank patting Jacob's knee.

Frank was affectedly witty. He larded his speech with English and French slang. It was as if he was out to embarrass. But the two girls seemed to enjoy Frank's monologous 'conversation' – especially the elder of the two, staring at Frank with intense brown eyes, dipping and swaying with laughter at his jokes. And Jacob, as if the wine was rinsing his sight clearer, saw that she was not after all a girl, but a woman in her thirties. She swept a hand through her mass of honey-coloured hair and looked at him with a sort of contempt. He did not know how he had earned it. She must be drunk, he thought, to laugh so readily. It was as if she regarded this table, Frank, Gerald, their conversation as a private world and Jacob as a gauche, unwanted invader.

To make matters worse he had not even caught her name among Gerald's introductions – because he had been gazing at the girl.

She was small and delicately beautiful, like an exquisite, expensive doll. Her hair was black-blue, her eyes huge and grey, her nose finely flared, her mouth large and sharply carved. Her figure was slight, her perfect legs crossed, with one foot loosely swinging forwards and back, forwards and back as she smiled across at him. Her name – he caught this, and held on to it – was Katerina.

Then her head turned, her lips parted; she was laughing again at Frank.

Jacob wondered about their relations one to another. It was quite evident that Frank was not attached to either of the women; but totally unclear which of them was attached to Gerald. He sat between them, his dark forelock falling forward, turning to talk first to the girl, Katerina, then to the woman.

What did they have in common?

Sometime in the evening, Gerald explained.

'You're actually sitting in on a meeting of the English Theatre,' he said apologetically. 'You don't act, do you?'

55

'We're rather short at the moment, take anything,' said Frank laying his hand on Gerald's shoulder and again opening his eyes comically wide

The woman laughed.

'We're doing *A Midsummer Night's Dream*. By Shakespeare.'

'I've heard of it,' Jacob said idiotically.

'You wouldn't like to be Bottom, would you?' suggested Frank . . .

Walking, waveringly, home, he could think only of the girl, Katerina. And that the honey-haired woman was now called Anna, and why did she hate him? And that the café was the most wonderful place he had ever been in. And when he got home – a most foolish grin on his face revealed by the hall mirror – he said, answering his father's question:

'I found a most wonderful new place.'

'Indeed – where?'

'A café, Palace Square. Off Palace Square. Stieckus.'

'Oh, that place,' said his father. 'Our little Bohemia. You'll grow out of it. I hope.'

If anything he had grown into it. The café had been good to Jacob. It had given him two things he lacked: a friend in Gerald; and a lover – perhaps – in Katerina.

As he entered the café this lunchtime it held neither friend nor lover.

What if she didn't come? And for once he didn't want to see Gerald. Not that he feared him as a rival any more. The brilliant, handsome Englishman was, Jacob was sure now, having an affair with Anna. At any rate he seemed to have no interest in Katerina. It was simply that Jacob didn't want any of the theatre tribe who gathered in here at night to watch his midday tête-à-tête.

Two pairs of elderly men were playing chess at adjacent tables. Two middle-aged women taking coffee and pastries glanced up as he passed, then resumed their intense, whispered conversation.

Stieckus served him almost jovially. He pushed Jacob's coffee across and returned to the newspaper spread on the counter, humming tunelessly. Stieckus always kept a glass of Pils under the bar which, like the magic porridge pot, never emptied. As Jacob moved across to the newspaper rack he saw Stieckus take the glass from beneath, raise it to his lips, drink, and return the glass out of sight – in a motion that was at the same time slow and studied, yet accomplished so swiftly and smoothly that it could be taken for one of those illusions glimpsed at the corner of the eye, gone in a blink.

Jacob took down the German-language paper. It had become now completely pro-Nazi and anti-nationalist, writing in glowing terms of the new Fatherland and how unfortunate they were to be estranged from the wonderful place. Some of the *Volksdeutsche* had begun to bother the café. Gangs of muscular young men with party pins in their lapels or pinned to their brown shirts strutted in to insult the artists and the Jews. Fights had broken out, spilling into the street. The police, it seemed, were reluctant to intervene, arriving only in time to arrest assaulted innocents. There were complaints to Stieckus, asking him to ban the Germans and their newspapers from the premises. But Stieckus shrugged his massive shoulders and said, 'Not my battle, is it? Money is money. Would you rather have the Russians?' Like all good bar owners he was above politics or religion.

Raising the newspaper on its pole clear of the stand, Jacob turned to walk down to the tables under the window.

A man, about the same age as himself at twenty-two or three, had just come in. He wore a long open overcoat; under it a dark blue, well-cut suit. He was in Jacob's way, looking down at one of the chess games. Jacob halted between the tables, bearing the German paper like a standard before him.

'My apologies,' said the stranger, lifting his head. The most astonishing thing – his eyes were a deep violet in colour, surrounded by the most pure white. Disconcerted, Jacob indicated with his poled paper the way he wanted to go.

A rather satiric smile on his mouth, the other stood aside and gallantly bowed him through, going on himself to the bar.

Jacob sat at a window table and hid behind his paper. Reading of insanities, he tried to overhear the conversation at the bar.

The stranger's voice spoke in the local language and had inflections of the East – yet there was something else there, something added, unplaceable. Despite the Russian tinge the voice was pleasant, melodious . . . And surely *this* man could not come from the East – that wasteland of marsh and lake where the highest thing, they said in the capital, was the roofbeam the peasant banged his head on.

Jacob stole a glance round his paper. Side of rather round face, pale-dark skin, that was somehow radiant in the gloomy bar, as if light glowed through pale amber; fine, long-fingered hand taking change of small coins, for brandy. He buried himself again in the newspaper. The low talk at the bar went on.

Someone tapped on the raised paper. He lowered it in surprise. Katerina smiled across the table.

She had come in through the door and sat down without him noticing. Reflected sunlight shone through the dusty window onto her face.

'Gentleman here wants to know if anyone knows of a room,' Stieckus called.

Katerina half-turned in her chair, looking up at the bar. Was she pretending that she had not noticed the stranger when she came in?

'Who,' she asked, turning back, her eyes most marvellously full of light, 'is that?'

And to Jacob's annoyance – oddly tinged with a sudden fear – she called across to the stranger that, yes, she knew of a room.

What was she doing? That lingering farewell on the landing after the party. The parting kiss – was it an invitation to follow on, to chase; or merely yet another of those awfully casual theatrical farewells? Whatever it had been meant as, Jacob longed to repeat – to intensify – the feeling of intimacy in the shadows. This meeting in the café had been to drive the affair forward, into another gear. Now that damn stranger was coming across, slowly, his overcoat swinging lazily.

He halted, bowed to Katerina, and then to Jacob.

'Max Sawallisch,' he said. His eyes said, 'What are you to this girl, eh?' to Jacob.

Jacob stood, making introductions, sat down. Katerina invited Mr Sawallisch to draw up a chair.

'I would love to, really – but I do have an urgent appointment. Another time perhaps . . . ?'

So he did not sit down. Worse, he leaned with one hand on the back of Katerina's chair as she wrote down the street name and number of the vacant apartment.

'This is terribly kind of you. I'm quite new to the city. I do hope we may meet again. Madame. Sir.'

Jacob thought for one absurd moment that the man was going to kiss Katerina's hand. But no, he merely smiled down at her for a fraction longer than was necessary, then smiled in a subtly different way at Jacob, inclining his head again in a half-bow. Then he swept out.

'Why,' Jacob asked irritably, 'is he wearing an overcoat in summer?'

'Autumn.' Katerina corrected him. She leaned to one side to look through the window. 'It quite suits him.' She caught sight of Jacob's face, laughed and reached over and clutched his hand. 'Oh – dear Jacob. I do believe you are jealous . . .'

'A drive – but how?' she had said.

'By car of course,' he had replied smugly.

'*Your* car?'

'My father's.'

He stared at the book again, but his mind was in a mad flux of Katerina beside him in the car on the way to the coast, walking along the shore, sitting among the dunes – what? Dining afterwards at that big hotel, the Duke Archibald or whatever it was called. No, the Bulduri. He looked across the room. Be bold, Jacob, be bold.

His father sat at the desk, going through official papers. Each little batch was fixed at the corner by a green-and-white-striped cotton tag with brass keepers at each end. Turning the pages one by one, he read rapidly down the centre of each, his very sharp, hard pencil descending every now and then, like a conductor's baton, to initial or mark a phrase.

'I did tell your Mama, by the way,' said his father before Jacob could ask his question, 'not to worry. It was not *that* kind of make-up. But something you needed for your play.'

Jacob was put off his stroke by this.

'I'm sorry – you wanted something,' his father said.

'It . . . it's just that I wondered if I might borrow your motor on Saturday? Some friends . . .'

'Of course, my dear boy. It's of no use to me in the city.' He took two keys off a ring. 'That is for the ignition. That for the garage.' The car was kept in a lock-up a couple of streets from the apartment block.

Jacob came over and took them. 'Thank you,' he said, then, 'How did you know I had a part in the play?'

'You don't normally pore over Shakespeare or have stage make-up on your dressing-table.' His father laid his pencil fastidiously down alongside a sheaf of papers. 'I can't work on these any more tonight. I sometimes wonder if they have any relevance any more.' His hand reached up and raked through his hair, disordering slightly its grey mass. His other hand brought out his cigarette case from an inside pocket – his father always wore a suit in the house. 'Would you like me to test you on your lines?'

How kind his father could be sometimes.

'Get me my Shakespeare from the case over there.'

'Take mine,' said Jacob. 'My lines are marked.'

'Ah yes – that will be easier.' His father settled at the other end of the sofa, replacing his reading glasses on his nose. 'Let's hope you have a great success, Jacob. Who knows, you may become a great actor someday.' He laughed. 'Now tell me where to begin.' And his mouth assembled itself self-consciously, ready for the strange sounds.

5

The tall old houses seemed to totter down the narrow street, leaning towards each other and holding each other up, like drunks. Jacob left the car at the bottom. To his disappointment she was waiting in the street doorway. He had hoped to climb the stairs to the apartment.

Her appearance made up for the dashing of his first hope. She wore a simple fawn-coloured dress which fell to a little below her knee, a beige jacket with white facings and puffed shoulders that was drawn in and buttoned over her hips. A white scarf. Her hair was freshly dressed; her face delicately and carefully made-up. The mouth . . .

He was pleased. She had obviously gone to some trouble. As he had, with his green and grey, many-pocketed tweed suit, soft-collared shirt and striped tie. He was taking his girl out. For a spin, as they said in that English film he had seen last year. Out for a spin.

He could not turn the car in the narrow streets, so drove up into the Old Town until he found a timber-yard gateway he could turn in. They headed back towards the centre of the city.

The car was an Austin saloon imported from England. The country had many links with England – by centuries of trade across the Baltic, and more recently by the small force of soldiers landed in '19 to help with their fight against the Reds. Wasn't Gerald's father buried in the British Cemetery? A civil death rather than a military one, however – a heart attack – but still, buried in the earth that a grateful country had imported in a shipload from England, to reward the lives it had borrowed then lost. A small reward, as the first President unironically said.

They were leaving behind the huddle and muddle; on one side the great public squares lay open; on the other the river widened to meet the sea. They drove under the statue of The Liberator, that great modernistic figure – irreverently called The High Diver – of a young man soaring up from the embankment, his arms flung to heaven as he took off for the calm blue sky, ruffed with high white clouds.

They halted as a policeman directed traffic.

'Have you ever appeared there?' Jacob pointed across to the baroque facade of the National Theatre.

'Not with their company. They're terribly grand, you know.'

'With Gerald's?'

'The Jewish.'

'Oh.'

'I flit about a lot, I'm afraid. From one to another.'

He wanted to say, it's your looks. They all want you for your beauty. They all want to decorate their stages with your eyes, your mouth. But all he said, moving off again, was, 'I suppose that all makes for experience.'

'Um – I suppose so. But where does it lead?'

'Do you want to be an actress? I mean, a professional?'

'I don't want to be anything else. I can't *do* anything else,' she laughed.

'It's a pity we don't make films.'

'Why?'

'You'd look wonderful in films.'

'Oh no. Do you think so?' She relaxed back in her seat.

They were going through the docks, taking a short cut to the bridge he wanted. Cold stores, timber yards, warehouses with their crane ropes hanging from turrets down to the still, discoloured water. Across the top of one of the largest warehouses ran the name SCHWARZWALD; repeated another half-dozen times, he noticed, on doors, van sides, trucks. That awful man.

Now they were on the South Bridge, the one Jacob had walked over last weekend. Then his heart had been full of Katerina – now, as if as a tangible reward for his intense devotion, the girl herself had materialized beside him. He still could not quite believe that she would not disappear if his attention wavered from her for one moment. How unworthy he was, how utterly and unspeakably unfit he was even to venture to speak to this girl, let alone abduct her in his father's motor-car. How boring, how ugly she must find him after her friends. And his thoughts oscillated between this self-denigration to – not quite the other extreme – but to considering himself, well, not at all a bad catch. On balance. After all, discounting his own person, wasn't he the son of a most distinguished Government adviser, the heir to a small, but not negligible fortune? There was the large apartment in town; the house in the woods. His own position, which would surely not be unaided by his father's presence in the Ministry . . . But was he simply the sum of these social parts? What about himself? There he was puzzled. It is difficult to tell if many young men of twenty-two do actually exist as any more than a hollow armature round which a life is to be wound.

Those already in possession of some idea of themselves usually turn into one or another kind of monster: murderer; estate agent; professional soldier – people with so limited an idea of themselves that they constitute the *whole* idea of themselves; that they come to resemble almost at once, even as children, the person they will be until the day they die. No, Jacob was not yet defined. By himself or the world. The advent of Katerina and her world had confused him. He had even toyed – not daring to mention it to anyone – with the idea of becoming an actor himself. Of some sort. After all, Gerald had given him this little part in the play, hadn't he? And he could not be totally physically repellent, could he? Or Katerina . . . The thing Frank had said . . . Well, of course, the man was queer and frightfully witty and all that sort of thing but, well . . . No, he could not be so bad looking. It was a pity he had to wear his spectacles for driving. He hoped he looked like a young Chekhov or Trotsky with his hair brushed back. But his forehead was not broad enough and his hair, though thick, stuck up in a stiff brush rather than flowing in the beautiful waves of poets and playwrights and revolutionaries . . .

'Where *are* you taking me, Jacob?'

They were entering the forest. It was a quite different place in the day; as if a dark cathedral had had its outer walls removed, leaving only thin perpendicular columns and traceried windows and the air between them. Here and there, as the road curved, they glimpsed the silver sea.

'I thought we could take the boat from Poltava to Goda. If you don't mind, of course?'

'I haven't been since I was a little girl. How nice. Is that little café still there, just above the jetty? I remember my mother walking me right round the island. We nearly missed the last boat back. How nice it would have been to have to sleep there.'

'We used to sail across.'

'In your own boat?'

'Only a sailing dinghy.' He apologized for it. For their bourgeois riches.

'Not a steam yacht?' she said mischievously.

'No.'

'Did you see that absolutely *lovely* Swedish boat in harbour

63

last week? You could see the tops of the masts from Mrs Mikulis's back window.'

'Yes. He was a Swede. He came to talks at the Secretariat.'

'Where you work? In the Ministry?'

'Yes.'

'Oh – what was he like? Terribly rich?'

'A very nice man.' Jacob managed to give the impression that he had been included in the talks. But he had only seen the tall, stooping man with white hair yellowed again by age going into his father's office, the door shutting.

'You should have wangled us an invitation onto his boat. For both of us.'

'Oh no – I could hardly have done that.' Jacob was shocked by the un-civil-servant-like suggestion – but then pleased. That she had thought of them together.

They drew alongside the jetty. There were a couple of other cars and an excursion bus. Some bicycles leant together against the low sea wall.

The islands boat was in, against the wall at the end of the stone jetty.

She was quite long, *The Unicorn*, with a well deck at the stern covered by a striped awning; a storage compartment in the middle; one fat funnel like a half-smoked cigar; then the wheelhouse. Forward, another awning covered bench seats.

The boat plied along the chain of coastal islands delivering mail and supplies. There was a smaller motor launch that took trippers every other hour to Goda; but it was a matter of pride for Jacob to take Katerina on the bigger boat that did not make its way back through the islands until late evening. He would have liked to have gone all the way with it, as he had once as a boy. The boat was too big to put in to some of the very small islands. The fishermen would row out and goods be handed over the side while they looked coolly up at the well-dressed holiday-makers who would turn, half-amused, away from the deep-set, sea-cold eyes, and chatter among themselves. A shout to the captain; greetings and farewells in an unintelligible dialect; perhaps the cumbersome, time-consuming decanting of some fat, elderly relative from big boat to little. Then *The Unicorn* would give its refined shudder as the engines picked up and it glided on to its next destination.

Katerina went down the iron steps in front of him. She moved to the back of the boat and sat in a corner, patting the slatted wooden bench beside her.

The only other passengers were a couple who, by their air of superior shyness, looked to be English. Katerina smiled at them.

'Good morning,' said the Englishman gravely, in English. His wife nodded. Then they stared resolutely out to sea. Two more men hopped skilfully on board. Islanders, unmistakable by their rough clothes, combining the world-wide thick drab of fishermen and bright embroidered scarves knotted round their necks. At their feet they placed a wooden case. A young pig blinked his innocently wicked pink eyes through the bars in the front. A boy and girl about seventeen or eighteen came down the steps, carrying bicycles, talking loudly in German. They stowed their bicycles against the freight compartment and made their way forward, Jacob's eyes following the dimpled thighs of the girl in her khaki shorts as they mounted the short ladder, wobbled their way between the side rail and the cabin windows, to disappear somewhere among the awnings of the front deck. Guiltily, he glanced at Katerina. She gazed over the stern to sea, her eyes bright, her mouth a little stretched already in that smile that the sea and boats and movement towards some promise of adventure always bring.

'I think we are just in time,' said Jacob.

Indeed, large men were now inserting themselves into the tiny wheelhouse in an almost farcical manner. The boat trembled. Under the stern water frothed gently and they began to back away from the jetty.

The boat twisted and turned to the channel between land and island. As they drew out, Jacob gazed back at the black and green forest slanted above the cream-white beach. Further on, half-hidden by the turn of the coast, the capital appeared as a tiny, lead-toy city over which clouds were beginning to mass.

But above the boat the sky was a clear pale blue. The sun struck up off the water. A beautifully cool breeze was dragged across the boat. The huddle of men in the wheelhouse stirred and humped like a large benign animal in a too small cage. Beneath the forward awning the German couple lifted their chins against the blue sky, exalting in the air – as if on some propaganda poster they tilted their heads to the radiant future. To the approaching island.

6

The excursion launch was returning them, with the English couple, to land. They had explored the island chastely. Jacob had been a perfect gentleman, afraid to seize his moment. He wondered glumly if the German bicyclists had had better luck, if they were even now copulating with efficient, hygienic, Aryan zest in some grove, oblivious to the put-put of the missed boat pulling away.

Certainly they had seen nothing of the Germans as they made their way round the island. The English, on the other hand, they had kept spotting; walking ahead on the white dirt roads; appearing over headlands; buying chocolate in the little bar; each time acknowledging Jacob and Katerina with a tentative, reserved salute as if for the first time.

They have a sort of vacuum around them, Katerina said, laughing.

He had walked her all over the island; nagging at himself all the way whether he should take her in his arms here, there, over there . . . showing her the Fort, the Semaphore Station, the Pink Beach. It's only in the evening, he had had to explain, when the sun is down and you stand at a particular place, and at a certain angle, that the sand appears pink.

He looked back from the launch.

Tall, sparse pines gathered along the spine of the island. Hidden over the high end was the Quarry. Not a conventional scoop out of a hillside, but a long, deep ravine, widening where the stone had been followed into the island's body. Bushes grew thickly along its sunken edges.

Stone from here built the Old Town, he told her as they stood at the edge.

It's rather frightening. It's like a wound, she had said. Let's go back down.

Of course. Of course.

Had he shown her that cold, disused place as some sort of revenge for her light-heartedness, which seemed to dance in front of him, leading him on, but which he had not the courage to grasp, lurching in awkward pursuit?

A few minutes before they had stood in a small deserted cove. Oh, I do wish we could bathe, she had said.

But what about costumes?

No one would see them.

And how would they dry themselves?

It was still warm. Quite warm enough.

He would have had to give in – but for the English couple. As if by magic they appeared between the rocks, after presumably clambering down by a way only goats and the English would have attempted, the man raising his hand in that shy, repelling salute . . .

The harbour drew slowly nearer. He stood to disembark. Katerina gathered her jacket about her. Had she expected more of him? Had he been a coward? They would settle things later. Later.

They walked up from the jetty to the car. The English were once more ahead of them.

'What a divine place,' said Katerina, settling into the passenger seat. 'Where to now, Mr Balthus?' If she was mocking him she was doing it very gently.

'The Hotel Bulduri. For dinner.'

'The Bulduri? How grand.'

The car mounted on to the coast road once more and he headed south.

The evening was splendid; the sun hung over the sea. The clouds kept to the north; perhaps it was raining in the capital. A steamer smudged the horizon. The white triangular sails of dinghies spotted the sea as the car rounded a headland, and a long sabre of white sand curved in front of them. Then they were in the fringeing pines again, the sea and its boats flickering like a movie between thin trunks. The road swayed along low undulating cliffs that disclosed bay after small bay of white sand, with bathers caught in the poses of postcards, towelling their hair, tripping high-kneed from the surf, their children castellating the walls of huge sand fortresses. Sights lingered in the eye, and were suddenly overtaken. The bright carnival tops of ice-cream stalls. Closed-looking fishing villages. A pink and white hotel or a verdigris-green-roofed church broke abruptly from dark gulfs of the forest inland. The sailing boats that had been tiny for so long, grew and appeared again and were populated with men and boys leaning back on ropes as they scudded over the blue, broken waves, the wind freshening and fetching up the tops of the waves like the white edges on broken porcelain. Outpacing the boats, they saw a line of white hotels, mock palaces made of icing, set in lush green parkland. The ornamental trees before the hotels cast long, intricate shadows back across the grass. Biggest and grandest of all the hotels, with no trees, but a great, empty fountain in front, was the Bulduri.

In two great four-storeyed banks, on either side of the colonnaded entrance, green-blinded balconied windows stared out over the gardens, the grey coast road, the beach huts, the faded coloured windbreaks on the beach, the sand and shingle, out over the insignificant sea.

They drove slowly up the gravel drive. In the long sunlight the shadowed side of the fountain looked grey and a little weary.

Although the season was at its end, the Bulduri kept up its style. As they parked in a short line of cars a man hurried down the hotel steps and across the gravel.

'Perhaps you could borrow his costume for the play, Jacob,' Katerina giggled.

The man stood a respectful distance off, weighing up the car's occupants with that mixture of obsequiousness and watchfulness that all hotel employees have. He was dressed in a superb parody of the national costume. His trousers were scarlet with pearly beads down the edges. A long green coat, with white flowers embroidered on the lapels and silver buttons. A tricorne hat – which he lifted as Jacob got out of the car.

'Welcome to the Bulduri,' he stage-whispered. 'You are to dine?'

'We are to dine,' said Jacob evenly. He was glad of his suit and tie, though they had made him feel hot and faintly ridiculous on the trek round the island.

The doorman's feet seemed to glide up the steps. They followed to the revolving glass door. He stood back to let them enter, snapping his fingers to someone inside.

Katerina looked up at the gilded, cherubed ceiling, then gaily back at Jacob. She somehow subverted the air of immense gravity in the huge reception hall – as if far away in one of the wings an emperor lay dying, and one of his mistresses, unknowing, had come to call.

From the warm evening in the courtyard, they entered a submarine world. Chandeliers let down from the ceiling's great height cast a discreetly weakened gleam. Thick piled carpet and panelled walls absorbed voices. A man, who sat reading a Swedish newspaper on the long leather sofa against the wall, obligingly yawned, his mouth working slowly and deliberately open and shut, like a fish feeding.

The doorman handed them over with much to-do to another functionary. Immensely tall, lantern-jawed, his face made pale by years of this aquatic life, this man was dressed in a black suit which encased his frame as if he had been put into it as a youth and had stretched it with age. He conducted them up the wide stairs to the art-nouveauish doors of the restaurant. He held a door open. Then he backed away, somehow disappearing into the wall. Perhaps he feared the light.

For the restaurant was radiant. The last of the sun shone horizontally through the open balcony windows, blinding Jacob.

A white impression of a waiter materialized at his elbow.

'You have reserved, sir?'

'I have reserved.'

The reservation seemed a foolish redundancy. The place was almost empty. Not quite. In one corner by the window, half-hidden by the blinding aureole of sunlight, a family sat; heavy, jowled father and fat mother upright, their hands in

69

their laps, and two children, a boy and a girl, slumped, pale in the frosty light cast up from the white tablecloth.

Obviously out of their depths. A treat gone wrong, Jacob thought snobbishly. He pointed, or, rather, dabbed his finger towards a table in the far corner.

'May we . . . ?'

The waiter squinted round also, chewing gently at the damp bottom of his moustache – then seemed to make up his mind. 'Why, certainly . . .' He led them between the tables.

They talked over the menus, picking dishes – Katerina leaving the wine to him. Jacob loved this. It was as if they were – a couple. A man and his mistress. The presence of Katerina across the table was an emblem of his ability to capture such beauty, to command it to appear, and he felt entitled to stare boldly at the waitress who came to serve them.

I know women, his eyes said, I could have you too, my dear.

The waitress stopped her ducking and weaving for a moment and stared back.

'Sorry . . . ?' she began.

He dropped his eyes and pretended he couldn't find something on the menu. Ah, there it was. How silly of me. Thank you.

The waitress smiled neutrally.

The restaurant began to fill. The sun had dipped into the sea when they finished eating. The chandeliers shone brilliantly. Each table was covered with immaculate snow; glasses and silver caught the lights and made the faces gayer, the eyes brighter, the hair crisper, the cheeks of children pinker, their parents browner.

When they came down, the same doorman hastened to guide their way. Descending the steps, the sky above was still blue at its height, with a few tiny salmon-tinged clouds; the flowers in the borders smelled fuller and sweeter.

It was amazing how light and easy he felt now. He had even asked her over dinner if she thought that man – what was his name? Swordfish? Wallfisch? – had found his room yet?

Which man? she had said.

They drove back along the darkening coast, the lights of the city becoming visible ahead. Katerina chattered happily about the island, the drive, the hotel. They laughed at the tall black-suited man.

'Why now – look. How beautiful. Look,' she suddenly cried out. 'Stop the car. Oh do, Jacob. Do.'

He pulled the car into the verge. They were on a grassed headland, just before the road curved back into the forest.

'Look,' said Katerina. 'It's the Swedish boat I told you about.'

The schooner stood out from the harbour. The white mainsails were like three pages of a book fanned open; the two triangular jibsails waved handkerchiefs in farewell. Tiny figures moved on her.

'Come on. Let's wave her goodbye.' Katerina scrambled out of the car and ran up on to the point, to the top of a dune. He followed her slowly. She stood tiptoe on a little hill, waved her handkerchief, and shouted, 'Goodbye. Goodbye.' The white boat sailed on, silent and beautiful and unrecognizing.

As he came up, she stumbled backwards. Into his arms. They kissed for the second time, but this time Katerina clung warmly to him. She took his hand as they walked to the car, looking back once to the schooner, its sails luminous in the failing light.

'Oh, wasn't it beautiful? Wasn't it grand?' sang Katerina.

'Yes. It was,' said Jacob, letting out the clutch.

Above the spires of the capital, clouds mounted massively, orange on their billowing tops with the last slanted rays of the sun. As they drove near, the clouds stained slowly grey and the last of the blue went out of the sky. In the city neon signs blazed above the big stores.

They bumped up into the Old Town on cobbled side-streets.

'You can leave the car in the gateway to Abraham's Yard,' said Katerina. 'There'll be no one there until Monday.'

His mouth was dry as he locked the car. She came round and stood a little way up the street, waiting for him to catch up.

'Do you want to go to Stieckus's?' he heard himself say.

'No. I don't think so. Come on, Jacob, don't be shy.' And she walked on quickly, a pace ahead, hips swinging a little jauntily, up to her street door.

7

'. . . the Communists are banned. Well and good. But they intrigue. The *Bruderschaft*, the *Hakenkreuz* are banned. And what do they do? They parade openly in the streets with their swastikas. Because the Germans have said they will protect us. Do you know what the Polish Ambassador said to the President? "Under the Germans we will lose our liberty; under the Russians we will lose our souls." ' His father's hands gripped the chair arms.

'. . . as if their word could ever mean anything. We cannot look for our salvation there. We have been through all this before. Why, in '19 they wanted to settle the unemployed, the scum of Berlin, up here. We were to be a colony even after they had lost *that* war. Then we had the Reds . . .' He had been talking with this sort of repetitive exasperation for half an hour now.

'Our democracy is fragile enough. We had sixteen Prime Ministers in fifteen years before Kubin took over. Things were under control at last. Now our future is in the hands of others again . . .'

The telephone rang. Lately there had been a lot more work at the Ministry. Jacob moved towards the door.

'Where are you going?' – his father capped his hand over the mouthpiece, glaring at him.

'It's the final dress rehearsal. I must go. It's past six . . .'

His father spoke irritably into the instrument. Jacob smiled, backed through the door, and shut it behind him.

This was the third of these lectures in his father's office, after his own work was done on a lower floor of the Ministry. Well, the world might be worrying itself to death – it did not worry Jacob as he swung blithely down from the tram on the very edge of the northern suburbs.

Following Gerald's instructions he walked along an avenue of limes. The last, large houses spread their roofs among the trees, each roof marked by some eccentricity of design: a fretworked pediment; a row of carved crescent moons on their backs along the ridge roll; a bell tower; a dovecot. The avenue petered out to the hedges of smallholdings with here and there a glasshouse or chicken coop. A few stones fallen from a wall into the ditch signalled the end of the city.

The evening was warm. He looked back at the trees and then went on. For days he had felt the ghost of Katerina's body clinging to his; the murmur of her fingers on his back; the smell of her hair. The world was beautiful. Who could wish to destroy all this? It was madness. Nothing would happen. By the force of his great love, the world would remain the same. Jacob strode on, feeling he had solved some problem that had perplexed all others; the suitor in the fairy tale who has slain the monster and may claim the eager princess.

This must be the turning Gerald had mentioned. A driveway between two stone pillars with rusted iron gates hanging off them. Part of some old, great estate; one of those broken up in '19.

He went between them.

Under his arm was the box of Leichner make-up; in a bag his costume – a peasant's green coat and a pair of torn brown corduroy trousers; a blue blouse and a pair of long peasant boots that laced up the sides.

The track was rough, tufted with grass in the middle where wheels had not ground. In the trees ahead were two white gateposts. On the green mailbox at the side was painted in neat white letters

STILLING
-HURST

The gate was open. He went on up a drive whose gravel looked as if it had been combed. A great plane tree stood on a lawn to his right, on his left was a high box hedge over which he could see the long green-tiled roofs of the house, the green and white chevrons and crosses and key-patterns of the wooden upper storey.

The windows were open, but no one was looking out. The place looked deserted. He mounted the steps of the front verandah. A buzz of voices came through the house from the back. He knocked loudly on the open door. A fat brown and purple sack moved convulsively on a cane armchair, growled and then relaxed, revealing itself as a dog as one great paw banged onto the floor. Across a bamboo table lay copies of *Punch* and the *Illustrated London News*.

Someone – a woman – was coming through the dark interior, heels clicking over the wood-tiled floor.

'Why – if it isn't little Jacob.' Anna, in her stage costume of Edwardian high-necked blouse and long grey skirt halted mid-way across the room as she recognized him. 'Come in, dear boy. Come in.' She turned and tick-tacked away without waiting for him. 'It's Snug the Joiner,' she called out to the murmuring crowd ahead.

He followed, hating her for her contempt. If Katerina loved him, why shouldn't all women? With the cynical eyes of a newly qualified connoisseur he studied her hips moving in the long skirt.

They walked through two shady, solidly furnished rooms and out onto the back verandah.

The cast was assembled on a long lawn. At its end was an orchard of ancient, heavily-laden apple trees.

Gerald had explained that the play was to be re-set in – almost – modern times. Just before the war, hence the costumes. *The scene: Athens, and a wood hard by* – why, that was the capital and the forest was it not? Theseus and Hippolyta – wealthy landowners, of the German sort, doomed to lose their great estates with Independence. The play takes place everywhere and nowhere, said Gerald. This way gave it an added resonance for an audience who would watch it at the Palace. Almost Chekhovian, he mused. A sort of Midsummer Night's Cherry Orchard, giggled Frank.

The boy and girl fairies were in national costume. To heighten the comedy, the rustics were to be played with the uncouth accents and manners and dress of the Eastern Russian peasants – whom the city regarded as shiftless, dirty and backward.

The quartet of lovers? Katerina as Hermia; Anna as

74

Helena; the tall blond German as Demetrius; Gerald as Lysander.

Gerald broke from the crowd and came towards the verandah. Dressed in a white uniform, like a Ruritanian general, his face was cut with a smile of genuine welcome.

'Jacob. You found us then?'

'We thought you'd come in costume,' Frank said, bobbing behind. 'How very disappointing.'

Frank wore a silk shirt of red and green lozenges and black ballet tights and pumps.

'No . . . I would have looked ridiculous.'

'Surely not,' said Frank smoothly. 'What are you anyway? I've forgotten. I'm Puck. As you may have realized.'

'He's a rude mechanical,' said Anna.

'Don't you adore it, Anna?' Frank opened his arms and pirouetted before her. 'I modelled it on one of Picasso's acrobats – you know, the Saltimbanques – the tall, *triste* one who doesn't know what to do with his hands.'

'It's gorgeous . . .'

'You're a little late.' Gerald took Jacob's arm. 'I'm afraid you'll have to hurry,' he said as he led the way back into the house.

Stairs rose between the two rooms.

'Up here.'

'Gerald?'

The voice was loud and commanding. An elderly woman stood on the landing, looking down at them. She was quite tall – or perhaps it was the angle and her ferociously upright bearing that made Jacob think so. She had a large oblong face rather like a horse and determined grey eyes that fixed first on Gerald, then on Jacob.

'Mother, this is Jacob. Jacob Balthus,' said Gerald as they came up to her. 'My mother.'

'Good afternoon.' Her grip was firm, the hand cold. 'Which one are you, Mr Balthus? You *look* quite normal.'

'He's our Snug.'

'Oh – one of the funnies. I'm afraid I have never found Shakespeare in the least amusing. You must excuse me. Are you staying to tea?'

'He's in the number, Mother.'

'One of the five thousand. Don't let me keep you from your play, Gerald. Mr Balthus. I only hope the President appreciates it,' she said as she stumped down the stairs.

'Through here.' Gerald opened a door.

'Will your mother be coming?'

Gerald sat on the edge of the neatly made single bed and lit a cigarette. 'Couldn't keep her away. Not for the play, of course. A chance to swan it over you bloody foreigners. Doyenne of the English community and all that.'

'Foreigners?' Jacob shook out his costume.

'To an Englishwoman everyone else is a foreigner. We carry England about with us. Like a tent.'

As he changed, Jacob felt as if he was undressing on a crowded beach. Gerald lounged back on the bed, smoking, watching him with a total lack of curiosity.

'By the way,' he said. 'You don't know where Katerina is?'

'No – afraid not,' Jacob answered. So the two of them were linked in the minds of others. Jacob and Katerina. Katerina and Jacob. I am the man who has slept with Katerina Osters. Miss Osters kept herself for me. Miss Osters is in love with me . . .

'Thought she might have come with you. If she isn't here soon, we'll have to start without her. Bloody awkward.'

'Sorry,' said Jacob, man of the world, casually misplacing his women.

'OK,' said Gerald. 'Ready?'

Back on the verandah, Gerald clapped his hands.

'Ladies and gentlemen, boys and girls.' They started to drift towards him. 'Is everyone here? Can we now begin?'

Katerina had arrived in the mob of frock coats, long dresses and peasant costumes. Jacob gazed down at her. She looked ravishing in her costume. Had she come in it? People must have thought she was a beautiful ghost.

'Now, as you know – Jacob, sorry, could you join the others on the lawn?' Gerald pointed down the steps.

'Oh. Of course. Sorry.' Blushing, he clattered down.

'As you know,' Gerald began again, 'I've had to cut quite a bit of the play so we can fit it in the time allowed. Besides which, I don't know how long the President will be able to stand it.'

There were isolated laughs from the people in front of him.

'Are we allowed to say that? So – I've cut quite drastically. The principals are quite secure on their lines, I think. But for some who are not quite so used to things, we've thought up a little wheeze. All the peasant types can read their Pyramus and Thisbe from these sort of rustic cue boards we've made. They're mounted on sticks.' He held one up. 'We can work up a bit of business mis-reading and so on. It is to be *hoped* it will make it funnier. All right? So – a quick run through for positions.'

The State Room of the Palace was represented on the lawn by white tapes arranged in a large rectangle. Long shadows were cast across it by the larches at the side of the garden.

Gerald strode into the middle, resplendent in his white uniform.

'Can we go from the opening I've underlined in red?'

Egeus was an English businessman in an elderly tweed suit. He coughed. 'Sorry, old boy.' He put on a pair of spectacles to read his script. 'Ah, yes.' He coughed again. ' "Happy be, Theseus, our renowned duke . . ." Sorry, Gerald – do I say that accent?'

'Yes, "renownéd".'

Theseus, the commercial attaché at the British Embassy, stepped forward in a frock coat. ' "Thanks, good Egeus. What's the news with thee?" '

'Ah . . . "Full of vexation come I . . ." '

Jacob waited for Hermia's opening speech. First violin in the quartet of quarrelling lovers. Then she began:

' "I do entreat your grace to pardon me.
I know not by what power I am made bold;
Nor how it may concern my modesty . . ." '

How sweet and strange her voice sounded in English; the alien vocables lifted into the air and drifted to the sky, into the orchard, back along the verandah, where Mrs Stillinghurst had sat down, book on lap, her rather severe face under a broad-brimmed summer hat staring out at them.

The light going, they finally broke up. People drifted upstairs chattering, relieved, triumphant, to change and come down again through the shadowy house, for tea. Jacob wanted to sit by Katerina on the verandah. But she was deep in absorbing, excluding conversation with Anna, the two of them, viewed from across the room, looking like conspirators.

He had been rather terrible, he knew, in the rehearsal – made more miserable, as he stumbled over another line, by seeing Katerina's understanding smile from the edge of the white tape.

Gerald circulated among his guests. To try to regain some face, some intimacy with his friend, Jacob waited until Gerald was at his elbow then whispered eagerly, and in revenge, 'Surely Frank isn't going home like *that*?'

Frank sat on the floor at Mrs Stillinghurst's feet. He was still dressed in his acrobat's costume. He leaned forward, arms folded on his knees, and gabbled up at Mrs Stillinghurst and an English friend of hers, who had joined the party from a house nearby, an elderly, faded woman in a faded dress decorated with tiny red flowers.

'Why not?' said Gerald. 'He's going on somewhere, I think.'

'I can imagine,' said Jacob.

'What?' Gerald stared at him. 'Jacob – you really should consider growing up a little. You know.' And his best friend left Jacob's side and strode away.

Laughter – an unusual sound – came from Mrs Stillinghurst and her friend. Frank was being politely outrageous, no doubt.

Jacob was determined to seek comfort. He went over and stood in front of the big cane chair in which Katerina perched, with Anna sitting on one of the arms.

'Katerina. I would like to speak to you for a moment. If I may?'

She looked up at him in a slightly puzzled way.

'Of course you *may*, Jacob.'

Was Anna suppressing a laugh? She got up.

'I'll see you later, darling,' she said to Katerina, and smiled coldly at Jacob. She strolled away down the verandah, people turning to talk to her.

'Sit down,' said Katerina. She tapped the arm of the chair. It shifted and creaked complainingly under his weight. For a moment they both sat staring in front of them, Katerina glancing up at him once, quickly, like a bird, an expectant smile on her lips. But he was not happy, and he was nervous.

From down the verandah scraps of conversation drifted back to them; the conversation turning, inevitably as it did these days, to the political.

You have to admire him.

. . . he has such extraordinary eyes

Like a wolf

Saw them in the last lot. Cardboard boots, half of them. Those that had them – the rich, fruity voice of Egeus. The ones that did. Cardboard. Cardboard boots. Mean to say . . .

Kubin is a Fascist

Sh . . .

There was a sudden silence. It spread down the verandah. Everyone looked at their neighbour. Then someone laughed.

Tut, said Mrs Stillinghurst. As if they could not say precisely what they pleased.

It's best to be careful.

God save us from the Reds again . . .

Times have changed. No one *wants* a war.

Boots made of cardboard . . .

Look at the trade we do . . .

. . . with both . . .

What if?

No one could be so foolish.

A game of bluff, I think you'll find . . .

From the far end, Frank's voice rose shrilly in the climax of some story and the horrible laughter erupted again.

Then Katerina said, her voice lowered, 'Did you get home all right, the other night?' All the half-fears he had had of her crumbled. His smile was a smug wrapping over his mouth that he wanted to be rid of, but that persisted, growing more and more idiotically triumphant.

'Yes,' he whispered in return.

He tried again to hold her hand, but it slipped casually into her lap. He must really not be so naive. To sit holding hands was hardly sophisticated conduct in this circle. He wished them all gone; the two of them to be left alone on this verandah

79

until the true night came, and candles were brought out, their reflections wavering then steady in the windows, the Pole Star burning through the glass roof . . .

But the evening darkened and grew cold and they all moved, chattering still, into the room behind, and Katerina was once more separated from him. Sitting between Frank and Anna on a sofa, she seemed greatly – treacherously – entertained by Frank's incessant, brittle wit.

The party began to break up with great floods of good wishes to each other in the forthcoming performance. Goodnight, Mrs Stillinghurst. Goodnight, Gerald. Goodnight, Frank . . . Jacob saw Katerina gliding out. He caught her up on the front verandah. Why hadn't she waited for him?

'Katerina. You're going? There's no tram back to town for half an hour.'

'I have to take a lift, Jacob.' Huddled inside her thick coat, over the stage costume still, she smiled up at him.

'But, I thought . . .'

'Jacob.' Gerald called to him from the doorway connecting the two big rooms.

'Someone brought me,' she said. 'I did promise to go back with them. It's my family.' He had never thought of her as having any family. 'We'd give you a lift, but I'm not going back to the flat tonight. You do understand? I really must hurry.'

She bobbed up, kissing him fleetingly on the cheek. Then she was gone.

Where was the car for her lift? Presumably out on the road. She disappeared among the trees.

Gerald's voice came from behind again. 'Jacob – we're not holding you up? It was just on a couple of the words. Pronunciation.'

'No, no,' he said. 'That's quite all right.'

He went back into the house.

8

There are great events in our youth. Nothing but great events.
Past and future are disregarded. Only the present burns.

On the night of the performance Jacob walked to and fro
at the edge of the lake in the Palace grounds.

Tonight was the last perhaps of the true, marvellous, late
summer nights. The rich oaks towered. Further on, the cedars
swept like capes across the Palace walls. Over the lake the
moon hung a huge orange globe. From the Battery wall arcs
in the searchlights began to sputter into life. You could hear
the 'snap' as a glow blazed suddenly and a beam of light was
thrown up and fixed on the upper storey of the Palace.

On the lake, from a boat whose rowers were obscured in
grey cloaks with black masked faces and gloved hands, one
by one, candles were floated on the lake, and lit.

The walking, the beauty of these scenes, concentrated
his thoughts. On Katerina. That story last night at the
Stillinghursts' – of a lift. Family. He did not believe a
word of it. But it had robbed him of sleep. If he had not
caught her up she would have gone off without telling him.
Him. But after thinking half the night and all the day – now
he understood. Last night she had wanted to get away from
him. So he had suffered all that misery. But tonight – tonight
he at last understood all. Tonight then, said Jacob, halting
at the lake's edge, punching his right fist into his left palm
in excitement, tonight everything will be put right.

This was the Great Event of his life, no doubt of that.
Tonight he would introduce Katerina to his parents. Before
coming out ahead of them this evening he had blurted out
that there was somebody, somebody special, he wanted them
to meet. After the play. They would be up there on the terrace,
with the other guests. After the play he was going to ask her
to marry him. That was what was needed. That was what

she wanted. He had thought long and hard about it, until the truth had at last crystallized in his mind. He had not seen it, tied up in his own selfish infatuation. How cruel and thoughtless he must have appeared to her. He had not asked her the one indispensable question. Poor girl – it must have seemed he had seduced her so lightly. No wonder she had been talking so urgently to Anna. It even made him view Anna in a better light. The best friend. But now he would take matters in hand. Become master of the situation. And she would be his forever. Clenching his fists in an ecstasy of determination, he stalked up the Palace lawn, away from the lake.

On the terrace, doors stood open to the State Room. At one end of the terrace a buffet had been laid on white-clothed tables. People were using the low stone walls as seats. Or they stood in little, murmuring groups, manipulating glasses and cigarettes against the dark, as if they were training fireflies. When the candles had first been lit on the lake they had turned, and a low 'ah' had come from them, an exhalation of delight. But now the hardly wavering yellow lights, reflecting lonelier and thinner in the black water, had become as much a part of the night as the ignored stars above.

Jacob moved – a graceful, forgiving angel – between them. The conversations sounded happy. Nothing could give offence tonight. Tonight the world was at its most perfect. The forthcoming performance no longer held any terror for him. So what if he made a fool of himself? The world should be made for fools and lovers.

'Jacob? Look Minna, he walks straight past us.' It was his father and mother, both sedately handsome in their evening clothes.

His mother smiled at Jacob and said, 'Don't tease him. He's probably trying to remember his lines.'

'Shouldn't you be in there?' His father nodded to the ballroom. 'Getting ready or something?'

'No – there's still time. You . . . you're not rushing off afterwards or anything? Not straight away?'

'No, of course not.'

'You said there was someone you wanted us to meet.' His mother smiled conspiratorially at Jacob.

'I like a good party,' said his father. 'I hear your Mr Stillinghurst has a few surprises in store for us.'

Surely Mr Stillinghurst was dead? Then he realized his father was talking about Gerald. What his father really meant was that he had been finding out about Gerald.

'A few perhaps.' Jacob looked about him for the first time that evening.

Tonight was part of the week-long Independence celebrations. A special year this – twenty years on from the first meeting of the first Republican government – and tonight a special one to mark the help they had received from the British people in those times, and since.

Most of the English community were here tonight; Mrs Stillinghurst's stern head rose out of one group. They normally kept a little aloof from those they patronizingly called the 'locals'. They had their own church; their imported Bath Olivers. Tonight was no more than their due. Though why, some complained, they should have to be subjected to *Shakespeare*, of all things.

A quiver of annoyance, of snobbish irritation passed through Jacob as he recognized somebody else who was here tonight. How had *he* got in?

The Sawallisch man. With a blonde-headed girl. He was waving at him. Making his way towards them. What would his father think of this acquaintance?

But before he could make any prefatory, apologetic comments, his father had raised a hand in salute and was saying cheerily, 'Mr Sawallisch. So glad you could come.' And he was chatting away as if they were old friends. Introducing wife, son . . . 'Oh, you've already met? Small town.' And who is this?

The girl was Miss Witkowska. Ella Witkowska. She was dressed inappropriately in a summer frock, with only a woollen cardigan draped over her shoulders to keep out the night chill. She was passably pretty, Jacob thought. But after Katerina . . . Her rather sullen face was smiling now, at something Max Sawallisch whispered to her.

For this was, evidently, what they were to call him. Max. His father called the stranger that. Max, Jacob's father explained, was working at the Reuter's agency in the city.

A journalist, specializing in politics and economics. He has, he said, been most useful to us. Most.

Jacob began to look at Max in this new way.

Max was splendidly handsome in his evening suit. The faintly shabby air that had hung about him in the Café Stieckus had entirely disappeared. He was an affable, confident man of the world. The hair was well-dressed; a rather flashy ring shone on one hand. His cigarette case was gold; his manners impeccable. Jacob's mother was obviously charmed with him. He must come to dinner with them. And Miss Witkowska too.

Jacob wondered if the girl was Max's girlfriend. It was difficult to tell. She worked in the same agency. They had come here together. But there was some reserve in her that kept her apart. And Max was only as professionally charming with her as he was with everybody.

'Where . . . ?' Jacob's mother whispered to him. Where is the girl you asked us to meet? Was that it? Before he could hear the rest of the question they were interrupted.

There was movement between the biggest pair of doors into the ballroom. A man stepped out on to the terrace and announced, 'The President.'

The murmuring ceased. Everyone looked at the doors. The people sitting on the low wall got up.

The silence was a gesture of respect rather than of excitement. In such a small capital and country the President was almost ubiquitous in his presence: dedicating memorials; unveiling plaques; taking the salute at parades of soldiers, farmers, milkmaids; attending the Lutheran cathedral, the Catholic cathedral, the Synagogue – even shopping, when he was noticed but politely ignored.

The country needed a strong man. That was what was said at the time of the coup. And Kubin certainly looked the part. Built like a farmhouse wardrobe, he had, he said in his first speech as President, 'seized the country by the scruff of its neck and lifted it, kicking and struggling, above the pack of dogs who would devour it'. The capital had said he would not last, but the country said, look, we have sent you a peasant – and peasants know how to look after themselves.

There was no great fanfare now. The President seemed to

wander on to the terrace as a man might into his back garden. Short, broad shouldered, a massive head with cropped white hair – dressed in a grey suit with a couple of Orders pinned to it, he looked what he had been for many years, a farmer.

Tonight Kubin had the wife of the British Ambassador on his arm, a thin, fair woman whose bones seemed to slide just a little too elegantly in her bared shoulders and back. Madame Kubin came out behind them, with the Ambassador. She was a small fat woman who looked always a little surprised to find herself inside the Palace. She reached up to the arm of the Ambassador and he – tall, lanky, with a Sherlock Holmes nose – leaned forward to accommodate her.

A gaggle of officials and Ministers walked out with their own wives. A polite patter of handclaps greeted the Presidential party. The President smiled. Behind him, General Eichenfeld, leader of the Army, scowled. The people were drawn along the terrace. The President walked down, shaking hands, the Ambassador whispering in his ear.

Mrs Stillinghurst, in a royal blue silk dress, presented a book to the President. A little girl handed a bouquet to the President's wife.

Jacob looked round one last time for Katerina. No – none of the theatre people could be seen. They must all be inside by now.

The President held up a hand. The President was going to make a speech. Jacob sidled through the crush of people – all their faces turned to the front, levering themselves up on their toes to catch a glimpse of the Old Man. The President began to speak. Jacob slipped between the curtains of a door into the ballroom.

The President sat with his hands folded on his stomach, his face illuminated, a serene and immobile Buddha. The raised stage came to within a few feet of the front row. Squinting through a hole in the forest backdrop Jacob saw the President lean over and mouth a question to the Ambassador's wife. Puck capered before him. He blinked. Jacob and the other yokels were greeted in silence – the attempted rough accents, approximating to the President's own, were – it was obvious – found unfunny, even offensive. The generally good but unShakespearian grasp of English of Jacob and the others did not reveal the humour of the lines. He hurried through, gabbling.

The applause at the interval was tepid and soon faltered to a halt. As soon as the curtains had settled – drawn to by two girl fairies – Gerald began to have a row, quietly, with Oberon. Jacob stood, feeling the clown he was supposed to be, in his peasant costume. A girl went past, carrying a cardboard bush.

'Can we have the stage area cleared, please,' Gerald hissed, 'so we can remake the set.'

The ceiling soared away above the curtains on their make-shift rails. Jacob could see the great chandeliers of the room beyond the stage and hear the chairs pushed back, the rising, relieved chatter of the audience.

The actors moved back to the rooms they had been allo-cated. Jacob could still not get near Katerina. The women were in one room, the men in another. He had hoped to draw her to one side in the interval. How romantic for his purpose, this shadowy mock-Arcadia. She had gone straight to the women's room. He would simply have to wait. Unbuoyed by success, he made ready, putting on his heavy Lion's head. Unfortunately, the eyes did not quite line up with his. Not until he stumbled onto stage, clasping his bark crib, and turned the wrong way did he see that of the four front chairs the President's was empty. How awful – he had not been able to stand any more or had been offended. Anyway, he had gone. But his absence did make the audience more relaxed. Jacob actually managed to raise a laugh – unintended – when he had to raise the crib to the Lion's left eye – and found that he could not see his lines . . .

'But *where* was the President?' Frank wailed, as they backed off after the quite sustained applause of the second curtain call.

'Business,' said Gerald grimly. 'They say he was called away on business.'

'Do think he could have made the effort,' snorted Frank.

Now Katerina and Anna and an English woman who had played Titania were receiving flowers from a little girl. They stepped back. The curtains were rushed to for the last time.

Jacob picked up his Lion's head. They were all to join the party for a buffet in the Great Hall. He must hurry.

Gerald came into the changing room, tearing at his general's uniform. 'I shall go and find out what happened to the President,' he said. When he had dressed and rubbed his face pink with a towel he strode out, saying again, 'I shall find out.'

'Well, what do you say? Not so bad, eh, old boy? Jacob, isn't it?' It was the businessman, Egeus, carefully peeling off his grey beard. 'Went quite well. All things considered, eh?'

'You haven't seen my trousers?' Jacob asked rather testily.

'Trousers? Trousers? Can't go out without them, can you. Mean to say . . .'

Jacob began to paw through the piles of clothes on either side of his.

'What *are* you looking for?' said Frank breathily by his ear.

'Trousers. Chap's lost his trousers.'

'Shakespeare, my dear. Not Feydeau.'

Jacob saw the trousers; they had slipped to the floor. They had been trodden on.

'Oh God – look at them.'

'Soon fix that,' said Egeus. 'Only a bit of dust. Hold 'em up. I'll give 'em a bit of a whack with my staff.'

Jacob, now in his white shirt and dinner jacket, held up the trousers and Egeus began to beat them with his stage staff. Jacob looked at his watch. He had been in here ten minutes? It would take Katerina longer to change. He hoped. He rescued his trousers from their enthusiastic flagellator and hurried into them. Egeus seemed quite disappointed. 'Sure they're all right?' he asked, inspecting Jacob.

'Quite sure, thank you. I really must go.'

Frank, stark naked, stood in front of him as he turned.

'Sorr-eee,' he sang out. 'Always seem to be in someone's way, don't I?' His unpleasant, mocking laugh followed Jacob out.

He waited at the women's door.

Five minutes. Ten. Come on.

Beyond the curtains the ballroom was silent. The scenery boards showed their plain backs to him.

Frank and Egeus came out.

'Coming, old boy?' Egeus called.

He smiled and shook his head. They disappeared through the curtains, giving him a glimpse of the rows of empty chairs.

He waited and waited. Distantly, from the Great Hall, came the sound of dance music.

He moved towards the door, stiffly, as if conscious of someone watching him. But he was quite alone. He laid his ear to the door. There was no sound, but then the doors here were thick and heavy. He waited a moment and then knocked boldly. The sound echoed like a hammer round the stage. He turned the handle and timidly pushed open the door a little way. He coughed.

'Sir?' A rosy little face above a maid's uniform looked up at him.

'Ah, I'm sorry. The ladies . . . ?'

'They're not here, sir. They've gone in to the reception in their costumes. The President's wife asked to see them. I'm just looking after their clothes.'

'Th . . . Thank you . . .'

What a fool to stand all this time waiting outside an empty room. They would wonder what had happened to him. He hurried towards music and voices.

The scene in the Great Hall did not look as merry as the chunking rhythms of the band had led him to think. People gathered in tense little groups, their voices low, talking seriously to each other. Perhaps the President was ill?

He saw his father and mother and began to make his way through to them.

'I say, where *have* you been?' Frank caught him by the arm and detained him. 'People were beginning to *speculate*.' Why did he have this atrocious habit of elongating certain words as if they were somehow suggestive. 'And no Katerina either! You've missed all the excitement too. Or have you?'

'What excitement?'

'Seems the Russkis have done a deal with Herr Hitler.' It was the amiable old fool, Egeus.

'What?'

'They've signed some sort of friendship pact,' said Gerald. 'Sounds perfectly bloody awful for you people. That's why they called the President away.' Gerald sounded satisfied that his production had not been the cause of the President's absence.

'Quite put a damper on the party,' said Frank.

'What did you say about Katerina?' Jacob asked Frank.

'Not a thing. Thought she was with you.'

He looked round. His father beckoned to him, irritably, Jacob thought. Anna was talking to the President's wife. Had he got to ask her? He began to push his way through, avoiding his father's eye.

'Mr Balthus, isn't it?'

'Miss Witkowska.'

She was looking lost, floating between two groups of people, blocking his way.

'I wondered if you'd seen Max?' she said, looking round in her turn. 'We must have got separated.'

'Yes.' There didn't seem a great deal else to say. There was no point sailing on. Katerina was not in the room.

'Perhaps you've seen the other young lady who was in the play.' He pointed to Anna. 'She came out here with that woman over there.'

'No, I haven't. The pretty, dark one?'

'Well yes . . .'

'Seems we're both searching for someone. It's always the same at these big parties, isn't it?'

'Well, they must be here somewhere, mustn't they?' He tried to make it sound a joke, to deny the terrible suspicion growing in his mind.

But for the time being it seemed he was stuck with Miss Witkowska. Ella.

'May I get you another drink?' he asked. Then, after a discernible pause, 'Ella.'

'Jacob!' His mother's voice swooped down on him. 'This is quite scandalous.' Her tone was jocularly scolding, but still scolding. 'I came to see why you are avoiding us. And I'm quite on my own. Good evening, my dear.' She looked keenly at Ella, then at Jacob.

'Miss Witkowska, this is my mother. Mother . . .'

89

'It's a pleasure, my dear. We have already met on the terrace, Jacob. But it's *still* a pleasure, my dear . . . ?'

'Ella.'

Jacob could see that his mother had all this time been taking in Ella, appraising her as a proposition that had appeared in its own right, not simply as the rather dim accessory to an escort on the terrace earlier. By now the girl's clothes, body, face, hair, voice, make-up, carriage, charm or vulgarity would have been broken down and evaluated.

He felt sorry for the girl. The summer frock looked awful, outlandish among all the formal clothes. An ugly red spot on her chin was inadequately covered by powder.

'Has Jacob got you some refreshment, dear? Aren't these men appalling. His father has been called away on urgent business . . .'

And while she prattled, she smiled emptily at Jacob, her eyes holding the question, 'Is *this* the girl you were so anxious for us to meet?'

'Excuse me,' Jacob blurted out. He must get away. Find Katerina.

'How extraordinary . . .' he heard his mother say. He pushed his way through the crowd towards the tall glassed doors.

The faces were concerned; the conversation seemed to have a new urgency . . . Hitler. Corridor. Surely not. Reds. What? Kubin. Where is Kubin? Kubin will. Borders. Shores. Oh – rubbish. This wine is corked. They would not. The English. Surely . . .

'The English will fix something up, you know.' Egeus swam up before him at the windows. 'S'pose they may have to fight. Though it's a damn shame. The Germans are a fine people. Fine people . . .' Egeus's commercial empire dwindled away in front of him. 'God knows what it will do to trade. It's so senseless. Senseless. I've had Germans in my factory. Been to theirs. Mean to say . . .'

Jacob slid past him and out through the french windows.

On the terrace a couple walked up and down, uninterested in history. Another couple hung on the pale stone wall and gazed down the dark intervening lawns to the candles that still burned steadily on the lake. But neither of these couples were

Katerina and . . . and? Max. He hurried past the windows of the Great Hall, glancing in at the crowd, wine-glasses in hand, cigarettes tilted, their backs turned to the night.

He was at the end of the terrace and went down narrow steps to the gravel path that led along the side of the Palace. A tall window stood open. He hesitated for a moment – he wasn't quite sure what he was doing, should he go looking for her? For *them*? Or go back to the reception? What could he expect to find – and where, in this whole huge building? He stepped inside the room. A dim light came under a door from the corridor. Jacob almost fell over a chair, reaching out a hand to save it from falling.

'Oh,' a woman gasped.

He turned. There was movement against the wall at the side of the window. A man and a woman. They must have been hidden in the long drapes. The man backed out, towing the woman by the hand. She stumbled slightly on the terrace, smoothing her dress with the other hand, until she was suddenly tugged out of sight. They were not the two he sought.

He crossed the room and opened the door. The junction of an L-shaped corridor. From one way came the clamorous murmur of the reception, the other stretched past heavy closed doors. He hastened along, away from the party. A staircase led upwards. They must have gone this way. Might. They might have left the Palace altogether. In her costume? Perhaps she had doubled back to change? He would have seen her. Tortured by the thought that the whole Palace was full of lovers he would discover, uncover, or otherwise disturb, he made his way up the stairs.

A man came hurrying down, a piece of paper in his hand. He glanced at Jacob – who tried to look purposeful, as if he had business up there.

Off the landing ran another corridor. He went down this one. Doors with brass labels; offices of this, commissions of that; he opened each of them. They were all empty. Well, of course, at this time of night they would be. And empty of what? Of secretaries, civil servants, typists, clerks? He stood in the doorways, hardly daring to breath, listening for the whispers of lovers; straining his eyes to see any movement among the lumpy shadows of desks and chairs and cabinets. They weren't here. But elsewhere? Was the whole Palace full now of concealed couples like the one he had disturbed downstairs; the illicit pairs peeling off from the celebrations until there were left only the too old, the too drunk, the uninterested and the incapable? The whole Palace a whispering, caressing, fondling mass of unfaithful lover with unfaithful lover? From door to door he pursued shadows and whispers.

He was at the end of the corridor. One last door; massive, with no name plate. He put his ear to it. Through the thick wood he could not be sure what he heard. Something. A low voice. Another. Max? He turned the knob and pushed the door softly open.

At the end of a long room half a dozen, perhaps more, men stood behind a table, looking down at a map over the shoulders of the only man seated. His father was one of those standing. The man seated was the President. He raised his head as the door opened. The sharp little peasant eyes glared over reading spectacles.

'Ah . . . ah. Excuse . . .'

'Get out,' said the President harshly.

'Get out. Get out.' His father's voice chimed in with the others. 'And shut the door after you.'

III

It is beginning to rain. Red fades from the dahlias.
The murderer washes his hands at the well.

Vladimir Holan, *The Hour*

I

Gerald and Frank were leaving for England.

Jacob got the news, quite by chance, from the English businessman who had played Egeus. He had not seen any of the theatre crowd since the night at the Palace, but now Egeus backed out of an office doorway in the Ministry as Jacob came down the corridor. Egeus moved towards him and stopped, blinking in an amiable, puzzled way. 'Ah – it's, ah – Balthus, isn't it?'

Hadn't seen much of, old boy. How keeping? Good. *Good.* Not that seen much of anybody. Whole place seemed cracking up, people leaving right, left, centre. Know Gerald leaving? Joining up. Make fine soldier. Father a soldier. You know? And other chap, friend . . .

Frank?

Going too. Though don't know about him. Odd fellow – know what I mean?

And . . . and the others?

Others?

Katerina?

Oh – dark, nice. Seen her once. Got flash new boyfriend. . . . I must be going.

Must be off self, old boy.

The old fool wandered away.

Jacob could do no more work that afternoon. The new friend could only be Max. Should he go and see her? Go to her street, hide in a doorway and spy? Convince himself of the truth. Whatever was the truth. The bitch. But he must *know*.

Who could he ask? If Gerald was leaving – if he was *leaving* – he could confide in him. Ask his advice. And it would not get back to her. Yes. He would go to the Stillinghursts' this very evening. He would not even telephone first. Let it be a surprise. A surprise of friendship. After all, even if the man had been rude to him once, he was going away to a war.

I have come to bid you farewell, Gerald.

The thought of some constancy left in the world, of his own generosity, made him feel a little better.

He stood at the white gate. Against a huge, flat, yellow-grey thundercloud, the house reared like a stage set. He expected, on the cue of his arrival, for a head to pop out of an upper window and 'hallo-oo' him, or a figure to step on to the verandah and beckon him to approach. The house remained closed and silent. He walked up the gravel path. This time, there was no murmuring of voices from the back. No dog on the cane chair. At one end of the verandah, storm-windows were stacked ready for winter.

The front door was again ajar. He moved through the shadowed front room to the living-room.

The back door was wedged wide open. Boxes of apples covered half the verandah floor; a table was laid with six places. He stepped forward. Among the trees at the end of the lawn, two women moved. One was Mrs Stillinghurst, her broad hat bobbing. He could not make out the other, deeper in the orchard, obscured by the heavily laden, drooping branches, except to receive the impression that she was younger. Should he shout to them? His mouth opened and closed, but no sound came. He was beginning to regret having come uninvited.

There was a giggle. Somewhere buried in the house. Somewhere over his head. He turned. No one. He stared back through the dark rooms, to the vertical flag of the front doorway, striped with grey gravel, green hedge, blue sky. No one. It must have come from above. He turned to his front again.

And here came Mrs Stillinghurst, tall and terrible, the big hat on her head, a basket of apples held before her unswaying body, stalking on to the lawn, towards the house. He stepped back in the shadow. The giggle came again. An ugly black clock that looked as if it was made of iron ticked loudly on the mantelshelf. In a moment she would be on the verandah. He was at the foot of the stairs. Another sound. Gerald must be up there. He mounted the stairs quickly and silently.

Gerald's bedroom door was shut. Jacob would surprise him. Did he think to disturb him? To find him, for once, at a disadvantage? If he did, it was quite unconsciously, and almost without malice. He turned the door knob slowly.

What he saw was impossible at first to take in. There were two figures in the bed. Gerald's bare back, surprisingly broad across the shoulders, was twisted above the white sheet. His head bent. Kissing? A girl? Oh God, let it not be Katerina.

Gerald's head lifted. In one of those instinctual moves Jacob had seen in people – when, looking down from the apartment window at a woman in the street, it was as if you somehow made her look around – Gerald twisted suddenly. His eyes were large. He stared at Gerald. There was no girl. Frank's was the face that appeared round Gerald's shoulder.

'What . . . ?' Gerald rolled over and fell out of the narrow bed.

Frank supported himself on one elbow on the pillow. He began to laugh. His body shook.

'H . . . hello Jacob,' he choked.

A cross-hatching of black hair ran down the middle of his thin muscular chest, disappearing under the single sheet.

'I mean – what the hell?' Gerald spluttered. Clutching up a shirt from the floor to cover himself, he backed across the room in a quick shuffle.

'Oh – if you could only see your *face*, Jacob,' Frank hooted.

'Up half the night . . .' Gerald grumbled, thrusting a leg into the pair of trousers he had seized from the pile of clothes on the window seat.

Frank rolled on the bed, set off into a fresh spasm of laughter.

'. . . war news . . . and all . . . Can't you see we're changing?' Buttoning the trousers, Gerald glared across at Jacob. 'What the hell do you want anyway?'

'I wondered . . .'

His face pressed into the pillow, Frank's laughter came now almost as a sobbing.

'For God's sake, Frank,' Gerald hissed. He sat down heavily on the window seat, jamming a foot into a sock. 'Would you mind *terribly*, Balthus, waiting *downstairs*. While we finish changing.' His face red, his mouth set as if he were grinding his teeth together, Gerald addressed the floor vehemently.

Jacob backed out, closing the door.

A released squall of laughter came from Frank; a hoarse, pleading admonition for silence from Gerald.

Jacob stopped on the landing. What on earth had they been doing? He could not believe what he had seen. Perhaps, if he opened the door again, the two of them would be sitting on either side of the fireplace, smoking and reading, two *good chaps*, like the ones in the line drawings to the English school stories he loved to read. Two good chaps. Surely things could not be as he had seen. They were friends, for heaven's sake. That such . . . *things* . . . took place he knew as theoretically possible. But *Gerald*? He stopped once more, on the stairs, and looked back up. He could see only the top of their door. Their door. That two naked men should lie on a bed on a September evening . . .

'Mr Balthus, is it not?'

Mrs Stillinghurst stood at the foot of the stairs, a white cotton glove on one hand, an apple in the other.

'You've come to see Gerald, I suppose. Like an apple?'

She tossed the apple to him. He had to fumble to catch it.

'Yes. Thank you. I was just on my way out.' He felt as if he, not her son, had just been caught in some shameful act.

'Out? But you have only just come. I was in the house an hour ago. No sign of you then. You'll stay for supper?' When he didn't answer immediately, she said, 'Good. Settled. It's such a long way from town, isn't it? Or have you a motor-car? Come and help us pick the apples.'

She turned on her heel and walked back towards the verandah, still speaking, evidently confident that he was following.

'My late husband had a motor-car of course.' Her explanation floated back as she strode across the lawn. 'But I sold it. I generally take the tram, otherwise my friend, Mrs Frobisher's, husband gives me a lift. Here we are. You know Anna of course from your theatricals.'

Of course. Of course Anna was the other woman in the orchard. She had to be, to render this thoroughly miserable

98

day utterly worthless. For a moment a dull hope ran through him that Anna being here, perhaps Katerina was expected. But that too was extinguished when Mrs Stillinghurst looked at her large wristwatch and said, 'I shall have to leave you two to finish, I'm afraid, and go and supervise the food. One of the Polish refugees is staying with us and God knows what she has done for us. Probably "do" for us, eh Mr Balthus? Now – how many are we? You, me, Mr Balthus. The two boys – wherever they are. It's most lucky you came, Mr Balthus, as Anna's friend could not accompany her.'

How could such a blank face as the one Anna presented to him somehow conceal a smirk? Katerina had been expected. Wasn't coming. In a way he was relieved. But he had been a coward not to have escaped when he could.

Mrs Stillinghurst went off to supervise the Polish supper. Anna, with no attempt at conversation, drifted to the far end of the orchard to begin methodically picking apples again. Gloomily, the prisoner Balthus began to pile apples into a basket.

The supper was of cold soup and pickled herrings, cold meats and salad. 'Quite a relief,' Mrs Stillinghurst whispered jokingly, as the young Polish girl, blushing, sat down at the other end of the table. 'Bravo, my dear,' Mrs Stillinghurst said in a much louder voice. 'Very well done.'

'Shut the door will you, Gerald,' she said as he came in. He looked in a bad temper. 'It is getting chilly in the evenings now.' She turned to Jacob. 'We're awfully late with the apples this year, but none of the *Volksdeutschers* or whatever they call themselves would lend a hand, as they used to. You know, I've a good mind to break out the Union Jack we flew when Gerald came home. We will have to when he and Frank leave. Oh dear, Mr Balthus, your father's in the government, isn't he? What's going to become of us all? What do you think?'

Frank drifted in and sat down beside Anna on the other side of the table. The only spare chair was beside Jacob. Gerald lowered himself into it and stared moodily in front. Frank beamed across the table at Jacob.

'I hardly know . . .' Jacob began.

'I mean – I follow all these little maps in the papers that

show the German and the Polish armies and it seems every day that the poor Poles lose ground – it's all right, Mr Balthus, Janka speaks hardly any English – I would not like to upset the girl. But do you think they have any chance?'

Frank snickered, turning it into a cough behind his napkin when Mrs Stillinghurst glared at him. 'Something in my throat,' he explained.

Anna sat back and fixed her eyes on Jacob, a sardonic smile on her lips, as if saying, 'Come on – we're waiting for the oracle. Speak oracle.' Why did she hate him so?

'From the reports we have . . .' how pompous that sounded, but he ploughed on. He at least knew something they did not. Not with all their cleverness, their artistic . . . nonsense. For that's what it was. Oh yes. Faced with reality they played. Two men. Naked. White sheet. Hair . . .

'Yes?' said Mrs Stillinghurst.

Frank widened his eyes to Jacob again, in that ridiculous, affected way.

He would go on.

'I do not think there can be much hope. We heard in the Ministry yesterday that the Russians have advanced into eastern Poland.'

'I suppose one should have expected that, with this wretched Pact of theirs. But what happens when they meet? Do you think they'll scrap?'

'Scrap?'

'Come to a fight. Between themselves? The Bolsheviks and the Nazis. One hardly knows which of them to dislike the more. Their word is scarcely to be trusted.'

'Oh no. I don't think it likely they will fight with each other, Mrs Stillinghurst. The Russians have bought themselves a little time and spared Hitler the trouble of thinking about having to fight on the eastern front. But what they will in fact establish is the beginning of an eastern front, and the Germans will have to commit troops to defend *that*.' Thank you, Father. 'To put it purely cynically, while the Russians are engaged down there and in Finland, they won't bother us. Why, Mr Zallner has been invited to Moscow only this week to sign a new Trade Agreement.'

Mrs Stillinghurst looked at him curiously. 'I suppose you

do have to put it "cynically" in your line of work, Mr Balthus, but,' she appealed to the table at large, 'one's heart does bleed for them, doesn't it? The stories one hears! Quite unbelievable. The cruelties, the horror . . .'

'I should not believe all you hear, Mother,' said Gerald irritably. 'A lot of these atrocity stories fly around all the time. Look at the last war. All the babies bayonetted in plucky little Belgium.'

'Well it *was* plucky little Belgium – if you are pleased to sneer about it. And the Germans played some dirty tricks in that war, I can tell you. You young men are the ones who have got to fight, so I'll say no more. I hope to God that no one has to go. That they patch up this nonsense somehow.'

'I think we are quite safe in our little backwater here. Quite safe. For the time being.' He sounded, he thought, like a wise old man.

'I hope you are right, Mr Balthus.'

They began eating again. This time the conversation did not include Jacob. Between Frank and Gerald and Anna, with occasional interjections from Mrs Stillinghurst, it seemed indeed to slyly *exclude* him, as if they had agreed among themselves to leave him moored in his backwater.

He wanted to be away from here. He tried to avoid looking at Frank and Gerald. He knew a secret between them. It was not knowledge he had sought, or that he wished to keep. Two men, naked, on a single bed. What malicious god was responsible for leaving such sights about? For putting such thoughts in his head, such awareness?

All at once he experienced a terrible vacancy in himself; as if his blood had drained away. It was an astonishing, shocking feeling. Quite unawares he had come to one of those terrible moments, which we learn to disguise in later memory, when we go suddenly forward from one phase of life to another. It was as if he lurched forward, through an archway, and a door shut, with an atrocious *slam*, behind him.

And no one else at the table noticed a thing, except Mrs Stillinghurst, who saw an odd paleness pass across young Mr Balthus's face.

2

At the end of September, first Warsaw, then the great fortress of Modlin fell and Poland surrendered. The Germans and the Russians met at Brest-Litovsk on the River Bug and agreed how the country was to be partitioned. The trickle of Polish refugees stopped altogether. The war seemed to be over. Would the English and French now do a deal? In the capital, the newspapers said that the French were digging in along the Maginot Line; the British were training. It seemed that the Germans were to be left to digest Poland, along with their new, unlikely allies.

But – two dogs, after tearing at a third, lift their heads, and scent for fresh sport.

First, the Russians.

On a bright cold October morning three brown bomber planes with red stars on their wings appeared above the capital. They circled lazily over the the Presidential Palace, the National Theatre and the docks. As if their circlings had some magical effect, those few people not staring into the skies would have seen the long grey shapes of two destroyers slide round the Head and stop perhaps two miles outside the harbour.

About an hour later, while the bombers still circled, now higher, now lower, and the ships remained motionless, Mr Zallner put a call through from Moscow to President Kubin. It seemed that their hosts in the Kremlin had not, as anticipated, presented new proposals regarding the import and export of timber; instead Molotov himself had appeared and read to them the terms of a new treaty, a Treaty of Mutual Assistance. Under this, the Russians demanded naval bases on the Baltic coast and army garrisons in the countries bordering the Baltic. In return the Russians would lend assistance in case of attack by any other party; the naval and army personnel would be restricted to their bases, and the number of their troops was not to exceed twenty-five thousand.

The trade delegation was given twenty-four hours to consult with their home government. To help make up their minds Molotov announced that the troops in question were handily placed on the border already; the three planes over the capital were joined by four more; and a battleship steamed genially down from Leningrad to join the two destroyers in the bay. The treaty was signed before morning.

'. . . it was not cowardice,' said Jacob's father. 'How could it be? General Eichenfeld wanted to fight. Kubin overruled him. The capital would have been flattened – a few thousand dead men would have been heroes.' His father had returned, grey-faced, from the Ministry at seven in the morning.

Before dawn the Russians had crossed the frontier and were heading for their requested bases; column after column of grey trucks and light tanks. Their ships, signal lamps blinking against the lightening sky behind, put into harbour as the high tide lapped against the walls; the last bomber droned away. Wakened by the noise on the roads outside, country people peered through their shutters at lines of trucks, the stone-faced, raggedly-uniformed soldiers glaring steadfastly out over the tailgates as they turned up back roads, disappearing out of sight.

The day after that, the day after *that*; day after day the Russians kept to their word and to their bases. People became more cheerful. Perhaps things would not be so bad after all. Perhaps Kubin had done a deal. Wily old Kubin, wouldn't put it past him . . .

Indeed, the worst seemed to have passed with singularly little change. The few Russians who appeared in the capital were officers and men from the warships anchored in the harbour. Their behaviour was reserved and wooden. But the treaty had given them a very advantageous rate of exchange for their roubles and they quickly discovered the shops, buying up shoes and pens, shirts and watches, stockings and cigarettes as if they had never seen such things before.

The people began to feel almost sorry for them. They were somehow comic in their awfully made uniforms, their lumpen manners; the Mongoloid barbarity in the faces of the enlisted men. But they behaved themselves.

A few days after the Russians settled in, the other dog lifted its head and howled.

Hitler Ruft – Hitler Calls – shrieked the front page of the German-language paper, *Mittag. Wir Folgen Den Weg Des Führers*. We follow the way of the Führer.

Hitler called home all those of German descent, of the true blood – *Blut*, the word itself seemed to well and swell in their veins. All those living in the Baltic states were to make immediate preparations to leave, to sell up their homes, their furniture; to liquidate their assets. No one must remain behind. No one to fall under 'a regime which, sooner or later, means their complete destruction'.

All must go. A Resettlement Commission was leaving for the Republics; its agents would ensure fair dealing and compensation. All money raised by the sale of what had to be left behind would be collected and paid into the German bank and refunded to them in their new land, their homeland. Ships – fleets of ships – would be sent to collect them. And – miracle of miracles – a perfect replica of everything they left was being put into place in the newly conquered land of the *Ostreich*. The Poles were being cleared from the sites of the new towns. Each family would step into a home at least equivalent to the one they had left. The farmers would have the same fertile hectares; the doctors their surgeries; the policemen their duties; the shopkeepers their tightly packed shelves. Even now the homes are being furnished . . .

But all must go.

The exodus began.

It was delayed then slowed by the first cold weather that came unseasonably early. But after a month, most of the Germans had gone.

They woke in the capital – those who were leaving and those who were not – to find a heavy snowfall on their roofs and window ledges and lying in great curved blue-white hammocks between the trees in the parks, with the trees still in full leaf. It was as if the war, unable to visit them in person, had blown a cold breath across the border.

This morning the main street that ran along the edge of the harbour, overlooked by the backs of the Ministry buildings, held a steady stream of horse-drawn and hand-pushed carts churning and displacing the muddy slush that had been snow in the night. Carts loaded with suitcases, with bundles tied up in blankets and bedsheets, with clocks, framed pictures, a harmonium, vases and pots in wooden cages, like fat tropical birds. These were the people from out of town. Every now and then came a car with a travelling chest and cases roped to the roof; trapped between carts it inched forward, came to a halt, inched on again, venting its frustration with a blast on the horn. A busload of very old people, their heads slumped against the windows, a row of grey, scanty and bald heads, moved slowly into the line from round a corner.

Then came more cars; a rich village. *Hitler Ruft* was chalked on the sides and bonnets of these and from their back seats overcoated children leaned out of the windows and waved little swastika flags. A dog barked. On the top of a huge heap of luggage on the back of a truck a man blew lamentably lowing, cow-like notes on a silver cornet – *moove-booove, moooove-boove* – over and over again. Most of the people's faces were smiling, but some on the pavements pressed forward anxiously – like people on a station, unused to travel, they wonder whether this is the right platform, the right train, looking round for someone to reassure them, so they can at last board.

'I knew the Germans were mad, but this is insanity of a new and altogether ludicrous nature.' Jacob's father stepped back and shut the balcony window. The cornet bleated distantly.

'You know your grandmother Clara telephoned to say she was going,' he went on, still looking down at the street. 'She is eighty-three years old. Her family has been here for two centuries. She says she must. It is her duty. A matter of blood. She thinks the Nazis will give her her estates back, I suppose.'

The estates of Grandmother Clara had occupied all of her conversation – all that Jacob had heard anyway. And it was made plain to the very young Balthus that his mother, Clara's daughter, had married beneath her. His father did not accompany them on the visits to what he derisively called the 'Schloss' – a large, rambling farmhouse up in the northernmost corner of the land, where in winter the coastline resembled the rind on grey meat, where the fires barely cast their heat into the huge, stone-flagged rooms, and where Grandmother Clara sat mourning her lost domains; her servants; the old life when people knew their place.

'She thinks she will have it all back again. They all think that. The Poles will be their slaves. Not from what I hear.'

'There's the *Aurora* again,' said Jacob, staring out over the harbour.

Like a large toy boat in bath water, dwarfing the headland and its lighthouse, anchored outside because it was too big to enter the harbour, lay the ocean-going liner, *Aurora*, that for the past two weeks had served as a ferry to Hamburg. Two smaller steamers, bound for Danzig, hugged the wall of the long embarkation pier, German flags lolling off their sterns. The Russian frigates on the other side of the harbour were obscured by dock buildings, but you could see the bridge of one, and a Russian officer looking steadfastly through binoculars at the German boats across the bay.

Under the window a great bundle, dwarfing the cart that carried it, swayed under the balcony like an elephant roped under a tarpaulin.

They turned away from the window at almost the same instant, Jacob's body unconsciously following his father's. He really wasn't very interested in what his father had to say. He was worried about what would happen at Stieckus's at lunchtime.

Ella, *that girl Ella*, had telephoned twice, his mother had informed him. Each time he nodded absently and each time she sniffed, put on her reading glasses and picked up her book.

His father sat down at the desk. 'What's happened to Max Sawallisch, by the way?' he asked. 'He was supposed to come and see me. All these things,' he waved a hand towards the window, 'they have upset everything. Very intelligent fellow. Very shrewd. He confirmed a lot of what I've always said. He's no idiot.'

Jacob, standing in the shadow of the long window drapes,

remained silent. He didn't tell his father that he was seeing Max for lunch at Stieckus's.

For that had been the burden of Ella's calls – contacting him at the third attempt. His friends wondered what had happened to him? Had he been ill? Abroad? Thank you for the taxi-ride home. Katerina asked if you were upset with her? Her apologies – she had had to go home urgently. And Max? Max said please, please bring Jacob along. They had got on famously together at the Palace . . .

Jacob had been coldly polite on the telephone; only when he put it down did he wonder quite how Ella had become friendly with Katerina? Surely they had not even met on the night of the performance. It could only be through Max. Bitterly – and confusedly – he mixed the three in their possible combinations – Max-Ella; Ella-Katerina; Max – and Max-Katerina, Max-Katerina kept thudding in his head till it became nonsensical, a single name Maxkaterina. Two-backed beast. Suddenly – unbidden – into his head Gerald rolled naked out of bed. Frank laughing and laughing . . .

'All that stuff they have with them – they won't be allowed on the ships with that.' Frowning, his father picked up first one piece of paper then another, looking for something. 'End up in Schwarzwald's warehouses to be sold off by your Commission – how are you getting on with our German colleagues? Come over here and sit down.'

'I have to go soon. To meet them.'

'What are they like – your Laurel and Hardy?'

The description appeared to amuse his father, but was not particularly just, Herr Tischbein of the Resettlement Commission being admittedly stout, but short, and Herr Zech slim, but very much taller. Jacob felt a need to defend the two officials he had been assigned to as Ministry liaison man. His father's cynicism was rather surprising. He had never been one to pick sides – it was the civil servant's duty, he had always preached to Jacob, to preserve his impartiality. He had a lawyer's distaste for moral arguments. Perhaps it was the anxiety that was beginning to irradiate the capital, the difficult act of juggling two giant, threatening neighbours in public affections, that was causing the Service to grow cynical in private, the procedures becoming slightly slapdash – as if whatever they did, or neglected to do, or decided, would not matter in the long run.

'Ah, here is what I wanted to show you.' He held a piece of paper away from him – he had started to wear reading glasses at home but would not bring them to the office. 'This was on the radio from Moscow last night.' He read, ' "The pacts with the Baltic republics in no way imply the intrusion of the Soviet Union in the internal affairs of these states. These pacts are inspired by *mutual* respect for the governmental, social, and economic situations of each of the contracting parties. Foolish talk of the Sovietization of any of the Baltic states is useful only to our common enemies and to all kinds of anti-Soviet provocateurs. The execution" – note the word, Jacob – "the execution of our pacts with the Baltic states is proceeding satisfactorily and creating prerequisites for a further improvement in relations . . ." So on and on. See, they mean us no harm. Well – perhaps. Those Germans out there don't seem to think that, do they? They're clearing out fast. The Führer has told them they'll all be murdered in their beds if they stay. But the Russians seem to be behaving themselves. A little too much, you might say. Did you hear that they shot a party of their own sailors? They got drunk down in the docks. The police picked them up. Rang their ship, to see what they should do with them. The officer said, cool as a cucumber, "Shoot them – it will save us the trouble." Our policeman said, "Good heavens, we can't do that." So the Russians came and picked the sailors up – the man who told me this said that the poor devils knew what they were in for. They took them back to the ship, and before our police got down the gang-plank – bang, bang – they heard a volley of shots. One way of keeping your people in line, um?'

Jacob listened and didn't listen. He smiled thinly at his father's story, but only to please his father. He wanted to get out of this room. To see what the Café Stieckus held. Now his father had one foot negligently up on the corner of the desk. Things were getting sloppy. Carelessness was becoming the upside of the fear that people carried around and would not acknowledge to each other or to themselves. Jacob was sick of it; sick of most things. That's why he was glad now of this job with the Commission. At least he was *doing* something. And it kept your mind off . . . Two men on a bed . . . Katerina in her bed . . . off himself, when he lay alone in his bed, wanting to scream, beating his head against the pillow, cursing her as a whore, a strumpet.

Then, considering – washed, dressed, all correct – whether or not he might be mistaken, putting a grotesque complexion on a series of quite ordinary events. That he might be misjudging her. She could not be . . .

'Yes, most correct,' his father was going on. 'It's not the best deal we could have,' he sighed. 'It's the *only* deal.'

'I must go,' said Jacob, and got up abruptly.

His father looked up in surprise. The piece of paper dangled from his hand a moment longer, then he tossed it on to the desk. 'Very correct. That's all our work is at the moment. Receiving their assurances. Politely bowing. They're sending the ballet here from Leningrad next month, you know that? Exhibitions. Concerts. The best of pals.'

'I *must* go.'

'What is it this afternoon? Laurel and Hardy again?'

'The Commission – yes.'

His father gazed up at him, then said, 'You know – I think you are enjoying this job. Are you?'

Jacob shrugged. 'It's something to do.'

'Yes. Don't get too close to them, my boy. They are not to be trusted.'

His father was a diplomat, that is, he trusted no one. But it was new for him to declare openly and with obvious seriousness any such opinion.

'And,' he said, in a lighter way, 'I hardly think they would sit well with your theatrical friends.'

'They are no longer . . . I mean – they have broken up. Most of the English have left. The others . . .'

'Um. There was a girl you were with, the night of the President's party. Your mother told me. What's happened to her?'

'I have not seen her.'

'Ah.' There was a pause. 'You had better run along then, if you have to go. I have work to do too.' His father sat back and lit a cigarette. 'Will you be in for dinner?'

'I'm not sure.'

'Please try to be a little more definite than that, Jacob. You know your mother has no maid again. Will you or won't you?'

'Well, then – no.'

'I'll see you later in that case.' His father leaned over the desk once more and began to sort ostentatiously through his papers. He had been looking forward to one of his long chats with his son, Jacob knew. It was with relief that he closed the door and went down the corridor.

To avoid the crush at the back of the Ministry, he made for the main exit into Palace Square.

It was astonishing how quickly the world changed – and how quickly one accepted the changes, so that, looking round, it seemed that this was how the world was destined to be, had always been, and his life, till now a charming, ineffectual interlude, was to be closed off. A silly little vision came to him of himself shrinking, like the absurd tramp toddling into the sunset, in the closing iris at the end of a film. Easier perhaps, he thought bitterly, to accept change and destruction in the world than in your friends.

He thrust his fists deep into his overcoat pockets as he went down the Ministry steps, and stalked heavily to the edge of the broad pavement.

3

A green store sign glowed against the sulphurous, snow-heavy sky. Cars cruised gently along the slushy road. Jacob crossed, taking a short-cut across one of the rectangles of snow-covered grass instead of keeping to the cleared paths, his rebellious pioneer footprints marring the white.

The world demands allegiance of us, and is unfaithful in return. Yes, that was the word – unfaithful. Something had not kept faith with him; the people he knew had failed him, had failed his vision of them. He had not expected so much, surely? Were they so incontinent, so promiscuous, that they had to rut and couple like animals; so devious that he could only discover them by the hints and giggles, sighs and looks, of others? To his horror his mind went away again, away from his control, inventing erotic combinations in shameful but curiously unspecific detail as Max and Katerina *did* things to each other. As Gerald and Frank . . . Did what? His mind sheered off again from the outrageous *details*. No, no. It could not be. His imagination attempted to re-order his memory. Two men changing. Unashamed *friendship*. Body.

Someone looked queerly at him as he stepped off the grass. He scowled back.

With the leaving of the Germans there seemed to have been a general dissolution, or perhaps only a dilution of the customary good manners of the capital. The streets, which had exuded an air of easy, prosperous satisfaction, where the policeman yawned discreetly behind his hand on the corner, had become raucous, sometimes dangerous. Last week a bunch of young *Volksdeutsche* had started a fight in Stieckus's with four Jews. A couple of tables turned over. A knife seen. There had been other clashes in the streets as long latent feuds resurfaced, or ancient blood rivalries were installed by some mysterious agency in the veins of the young, causing them to clash with others over such things as the shape of a nose, the pronunciation of a river's name, the circumcision of Christ, a red necktie, the precise way to rupture a kidney, the book an old man was reading in a park . . . A couple of nights before, the air raid sirens had been tested for the first time. Was there not something a little hysterically forced about the muffled laughter in the dark, the edgy too-good humour as the people piled down, bumping against each other in the cellars under the apartment blocks? That night, in the completely blacked-out city, two murders were committed.

He made his way up the side street to the café.

There was little sign of damage from last week's fight – except to Stieckus himself, who wore a sticking plaster above his right eye. As always, the two pairs of elderly men sat at the chess tables. They were like old, paint-flaking automata that performed only when your eyes were on them, one raising a pipe, frowning, a thick-veined hand trembling over a king.

A couple of dockers stood against the bar with their Pils and aquavit. Serdyuk the poet leaned forward over a table, talking intensely to his latest muse, a dark rather plain girl gripping her hands tightly together on her lap under the table, as if she feared she might strike him. Serdyuk's eyes flickered up as Jacob passed; not that they were interested in Jacob, but they casually but boldly demanded that the passer-by recognize *Serdyuk, the poet.* Jacob did not understand or like poetry of any modern sort – but Serdyuk was a hero of the café. He had served a week in the Fortress prison for his satire on the President – 'The Vladkin'. So Jacob nodded as he went by; and immediately Serdyuk lowered his eyes, satisfied with the tribute, but not wishing to waste time on some nonentity. He gazed back into the girl's face, fingering his ginger beard, speaking in his impressive rumble.

Ella sat right at the back of the café at one of the tables in the small dining area. Food was prepared by Madame Stieckus, somewhere in her impenetrable region behind the glass-panelled doors.

He bowed. They shook hands over the table and he sat down on the other side.

She looked different. He nearly said it. She had obviously bought smart new clothes in the city. Her blonde hair had grown and was pinned back. There was lipstick on her mouth. He felt as if she had called him here to help her sort something out. Perhaps she was going to break down, weep, and confess that she loved Max. That Katerina had rejected Max – it had only been a mad temporary infatuation. Katerina had cried, No, no – I love only Jacob. And now I can see him no more. Please, please, take Katerina away from Max again. Let him recover his sanity. She needs you. She wants you. Only you ... His mind teemed with this shop-girl's novelette. How stern and coldly forgiving he would be. The young eagle. Katerina would bite her lip. Max, sobbing, would clasp his hand. Shall we not be friends henceforth?

A stick-thin waitress dressed in black stood at the side of the table.

'We are waiting for some others, thank you,' said Ella.

The girl went back up the steps and slid between the doors like a feather.

Yes, Ella had definitely tried to improve herself. Did she find him attractive? She was not so bad at all. He could forgive even her awkwardness at the Palace if she was to be the instrument for bringing Katerina back to him. With all the vanity of the maladroit lover he spoke a little more brusquely and loudly than he intended.

'Well, how are you, Ella?'

'Very well, thank you.' She shifted on her chair, and smoothed her skirt.

'How is the – what is it? – the press agency? The war must have made you busy. It has with us at the Ministry.'

He caught himself gazing at her eyes. They were a rather cold pale blue and the quick twitch of her mouth that was meant as a smile did not warm them at all.

He scored lines in the tablecloth with his thumbnail, glancing up at her. Her mouth twitched into that smile again. Very slightly wider this time?

'Your poor . . .'

'Thank you . . .'

Their voices clashed. No . . . no . . . you first. No . . . no, I insist.

'I was going to thank you properly for dropping me home in your taxi the night of the play. I'm afraid Max has a habit of disappearing.'

'Then, you and he . . . ?'

'Oh no.' She laughed. 'I merely work with him.'

'And I . . . I meant to say – your poor country. It is Poland?'

'Yes.'

'I hope your people – your family – they are all right?'

'They moved to the eastern part. They are safe from the Fascists. Have you a light?'

'Of course.' He offered his lighter. 'But the Reds. Not much better, surely? The Soviets?'

'I think they are safe.'

'Not that I have anything against Communists. Quite a number come in here.' He dropped his voice. 'Quite a few are Reds. My father's generation feels differently about these things, about the things done in the past. But that was Revolution, Civil War, wasn't it? Both countries were a great deal more backward and uncivilized than they . . .'

'Here they are.' Ella was looking past his shoulder up the café.

He turned, attempting to get up in the cramped space between chair and table.

They were coming down the centre aisle, Katerina in front, head confidently back, shoulder-bag swinging on her hip. Max followed, smiling amiably, undoing his overcoat as he came, nodding in a familiar way to Serdyuk – who raised a palm in salute.

They arrived at the table as Jacob was still trying to extricate himself. He felt as if he were crouching before them.

Ridiculously, he offered his hand to Katerina. She took it lightly in hers, leaned forward and kissed him on the cheek.

'Jacob, where have you been?' Her voice was gently chiding, as if speaking to a fondly regarded child after a long absence.

'I wonder . . .' said Max, and like an illusionist he performed the trick of somehow rearranging the table: drawing Jacob into the aisle with a firm friendly hand, at the same time motioning to Katerina to sit in Jacob's vacated chair, and then himself sitting down beside her – so that the only place left for Jacob to sit was by Ella. And that was where, to his surprise, Jacob found himself sitting.

'What – nothing to drink? What *have* you two been up to?' Max joked. He half turned in his chair, and shouted, 'Joseph. Four beers – beer all right?' His eyes flashed round them. 'Four beers, my good Joseph.'

Jacob had never ever heard Stieckus referred to as anything but 'Stieckus'. The possibility that he had another name and that anyone would have the temerity to use it, came as a shock. But the great Stieckus took it in his stride, with his customary, grudging 'All right. All right. Fast as I can. Fast as I can.'

Max faced them again. 'And what are we eating?'

Jacob opened his mouth.

Max held up a hand. 'Before you say anything, my dear

Jacob – this is my treat.' He patted the breast of his fawn-coloured suit. 'Expenses. I've put you down as the Senior Counsellor. You owe your father a lunch.'

The beers were brought. The black-frocked girl appeared again and Max even managed to draw a wan smile from her. 'The salmon? No? No – the crawfish. Yes, the crawfish. And with them the Kümmel. Yes. Yes. And strawberries. And to start – the stuffed pancakes? Oh yes. Yes.'

Katerina sat smiling radiantly on this wonderfully vulgar man. Any hope Jacob might have had that she was still his died when, the order completed, Max slapped the menu down and Katerina's hand fell quite naturally and lightly on to Max's sleeve.

Jacob looked away, down, at Max, answered a question from Ella absently – anything to avoid looking at Katerina. If he caught her eyes his own would fill childishly with tears. What did he expect of her? The little tart. The little Jewish tart. And the word surprised him. Why did he say that? Jewish tart? Why that – Jewish? He drove through the night in Schwarzwald's car; he listened again to Tischbein and Zech, ticking their lists, muttering about Jew-filth, Jew-filth. He felt ashamed of himself. What had that to do with anything? Little Jewish tart – it hammered again in his head. It was as if it had lodged there, against his will, and now he could not be rid of it. Disgust. Involuntary. What else was she? Achingly beautiful ... the essence of sweetness ... all he desired ... ever would ...

'I said, Jacob, you must be busy at this time.' She was talking to him. He realized he had been sitting bolt upright, staring at her. For how long?

'Miles away, Jacob?' Max laughed.

'I know Max is. Terribly busy,' Katerina went on. 'Dashing about all over the place.'

'The Ministry is – yes – very busy –' The words were merely markers, disconnected and meaningless.

'And your father? How is he?' Max was all at once serious, a concerned look on his face, one man of business addressing another.

The pancakes arrived. Max ordered fresh beers.

Jacob had composed himself. 'We are all most concerned about the situation vis-à-vis the Soviets,' he announced.

'Why?' asked Max. 'They seem to be doing just what they said – keeping to their bases.'

'They're sending their ballet next week,' said Katerina. 'Why don't you two come? Max can get tickets.'

Which two? There was, obviously, a tacit agreement that Ella was his 'girl'. That here were two men of the world out with their women. It seemed, like many assumptions by the outside world, to have crept up on him, presenting itself as an accomplished fact, as if someone called *Jacob Balthus* had been living an independent life he knew nothing about.

'Wouldn't you say though, Jacob,' said Max, buttering a piece of bread, 'that their conduct has been exemplary so far? That they have earned a little trust?'

'I would so like to see their theatre too.' Katerina was talking to Ella. 'Some of their actors . . .'

Jacob left them to it. Let the men speak of the serious things.

'I don't know,' he said. 'We may, I think, have more to fear from the Germans. After all, it is they who are at war at the moment in Europe. The Soviets may well not be in a position to embark on any military adventures. Look how they are tied down in Finland.'

'Yes. Yes.' Max's face expressed deep interest, signalling by his slightly furrowed forehead, the serious set to his mouth, that he took these remarks of Jacob's to be of great importance.

Warming, Jacob went on, 'It may well be' – says my father – 'that if they can hold to the Mutual Assistance Pact the Soviets might want us as an ally in the near future.'

'You think they will fall out with the Germans?'

'Undoubtedly. And one cannot help feeling that it won't be long before the Germans start fishing for peace terms again. After all, they've got what they wanted – the Corridor; an eastward and southward expansion. It will take some time for them to swallow what they have bitten off, and in the meantime there are Britain and France to contend with. Hitler after all is a realist.'

'So you think it will all be over soon?'

'Is that why the Germans are leaving?' asked Ella.

'Well, that is another matter. They have always wanted the Baltic – now that things aren't going their way, they're clearing out. I understand their motives – I really do. After all, I am half-German myself. In blood.'

'But you are not leaving?'

'No, no. It's only my mother who is German. I feel no loyalty to their *Father*land, as it were.' His joke fell flat.

'Oh, I'm so glad you're not leaving, Jacob,' Katerina cooed. 'The place wouldn't seem the same without you.'

'The place wouldn't seem the same without you.' She sounded genuinely concerned about him. Surely she could not be so cruel as to be mocking him? No. No. He saw then how easy she was with Max – how he himself was an outsider to their public intimacy. He guided his thoughts away from the *private*. Max was asking him another question. At least there was something he could teach the fellow. Perhaps he was not such a bad sort after all. And – when all was said – Jacob thought, I hardly advertised my rights in Katerina, did I? Oh, I was a fool. Perhaps, still, she was playing a long and complicated game with Max. Wait and see. It was quite civilized to be able to sit and talk like this to each other. Quite civilized. In his head Gerald said again, 'You really should grow up, Jacob.' He squared his shoulders, delivered another carefully worded political statement to Max, and pressed his fork into the crawfish.

So, they had the conversation that was going on in a score of cafés that day, a repeat, with slight variations in tension, of the conversation of yesterday, and a foretaste of tomorrow's – the talk that was to bury further the hidden anxiety, to revive the hope that comes from manipulating optimistically in the mind events over which you have had and can have no control.

The beer and Kümmel, the vivacity of the others, cheered him. He talked to Ella at his side. Her poor country. Anything he could do, he would. She smiled at him. He took another swig at his beer. What a dog he was, to have exchanged one mistress for another. Not effortlessly. Sure, he had felt bitter and confused. Better to take these things lightly as Max seemed to. What the Viennese called *La Ronde*. He caught sight of the clock. He was late for his appointment with the Resettlement Commission.

'Oh, poor Jacob.'

'Must you?'

'It has been a great pleasure.'

Katerina. Max. Ella. And before going he just had time to agree a date with them for the ballet, to shake Max's hand, though not Katerina's, to offer – and be refused with mock severity – to pay the bill, to pick up his overcoat, and to be off.

Serdyuk had gone – no doubt to induct his latest into the mysteries of free verse and free love.

The chess players bent over their interminable games.

Holding open the door, he looked down the length of the café. Max and Katerina had their backs to him; at that moment Ella looked between them and saw him at the door. Her mouth twisted in that peculiarly cold smile again.

Better than nothing.

He stepped out into the cold wind.

He had only a few streets to walk, but hurried. They were working in the Old Town this afternoon, visiting those who had not turned up for the morning's embarkation. They must be seen, and their reasons noted.

He turned a corner and there they were, waiting for him, in their long overcoats and soft hats – regrettably not bowlers – his Laurel and Hardy, Tischbein and Zech.

4

These professions and occupations, ways of life and death, appeared on their lists. *Specify which of the following:*

Accountant, Acrobat, Actor, Actuary, Advertiser, Aeronaut,

Aged, Agent, Alcoholic,* Architect, Artist,* Astronomer, Auctioneer, Baker, Banker, Biologist, Blind,* Book-keeper, Bookseller,* Bootmender, Brewer, Builder, Carpenter, Carpet Weaver, Chemist, Child, Chiropodist, Clerk, Coalman, Collier, Communist,* Confectioner, Convict, Corn Merchant, Cowman, Cretin,* Cutler, Dancer, Dentist, Dramatist,* Dyer . . .

Jacob's eyes ran down the columns, fascinated by the thoroughness.

. . . Hairdresser, Hatter, Homosexual,* Housewife, Insurance Agent, Invalid,* Jew,* Jeweller, Judge* . . .

Separate returns should be submitted for those categories marked by an asterisk.

. . . Policeman, Potter, Printer,* Quarrier, Railwayman, Roofer, Salesman, Seedsman, Silversmith, Soldier, Surgeon, Tailor, Teacher* . . .

Lists of what they might take:

Books (to be examined); Food, for voyage; Identity, Proof of; Sentimental Nature, small portable objects of; Toilet Requisites . . .

What must be left behind:

Beds, Baths, Bicycles, Blankets, Blinds, Books (unless permitted), Cabinets, Carpets, Cars, Cats, Chairs, Chests, China (see Sentimental), Clocks, Cooking stoves, Curtains, Cushions, Desks . . .

. . . Rugs, Saucepans, Saws, Scales, Sheets, Sinks, Tables, Tents, Tools, Typewriters . . .

'Those are your copies for today, Herr Balthus. You are late. What?' Tischbein did not wait for his answer, but tapped Zech on the arm, encouraging him to lower the map, which they then proceeded to consult in silence. Zech had marked off the streets as they were dealt with. A green pencil line along one side of a street meant that it had been completely cleared of *Volksdeutsche*. A red line marked streets of no interest. A blue cross marked houses where there was some query. A black ring surrounded those who had chosen not to move. There was an eagle mounted on a swastika printed in the top right corner of the map – as there was on every document Jacob had seen.

His job was to act as their guide, translator when they had to refer to non-German speakers, and to witness with his signature each house inventory. Everything was most scrupulously done.

Today they were in Mannheim Street.

'Today we are in Mannheim Street,' announced Tischbein. Zech rolled up the map with a solemn flourish and tapped each end on his briefcase before dropping it in and zipping the case.

The last family left were due to leave on one of the ships tomorrow. Name? Kirdorf.

Their house must be measured, the contents listed and valued, the Kirdorfs issued with their boarding cards; details of their destination.

Herr Kirdorf was a kindly-looking pink-faced man of perhaps seventy; his hair had turned that peculiar white-yellow that affects some of the old, as if they are turning into blond children again. There was a yellow tobacco stain like a flame on one side of his thick moustache.

He was a retired baker. Being retired, Tischbein explained jovially, he would unfortunately not be entitled to his own bakery again. Not in Poland.

No, no, Herr Kirdorf agreed and laughed, though there was nervousness behind his laugh.

The Commissioners had squeezed into the small living-room. Cold outside, the fire in here was too warm. Presumably their last on this hearth, it had been built up. Tischbein and Jacob had the two good armchairs; Zech was upstairs, taking the first part of the inventory.

On their first visits, Jacob had diligently followed Zech through every room of every house, watching as he listed every last stick of furniture. But, however seriously Zech took it, the work became tedious to Jacob. And if Zech occasionally got it wrong, over- or undervaluing a family's possessions – well, Germans were paying and Germans receiving. It was little to do with him. And Zech was so patently, so painstakingly honest. They had visited so many hundreds of homes now, it was impossible not to be bored by the whole nonsense. But not Zech. Even in the houses of the haute-bourgeoisie, where they would often be presented with a full, beautifully typed inventory, Zech would still insist on checking every item, reducing the owners to fuming, silent fury. It was necessary, Zech explained, to guard against fraudulent over-claiming. However, he declared proudly, he had not yet found a single case that could not be put down to simple clerical error. That is the sort of people we are, Herr Balthus. The *Volk*. Strong and honest. Prepared to uproot themselves at a moment on a word from the Führer.

That kind of people.

Jacob had to agree, *this* sort of people was no trouble at all. They were like his own family; confident and competent in their affairs. But the Kirdorfs?

Jacob had never been in the house of anyone poor. Not that he supposed that the Kirdorfs were really *poor*. It was simply the dull sufficiency of their home: the dark, heavy furniture, the few, cheap ornaments, the vilely coloured and sentimental oleograph of Virgin and Child that hung above the small dining-table. All was heavy and dull.

Like Kirdorf himself. His head nodded in anxious agreement as Tischbein ran through what could and could not be taken.

'Your boarding cards. Your ship, and time of embarkation.'

Tischbein handed them over.

Again the head nodded, the big hands turned the boarding card over and over as if half-expecting to find more than two sides to it. Kirdorf looked over in a sheepish way to his wife.

She sat, straight-backed, at the dining-table.

'We have been here so many years,' she began. 'What about our things? Our furniture? Our home. We have heard so much about Poland – that things were not quite as planned. Do you know anything of this?'

Kirdorf lowered his eyes again, his fingers playing with the card, embarrassed by his wife.

'A new beginning, my dear lady,' said Tischbein. 'It is bound to be unsettling at first. But wait until you are sailing. You look back – and what do you see here? There is no future here – forgive me, Herr Balthus – but there is really *no* future here for Germans. You are going home, Frau Kirdorf. You are going *back* to your home.'

'But our things?'

She gestured at the contents of the small dark room.

Tischbein frowned. Then he put on a patient smile. 'They will be stored, my dear. And either shipped to you, or sold and a credit lodged for their value in a homeland bank. Your new apartment . . .'

'Where? Tell us where again please, Herr Tischbein.'

'Posen.'

'In Poland – not Germany,' said Frau Kirdorf.

'I do assure you my dear lady that Posen was very much a German city until the banditry imposed by the Versailles treaty, when this ludicrous entity *Poland* was born. There is no more Poland. There is only the Greater Reich.'

Silence fell in the room. Frau Kirdorf did not look convinced.

At last she spoke. 'You say there are apartments? New apartments?'

'The prettiest, neatest, newest apartments you have ever seen, madam.' Tischbein's voice delighted in the newness, the prettiness of the new homes. 'Now – unless you have more questions . . . ? Good.' He whisked out one of the printed sheets from his attaché case and handed it to Jacob. 'The inventory then. Everything in good order.'

The small fat man capered around the room. Table, dining, small. A little sticky white label pulled off a bunch, licked and slapped on a leg. 104543 its number, like an auction lot. Jacob noted it on his sheet. Carpet, red, worn – 'No value', Tischbein said under his breath. Clock, nineteenth-century, late, German. Vases, three, assorted. Chairs, dining, two. Sideboard, mahogany, heavy. Pictures of family, 'Frames only of value.'

104544
104545
104546 . . .

'They'll be all right. Salt of the earth. Long as they've no skeletons in the cupboard.' Outside the house, on the pavement,
under the grey sky, Tischbein twinkled behind his round
spectacles. Zech studied his map.

'Skeletons? I should hardly think a couple like that . . .'

'Long-nosed skeletons. You would be surprised, Herr
Balthus.' Zech tucked the Kirdorf inventory into his case.
'Some of the people we received down in Posen were found
to be non-Aryan.'

'Non-Aryan? You mean Jewish? But surely – in view, I
mean, of your government's policies on this matter –' It was
best to be diplomatic in these matters, '– surely they were
foolish to go.'

'They would have been mad to go – if they had *known*.
Many of their families, it seems, converted to Christianity in
the last century. Regarded themselves as Germans. Protested
they did not know . . .'

'But that hardly makes them Jewish?'

'Or they had a great-grandmother. Grandfather.'

'Anyone is considered non-Aryan who is descended from at
least one non-Aryan grandparent, or whose grandparents are
themselves of non-Aryan origin,' Zech recited.

'But – if they had converted?' said Jacob.

' "What you believe is no disgrace, The swinishness is in the
race," ' sang Tischbein, executing a little dance-step. 'We even
checked you out too, Herr Balthus. A name like *Jacob* – you
know? But you were clean. Clean as a whistle. Eh, Zech?'

To Jacob the whole conversation smacked of a silly vulgarity. He was quite used to the dry, witty jokes concerning the
alleged cupidity and sharpness of Jews that passed sometimes
between his father's friends; of the lofty class disparagement
of the race by Grandmama Clara and others of the Germans
who regarded themselves as the last survivors of a deprived
nobility – but then Grandmama Clara looked down on everyone except the late Kaiser and his family. He had read and
heard tales of the anti-Jewish laws in Germany, but most

123

people considered that Herr Hitler had to toss a few bones to his more ignorant followers. To actually meet anti-Semitism expressed, not cynically, but with all seriousness by such obviously educated men, civil servants like himself, was both amusing and alarming. He could not help feeling a twinge of relief that Tischbein had cleared him, had given him a certificate of good health, as it were. And, he supposed, you did feel a certain sympathy for their viewpoint, crassly expressed as it was, when they told him how their economy, their professions – their whole culture had been dominated by an alien race. But, it was all in such poor *taste* – either the cold vindictiveness of Zech, or the crude jokes of Tischbein. And yet – and yet. Against his own best inclinations, Jacob's mind again began to toy with their ideas. After all, there must be something in it. Was there? Perhaps the Jews had got too cocky; overstepped the mark; needed to be taught a lesson? No, nonsense – and what is more, wicked nonsense, said his reason. But the human mind generally prefers irrationality to the constant self-questioning that reason demands.

Many times it had been on the tip of his tongue to reprove one or the other of them for their more absurd comments – but . . . they were older than him, he was supposed to be assisting them. It was only a job after all, you can't always pick who you will work with. So he joined in, dutifully laughing at Tischbein's less unpleasant jokes, turning away, pretending not to hear the grotesquely obscene; busying himself at something; giving a wry little smile to Tischbein if the German was so taken with his own wit that he insisted on repeating the whole joke to Jacob.

'The ones who disguise themselves, or even live in ignorance of their state are, in a way, worse than the overt type. They lie in wait.' Zech's cold eyes searched Jacob's face.

'What happens to those identified as non-Aryan?' asked Jacob.

'They are separated,' said Zech. 'Now – if you are ready – we have more to see.'

Before he could draw his green line.

In the last street, men were loading furniture onto Schwarzwald company trucks.

The people here had left a few days before, the Commissioners sealing the doors.

Outside a draper's, an unclothed mannikin had been abandoned, her arms outstretched in invitation, or appeal. Further along the pavement, a typewriter. An umbrella. A lobster pot.

'You go with the first lorry, Herr Balthus,' said Tischbein. 'We shall wait for the second.'

Jacob heaved himself up into the cab that smelt of warm oil. The driver grinned at him – he had two yellow teeth wedged loosely in his upper jaw. They went down towards the dock warehouses.

Schwarzwald himself was in the yard when the lorry drew up.

'No more. No more,' he shouted, a great grin on his face, waving his hands in mock fury. 'No room. Good afternoon, young Balthus. Who would have thought there was so much furniture in the city, eh?'

Jacob clambered down. 'There's another truck on the way.' It came through the gateway as Jacob spoke.

Schwarzwald went to greet this too.

'Tischbein! Where is Herr Zech? Come along. Come along – not yet more coming with Herr Zech? Where shall we put it all? Squeeze it in somewhere, eh?' He seemed in huge good humour. 'Squeeze it in somehow, eh young Balthus?' And he manoeuvred the two men on either side of him and laid his arms across their shoulders. His beefy hand – literally, the fingers like hairy sausages – closed on Jacob's shoulder and squeezed.

'Keep your eyes on this one, Herr Tischbein. Smart young feller. Coming man. Get that stuff off. Come on,' he yelled at his men, his beery breath roaring past Jacob's cheek. 'Know his father well. And old Clara Hugenberg, his grandma. Fine lady. Fine. In Berlin now, I hear. Lucky her, eh? And I'll be going soon. Leaving all this – built it up – but I'll keep in touch, tell your father, Jacob – I will keep in touch. Never fear.' His grip did not relent. They watched the men unloading the trucks.

'Shame to go. In a way. But I know where my duty lies. Blood's thicker than water, eh? But, look here, you lads.'

Tischbein, thought Jacob, could only be a year or two younger than Schwarzwald. Somewhere in his late forties. 'Look – I'm giving a party. My town house. Friday night. Come along, both of you. All of you.' Again his voice blasted out. Zech had arrived in a third truck.

'Party, Zech – you're all invited. Bring your girls. If you have 'em. If you haven't, there'll be plenty there. Jacob?'

'Thank you very much, Herr Schwarzwald.'

'Many thanks. A party – that's fine. I love parties,' said Tischbein.

Zech bowed. It was not entirely evident that he knew what a party was. Apart from the Nazi variety, that is.

5

They had come to the theatre early, but already the auditorium was filling up. Getting to their seats, still standing, people looked around them, lifted their programmes in greetings to friends in other rows, and then settled themselves down, adding their voices to the excited, muffled conversation that arose from the audience but seemed to sink back and be absorbed in the plush seats, with only, every now and then, the higher voice of a child escaping and floating up to the gilded cherubs on the ceiling.

Jacob sat staring down at the empty orchestra pit. Ella was on his right. The two seats on his left, reserved for Katerina and Max, were empty.

Jacob thought gloomily about his Germans. He was glad now that the job was coming to an end. He had not told Ella he was working with them, although the chance of keeping anything secret in this city was negligible. But it would all be over soon; it was best left as one of the areas of which one does not speak.

The day had started badly when, in the office allocated to the Commissioners, he had read a letter from a woman who had been resettled in Posen. Things were not as rosy as painted. Two or more families were having to share a single unheated flat or tiny house. They were waiting still for the extra police who had been promised.

> . . . some of our men have been attacked and one or two murdered by Polish bandits thankfully they have been hung in the open square but still the bad feelings go on against us. These people are barbarians . . .

Later he had to accompany Tischbein and Zech to the big mental asylum on the northern edge of town, to supervise the 'simple transfer' of all the German mental patients to the hospital ship in the harbour.

'Quite why they should need any more lunatics in their country, I don't quite see,' his father had said drily when Jacob told him of their task. Not funny in practice. He preferred not to think about it. That man with no eyes – simply the skin over where they should be; the fat, flat-faced overgrown child of thirty-five; the two, three, four twisted, dribbling mouths making sounds at the sky as they were wheeled out.

'Unpleasant. Unpleasant,' Zech had kept muttering, striding up and down until the ambulances were filled . . .

The first musicians entered the pit, creeping, bent over, to their positions, heads bobbing up and down as they got out their instruments, adjusted music stands. The conductor arrived, the side of his face lit in a ghastly way by the rostrum lamp as he bent over the score.

The two seats beside Jacob remained empty. The rest of the theatre was almost full. They were most probably in the bar. Noises; scrapings of violins as they tuned, little wisps from the woodwind like bird calls, arose from the pit. Two of the musicians talked, craning towards each other, under the soft lights on their music stands.

Those poor bloody lunatics.

In the docks today he had seen horses loaded by slings into the holds of cargo ships. Earlier a shipload of convicts had left

for Germany. 'A day of odds and ends,' said Tischbein con-
tentedly on the quayside, rubbing his gloved hands together.
'I could do with a cognac.'

So could I, so could I. Jacob had had several.

And now wished he had not. The theatre was too warm. The
pit became cacophonous and then eerily silent. The doors into
the auditorium were shutting. Where were Max and Katerina?
The last door shut. The house lights went down. For a moment
the audience was in almost total darkness. Then the orchestra
pit showed as a dark pool ringed with dimly luminescent faces,
as if people on the bank were kneeling and staring at their
reflections. The curtains began to rustle back and light from
the stage glowed softly out on all the faces.

Violins sawed; the woodwinds blew; well, the music was
nice. He began to relax a little. But what he had not reckoned
on – as no one ever does, except the dim romantics who
would live their lives in it – is the quite inordinate length and
dramatic tedium of Tchaikovsky's *Swan Lake*. The nice music
droned on. The white dancers on the grey stage hypnotized
as they twisted and turned under their following spotlights,
and – as the damned thing dragged on and on, he began to
feel drowsy and had to struggle to keep awake. He shifted
his backside in his seat, pinched his leg, tried to read his
programme by the stage light to find out exactly where
everyone down there had reached. And all the time, in the
soporific darkness, Ella sat bolt upright. On his other side,
the two seats remained palely, mockingly empty. *She* at least
should have been here. Jacob Balthus, satyr, between his
two women. Past and Present Conditional. His mood swung,
with the bathetic music, between self-esteem and self-pity,
desire and hate – was it? While, down on the stage, that
fool of a too-large, balding Prince Siegfried stood on his
toes, arms outstretched as Odette-Odile and her maidens
fluttered, fluttered, fluttered until they were at last out of
sight behind the side flats, and the Prince stood and stood,
arm stretched after them, eyes staring up as they turned
to swans and flew, flew (his hand twitched), circling away.
Only, we know, thought Jacob, all the time it is nonsense.
There are no swans out there, though the music begs us to
believe so. When Prince Siegfried stands, his hand stretched

out in such poignant longing, all he can *really* see in the wings
are a couple of stagehands with mops and brooms, a lighting
man up a stepladder sliding a new gelatine into his lamp, the
tutued, flustered girls cooling down, giggling, drinking lemon-
ade from a huge white jug, the ropes and pulleys descending
from the flies; all the mechanics, the delusions of art. Again
Jacob was aware of that odd feeling of blasphemy, of some
transgression against what he knew it was *right* to feel. And
here came Prince Siegfried again, audibly thumping across
the stage, the stage just half a foot not wide enough for his
last stride.

Jacob stole a glance at Ella. She was rapt in the goings-on
on stage.

The house was full. All were agog. He searched for beautiful women. There were many. Their faces were all turned
to the stage.

He shut his eyes and tried to concentrate solely on the
music. Why should *she* prefer Max to himself? There was
an obvious gloss and animality about the man. The eyes
that shone brighter at the sight of a woman; the hands that
were long and strong; the too large, sensual mouth. Maybe
Max too was a Jew. There it was again. That word. His
eyes snapped open, in protest at himself. What had that to
do with anything? His mind was playing shabby tricks. The
music was nice. The dancing pretty; dull. He looked at the
ceiling, at its baroque angels, their hair flowing back, cheeks
rouged, blowing long trumpets – horns? At his watch. At Ella
again. And she looked back at him. Was that a smile? Her
head turned back to the stage. He closed his eyes again and
prepared to let the music carry him away. But his drowsiness
had left him and all the time his brain worked.

What was he to do with Ella? What did she want him to
do?

Oh dear God, Katerina – why have you left me? She
was farther from him now than if he had never set eyes
on her. If she lived a thousand miles away she would be
nearer. The white legs of the girls on the stage. The little
red buds of *her* nipples, the pink tinily dimpled surrounding
aureoles, the ineffable sweetness, softness, yielding – and his
almost instantaneous coming as he entered her bewitching –

what can you call it? And she whispering it doesn't matter, it doesn't matter, and he, confused, her lover, stammering it will be better next time, next time. And her soft never mind, never mind, there's always another time. Only there wasn't. There had not been. There never would be. Time had moved both of them on. The music swelled, ennobling him. O dear Katerina – forgive my unworthy thoughts towards you. The obscenities in my mind. All this . . . this filth. And, noble, he rose with the soaring violins, and fell with them, and opened his wet eyes.

Here come the hunters. The swan is shot. She dies slowly, unendurably; fluttering and sinking. Only one tiny backward slip betrays the dancer behind the dance. It is recovered; the music overwhelms. The swan dies. The lights dim.

Jacob closed his eyes and willed the last few bars to make him *feel*. And, at last, he achieved an all-pervading sentimental melancholy. The music stopped.

The applause thundered. In his box the Soviet Ambassador rose and stood beaming down and clapping his hands in that stolidly arrhythmic way Russians do. All the gentlemen and ladies stood applauding, nodding and gabbling to each other. Flowers were given to the principal ballerina who had died so prettily and almost without mishap.

Ella was full of chatter now as they came down the marble staircase and into the Parade. The night was cold and brightly starred. Weren't the dresses pretty? The prince a prodigious leaper? The music sublime? The ballet seemed to have released something in her so that she appeared prettier and less cold.

Less cold indeed. Half an hour later they were in bed together in her hotel room. This time there was no failure on Jacob's part at the first moment of bliss. He drove and drove into her for, it seemed, hours and she moaned and clung to him and bit into his shoulder. Her eyes wide, her body rose and fell in time with his, her hair, splayed loose, shuddered as again her head convulsively rose from the pillow and she screamed.

Jacob had discovered the pleasure of making love to a woman he did not love. The importance of impersonality. Almost, of contempt.

*

Perhaps he had, at last, grown up. The new realist Jacob certainly was no longer happy. The next evening his home seemed constrictive, the preoccupations and anxieties of his parents timid and bourgeois. He had frequently heard the word used sneeringly by Ella and others in the café, but he had never taken it to refer to him. And really, he thought, surveying his father bent over his official papers once more, what life had they ever seen?

When his mother chided him gently with yet again not appearing for dinner, he said, with all the cruelty of the newly freed, 'That need not pain you much longer. I shall, Mother, be moving from home shortly in any case.'

His father looked up, astonished.

6

The wine was sweet and whatever coolness it had got from the ice-box had melted in the warmth of the room.

Or rather, rooms. Schwarzwald had opened the double doors joining his two large living-rooms. People sat, or perched on the arms of the chairs and sofas pushed back against the walls. More stood about chattering in little knots, glasses in hands, while the sweetly intertwining strains of the Trout Quintet on the gramophone – and two maids with trays of drinks – moved among them, serving.

Nearly all of those at the party were German Balts – they were all leaving soon, he gathered from their excited talk. But *these* were not leaving for cold-water flats in Posen. Their money and relatives were taking them home – to the Fatherland itself. It was as if they were waiting on a sunlit quay for a white ship to scoop them up and take them on an endless holiday.

The electric chandeliers shone brilliantly, the music flowed between them like water; the whole dead dark night stood like an ocean outside the tall windows.

Jacob felt fraudulent at being in this company; he clung to his blood line with Grandmama Clare – Omama, as she liked him to call her. Could there be anything in it – in these loud voices, superb confidence, sweet wine, music, the image of an endlessly sunny modern Germany in their eyes, a land of broad autobahns, of fine young sunburnt men on leave from a victorious war? What if they were right?

He was alone. He looked about him. It was the first time he had been to the home of a really rich man. It was a shock to see that it was not the same as that of a man with taste. All was sumptuously leathered, chintzed, varnished, gilded, and everything was somehow out of place, as if he had stepped through the screen into a Hollywood studio version of an antechamber in a palace.

On the walls large oil paintings showed large, naked women with large globe-like snow-coloured breasts and no other evidence of sex; the smooth flesh between their legs curved as chastely and unbrokenly as the curl of a Mercedes mudguard. These maidens stood their ground, sword in hand, against dragons; held grapes untantalizingly above their mouths; here one swooned on the sandy floor of a cave . . .

'Ah – you're admiring my nymph. Fine picture, eh?'

Schwarzwald stood close behind him and put a heavy hand on Jacob's shoulder.

'We Germans certainly can paint, eh Jacob?'

Yes. He supposed they could.

'Not like this modernistic rubbish. You know the Führer put all that stuff into one big exhibition – all that stuff, the monkeys with three eyes and the yellow trees and the women with purple tits into one exhibition. Called it the Exhibition of Degenerate Art. Right, eh?' Schwarzwald snorted.

Yes. He supposed so. Never really taken much notice of art.

Jacob had seen some unframed canvases that Otto whatever-his-name had brought into Stieckus's once. Otto was supposed to be good by all his friends; Gerald and Frank and . . . and. Gerald had bought one. All squares and triangles and bits of gauze and labels stuck on. Why it was like that Jacob didn't know. He felt it was vaguely ridiculous. But in those days, in Jacob's eyes, Gerald knew all about that sort of thing. And Otto seemed a decent enough chap, if scruffy. Hardly degenerate . . .

'All be crated up tomorrow,' said Schwarzwald. He and Jacob gazed up at the woman in the cave a moment longer.

'Know why I asked you here tonight, young Jacob?' Schwarzwald spoke in a surprisingly quiet voice.

Why had he asked him here? His father? Grandmama Clara? Schwarzwald was evidently acquainted with Clara, but Jacob could hardly think that Omama, who counted her ancestors back to the Teutonic Knights of the Middle Ages, would have welcomed this parvenu – was that the right word? – this *Schwarzwald* to her home. But – Schwarzwald was German. And that was all important in her eyes. In these days.

'What I wanted was to make you an offer. There now. I'm a blunt man, eh? No point beating about the bush. No – no.' Schwarzwald motioned a waitress and her tray away. 'Hired for the night. Not my regular people. You know that I'm leaving. Got to sell up and all. That's part of the deal. But, the place doesn't disappear overnight, does it? In a puff of smoke. And I'm not going to sell. Not to a bunch of dirty Jews.'

It was common among the Germans, Jacob had noted, to use the most foul and abusive language about Jews, as if no one in the world could possibly object or disagree. And, to his shame, he did neither. It was the new normality perhaps, part of the way the world was going.

'No – what I want,' Schwarzwald purred on. And it turned out that he needed to appoint a couple of managers to run his timber business by proxy. 'You know the import-export side from the Ministry. Interested, young Balthus? Seems to me you have a sound head on your shoulders. Think you could handle it, eh? Eh? Come and see me in my office tomorrow.'

Through all this Jacob nodded, smiled, said um and yes and well, I don't know . . .

'Come and see me. No obligation to buy. By the way –' Schwarzwald looked at him in that suddenly searching way that fat jovial cunning men use to catch someone

133

out. '– don't still frequent that terrible place, the Stieckus café?'

'No . . . no. Not much.'

'Drop it. Want my advice – drop it. Do you no good. There's only one way to live, my dear young Balthus. You'll find that out soon enough. And best to do it young, eh? Before it gets painful. Now –' For emphasis, Schwarzwald tapped Jacob's arm with two plump, rigid fingers. '– let's join the party. It's my bloody party, after all, isn't it? Ha.' He spoke with his usual loud blustering voice and laugh. With their release, he looked about him, his eyes shining, his small lips wet and moving slightly as if he was rehearsing some simply wonderful joke.

Close conversation was becoming impractical. The party had passed its first stage, its overture, when the guests gather, tentatively greet half-strangers, circle the room to avoid the disagreeable, coalesce in gabbling, happy groups – or stand, lonely, pretending to look at ornaments and pictures as Jacob had done. Now the room was almost filled, the first themes of conversation had been aired and people had once more begun to move about, detaching themselves from one group, attaching themselves to another. The variations swirled and babbled. The music played on the gramophone became inaudible, escaping only as snatches in those mysterious silences that every now and then fall on a crowd – and are a moment later vanquished by a great clash of laughter and half-shouted relief.

Jacob started and did not finish many interchanges of polite banalities with total strangers or imperfectly remembered acquaintances. No, he explained with various impersonations of brightness, shame, or casualness, no, he would not be leaving for the Fatherland soon. Was that a look of contempt, an inclination to turn away from this presentable but un-Germanic gatecrasher, that he saw in his questioners? With some desperation he would say, Yes, Yes, he was half-German. His mother. Perhaps you know my grandmother – Clara Hugenberg? He brandished Grandmama Clara like a flag of surrender.

Tischbein and Zech had arrived. He saw Zech's pale red hair and freckled face moving through the crowd and presumed that Tischbein must be following in his wake. Yes, there was his head now. Zech spotted Jacob and changed course towards him.

And just then, another door was flung open in the lower of the two rooms and a great call of 'Food!' came from Schwarzwald, standing in the doorway.

The pressure of people eased as they began to queue to pass into the dining-room, so that Tischbein and Zech came ahead at speed.

'In time for the food, I see. Good. Good.' Tischbein rubbed his hands together. 'But – will there be room?' he asked anxiously, gazing at the crush trying to get through the newly-opened door.

'It's a buffet,' said a woman loudly.

'Ah buffet. Buffet. Splendid.' His face brightened again.

Evidently the dining-room opened onto the hall, because in a few moments the first people began to stroll back by way of this circular route, into the top end of the room, carrying their plates loaded with cold meats and cheeses and 'Oh, good – beetroot,' Tischbein said excitedly, examining the plates with delight.

Now the record of the quintet had been replaced. Something lighter, airier – Mozart? Jacob thought – drifted through the rooms. Little silver forks and ringed fingers rose from plates to mouths and fell again, emptied. Glasses were balanced precariously on the sides of plates, or held tilting between the middle fingers. Jacob, Tischbein and Zech filed through the dining-room, helped themselves to food and rejoined the party. Everyone ate. The music swooped and trilled and joked with itself. A wine-glass fell from one of the marble mantelshelves into the tiled fireplace, shattering with a tinkle that sounded part of the music. The log fire was revealed as people parted and drew back to let through a maid with a dustpan and brush. The long drapes were drawn against the night.

This second stage of the party lasted, it seemed, a long time. If a sober outsider had been able to conceal himself somewhere to observe the crowd he would have noticed little change in behaviour from moment to moment, but over an hour, an hour and a half, two hours, he would have seen it build up to little climaxes of laughter, each time a little shriller than the last, would have seen the faces flush and the eyes become brighter, the attention-drawing tugs at sleeves and the digs with fingers get harder and more vehement, hear the voices grow louder and more demanding – but for those *in* the party it would seem that time stood still, or even reversed, and they did not change at all, only to become simply more pleasantly *themselves*.

Seated at a table, Tischbein showed a picture of his family to Jacob. A plump-faced woman with a plump, blonde-mopped little girl on one knee. Magda and little Ida. Are they not beautiful?

Jacob smiled, feeling not a little superior and amused. That such *ugly*, middle-aged people could think they were in any way beautiful!

The Mozart was long over. The new music was lush, heavily and insistently seductive, like a thick perfume. There was now, it appeared, room for everyone to sit down. The women looked prettier, younger, between the large confident men. The staid matrons and respectable husbands had all gone home. Schwarzwald walked up and down between the rooms, lifting his glass in salute to this table, then that, saying again and again, 'Good times ahead, Herr . . . My next greetings in Berlin, Frau . . .' Or, as it seemed to Jacob, *marching* between the rooms. Jacob was sweating; he had had a lot of the wine already. The waitresses went up and down, the smiles now fixed on their faces with weariness.

The music expanded in the slightly emptier rooms.

'This,' Tischbein announced across the table, 'is our divine Wagner.'

Even Zech was smiling; though on his face the smile was turned inward in some secret way, as if while he smiled he examined himself, saying Yes, yes – that is how they do it.

Then he leaned forward, or rather his whole long torso in its buttoned-up suit jacket tilted and he picked up his glass.

'To our beloved Fatherland. Heil Hitler,' he said in a loud, solemn voice, raising the glass.

'. . . Fatherland . . . Fatherland . . .' The call was taken up and rippled away from them along the other tables, drinks lifted in the toast, a girl's mischievous eyes serious for a moment over the rim of her wine-glass.

Tischbein stretched his glass forth to clink against Zech's. Jacob, again half amused, but feeling it expected of him – and why not? it was their party – did the same.

'. . . Hitler . . .'

Schwarzwald stood before their table, standing at attention.

'Heil Hitler.' Then he too drank, the whole glass, and banged it down on the table. There, lads, there. But somebody called. He must go to his other guests. Excuse. Be back, lads. Bring you another bottle. Two, he called over his shoulder, his face splitting again in a huge smile.

Zech drank his wine rather prissily, as Jacob imagined an English spinster might – his little finger extended at a right angle, the stem of the glass clutched delicately between thumb and forefinger.

Tischbein wiped his mouth with his free hand and looked disappointedly down into the empty glass balled in his fist. 'This is all very well, my dear Zech,' he said. 'But is there no beer? Beer is my drink. This is very nice – but a little for the ladies. Is there no beer?' he appealed to Jacob.

He said this just as Schwarzwald was re-passing.

Beer, gentlemen? Beer? Why, of course. You should have said.

Beer was brought – a whole barrel mounted on a sort of barrow was wheeled into the centre of the floor to hearty cheers.

At last, under the beer's influence, Zech began to unwind. He loosened his tie that had seemed welded to his collar, silently downing litre after litre of the cold, sharp beer.

A girl came round each table and placed a candlestick in the centre and lit each thick white candle. The electric lights were switched off. A girl screamed. Then, gradually, in the isolation of each group in its own yellow pool of light a new order, a new life began to emerge; the last few shrieks of laughter died away, some people continued to talk for a while, until they were shushed into silence by their neighbours.

For Schwarzwald, like a large fat bear in a cave in the alcove that held the gramophone, had put on the prelude to *Tristan and Isolde* and the music held them in a dream.

Undulating, gross, caressing waves of passion washed over them; great soughing rich chords like storm clouds passing among the gods on their mountain tops elevated each of their souls. For five minutes – until the needle clacked in the last groove – they were all held in a spell of tender, intense passion. All were informed, sublimely, of their place in the hierarchy of lovers – our secular angels. And when it was over they remained silent. They waited for Schwarzwald to turn over the record and continue the vision of Paradise they had been given. But Schwarzwald had gone out of the room. No one else approached the gramophone. The needle remained knocking in the groove. Someone began to whisper at one table. Then at another. Schwarzwald let a shaft of electric light in from the hall. 'What – music over?' he shouted. And it was. Released – relieved – from their rapt attention, table after table began to chatter and drink again.

Zech's body tilted back, his eyes shining on Jacob.

'Was it not great? Was it not – noble? What a man Wagner must have been. That is German art, my friend.' These were the first words not directly connected with their work together that Zech had spoken to Jacob. 'The Germanic soul will ennoble the world, that is what Wagner said. Ennoble.'

A girl brought another jug of beer and refilled their steins. Schwarzwald came out of his cave. He had put something from *The Merry Widow* on the gramophone. On his way back he caught the girl and whirled her down the room to cheers and claps, between the tables, and out the door at the end. At her table Frau Schwarzwald's bosom heaved. 'That's my Heini,' she snorted, laughing.

Zech went remorselessly on.

'It is the artist like Wagner who shows us the true nobility of man. Of the higher man, Herr Balthus. Not the common herd, the *Untermensch*, but the Aryan who alone searches always for the truth. The Higher Truth. That is our destiny as Germans. Oh, if I could only explain. The beauty of it. Our Führer has said it, "Art cannot be divided from blood. It is the expression of the psychic feeling of the people." When you think of such things made by *our* people. Such perfection. Why should we need new art? Such perfection. History should come to an end, Herr Balthus. There is no need for any more. With all these things . . .' His face twisted with distaste. He leaned forward. 'But, you must

138

know, it is the Jew prevents us. He is at the root of all our problems. All.'

Across the table Tischbein nodded, a seraph of happiness, agreeing.

'The German people invented the art of writing. Did you know that? Our ancient Runic script. That the greatest of painters, musicians, scientists – all these have been of higher racial type. And all of this – this beauty – we have allowed to be corrupted by the Jews. Oh – oh – you people make me so angry. You live your lives in a dream, unable to see our true enemy.' Zech was most extraordinarily wound up; his forefinger stabbed towards Jacob. More beer came.

The music had changed to a Strauss waltz. Some couples came onto the floor to dance. Time would pass quickly for the dancers – here, at this table, it moved sluggishly, impeded by Zech's laborious, mad lecture. More and more beer came until Jacob felt gorged. He was drunk. Zech's voice invaded his drunkenness.

'. . . Germanic peoples most gifted . . . highest . . . Aryan. Not though that every German Aryan . . . Not by any means.' The voice was raised. 'Are you listening to me, Herr Balthus?'

Jacob gave him a sickly smile.

'The true Aryan is not common. It is the sacred task of the German *Volk*, Herr Balthus, to make him more frequent and dominant. How marvellous it would be,' his face was ecstatic, 'if the world could be run by the most gifted, the strongest – a league of Supermen who would stride the world, leading the nations, cleansing their blood. You are blind. You people are blind. The secret of life is to know your enemy. Believe me, when I woke I knew, I *knew*, with a blinding flash who our enemy was. And is. The eternal, fornicating, creeping, sly, slimy Jew. Like worms they bore through our civilization. They have. But no more. No more. They have degraded our people, poured their filth over this, all this –' he strove for the right word '– this *beauty* – what is it to their filthy caterwaulings, their stupid meaningless pictures, their sneering slanderous books. But – no more. *No more*.' Zech smashed his fist down so hard on the table that the glasses and steins and empty bottles rattled and shivered together.

'Steady on, old man,' came a call from the sofa across the room. A pair of dancers stopped and stared over at their table.

'Perfectly right, Zech,' said Tischbein. 'But we've made 'em sweat. They have to do honest work now. What was it the Führer said – a good joke this, Balthus, you will like this – "The Jew is assuredly the member of a race but, but ..." ' Tischbein's voice bubbled with good humour, his face seemed to expand with the anticipation of releasing a rich gust of laughter, 'but, "but not the *human* race." Good, eh? Good. Ha, ha.' Laughter broke out of him. Zech managed a quick humourless twitch of the lips. Jacob found himself smiling.

Now some jolly military band music was playing. Tischbein sat, beer in one hand, the other vigorously tapping out the rhythm on his jigging knees. Zech was downing more beer. He put his stein on the table, his hands clasped round it as if he were holding it together.

He began to speak again, quickly and insistently, in a quiet voice that could hardly be heard above the oompahing music. As much as Jacob could hear, Zech seemed to be continuing his tirade against the Jews – but the whole now totally obscene and scatological; blood and filth, rape and child-murder, usury, and matzos dipped in the blood of Christian children and blood and blood and blood . . . And so Zech went on, while Tischbein's knees jigged up and down to the trumpets and drums of another and another record. Jacob tried to listen to the music, to drown out the mad muttering at his side. But the room swayed. The candles were burning down. A gale of laughter swept across the room. The music stopped and he could hear Zech again.

What was this he was saying? He had done something. The asylum. The lunatics. We have a way to clear such places. Not for the squeamish. A duty. Duty. No point in them living. If you could have seen them. Have to swallow your pride. Do your duty like a man. If you ever have to drown a man in a bath. Shoot. Gas. You would know what I mean . . .

'What do you mean? Shoot? Gas?' Jacob tried desperately to gather his wits about him, but, like a drunk comedian in a film, they slipped and slithered away from him. Was Zech saying . . . ? That he had . . . ?

'Zech!' Tischbein had shifted round in his seat, and grabbing Zech's arm he pulled him forward and whispered fiercely into his ear.

Zech stared ahead, his thin lips now tightly shut. He heard Tischbein out, then stood suddenly and bowed, first to Jacob, then to Tischbein. All joviality again, Tischbein reached across the table and laid his hand on Jacob's. 'I'm so sorry, Herr Balthus. My friend cannot take his drink as well as some of us . . .'

Zech took a staggering step backward, nearly falling over his chair. He circled the table and marched stiffly away towards the door to the hall.

Jacob cleared his throat. 'Squyrallright,' he said.

'Yes,' said Tischbein, rising from his chair. He seemed quite unaffected by the wine and beer he had drunk. 'If you will excuse me, I will bid you goodnight. Until we meet again.' He extended his hand across the table. Jacob shook it, or rather, was shaken.

'Goodnight.'

'Guni.'

Jacob was left alone at the table. From then on things became confused. He remembered sitting at the table alone. Then, sitting at the table. Alone. Deciding something. To go. Sitting at the table. The lights went on. The main, electric lights. He was standing at another table. He was effusively bidding Frau Schwartfall a ver gunnigh. An thanyou, lovely party. Thank you. Must see Herr Fartschawl. Not here? Not here, in library. Found himself outside another door. Opens. Fat bear embracing ice maiden. Waitress. Maid pretty. Beer. Sorry. Sorry.

Then he is in the street, reeling warm through black icy night. Then in corridor. Outside room. Number? Ella opens door. He says simply, 'I have come.' Walks in. Stands in centre of room swaying, and all he can say is, 'Germans. Germans. Bloody Germans. Sorry.'

Then all is blackness until the morning.

IV

Leontion, son of Aglaion, was on his way up
from the Peiraeus, outside the north wall, when
he noticed some corpses lying on the ground
with the executioner standing by them. He wanted
to go and look at them, and yet at the same time
held himself back in disgust. For a time he
struggled with himself and averted his eyes, but
in the end his desire got the better of him and
he ran up to the corpses, opening his eyes wide
and saying to them, 'There you are, curse you –
a lovely sight! Have a real good look!'

Plato, *The Republic*

I

The day after the last German ship left snow began to fall
again. It seemed it would snow forever. The whole country
lay under this soft, translating beauty; roofs rounded at their
edges, roads as valleys between banks of snow higher than
a man, the bare trees charged with beauty, changed to the
most richly rhythmical charcoal drawings; the telegraph poles
radiating white lines like stars. Dogs plunged joyfully, their
heads tossing like swimmers' in the park snows.

Then the snow stopped falling and everything froze. The
heating was turned to full in the apartment-block radiators
but you felt cold if you took a single step away. Breath snapped
in the air. The city and its reversed archipelago of snow-filled
parks, and lakes, its frozen river and sea lay at night like a
great broken mirror reflecting the moon.

In the forests birds froze in their nests, turning to stone.
More rarely, one would freeze to its perch, and in the day,
when the sun shone enough to melt a little snow in a wind-
less corner, the water droplets – each enclosing its own tiny
crystal of inverted forest – would drip onto the cold small
body, freeze again in the darkening afternoon, until layer
by layer ice formed a case around the bird. Usually these
were misshapen cloudy eggs that gave only glimpses of the
bird inside and they would topple off by their own weight
and be picked up by children. Hurried home as curiosities,
placed on a table, in the warmth of the house they would
melt, leaving only a wet bedraggled body, to be thrown out
or buried with some little ceremony in the snow. But, once
or twice in a winter, in some deep and undisturbed part of
the forest, a perfect ice-egg would form about a bird so that
it seemed to have fallen asleep in a perfect crystal. And, by
virtue of its own coldness and the shade where it happened
to be lodged, it preserved its shape and transparency until

well into the spring, only then beginning to melt and fall away, shrinking and clouding until the bird could no longer be seen.

How interesting. It was a pity you could not keep such a thing. As a curio. Conversation piece. In an ice box you could. But out it would melt. Pity.

Jacob's father turned over the magazine page on which the photograph of the frozen bird appeared. That awful winter. From before Christmas until well into April not a morning had passed without a hard frost. Even when the sun shone from a cloudless sky the ice and snow only seemed to *perspire* a little. At least it had slowed the war down. For a while. He had picked this old magazine up to avoid reading the dreadful news in the paper.

For, with the end of winter, the war had begun to flow again, like a melted river. In March the Finns, after their stupendous, unequal struggles, were forced at last to surrender to the Russians. In April the Germans crossed the borders of Denmark and invaded Norway. The two powers circled about *this* country as if they could not see it. Are we invisible?

Across the room his wife, Minna, coughed. He gazed at her for a moment. She was reading yet another English novel. Arnold Bennett? Galsworthy? Why did women like so much to read of the minutiae of domestic lives? Why couldn't they read of the big things? He had tried to interest her in Mann – 'Too boring.' In Proust – 'He knows nothing of life.' Chekhov – 'Too sad.' Oh well, that was her taste. Or lack of it. It no longer irritated him. She was his wife, and that was the way she was. His gaze wandered to his books, shelved to the ceiling along one wall.

When young he had harboured a secret half-wish – no more – that he might himself be a writer one day. As an adolescent he had written poetry of course. And, later, a few private poems for Minna, that only she was to see. He was not supposed to know that she kept them still in her drawer upstairs. Not that he would dream of reading them again. And little plays and stories for the toy theatre he had built for Jacob. The little gentlemen and ladies, soldiers, dragons, all mounted on sticks, the scenery and oh, whatever, picked out of a catalogue and ordered by post from London. Very old shop. What was their name? Potter? Pottle?

'You look happy,' said Minna.

She smiled across at him.

'I was thinking.'

'When did you say Jacob would come?'

'I don't know. I've asked him to the office. I don't know if he will come.'

'To go and live with that girl.'

'She is not that bad, I'm sure. Jacob is grown up now.'

'It's immoral.'

'Times change.'

She put down her book and sighed. 'Go and see him. See if there is anything he wants. Tell him not to be ashamed to come back. If he wants.'

'Yes, yes Minna. I'll arrange something.'

She went into the kitchen to make some tea for them. Outside the sun shone. It was warm enough already to have the windows open. How marvellous – despite the news from the world surrounding them, the sun shone. The shadows of the curtain edges trembled gently across the carpet. How good it was to see the green and red and blue tiled roofs again after that awful interminable white. Pretty enough to begin with. He picked up the magazine. It fell open at the picture of the bird encased in ice. Perhaps he could write a little poem about that. Yes.

Yes. He had not felt so young for years. Ridiculous statement. But true. Perhaps anxiety did fall away in the end, exhausted by itself. Perhaps anxiety was simply cowardice. War released the frisson of renewed youth to the middle aged – but you sent the young to face the actual dangers. In that case rather shameful. To be denied. He entertained himself with easy philosophical thoughts on the nature of war, of pacifism, neutralism – the advantages of a man standing apart. He knew the thoughts were facile but the afternoon was really too sweet to tax oneself yet again. He confirmed again to himself the suspicion that all these, what? these skirmishings in Norway, in Finland, were only urgent grabs to establish negotiating positions – the more you had the more you could afford to give up. And, until peace came

– well, it was exciting. And this afternoon. Yes. Yes. His
fingers itched for a pen. He would write a poem about that
bird. About winter. Beauty. And tonight he would take Minna
out to a good restaurant – Oswald's. With good wine. Good
food. Enjoy it. And then . . .

The before-dawn hours are the favourites for Death, thieves,
secret policemen. Lovers, however indefatigable, snatch an
hour's sleep. The old die, if lucky. Insomniacs once more
cease to believe in life. Child, respectable wife, drunk, swim
deeply in their dreams.

But soldiers, rested, eyes clear, look forward to a clean run,
the scent of fear just pricking through their thick tunics – a
huntsman's excitement.

Before dawn, while Jacob's father twisted slightly in sleep
beside Minna, German armies and airplanes invaded Holland
and Belgium and Northern France. From then on, May morning after May morning, they tore and smashed stone and flesh
in a jubilant orgy. Everywhere was this invasion, this victory
of young men, bringing the summer.

In Rotterdam the front of an apartment block dissolved;
all the rooms exposed to air.

Hours later, in the street, a dog timidly, tentatively sniffed,
then licked blood from a wall.

2

At a table in the window of one of the smartest newest
restaurants in the capital, Katerina sat waiting for Max. As
yet, only a few of the other tables were taken. People lunching
on their own pored over newspapers, or, if in a group, talked
in endless, anxious speculation about the war. What would
happen now? Things were getting worse, weren't they?

Katerina had no newspaper. She could not bear to read of

such things. It was better to try and put them out of mind if you wanted to be happy. What could you do?

The waiter brought her coffee, and a clean ashtray. She smiled up at him – a quiet, enchanting smile with just a hint of pain behind it. That was not insincere, was it? What was wrong with showing people you sympathized? Trying to cheer them a little. It was not hypocrisy. It was, if you like, acting. Well – she *was* an actress, wasn't she? She took off her grey gloves and laid them beside her plate. She lit a cigarette.

The noon sunlight slanted down the empty chair on the other side of the table.

Max had asked her to lunch with him here over the telephone this morning. He had spent the night at her apartment but left early to go to the agency. Isn't it terrible – the news, she had said. What news? The Germans have taken Paris. Terrible, yes terrible, he said almost absently. Then he said, Meet me for lunch. I'll cheer you up. Look beautiful. You always look beautiful – but I want to see you especially so.

Thinking about the call made her smile again; an inward smile, a reflex of pleasure. She tapped the cigarette on the side of the ashtray. Well, she *was* beautiful. Men told her so often enough. She was, she supposed, bright too in a way – though this was less interesting to them. To please men you had to be reasonably cultured, though not clever; humorous, but not witty; you must know enough about food to cook and serve it properly, but leave the reading of a restaurant menu to them. You had, in short, to be an actress in life, as well as on stage. A better one.

She had dreamed of herself as the Great Actress; as Camille, Ninotchka, Lulu – her own small, dark face miraculously reforming and resolving itself into Garbo's. You had to get down to it, to work at your vocation. Your art. Oh, she knew that. There was time for that. She knew she would have to leave this little country, as she had left her parents' home, to make anything of herself. She had dreamed of Paris . . . America even. But it had never seemed quite the right time to go. Now it was too late for Paris. They would hardly be welcoming Jewish girls now, would they? Not that she bothered with the Jew thing. Nor had father. A Radical, he had been proud to call himself an atheist, to ridicule his religion as 'mumbo-jumbo'. She sometimes dimly resented the fact that her parentage had left this faint stigma on her. But that's all it was. Faint. Really, did anyone care any more? Perhaps Sweden might be better for her than here. A bit more cosmopolitan? Exciting. But then, the Germans were in Norway. They might cross over at any time. Not that they were all bad.

That was part of the problem she was in now. The leaving present her rich German had given her before he went away was all gone now. Max didn't live with her. Anyway, she didn't want to ask him for money. It was wrong somehow. And he wanted to keep his own apartment. That awful poky little place. No, no – she couldn't go there. Yet she owed two months' rent on the apartment. She would have to move in with Anna again.

Well, Anna was nice enough. But her flat had only the small bed in the tiny spare room. What a shame to have to leave. She had loved the apartment. So airy and light, with such nice things. Her German – 'her uncle' he liked to call himself. 'Think of me as your uncle,' he had said, stretching back in the armchair, putting up his big hands to draw her down to his lap. Uncle. Well, well. At least he didn't want her to dress up as a nun or a little girl or do anything funny. Not bad for a German and very generous.

Perhaps it was as well he had gone though. Had he known about the others? *He* was very discreet. About Peter and Vares and Axel and Jacob? The German had stopped coming to see her just after she met Jacob. That was right. And before Max. There had been no one else since Max. Jacob had been the last before. She had liked Jacob. She had been nice to him because he had been nice to her. That had been a lovely day at the sea. On the island – though, she knew now, even then her mind had been on Max. All that day she had been puzzled as to why Jacob didn't make a pass at her. She had gone to the lavatory in the little island bar and looked at herself in her hand mirror to make sure her face was on. But some of them are like that first time. She had made all the running in the flat too – when she genuinely wanted to please him. And really he was quite sweet, with his dark hair and long clean hands and the appealing oddness of his eyes when he took off his glasses. He was a very timid lover – then all at once too excited. It lasted no time. She had hardly felt him at all. Then, when he could have rested and tried again – he had left. Poor Jacob. He had Ella now. Fancy them going to live together like that. She couldn't do a thing like that. Not openly. Never thought Jacob had the nerve. Hadn't seen them since that night she and Max hadn't gone to the opera or whatever it was with them. Max had said he'd rather go to bed. Ella would suit Jacob better. Yes – she was clever. And quite pretty.

Here came Max at last. Quite pretty. Half-way across the restaurant floor he stopped to talk to a seated man. He seemed to know *everybody*.

'Sorry I'm so late. The wires are red hot at the moment with this French thing.' He pulled the chair out and sat down.

'Oh Max – isn't it awful?'

'Yes. Terrible.' He reached over and took her hand in his. 'Terrible.' He released her hand. They were silent for a moment.

'A man was crying over there.'

He looked over at an empty table.

'A little earlier.'

He shook his head. 'That's no good. No good. That's what the Fascists want, you know. No good giving in, is it?' After trying to subdue his natural high spirits and to look suitably depressed by bad news, his natural robustness reasserted itself. He flung his hands out in a gesture. 'What is it men cry out in front of firing squads? They don't moan and whine, do they? *Vive la Republique!* Liberty! Death to all tyrants! No good crying over spilt milk. Have you ordered?' The waiter stood by his side. He went quickly through the menu. 'What about some champagne to go with it? What d'you say?'

'People would think we were celebrating. How awful.'

'Well, we are celebrating. We're celebrating us.'

The bottle was brought. The cork popped loudly. People at other tables did stare over and whisper to each other. A man going past their table tutted in disgust.

Katerina felt constrained, embarrassed to be so publicly festive on such a day. But Max was at his most ebullient. He refilled his own glass and then hers, despite Katerina shaking her head. He smiled and filled it anyway. And everyone in the place, sad-faced and fearful, could see that here at least was one man who seemed to have received good news.

3

Schwarzwald, rosy, but with no hangover from last night's victory party at the barracks, arranged the beautiful green leather-bound sets of Goethe and Schiller, that Father had left him, along the shelves of his new house in Posen.

It had been the home of a rich Jew store-owner and his family. They were away on 'holiday'. Ha. Serve them right too. They certainly knew how to live, those Jews, though. The swine it seemed had traded or sold most of their own books for food when they couldn't get any legitimately under the new anti-Jew laws. Furniture too, and pictures. Schwarzwald had managed to fill the gaps from other houses in the area, but then, of course, other new owners wanted their share too.

He got down from the chair and admired the green spines glinting with gold lettering and decoration. Handsome. Handsome. The big nursery upstairs. Difficult to know what to do with that. Steffi had had all the toys packed up in chests and sent them off to an orphanage in Hamburg. Lovely things. Worth money. But a nice gesture. He had considered a billiard table up there but was worried if the floor would stand the weight. Still, a solid enough house.

Humming he got back up on the chair and pushed an errant volume back. A dead straight line. Perfect.

Young Balthus seemed to be running his end of things satisfactorily. It was difficult to keep wholly up to date with the telephones not working half the time and the mail not getting through, but from the reports Balthus sent through the Legation trade was going on. Very sluggish. Difficult to move neutral vessels about now. But most of the warehouse full of furniture and stuff had been flogged off. The commission on that was good. The factory here was going well. Unit labour costs practically non-existent – the factories back home were complaining of unfair competition. He chuckled. Business is business.

Yes, young Balthus was not bad. Drunk that night coming into the room when he was feeling up the maid. Brought it up – obliquely – when he came to the office next day. Didn't seem to remember. Remembered his appointment all right – why not the scene with the maid? Perhaps he did though – too subtle, too cunning to bring it up. People stored things up to use against each other. Well, he knew a thing or two about people too.

Get a German maid? Can't trust these bloody Poles. But then again you'd have to pay a German girl.

He looked round the room, elegantly furnished, up at the prettily plaster-decorated ceiling.

Above, in their bedroom, his new uniform, for his promotion, lay in its tissue paper on the bed. Very smart. Had to wait a bit for a commission, but no problem in the end for a man like him. Captain Schwarzwald.

4

Gerald was a new man in England. How jaded he had become; how lacking in purpose. The war clarified things. What was that poem they had learned at school: 'Like swimmers into cleanness leaping . . .' ? Something like that. Last war. Perhaps you wouldn't say that now. But six months ago he would have scorned as jejune patriotism what he felt now. It was positively a relief to get into uniform. To know everybody was in the same boat. The war had magically dissolved all that doubt and dreadful, gnawing fear – better to know you were perfectly fit and healthy but that at any moment you might die, than to suffer that cancer.

And he was glad – God, he was glad – to be away from Frank at last. He'd heard Frank was in the Army. God knows what they would make of him there. How awful life had been. The idea occurred to him, and cheered him, that all that theatre business had been more a desire to command, to manipulate, than anything to do with *art*. Admittedly, Lysander's uniform had been more elegant than the one he wore now. Anna had said he looked like one of the Tsar's sons in an old photograph. And it had been quite a feat to arrange and mount that whole thing at the President's Palace – even if no one over here had ever heard of the place. How terrible if these new comrades of his, these wonderful, smiling crusaders he was with, how terrible if they should ever know, find out – about that afternoon. Just one bloody afternoon. A sort of madness. He wasn't really. What did it amount to? Except at school a few times. Frank was. Oh, Frank was. Most definitely was.

That creep Balthus was the only one who knew. Who had seen. Perhaps he was too witless to know what he had seen. Put it down to youthful peccadilloes. Only he didn't feel so young these days. At twenty-six he was older than most of the other trainee pilots.

They wouldn't get to France after all now. It was over with the French.

He looked out of the window. The others were walking towards the aircraft. He didn't want to be last. None of the instructors was out yet. Mackay. He hurriedly zipped up his jacket and picked up his helmet . . .

Sergeant Mackay sat behind him; his Scots accent barked hoarsely through the speaking tube.

'I'll take her up. Let you know when you have control.'

They mounted up over the flat Leicestershire countryside. The land started to roll upwards to the east.

'Take over will you, Mr Stillinghurst.'

There was fear and exhilaration about this moment. The stick in his cockpit came alive. The aircraft juddered.

'Watch it,' said the calm, hoarse voice.

'Sorry.'

154

He eased back the stick and twitched the plane awkwardly into the wind. The engine cut out. That's not right, his mind said. They began to lose height, gliding down smoothly. Instinctively Gerald tried to bring up her nose.

'Leave her to me. Leave her to me,' the voice behind shouted. They were descending in a great sweeping arc towards the village.

'What is it?' Gerald shouted, then felt ashamed rather than afraid. Mackay was shouting something from the back. He couldn't hear a thing for the wind. The starter dial jumped. And then again, but the engine did not fire. They were gliding down fast. There is no time for fear, Gerald's mind said. This is a test. You have to learn this thing too. A river flashed towards them like a scythe . . .

Where did you go for advice? How to express yourself? The squadron leader thought of those manuals that told you how to make a speech as best man at a wedding, or write a letter of thanks after a visit. Not much bloody use in this case. Must be something in regulations about the form to use. He re-read his effort:

> . . . almost certainly saved a grievous loss of life in the nearby village by their prompt, unselfish action . . .

Well, no doubt Mackay had tried to bring the plane down. Just hard bloody luck. Power cable or something – how had they missed that? Damn planes were practically uncrashable. Who knows what went on up there. What did a little bending of the truth hurt?

> In the short time I knew Gerald I valued his contri-
> bution. Knowing of his interest in the theatre I can
> wholeheartedly aver, in the words of Hamlet,
>> He was likely, had he been put on,
>> To have proved most royal.
> With deepest condolences

He signed the letter and dated it 15.VI.1940. He copied the address carefully from Stillinghurst's file onto the envelope. Damn queer-sounding place.

5

Unlike Gerald, Mrs Stillinghurst had no reason to think of
Jacob Balthus. Not as an individual. He was simply one
of the dimmer figures in the constellation which revolved
around Gerald. There were some pretty girls – well, there
had been – one or two English, the daughters of businessmen,
but none of them very suitable. Now they had all gone back to
England. Even Mrs Frobisher and her husband. And Gerald.
She could have wished he were in the Army, but remembering
the last show he was probably a deal safer where he was. His
father had been a good soldier. Everyone had said so. And
whatever you said about the young – well, the awful thing
was up to them again this time. They would not fail. She
wondered if he had had her last letter and parcel. They said
the post might even stop altogether. There was simply no
one to ask. She did not like to bother the Consulate – they
had far too many other things to think of. And what to do
about the garden? Here it was, nearly midsummer and such
a mess. Very well – no good repining. She must get on. You
must set an example. If only to yourself. Where were those
gloves?

6

Jacob was proud of the fact that he and his father could
now meet on equal terms. Men of the world. So his parents
did not approve of Ella. That row at home, when he had

walked out to the accompaniment of his mother's tears, his
father's glaring silence. He could forgive and forget. He was
remaking himself – a new man. He had drunk no more since
that German party. Schwarzwald had said business and booze
didn't go together. That was at that rather odd interview,
when Schwarzwald in his sly winking way had asked him
twice if he remembered some maid or other. Pretty girl, eh?
Schwarzwald had repeated. What on earth was he trying to
do, fix him up with her? He had not remembered her in
the slightest, but he pretended to the old man that he did,
chuckling appreciatively at the coarse remark Schwarzwald
made about her. They made a tour of the warehouse and
Jacob accepted the job of managing it in Schwarzwald's
absence. I am, said Schwarzwald, supposed to sell up –
but who is there to buy? A company had been formed in
the capital with a nominal local director – but Schwarzwald
would still control the enterprise.

To his surprise, Jacob had found that he quite liked the job.
Better at least than the Ministry. He discovered in himself a
liking for order, a sense of responsibility enlivened by the
absence of any real control . . .

He reached the door of his father's office, knocked loudly,
waited a moment for his father's shout, then went in.

'Jacob?'

It was most disappointing. Jacob had been expecting his
father to be at his most charming and warm, eager for a
reconciliation – here he was, looking surprised to see him.
His assistant, Margraz, a young man, slightly older than
Jacob, stood at his side behind the desk.

'We did arrange an appointment,' said Jacob. He had
interrupted his father in the middle of working; his coat
was on the back of the chair, his shirt sleeves hitched back
– something Jacob had never seen at the office before.

'Did we? Of course. I am sorry, Jacob. Things have been
happening. Margraz, come back a little later. Leave the
papers. I'll ring through.'

He said no more until Margraz, with his odd, dipping,
subordinate's walk, had gone out and closed the door softly
behind him.

'Sit down.'

No, Jacob would rather stand. It was his only way of maintaining his own ground in whatever was to come. His father picked up the cigarette from the ashtray.

'How are you, Jacob? You look thinner.'

'No. I don't think so. It's some time since we saw each other.'

'Yes. Well – have you heard the news?' There was a sort of ironic brightness in his voice.

'Of course. The French . . .'

'No – not the French.' His hand waved in the air, dismissing the French. 'No. There has been an incident on the frontier. Near Gaudas. The Russians say we have fired into their territory. They have issued an ultimatum. Haven't wasted a lot of time, have they?'

The office was shaded and cool. Outside, the sky was bright blue. For the first time his father looked as if age might be coming to him.

'It's all over, Jacob.'

'What do you mean?'

'This is not just another protest. They have presented an ultimatum which we must answer by midnight. Tonight.'

Jacob could see that his father was waiting for his reaction. All he could think was, Why should the Russians do a thing like that? 'They are here already, aren't they? What difference can it make?'

'Among many other things the Soviet Ambassador has accused us of military provocation, of concluding secret military alliances with our neighbours, of anti-Soviet propaganda directed at their garrisons. Presumably the fact that we have things in our shops they have never seen back home.' He ground out his cigarette in a slow deliberate way. 'So – we must form a government friendly to the Soviet Union; we must allow the immediate entry of more Soviet troops to safeguard that government against "unfriendly" attacks. You see – we must get rid of our Government and open our gates by twelve tonight. If we don't, our President has been informed by telephone, in an interesting supplement to their public announcement, that our capital and other major towns will be bombed.'

'Does this mean we will fight? That we will have to fight?'

'No.' His father stared at him.

Had he sounded such a coward?

'No,' his father repeated. 'General Eichenfeld wanted to immediately mobilize all our forces. All our forces! But the President told him that resistance was out of the question. They would obliterate our army in a few hours and God knows how many innocent civilians as well. Interesting word that – innocent. We say, "attacking an innocent victim" as if there were another sort – a *guilty*, a worthy victim. Don't you think that rather odd?'

But Jacob was hardly listening. He had made love that morning. The day was bright; the capital sparkling with flowers, and if the people scurried about with long faces and talked anxiously in the cafés, well, it could still not be as bad as all that, could it? He knew that a terrible moment had arrived. Or rather his body knew, as if it were a more sensitive and fearful receiver than his mind, which sought to rationalize, to minimize the sense of risk. And here, his father – with only a little less than his usual sang-froid – philosophized about words. Well, perhaps that was just his way of putting it at a distance. A trick. Perhaps inside he was just as afraid. Then why did he not show it as transparently as Jacob was sure that he betrayed his own fear? His father's very calmness seemed yet again designed to demonstrate superiority over his son.

'I do not think you still quite understand, Jacob. Our people say that many thousands of their troops are massed at the frontier, together with tanks and artillery. Their Embassy is not answering the telephone. A small fleet is standing out from the bay. They mean to crush us.'

'But, I'm sure . . .'

'They will come. They will take everything from us.'

'Perhaps it won't . . .'

'It's all over. Don't you see, Jacob? It is all over.'

7

The long days of summer are the best for war. The ground is firm. Fully-leaved woods and hedges offer cover for armour and infantry. The merciless light floods road and street, village and city for eighteen hours a day.

All morning Jacob's father and the other senior counsellors and officials had been assembled in the Minister's conference room awaiting instructions, awaiting news. Every now and then through the hot still morning a messenger appeared at the tall door, piece of paper in hand. One of the officials would hasten towards him, take the paper, turn and read it aloud. The reports came from police and military. They told of long, long convoys of troops moving across the border and out of the country garrisons; of aircraft landing at the civil airport just outside town. The Soviet ships in the harbour had trained their guns inland. The cruiser *Marat* stood out in the bay, surrounded by a necklace of frigates. At one minute past noon a man with a startled face thrust his head round the door and said that you could no longer telephone out from the city. Coincidentally, and comically, the telephone in the Minister's office began to ring. But the Minister had been called to the Palace and his room was locked.

The messengers stopped coming. Quickly the feeling gained upon them in that long room with its glowing rosewood-topped table, its view of the sunlit square, that while they were free *here*, their city was surrounded, their country cut off from the world, and that they were effectively caged. A wireless set was brought in. The set told them to listen at two o'clock for an important announcement. Music. It told them again, adding that the Soviet Embassy had presented a document to be read. Music. This was the first intimation they had had that the city itself had been breached, or had bred its first cancer of defeat.

At exactly two, the music terminated in mid-bar. The voice that followed was stern and unrelenting, a Russian voice declaiming, with accents oddly misplaced, in their own language. It repeated the allegations of yesterday's ultimatum. It stated that the government of the Republic had acknowledged its crimes and errors and that the President had accepted its resignation. Any unfriendly act towards the Soviet forces would be met with the utmost resistance. All civilians were to surrender firearms upon request. All communications were now under Soviet control.

The voice ceased abruptly. Music played again. Somebody switched off the set.

'Look. Come and look at this.' Margraz was at the window, looking down into the square. The rest of them crowded up to him. One of the long, balconied windows was opened. The sound of a drum being beaten came up to them. Of shouts, and then a ragged chorus of the Internationale. The few people strolling on the edges of the square – and they were few, even on this brilliantly sunny day, with most indoors, listening to their wireless sets – these few were gazing towards a ragged procession filing into the square from the shadowed side street between the Lutheran cathedral and the big Epstein store. The drummer led them, followed by a young man holding aloft a huge red banner, which for lack of wind lolled about its staff. Another white banner held between two men announced *Greetings To Our Soviet Brothers*. There were several hundred filing after them, moving over the pavement, the grass, and ranging themselves round the statues in the centre of the green.

'What are they chanting?'

At the window they tried to sort out the shouts but could only gain a confused impression of overladen cries. The banners, sagging between pairs, were more explicit and wordier. *Welcome To Our Comrades And Liberators From The Great Union Of The Soviets. All Power To The Greater Baltic Soviet States. Comrade Stalin* . . .

Another influx from the side street spilled across the green.

'These are not our people,' said someone.

'It does not matter,' said Jacob's father. 'They are their people.'

The impression was almost of *packets* of people being emptied onto the green – as if one was making a soup and adding ingredients. And the onlookers on the pavements multiplied as they came out of the shops and offices, or were drawn by curiosity into the square.

More and more the mob in the centre swelled outwards – but then the supply stopped, as if a tap had been turned off. The police had also arrived and began to press them back. Scuffles broke out, like flurries of dust. More police, blue helmeted, entered the square.

The first tinkling sound of broken glass came. One of the Epstein store's plate-glass windows shuddered and fell to pieces. The great red banner was draped over the statue of the founding president. A policeman could be seen attempting to drag it down. He disappeared beneath a mêlée of people. They appeared to be dancing inexpertly on top of him. At this the main police line made a concerted push, the crowd swayed back and then forward again, breaking the police line and spurting in hectic little groups across the outer green and into the wide roadway.

'They cannot be our people . . .' 'This is preposterous . . .' 'Who are these people . . . ?' 'Why don't they stop it?'

And in his heart Jacob's father wished vengefully that the police would bloodily clear the square. But another part of him begged no, no, do not go too far. Do not enrage them. They are the future.

And, as if in answer to his prayer, nosing out of that same side street came the armoured tracks of a tank. It obtruded the very front part of itself into the square like a dog sticking out its nose in curiosity. Then the tank rolled forward as if pushed from behind; wheeling, its tracks squealing on the cobbles, straightening round again so that its stubby gun faced the Foreign Ministry.

Oh God, not an heroic gesture by our Army, Jacob's father thought at once. It was almost with relief that he saw the red star painted on the turret. The tank was followed by another. Then another. A great roar of approbation came up from the crowd in the middle of the square.

The telephone rang and rang in the Minister's office.

8

'I have seen the President.' His father leaned across the table, talking in a low voice. His face, large, was pale under the tan, giving his skin a yellowish, aged tint. 'They say he is still in the Palace but I have no way of finding out.'

The Café Stieckus was half-full. The people all talked quietly and quickly, bending towards each other, as Jacob and his father were. The two chess players sat either side of their game, but were screened from each other by the newspapers they were studying with grave expressions.

Jacob had arrived early for this appointment set by his father and had already read his paper. The front was dominated by pictures of what it captioned 'The Welcoming Crowds For The Liberator'. The tone of the articles was of extreme abasement before the incoming Soviets. They were indeed so cringing that Jacob thought for a moment they might be parodic. But no, the whole paper was like this. Evidently the censors had had to hurry their work – white spaces, un-full of non-information, were scattered across the inside pages; here and there words were blacked out. The Russians had been here for two days. Supplies from the country into the shops had dried up. There were no fresh flowers on sale. The telephones worked again, after a fashion. The one in Jacob's office had rung this morning. His father. Could they meet? Most important. What is it about? I can't say. I cannot stay on the line too long. I will see you, twelve noon. At your usual place. What? – Jacob did not understand. Your *usual* place. The voice was insistent. Your artist place. Oh, you mean . . . Yes. Yes, the voice interrupted testily. Twelve o'clock. The telephone was put down.

Normally his father would have looked out of place in Stieckus's. But now his fawn summer suit looked a little crumpled. There was a dirty crease in one sleeve. He had not shaved.

'It was a long day yesterday.' As he often did, he gave the impression of reading Jacob's thoughts. 'I must apologize for my appearance,' he said with heavy sarcasm.

Jacob waved a hand, as if to say, Who will notice in here?

His father lit another cigarette. His fingernails were dirty.

'They mean to stay then?' Jacob asked.

'What – are you stupid? Of course they will stay.'

Jacob was shocked. It was the first time his father – his still beloved father – had called him a name, had insulted him. And his father did not hurry, as he would usually have done, to apologize, to charm hurt away with his smile.

'They say here,' Jacob pointed to his newspaper, 'they will guarantee our national way of life – our society.'

'They've started well then, haven't they? The government has been dissolved. A Soviet official – a high-ranking official – a pro-consul, if you will – is to visit us tomorrow to "discuss" the formation of a new cabinet. All the present Ministers are under arrest.'

Jacob shifted in his chair. He still felt resentment at his father calling him stupid, but – again, the old man was in touch with things he had barely felt, barely known. Some courtesy was due.

'You said you saw the President?'

'We were summoned over last night. The senior department heads. There were armed soldiers at the gates, in the courtyard, doorways, up the stairs, along the corridors – they are, alas, not subtle. We were led along to the big map room. You know? Perhaps not. Kubin stood behind his desk. They had removed his chair – how ridiculous. As if it were a throne or something. And behind him stood half a dozen of their officials. President Kubin said, "I have been asked to read you a statement. I do not associate myself with it." At that, one of the men behind him said, "Please stop." Please stop – in Russian, but not as politely as that, as a harsh expletive. And Kubin said to him, "Am I to understand that I am now a prisoner of yours and that I may not do as I wish?" This man, very hard, spoke again. "Clear the room," he said. "We must have a private conference." That was to us. All the Russians remained. We were ushered into the corridor.

'Five minutes later they opened the door.'

He was silent for a moment, then took a sip at his coffee, staring across at Jacob.

'Five minutes later they called us back in. God alone knows what they had said to Kubin. He asked us to listen while he read an official statement. He seemed very weary. Copies were handed to us.' He reached into his pocket and pulled out a folded paper and his spectacle case. Putting on his spectacles, he raised his hand to his forehead as if to shade his eyes. The café was its normal dark inside though the sun beat down in the street outside. He began to read.

' "The Government is dissolved. Its Ministers are in protective custody to shield them from the understandable anger of the working class of the Republic. The people demand a new government responsive to their wishes. The make-up of this will be announced within a very short time.

' "The form of the new regime will be strictly constitutional, though the content will be revolutionary, up to a point. All steps taken by the Government to be appointed will be strictly based on existing laws. Where necessary these existing laws will be revised according to the procedures set down in the Constitution to be established by the Government to be appointed until such time as the desirable dictatorship of the proletariat, seizing its due power, directs the full transition from Capitalism to Socialism . . ."

'I must apologize for the language, Jacob. It goes on –

' "Until that time the social structure of the Republic will remain intact, though domestic and foreign policy may undergo some change, in accordance with the Constitution and the existing laws . . ." '

His father took off the spectacles and slid them back in their case. He refolded the paper. His usual methodical movements seemed to take on an irony here.

'There is a lot more I will not bore you with, of an administrative, technical nature. Now that we can no longer be considered to have a foreign policy, your father, you will be proud to hear, Jacob, has been placed in charge of the Foreign Ministry. *Pro tem*. The Minister being unavoidably detained, as it were. Quite how long this fortunate state of affairs will last, I do not know . . .' His voice trailed off.

Jacob wanted to say, Now come, the statement did not sound as bad as all that. A Government. A Constitution. He could not insult his father by saying that he was exaggerating, but in the aftermath of . . . of an invasion? A military presence? How often he had heard impassioned arguments in this café, calling for reform, for greater liberties. Perhaps they would be *imposed*, but were they still not necessary? This was not 1919 after all. They were not at war with anyone. A Communist-influenced government – but *their* Government. After all, the Finns had struck a deal, hadn't they?

'Perhaps . . .' he began tentatively.

'Well, I do know. Perhaps I know.' His father ignored what Jacob wanted to say. Then he did an extraordinary thing, for him. He reached across the table, laying his hand on Jacob's hand and gripping it. 'I think, I think an offer is to be made to me. In which case, I cannot accept. I cannot work for the Communists. I will not. There is a meeting arranged for tonight. When we came down from the President's office I met Margraz, my assistant.' The grip on Jacob's hand relented, but the hand remained lying unbearably warm on his. Jacob felt embarrassed. He looked around quickly. But the other tables were engrossed in their own low-voiced conversations, conferring with each other's fear. Except, that is, for one table up by the window. There Jacob saw Serdyuk the poet, his head tipped back. His great laugh rumbled down the room.

Everyone went quiet. It was as if a thunderclap had suddenly burst overhead.

'Shame,' someone whispered.

Jacob's father took no notice.

'I was surprised to see Margraz,' he went on. 'I asked what he was doing there. I thought that he must have an urgent message for me from the Foreign Ministry. Though God knows what. Where would it come from now? Well, Margraz sort of coloured up. Gave me a sickly smile. He always was something of a crawler, I suppose.' A touch of his old acerbity came back into his voice. 'He had, he said, an invitation for me. Who from? From Pryubschin. An attaché at the Soviet Embassy. I had seen him among the men standing behind Kubin. What had this man to do with me? I demanded. He is co-ordinating things. What things? I asked. Until their man – the big man – comes from Moscow, Margraz says, suddenly bold enough, though still red in the face. It affects the Ministry, the Minister. So I said, well, well – as the Minister is not here I suppose I must accept. So Margraz bashfully gives me my instructions. I must be standing on the corner of Herzen Boulevard, by the park gates, at eleven o'clock tonight. They like their little night-time intrigues, the Bolos.' His grip tightened again. 'I don't want to go on my own, Jacob. I don't *think* there is any danger. I don't think so. But I want someone with me I can trust. A witness I can trust, in case they try to use my words. I would not ask if I did not think it was safe. But you are the one.' Now his grip relaxed, as if his father too felt embarrassed.

'Well . . . yes . . . Father.' The last came out as a strange-sounding word.

'You will come?' his father asked, insisting.

'Why, yes. Yes.'

'Good. Good. Do not tell anyone.' Then his father relaxed. He looked down at his hands, at his crumpled suit. 'I must go home. Your mother would like to see you some time, you know, Jacob.'

Jacob felt accordingly guilty.

'Well, I must go home at least,' said his father. 'Clean up. Must be smart for our new masters, eh Jacob? You will come tonight?'

'Of course. Father. Of course.'

As the two men made for the door, the party at the window table again became raucously merry. Serdyuk, his face radiant with wine and good fortune, looked their way but ignored, or perhaps simply did not notice, Jacob.

He went back through the interlinked squares. Tanks faced the public buildings, their guns raised, hatches closed so that the crews inside presumably broiled slowly in the afternoon heat. In Palace Square a red banner draped the statue of the first president. This was where, his father had told him, the first rabble had appeared. Exiled Reds had been trucked in with forward units of the invader; released from the holds of cargo ships in the harbour; augmented by local, underground Communists. There was still a small crowd surrounding the statue. They sang a song Jacob did not know. It was all rather like a sober man encountering the survivors of last night's drunken party. A couple of local policemen hung back on a street corner, evidently under orders not to interfere, staring stonily forward, their mouths set under their helmets.

He came away from the square. At the next street corner was a patrol of half a dozen of their troops, all looking slightly bewildered, poorly uniformed and somehow physically stunted. Were these the vanguard of the Revolution? One could feel almost sorry for them. Then, frightening in their ambiguity, he heard popping sounds, like the backfires from a motorbike, from the square he had just left.

He turned immediately off this wide avenue, and hurried down through narrower, darker side streets that led towards the docks. The sky was a brilliant blue bayonet diving between the tall warehouses, intersected by the extended beams of hoists, the cage-work of tall cranes. He was near enough to see the warehouse – SCHWARZWALD picked out in huge white letters along the slanting roof – when a troop of soldiers, Russians, in their baggy uniforms and big, red-starred caps, their rifles held slanted across their chests, ran round the corner and into the street. They took the whole width of the two pavements and the cobbled roadway.

For the first time Jacob experienced fear. He dithered, then stumbled up a step into a doorway. The door was shut fast. As in a nightmare it had no handle. He reached into his pocket, grasping a handful of coins to weight his fist if it came to a fight. A fight? Ridiculous. A dozen armed men clattered towards him. He flattened himself against the paint-peeling door. Here they were. They simply thundered past him. Without even a sideways glance, their eyes staring straight ahead with that terrible vacancy of men promised violence. Only when all sound of their running feet had gone did he step down on to the pavement. To his surprise he was trembling.

Another hundred yards and he let himself into the warehouse by a side door. He walked up between stacks of pallets and piles of the still unsold, or unsaleable, Commission-numbered furniture and bric-à-brac. There was someone shouting from the direction of the loading bays. Here came Kalamees, the foreman, his short, bulky body swaying between the high stacks in the huge shadowy warehouse. He glared suspiciously at the figure before him, then recognized him.

'Mr Balthus.' But his coarse, normally jovial face remained set in a sour expression.

'Where is everybody? What's all that shouting about?' As usual Jacob did not quite know how to address his foreman. The man after all practically ran the place, though Jacob was nominally in charge. So Jacob always phrased whatever instructions he felt he must give in a roundabout, almost apologetic way. Even now, he realized, his voice sounded jokey, hopelessly sub-dominant.

'They're holding a meeting of the workers,' said Kalamees. 'A bloody Communist. Telling us how bloody wonderful everything is going to be from now.'

'Can't you get them back to work?' Again he noticed with anguish that plaintive note in his own voice.

'The Russians have an armoured car at the gates. It's not just us, they're going round all the yards.'

'Well – in that case – I suppose we'd better let them have their meeting, eh? If they insist.'

Kalamees looked at him. 'I was going to make sure the office was locked,' he said. 'I know what soldiers are like. Nick anything not nailed down.'

'Yes. Yes. I . . . I have a meeting down at the harbour office soon.' He had made that up. Not very cleverly. Kalamees would know there was no business to be done down at the harbour. No ships had put in for the last two days except the Russian warships.

'I shouldn't go through the yard. They were asking where the manager was, where he lived. I said I didn't know.'

'Thanks.'

'I'd better get on to the office.'

'Yes. Yes please.' Did Kalamees think that he was a coward? 'You have the keys?'

'Yes.'

He let Kalamees go past. That is *your* job, Jacob told himself. Why let that man do it? Well, of course, because when anything serious happened, it fell to the Kalameeses of this world to sort it out, didn't it? The good sergeants of the world. He envied the man's strength, the simplicity of mind that enabled him to think clearly; the lack of imagination that preserved him from the luxury of fear. He had sat once as a child with his father in a restaurant with Petersen the boxer at their table. Petersen had told him – his big, handsome, slightly malformed face as if transmitted through a slightly rippled but very clear sheet of glass – that every child should learn how to take a blow at the earliest age, for then you are not afraid to take one later. Like conquering the fear of water when you learn to swim, he had said with his extraordinary thick-lipped smile.. These men, Kalamees, Petersen, swam easily in a physical world in which he was afraid to dip as much as a toe.

Then he was defiant again, with all the secret pride of the coward. I shall show who is afraid. He would re-cross the city – or that small part of it separating him from his apartment – striding out manfully. But all the way back he did not meet a single foreign soldier or any other evidence of occupation to test his courage. And when he closed the door behind him he hunted out the bottle of brandy they kept for visitors and poured a large drink – a thing he never normally did in the afternoon. He drank that and went and sat with another glass-full on the edge of the sofa, staring out of the window, blind to the facade of the building across the street, allowing the drink to fill the hollowness inside him.

He had slept. He was woken by Ella coming into the room. The heat and the unaccustomed drink. What time was it? He had a sense of disorientation. The room was gloomy. Night? But he looked at his watch. Ten. Half-past ten.

And Ella said, 'Asleep? What a storm. How could you sleep through that?'

He went to the window. The sky was leaden. Thunder rumbled in the distance. The roofs and pavements gleamed with the rain that had fallen.

'It's passed now,' said Ella. 'I tried to ring you but there was no answer.'

'Where have you been?'

'At the agency.'

He felt rather ashamed at being found like this, at a moment of weakness, so he was a little more brusque than he intended to be. 'I have to go out. An appointment.'

She switched on the light. It was as if he had been found naked. Where was the gently dying, brandy-hazed evening?

'I . . . I cannot say.' Making it dramatic; a secret, important thing for Jacob. Affairs of state weighing on him. Mere women would not understand.

'What do you mean – you cannot say? How absurd. Of course you can say. I was just about to get us some food. You can't go out *now*.'

'Yes. Yes. I must. A promise.'

With its curled, question-mark shape where his body had lain, the sofa accused him. The effect of the brandy had passed, leaving him feeling again empty and querulously dissatisfied, the way you feel after a brief, unhappy dream.

His father waited by the iron park gates. The bandstand in the middle of the park, normally lit and loud at this time of summer, was dark and empty, its white-painted columns spindly and skeletal.

As Jacob approached his father smiled and nodded his head as if in gratitude. Despite the storm the air remained very warm and heavy. The trees on the other side of the park railings gathered darkness inside them.

'We must wait for Margraz,' said his father.

A young, raincoated couple hurried into the park.

The silver road stretched empty in each direction.

Expecting a large black sinister car to draw up alongside in the best gangster movie fashion, it was something of a relief when a small absurd Citroen puttered to a halt on the opposite side of the street and an uncertainly smiling Margraz peered out.

His face fell when he saw Jacob following his father to the car.

'Mr Balthus – I don't mean to – but this was to be, ah, a confidential, a private meeting . . .'

'This is my son.' His father spoke briskly, plainly not in any mood to discuss the matter. 'Get in,' he said to Jacob.

Margraz took them through a maze of side streets, avoiding the centre of the city, coming out in the commercial district. Offices and light industrial factories, most built in the last ten or fifteen years. They stopped outside a modern, dingy-looking apartment block.

'Please follow me, Mr Balthus. Mr Balthus.'

They went into a small, meanly lit foyer. The lift gate was open. They went up in silence – except, that is, for the groaning of the open cage, which gave a view of the ceilings descending to meet you, of the landings falling away, the corridors' perspectives tilting, shortening and lengthening.

The lift shuddered to a halt at the fourth floor.

Margraz led them down the corridor to the last door. The label, crookedly inserted in the brass holder below the bell push, read *Sawallisch*. Sawallisch? Max? Surely not? Jacob felt a sense of relief that was almost comic. He had come up in the lift and along to this door with that fear and lack of hope that we feel in going down a hospital corridor towards news of pain and death. And they were here – at this, this absurd man's door. His father, reading the label too, raised an eyebrow in enquiry.

Margraz rang the bell. The door opened almost at once as if Max had been stationed behind it, waiting. He was in a white summer suit, his shirt undone at the neck, necktie pulled away from the collar. He had a glass of wine, half-empty, in one hand, the other waved them dramatically in.

'You are most welcome, gentlemen. Warm night, Mr Balthus. And Jacob, *mon vieux*. Come in. Come in.'

Jacob wondered why Max, though so extravagant in his greetings, spoke so quietly in his own apartment.

They stood in a little room almost bare of furniture except for two or three straight-backed chairs of different ages and designs. It was like a waiting-room. There were no windows. The only light was that falling through the half-open door into the inner room.

'Neutral ground, old chap. Neutral ground,' Max whispered to Jacob as he entered. Then, loudly and jovially, he said, 'Come on through, gentlemen,' and led them into the next room.

'Mr Balthus. Mr Balthus's son. Margraz,' he announced,

and there was somehow an added note of deference in his voice as he demonstrated the newcomers to the two men already in the room. 'Mr Pryubschin. Mr Serov.'

The Russians, suit jackets off, the sleeves of their white shirts pulled back, sat behind a bare dining-table. A single straight-backed chair had been placed on the other side of the table facing them.

The man Max had pointed to as Pryubschin – his large pink face rather incongruously surmounted by small rimless spectacles, as if a child had scribbled them on – this Pryubschin frowned at the introductions, looked at the single chair, at his companion Serov, and back at Jacob. Serov stared. He had a parrotish head; prominent grey eyes and a thin head on which grey hair stood upright making him look older than his – thirtyish? – age. His lips were pressed together. It was as if his whole intent was to convey a sense of sternness and gravity that his insubstantial face could not quite bear.

Jacob's father, practised diplomat, advanced to the table, hand outstretched. Neither of the Russians stood, but Pryubschin shook the hand perfunctorily, withdrawing his own quickly. Serov studied the papers in front of him, his hands flat on the table.

'A drink, gentlemen?' Max's voice had an unexpectedly speculative tone.

Pryubschin nodded.

Max clapped his hands and went to a sideboard.

This was a new Max; one who appeared to defer to others. Jacob was surprised at this. And at the room. He had expected Max to live in some style, his personality to express itself in good furniture – a seducer's couch at least; thick piled carpets; perhaps pictures, and ornaments of a flashy kind. But this room looked like one of those hotel rooms through which whores and commercial travellers pass. Under the window a single bed was imperfectly concealed by a thin, quilted coverlet. A cheap deal wardrobe. The table, straight chairs. Two easy chairs that looked uneasy. Max opened the sideboard. One of its doors had a split panel.

'Aquavit? Wine? Cigarettes?' He drew out a carton of Camels.

The Russians would have aquavit. Jacob's father waved his

hand. Nothing, thank you. Although he would have liked a drink, to reactivate the earlier brandy, Jacob said no. Margraz took a glass of red wine.

'Now – can we get on?' said Pryubschin. 'Who is this young man?'

'Ah, Jacob. Jacob . . .' Max began.

'He is my son.'

'Will he leave the room, please. And you Mr Sawallisch. Thank you for the use of your apartment, but these are private talks. If you would both withdraw.'

'My son will remain if I do. I don't know why you have asked me to come here and consequently I would prefer to have a witness to our conversation.'

'That is why Mr Margraz is here.'

'With all due gratitude to Mr Margraz he is not here by my choice but yours. I don't doubt for an instant his loyalty to myself or to the Government of which he is a servant.'

'Your government no longer exists,' Serov snapped.

Jacob's father blinked once, as if shocked by the coarse and abrupt way in which Serov had interrupted him. He recovered, and smiled.

'Under our Constitution – which I believe the Soviet Union has agreed to uphold – civil servants swear loyalty to the President of the Republic. President Kubin is still in office, I believe.'

'The Constitution will be framed by the incoming people's government.' Serov glared up.

'Come, come.' Pryubschin looked at his watch. 'We haven't all night. We have many interviews. Sit down, Mr Balthus. Your son may stay – but take no part.'

Jacob went and sat on the edge of the bed. He wished he had taken a drink now. Margraz sat at the other end, smiling that oddly embarrassed smile at Jacob, then staring across at the table, not directly at the Russians but as if he was studying other, invisible figures to the side of them. His lips were wet where his tongue moved out; once, twice. There was an air of suppressed, of barely to be expressed, excitement about him.

Although now the evening outside must have cooled, the room still ached with daytime heat.

Jacob's father took the chair at the table. As if this was a signal, Max said, 'Well, I have things to do.' He winked at Jacob. Don't take this seriously, the wink said. It's all a joke; a charade to amuse us. 'Please feel free, gentlemen, to help yourselves to drinks and cigarettes.' He went out of the room. They heard the outer door shut.

'First of all, I would like to know . . .' Jacob's father began.

'First of all,' said Serov, 'you should know that to all intents and purposes your country in its previous form no longer exists. Its government has been dissolved. The country has been released from the tyranny of a small oligarchy of reactionaries and plutocrats. We do not yet consider that conditions exist . . .'

'What has this to do with . . .'

'. . . exist for the dictatorship of the proletariat in this country. An interim state must direct the transition of your country from capitalism to socialism. Your working people will have the opportunity to elect a truly representative body, reflecting the genuine, unqualified will of the people.'

'May I carry on?' Jacob's father appealed to Pryubschin. It was not quite clear who was the senior of the two men, but it seemed that his father had opted for the elder. Pryubschin's hand undertook an Oliver Hardyish arabesque to indicate to Serov to remain silent, and for Jacob's father to continue. Did they always come in pairs, these people? The comic and the foil? The hard and soft? Like Tischbein and Zech? But, as with those two, the Germans, the roles were occasionally switched between them, to fool the onlooker, the questioned, so that Jacob felt obscurely that perhaps plump, jolly men are very much more sinister than the thinner, moody companions they bring with them.

'As I understand it,' his father went on, 'I am here only because my Foreign Minister is now under arrest.'

'Protective detention,' Serov said.

'President Kubin has placed me in control of the offices of the Ministry – not of policy, neither am I allowed to make any decisions affecting policy – until a new minister is appointed.'

'That is what we wished to speak to you about,' said Pryubschin. 'Serov?'

175

Serov held up a sheaf of typewritten papers. 'We have here details of your military alliance with the other Baltic republics and a secret agreement with the German government that you would side with them in the case of the Soviet-German Pact breaking down.'

'We have no military alliances with anyone. You know that. It was set down in the so-called Mutual Assistance Treaty you forced upon us last year.'

'I repeat – a secret agreement with Nazi Germany to come to their military assistance.'

'With what? Who has been telling you this nonsense?'

'In what way is it nonsense?' asked Pryubschin politely.

'It would have been suicidal for us to have entered into any alliance that would have provoked any of the senior powers.'

'Your government *has* provoked us. Why else should we be here?' said Pryubschin, smiling.

'Now – as to this agreement,' Serov cut back in. 'We have prepared a document giving your testimony that the agreement was signed in your presence by President Kubin and the Foreign Minister.'

'Which agreement?'

'What?' Serov frowned.

'The secret alliance with our neighbours, or the one to bale out the Germans?'

'Both, Mr Balthus. Both,' Pryubschin smiled again.

'This is absurd.'

'No, not absurd, Mr Balthus. Necessary.'

'I have no knowledge of any such agreements. If you are in any doubt why do you not ask the Foreign Minister?'

Serov flashed up another piece of paper. 'We already have the Minister's testimony. We require confirmation.'

'Everything must be done strictly to the law,' said Pryubschin smoothly.

'I do not believe the Minister would make any such statement. Show me his signature.'

'This is merely a copy,' said Serov coldly, and slid the paper under the pile in front of him.

'Mr Margraz – perhaps you would help us all to another drink?' Pryubschin's voice was unexpectedly soothing, but it did not appease Jacob's father.

'I say, then, that I would dearly love to see the original. With the Minister's signature.'

'Oh, you will. You will,' said Pryubschin.

Margraz was clinking glasses. Jacob's father waved away the one prepared for him.

Jacob saw Pryubschin gesture at Serov to be silent. Pryubschin rolled his glass between the palms of his hands.

'All we require, Mr Balthus,' he said after a moment's silence, 'is your additional testimony that these agreements existed and were ratified in your presence by the President and his Foreign Minister and that the rest of the administration's senior officials were informed at a meeting in August 1939.'

'You mean before the Pact imposed on us by yourselves?'

Pryubschin smiled again.

'Remember . . .' said Serov.

Pryubschin held up his hand and silenced his colleague.

His voice purred. 'Great events are happening in your country, Mr Balthus. You are an intelligent man. To create the new it is important that the mistakes of the past should be recognized.' He paused. 'As I say, great events. Those who cannot or will not move with them will be swept aside. Make no mistake of that. But for those who remain – well, great tasks will fall to them. Great opportunities. The new cabinet will be announced tomorrow. A new Foreign Minister. Um?'

'I am afraid, Mr Pryubschin, I am afraid I cannot help you. I could not possibly sign any documents alluding to events which seem to have arisen solely in your own imaginations.'

'We are going in circles,' Pryubschin snapped, his good humour gone. 'You think you cannot help us then, Balthus? You deny these agreements exist? You will not sign the affidavit? No? Good. The interview is at an end.' He pushed back his chair and stood up.

Jacob's father got up more slowly. 'I am free to go?'

'For the time being,' said Serov.

Pryubschin refilled his glass at the sideboard. 'We will be in touch with you, Balthus, to discuss this matter further. You would be wise to attend our next summons. You are after all a responsible man. You have a family to consider . . .'

Jacob had got up from the bed. He was suddenly aware that he was soaked with sweat.

His father's face was white. 'Jacob? Margraz? Ready to go?'

Margraz remained seated on the bed, grinned foolishly, and stammered, 'F . . . Fraid not, Mr Balthus . . .'

'Mr Margraz has further business with us,' said Pryubschin.

'Oh Margraz. Margraz,' Jacob's father spoke quietly, gazing down at the man on the bed. 'Jacob. Come along. Good evening, gentlemen.'

It seemed an enormous journey to the door, under the Russians' eyes.

'You will be informed of the next meeting.' Serov's voice came from behind them.

They did not speak to each other going down in the lift. As they descended into the lobby, Jacob looked down through the iron cage. Max sat in the one chair, a magazine open on his lap, a cigarette drooping between his lips. As Jacob rattled the lift cage back, Max rose in a curiously fastidious way, like someone alone on a stage.

'Down so soon, Mr Balthus? Jacob? How goes it? No trouble?'

'No trouble, Max,' said Jacob's father. 'Why should there be?'

Max gave his most charming white-toothed smile. 'A warm night. I owe you a lunch, Mr Balthus. These are odd times – what about it soon?'

'Yes. Yes. You must telephone me. If the lines are working and you can get through.' All this time Jacob's father was going towards the open street door.

'Ah – yes. Perhaps I could call at the apartment? But – everything will be back to normal soon. You see.'

'Yes. Yes. Good night, Mr Sawallisch.'

They were in the street. Max did not come out after them. A little way up the street a man stood, looking hard into an empty, dark shop window.

They began to walk the other way. Jacob looked back. The man continued to concentrate on nothing.

'What is Max Sawallisch's part?' his father muttered. 'Don't trust him, Jacob, not now. He knows these people.'

They walked on in silence. The new, grey district fell away, and they entered again the magical city of haunted

178

parks, avenues of trees grape-blue against pale stone fronts, of statues of now inconsequential heroes, the creatures of dead legends.

When they came to part, his father turned and faced Jacob. He put out his hand.

'Go carefully, Jacob. I wish you were home with us.'

Jacob felt a lump in his throat.

'Wh . . . What will they do now? This testimony they want you to sign . . . ?'

'As long as we remain firm there is nothing they can do. Remember that, Jacob. Do not do anything you know is wrong. Love your country.'

He had not expected anything so simple and direct from this cynical, clever man. They shook hands, firmly on his father's part, fervently on Jacob's.

He watched his father stride away across a small, empty square, then he turned and began to walk in the direction of his own apartment, tears unashamedly welling in his eyes.

9

The city was quiet again. Or, rather, quietened. It lay hot and dusty and shuttered under the July sun. The people were grateful for the cooling breeze off the sea, but everyone agreed that the summer was as extraordinary in its heat as the winter had been in its cold. It was as if Nature was adjusting its controls for some experiment.

Were things bad?

Things are bad, came the whisper back. It was not that anyone wanted to whisper. The instinct was to shout defiance, to proclaim what one truly felt. About the way . . .

With the surrender of France the war had entered a new and more terrible phase; of stasis; of tyranny in position there, and here. Political discussions gave way to complaints about shortages in the few shops still open; of the everyday difficulties of avoiding the occupiers' attentions. You spoke openly only to your closest friend or lover, wife or husband. There was a hierarchy of candour going down through these, through looser friends, and lastly to acquaintances and colleagues; from openness, to calculated comments, to lies. You did not speak out in front of your children. It was not safe, or fair, to load your burdens onto them. The schoolboy who took off his cap and bowed to the President's statue in Palace Square was arrested by Russian sentries. He disappeared. His distraught parents could get no word from the police. There was no power, the police said, to investigate any action by the Soviets.

The informers – some known, some never dreamed of – sat in all the cafés, listening, straining to hear the talk around them, rising to report in the evenings. Then, when darkness had filled the city, the dark green vans that looked black under the streetlights moved out from the back of the Fortress, taken as the Soviets' headquarters, and headed down through the city.

They hunted off the main boulevards, moving slowly along so that street names could be read; turning into the street required; stopping almost silently. Then the dull footfalls on the pavement; flicking beams of torches; whispers. The sharp, repeated knocking on the door. A short delay. House lights on. Door opened. The quick eruption of soldiers and plainclothes men into the hall. Soldiers running rapidly into each room, rousing those still sleeping. The assembly of the household in one room downstairs. The quick funnelling through the hallway to the street, up into the back of the green van. The lights in the house switched off. The van doors slammed shut, the engine restarted. The van driving, with that nightmare slowness, away up the street.

Nobody knew how many had been taken. A few hundred? A thousand? There was never any indication in the newspaper that any arrests had taken place. Not many now looked out of their windows at night if they heard sounds in the street. This must be borne. Perhaps the situation would ease when this spate of arrests came to an end. They must surely end, the new government assume more power to itself, the Russians come under some local control.

Not that it was easy to know how much reliance could be placed on their new government. It was a mixture of unknown exiles returned from Moscow and Leningrad; a number of obscure academics and intellectuals from the universities and a few Socialist and Independent members of the old, dissolved Parliament. President Kubin had not been seen since the Soviet invasion. In fact, the announcement of the government had been a source of some amusement.

What was Dr Paleckis, a zoologist, doing as Foreign Minister? Presumably to keep the Russian apes in order, said one wit in the Café Stieckus as they listened to the announcement on the wireless Stieckus had put up on the bar. He said his joke loudly. Those were the early days. Shh – let us hear. And Professor Chud as Prime Minister? A historian. Well, said the comedian, we must all live in the past now. But even he had no comment on the statement that Mr Serdyuk was to be Minister of Education. Mr Serdyuk? Serdyuk the poet? Everyone in the café looked round to see if he was sitting at a table, laughing in his cynical way at the coincidence of names. He was not to be seen. Serdyuk was at the Palace, drinking warm champagne, watching Prime Minister Chud announce the new Cabinet into a large black microphone.

The crowd at the Café Stieckus, attentive, and only now and then interrupted irritatingly by its joker, listened through the rest of the announcements over the wireless. The broadcast ended suddenly. Instead of the anthem, the Internationale was played. Stieckus let it go on for a few, decent seconds, then switched off the set and went back to wiping his bar. The conversation, the muffled, ceaseless chatter welled up again around him.

At the end of his broadcast, Prime Minister Chud rose from his chair, acknowledged with a slight bow the polite applause of his new colleagues, went out through the door, between two unsaluting Russian sentries, hurried along the corridor, down two staircases, across the red, blue-starred carpet in the columned entrance hall, out of the great double doors, and into the waiting car which was to take him to the Soviet Embassy.

Upstairs in the Palace that Chud had just left, after a long, hard session, a blood-stained mat was being rolled round a bulky object. It took four men to lift the fat tube. They cursed, carrying it towards the door. It had not been the ideal place for such a confrontation between the naked President and the interrogators of the NKVD – but who could deny them a certain piquancy in their choice of location?

10

Jacob's father took down the small leather-bound minute book which he had decided to use as a diary. Minna had gone to bed. He had difficulty in sleeping. It was cooler at night too. He arranged the lamp to shine on the open page. He closed the curtains, no light would be visible from the street below. He began, dating the margin:

4-7-40   Two weeks since my meeting with the Russians, Pryubschin and Serov. I have not asked Margraz what was said to him after I left and he has not volunteered any information. Nor have I received an 'invitation' to another meeting. I continue to go to the Ministry every day. No work is brought to my desk. The telephone does not ring. The Minister does not send for me. There is still no news of the President. Rumours abound. He has been murdered. He is in the Kremlin having talks with Stalin & Molotov. He has escaped and is in hiding in the woods. He is in Sweden. In America.

It is said the prison is full and other prisoners are lodged at the Fortress for 'special treatment'. God knows what that means. Still others have been shipped off to Russia. Some are released after one, two or three days, though rarely longer. They return to us pale and shaken and all they will say is that they can say nothing, that they have signed a document stating they must tell nothing of what has happened to them. What has? This sort of thing was bound to happen at the start. When things settle down? After the promised elections?

5-7-40   Dream of Jacob as he was as a child. And Minna as young. Minna and I have spent only two weeks at the cottage this year. Jacob no time. It does not look as if we will ever holiday there again as a family. Innocence lapses with age. It is so sad we have to dream. We may as well go – it is said that the best town houses will be taken as billets for the Russian officers and the wives they are importing. Compensation has been promised – but in roubles – at their fixed rate. This will give only a fraction of the true value. Tonight we opened a bottle of the '34 Ausone. That leaves three and who can say when we will get any more good wine? Minna's birthday – though she had to tell me.

6-7-40   Summoned to see the new Minister, Paleckis. I go to the fifth floor with all the best possible grace, but wondering what sort of foreign policy we now can be permitted to have.

   Paleckis is seated at the big desk. A picture of Stalin on the wall behind him. Smaller and differently shaped from the picture it replaced so that there is a pale surround of unfaded wallpaper on three sides. Oh – Balthus, he says. He does not invite me to sit down. Well, well, a little power gone to the head – what's that? The man is well known as a pompous professor at the University; a vague sort of socialist, but no sort of Communist. If this is the sort of man they are going to employ, we have little to fear.

   He looks at me for a few seconds – I suppose he thought fiercely – from under his eyebrows that stick out like grey wings. I wish you to read this, he says, and pushes a piece of paper across the desk.

My dismissal. With immediate effect. A very short letter, but I read it again with almost childlike slowness, because I know he is watching me and I want to collect my thoughts. At first I feel sick.

To be turned out is bad enough, but by these people! It is insufferable. I would not let Paleckis see this, however. I knew somehow that he was unsure and nervous as to what my reaction was going to be. Thank you, I said at last, but you do know, Mr Paleckis, that any such notice of dismissal addressed to a senior counsellor must come from, or be countersigned by, the President. We are not the servants of the government of the day but of the State. Only the head of state may dismiss a Department Head.

All he said was, Balthus, if you do not go now . . . Go now. Under the new Constitution the President assumes only a ceremonial, decorative role. You will find I have full powers in this matter. I said that I thought that these matters, constitutional matters, were to be settled after the election of a new Parliament in the elections we have been promised. It does not matter what you think, he said angrily. I repeat, I have full powers. If I pick up that telephone . . . You would not want me to pick up that telephone. Never mind. Things are necessary now, Balthus. It is not a cosy little country any more where we can play little games off each other. That dance is over. You do not grasp the inevitability, the historical necessity of what is happening about us. There is a new spirit. No room for those who do not welcome this change.

That was his speech. He waved his hand. A little short chop in the air to dismiss me.

This letter, I said. It says nothing about my salary. My pension.

There are no arrangements for all that at present, he said.

No arrangements?

At present. At present no arrangements, he said irritably. But for the first time, I think, he had the good grace to look a little ashamed.

I left him. I went back to my own office. I was light-headed, dizzy. Margraz was standing at my desk. I am afraid that I must leave you, Margraz, I said as jocularly as I could. It seems my services are no longer required. Excuse me, I must clear my desk.

Margraz drew himself upright. He attempted to frown at me. Frowning it seems is to be the fashion. Instead he coloured up like a girl as usual. But he managed to find enough in him to say, I am afraid that won't be possible. This desk is now mine. He sat down, or plumped down it might be better to say. As if we were playing musical chairs and he had narrowly got there first.

It does not take people long to adjust to the new situation.

7-7-40   Minna says, What will you do? As ever, she worries first about her family, not herself. Only women do that – do that automatically. I have not told her about the money. I have some; she has some from the Hugenbergs. We shall manage, I say lightly. I shall read; write. I can get a job somewhere. Perhaps teach.

8-7-40   I have told Minna that we shall slip away to the sea villa after the elections. Mrs Karner who has just come back from the coast says there is little sign of the Soviets there yet and that our villa is untouched. She has kept an eye on it for us. It will be good to get away. The capital is expectant. We do not know how much or what we shall get from the elections. The new Prime Minister has assured us they will be free, and despite a huge show by the Soviets with troops touring all the towns and villages in a show of strength nearly all districts have nominated independent candidates. It seems the Russians may be in for a shock on polling day. Reading Maude's Life of Tolstoy. Is that great old elephant of genius in their slender pantheon of saints?

9-7-40   I have said to Minna that now is not the time for feuds or recriminations in the family circle. Jacob has shown his true spirit by helping me when I asked him. I have proposed that he, and his young Polish lady – I do not even know her name – that they accompany us to the villa for a holiday. Minna baulked at this. No, no, I said, it is his choice, she is his girl. I think Minna winced at this. Where will she sleep? she asked. They certainly cannot share a room.

Candidates have been ordered – a decree over the wireless – to present their programmes to the government by six o'clock this evening, otherwise they will be disqualified. The government have put everything they can think of in the way of the non-Communist candidates, but it is difficult to see what more they can do after announcing so officiously that the elections would be absolutely free.

Minna compromises and says that I must invite Jacob and whatever-her-name-might-be (as Minna puts it) to dine with us. Then we can see what sort of girl she is.

From Tolstoy's diary, 1881 – 'Smells, stones, luxury, destitution, and vice. Malefactors have come together, robbed the people, collected soldiers, and set up Law Courts to protect their orgies, and they feast . . .'

10-7-40   We exist in the great, dark, infinite universe. In history – at some point along a wave. In our own immediate relationships. And again within the ambit of our own poor fragile domed skulls. And the spirit of God is what moves, mediating, between and through all these contiguous worlds. Amateur philosophy – but a surprise to me that I

186

had not lost the faith of my boyhood. It is a great comfort.

11-7-40   Disaster. The newspaper announces this morning that 'enemies of the people' have been prevented from standing in the elections. Of the eighty independent candidates twenty-one have withdrawn their candidature; three have been arrested – the charges are not revealed; the remainder have been disqualified for putting forward programmes 'prejudicial to the security of the state'. So that is that. We still have to vote – 'It is a citizen's duty. Shirking the elections would be a very imprudent step. In the present situation, a passive attitude might be viewed as hostility towards the people; only those opposed to the people will remain passive.' The wireless all day reiterates this nonsense. The tanks are out in force. A scruffy-looking man appears at our door to exhort us to vote in the 'free' elections. As I shut the door on him, I hear him banging on the next apartment down the corridor. Old Mrs Vardys – I am afraid she will eat him alive.

All our hopes it seems are to be rendered meaningless in the most cynical fashion.

Tonight, Minna reminds me, Jacob and his young lady are coming to dinner. Women retain a sense of proportion.

12-7-40   We vote on the 14th. I have told Minna that I shall insert a blank ballot paper into the box. This is a way of getting round the necessity of voting for only one farcical candidate. Minna says she will write the President's name on her paper. Jacob said he would do the same. His girl said nothing – which seems to be her customary mode of conversation. They arrived at half-past eight last night. I was annoyed as they must be gone before ten to avoid the dark. That is when the Soviets' police vans come out to play. So, he sensed my displeasure and was determined, I felt, to be on his best behaviour. And to try and show off the girl, Ella, to best advantage. She is quite a handsome girl; but inclined to heaviness in body and rather awkward in her movements. But she is quite well bred, educated. Her views, inevitably, are of the Left. But then, she hardly spoke. The whole evening was muted. Ella looked tired. Jacob said she had been detained by the Russians at the agency and taken to the Hotel Gregorius, which they seem to be using as a headquarters for their political police. There again, they have no legal validity for their activities. But our own police seem reduced to directing the traffic. Oh, my dear, said Minna with genuine concern, did they mistreat you? Of course not, said the girl in such a cold way that Minna went red. I had already issued the invitation to them both to come down to the beach. There are bound to be other such moments. I let it pass, helping them all to another glass of wine. I didn't pursue with the girl the rumours that are coming out about what goes on in the Hotel Gregorius and the cells of the Fortress. Beatings, and worse things which are barely credible. There is a counter theory – that such rumours are put about by the police to attempt to terrify us. Some hope, Minna says. So, it was a bad evening – for one which I had hoped would draw us all together. At first, I could see that Jacob was determined to make an effort; by leading Ella in her conversation, by talking her up. But the girl somehow subtly contrives to let herself down. And after a time he began to side with her and to drift away from us again. I am ashamed to say that I was almost glad when they left the apartment. But when they had gone I hurriedly turned out the light, and twitched aside the curtain to see them safely across the street. And there they went, tiny, foreshortened. Jacob's hands were gesticulating. It looked as though they were arguing. I turned and Minna switched on the table lamp and was suddenly lit and looked young once more, as in my dream.

11

On a Friday late in August something was beginning to happen. The tanks reappeared in the central squares, many more hundreds of troops disembarked at the station and were marched through the streets. The city, demoralized and shaken already, steeled itself. But the night, and Saturday, passed relatively peacefully.

On the Sunday Jacob was expected at his parents' villa by the sea. Ella was not going with him; things were not going well between them. He had packed a small bag. You're staying the night? she had asked, staring at him coldly across the room. Yes. She had shrugged and gone into the kitchen. Yes, on balance, he was glad to get out of town.

What did not look such a good idea was his decision to take the train out to the coast.

A long row of military lorries obscured the station front. The white wooden tower stood into a sky silvery-blue with midday heat. He had only five minutes till his train. He did not run. Nowadays it was best to be seen going purposefully, but not too fast, from one spot to another. He squeezed between two of the lorries. A few NKVD troops in the booking hall but no officer, luckily. They never did a thing without their officers telling them. He went over to the ticket grille. Not many travellers on Sundays now. There was one train only to the resorts. Leaving at one o'clock. From the farthest platform. He waited impatiently for the clerk; handing over his identity card so that the man could laboriously note his name, destination, when he was returning, apologizing quietly. That's how things are now . . . The large hand of the clock on the booking office wall clacked onto the hour. You'll have to hurry, muttered the clerk, not looking up. But that you did not do. Run. They might assume you were running from them. Jacob walked quickly to the footbridge. You could hurry up steps. His shoes rang on the iron bridge. At the far platform the engine fumed quietly, its nose jutting into sunlight. High in the roof the air smelt of sulphur and soot from the big trains. His little train seemed to bristle with expectancy. Of leaving the city. Of getting away from here – all this. He clattered down the steps and just made it to the train, swinging himself into a compartment as it jerked, then rolled forward.

The only other people in the compartment were a young couple. The girl's head rested on the boy's inclined shoulder. They came abruptly apart, the boy glancing round to see who had joined them. They burrowed together again into their private world as the girl replaced her head on the boy with just a shrug of irritation at the interruption. Jacob felt affronted, as only those who are generally unhappy can feel, at the sight of such mindless happiness. He walked on past them, swaying slightly as the train trundled slowly over the points, curving away from the great fan of lines that went east to Russia, south to Germany.

He settled two benches up from the couple. Behind him the girl giggled. He slumped a little behind the high seat back so they could not see him. He tried to concentrate on the view.

Idle Sunday factories and yards. Low walled garden plots brilliant with patches of flowers. Of perennial fascination – the backs of people's lives. The noise of the train's wheels changed to a cavernous rumbling as they crossed the river bridge. At last, Jacob began to relax, to feel charitable to the couple behind. Let them have their fun, after all. He forgave them their extreme youth with all the pompous magnanimity of a twenty-three-year-old man of the world. Over the river, the train ambled for two or three minutes through the suburbs, grinding gently to a halt at a tiny station. It seemed to wait an interminable time. No one came or got off on the platform or walked on the dusty road glimpsed through the fence. The white-and-pink houses had their blinds down. The sun edged fiercely, like a hot knife, into the compartment, heating the windowsill, the edge of the seat, so that Jacob shifted sideways into the cooler shadow.

Then they were off again, slowly, leaving the last houses behind. The train picked up a little speed. The fields rolled past; the edge of the sea forest swung lazily towards them. At the edge of the trees the train slowed again, entering between birches that crowded up almost to the windows on either side of the single line.

Jacob thought of Ella, less angrily now. She had flatly refused to come with him to his parents'. Last night she had not come home until ten minutes after the curfew at ten; slipping in, her face tense and pale.

'I thought you had been taken,' he said.

'Taken?' Though weary, her voice succeeded in also sounding slighty mocking.

'Arrested. People are taken. More and more of them.'

'Who would take *me*?'

'Can't you see I was worried? Where have you been?'

'The police. There was a query on my papers in the street.'

'You shouldn't have been out so late.'

'No, no – this afternoon.'

'A query? All this time?'

'They keep you waiting.'

'Well, at least you are back. Thank God for that. The streets are full of the brutes.'

As she went towards the kitchen, he said, 'We'll be out of it for a few days tomorrow. You haven't forgotten we are going to my parents? At the sea.'

Her voice came from the other room. 'Your parents? Oh no, Balthus. I couldn't stand that. Not at the moment.'

'I have promised.'

'Then you go.' She stood in the doorway.

'I will. I will. You see if I will.'

'For God's sake. If you want to – go. We said that each of us is free. I don't want to spend days with your mother looking down her nose at me and your father pretending to be jolly, pretending nothing is happening.'

'What else do you expect, the way you . . .'

So a whole, fruitless row had expanded into the small hours – into their bed. But this time, instead of making up in their usual way, by love-making of an extraordinary semi-brutal kind, an act of expiatory ritual, during which Jacob would say over and over, 'I love you, I love you,' as if to convince himself; this time he held himself away from her and she did the same, and they both pretended to be asleep, until they did at last sleep. In the morning she had already got up and dressed before he woke, late, at ten. After the breakfast she served silently, he had gone into the bedroom, swinging out of it with his small case in his hand, going towards the outer door.

'Well – I am going at any rate.'

'You're staying the night then . . . ?' she said.

He took off his jacket and folded it neatly beside him. He lit a cigarette. There were more packs and a few tins of food in the case. He would present them, lightly, as a gift. He didn't know exactly how his parents were placed for money, but it could not be well. The Russians had left Schwarzwald's yard pretty much alone; presumably as it was German owned, and under their wretched treaty with the Germans they didn't like to touch it. And his mother had managed to contact Grandmama Clara – without telling his father – and Clara had sent some money through the Legation. But after the election the first act of the new government had been to declare the triumph of the full incorporation of their country into the Soviet Union. So now they came under Soviet law – whatever that was. All land and most industrial concerns were nationalized. A moratorium froze all bank accounts; indeed, all deposits worth over 1000 crowns – a derisory sum, perhaps two or three months' wages – were declared the State's property. His father therefore had lost all his investment income, small though that was. All they had was the detested Hugenberg money.

The country was caught in a mad dream, but, looking out to the cool wood, it was hard to believe in that dream entirely. Presumably when the Russians had questioned everyone they wanted to, the arrests would stop. Even terror must have a term. They were the most extraordinary people, these Russians. They looked so inefficient and sloppy and drab, and combined this with a most ferocious bureaucracy. Well, his people would not be so easy to dragoon as backward, half-witted Russian peasants. He smiled to himself, remembering his Russian peasant in *A Midsummer Night's Dream*. How upset he had made himself over those two Englishmen. What did all that matter now? England anyway had the easier part of it. They at least were still free. Katerina, in the middle of the lawn, in her long dress, speaking in a high clear voice a foreign poetry. He allowed himself to think of her as that; visiting a secret picture he had hidden away. And he realized that he was still in love with her, hopelessly and irrevocably. What was this love? The knowledge that the beloved completed the fractured, intolerably divided self, making a whole. That only she could do that. Was this wallowing in self-pity? She was evidently not aware of her Platonic destiny. Not with Max, if she was still with him. She was a whore. She was his love. What did he think he was – a character in some bloody tragic novel? He tried to put her out of his thoughts.

In a little while the train began to brake again. The trees drew back, and the train halted in a clearing. Why, this was the little halt a couple or so kilometres above his parents' villa. He had dismounted here a few times as a boy with his mother, after his father had been detained in town and they had travelled up to visit him. But he would not get off here. He planned to go on to the main resort of Poltava further south on the coast and see if he could buy any liquor from Herr Kleiber at the hotel. You could get none of these things in town now. Well, they would be on the move again soon. There was no sound of slamming of doors. He looked out of the window at the trees and tried to find something in them to interest him.

The train did not move. After a while the sense of the great inert mass of the train sitting idly in the sun began to irritate him. As did the whispers behind. There was also someone talking loudly, outside the train, farther up the track, that oddly faraway sound you get on lonely, empty stations in the heat. Jacob got up abruptly and crossed to the window on that side. He glanced back as he did so. The eyes of the lovers – brown, doe-like, female; light-blue, hard, male – watched him over the bench. He nodded to them, against his will, forced down the window and stuck out his head.

The engine was pulled up ahead of the short platform. A man was standing on the track, talking to the driver who leaned out of the cab. The driver clambered down and hopped nimbly – for such a large, middle-aged man – up onto the platform. He spoke into the first carriage. From the second a woman's head popped out, then in again, then out again as the driver stepped along and began to explain something to her. Some of her words in answer floated down. She had a Swedish accent. 'But how long? . . . Why? . . . We *must* leave the city,' her voice rose sharply, with an edge of panic. The driver's voice rumbled. Shrugging, he ambled past the third carriage, evidently empty, and came below Jacob's window. Determined to show his country's coolness to the foreigners up the train, Jacob asked quietly, 'What is the problem, driver?'

'We can't go on to Poltava. Not yet. That man . . .' He pointed back up the platform. The man had disappeared. 'Wherever he is – he's come from there. Many, many soldiers, he said. Trucks and tanks crossing the line. The gates are shut. No one can enter or leave the town. He slipped through before they cordoned it off.'

'What are they doing?'

'God knows – begging His pardon. The forest to the south of the town has been closed off. We're to stay here. Not to move.' The driver did not sound or look worried by this news. These people never did; sturdy, resolute, they seemed to take everything in their stride, refusing to be worried, counting it perhaps below their peculiar sense of honour.

'An exercise? Manoeuvres? Do you think . . . ?' Jacob, anxious to appear insouciant, knew that he sounded only anxious.

'Who knows? Whatever it is . . .'

They both looked up the line. It was another five kilometres to Poltava. The pine and birch closed in again on the line and it was swallowed in the forest. Birds sang or whistled; in the distance a dog barked with a sharp, regular persistence.

'Can I get down here?'

'Of course, sir.'

That flattered him. He turned back into the carriage to get his case and jacket. The couple had been listening. The boy said, 'Aren't we going on?' in a loud, common voice.

194

'I am afraid not,' said Jacob. 'There is some sort of delay up the line. The Russians are evidently restless.'

Did the girl giggle?

Why did he have to sound so pompous? he asked himself angrily. He put on his jacket, picked up the case, face reddening, and without looking back at them swung down from the carriage.

He walked up the platform towards the wicket gate. In the Swedish woman's carriage a group of four people sat talking energetically. They looked at Jacob as he passed, as if he might be bringing news. A young boy hung out of the window of the first carriage, his face golden under a fringe of blond-white hair. He watched Jacob all the way to the gate, his face solemn.

Jacob's feet crunched on a gravel path. The trees met and enclosed him. He looked back and saw already only slivers and pieces of the train shining in the sun. The path went straight ahead to the sea; he had to bear to the south-west, following the sun. He turned off into the woods.

He had perhaps lost his way for the moment. The sky had clouded over. He was in a thick, wild part of the forest, where the resinous odour of the tall pines caught at the back of the throat, the birds' calls seemed to come from great heights and distances. He found himself searching for ways round and between thickets. Then, suddenly the trees thinned again, growing small, deciduous, sweetly green. Another noise came, the recurring, heavy drone of motor engines and he realized he had wandered near to the coast road. He stepped forward delicately.

The engines grew louder; their shapes flickered between the trees. He hid beneath the low-growing branches. Now the trucks could be seen quite clearly. About every fourth was filled with soldiers, sitting in two rows facing each other stolidly. The others, open-backed, fence-sided like animal trucks, were empty. Jacob stayed where he was. The trucks roared on, heading north for the city, seemingly endless. He squatted down on his haunches and felt hungry. He had had only coffee and bread for breakfast. He must have waited nearly an hour, the stream of lorries and some tanks coming in smaller bursts after the main convoy, at last dying out altogether. He went forward. He could hear nothing coming and scurried across into the farther side of the wood. He was scarcely among the trees before another vehicle buzzed along the road – a saloon car.

With a great sense of relief he struck almost immediately onto a well-worn path. The sky was still clouded over, but the road had given him a fresh bearing and he knew he was going in the right direction. He came suddenly in front of the first sea villa. He veered off, with a feeling of embarrassment at invading someone else's privacy. But there was not a sign of life about the place; the screen door hung off by one hinge. Back in among the trees, to amuse himself, his mind got to work with a tale of dereliction – a secret drinker; a violent marriage; an infirm elderly spinster. But the otherwise neat and clean appearance of the place fitted none of his scenarios. He pressed on. The clouds opened; ahead of him he saw a long wide clearing, the bracken, already beginning to brown, all at once flooded in sunlight. The sun shone strongly from dead ahead. He made for the clearing. At the far end a jay flitted up from the ground, disappearing, like a handkerchief in a conjuring trick, into a tall dark pine. About to enter the clearing he stopped, took off his jacket, draped it over the small case and slung both over his shoulder. Soon he would be back with his loving mother and father. Perhaps the capital, the trucks on the road filled with soldiers, Max, Katerina, Ella – all that now seemed suddenly so far away – perhaps they were all simply a price to be paid, tests in the rite of passage to what was called maturity, growing-up? If they had used him, he had used them – and now he knew he was superior to them all. Why, he could stand here and enjoy even the feeling almost of being a child again – facing this green and golden, sun-warmed clearing – when the world of innocent sensuousness is all.

The clearing clouded, and then shone again. The clouds were drawing a breeze off the sea and the shining trees rustled and moved at their tops.

About to step into the clearing he heard shouts; loud, hoarse, imperative. Then a girl came running into the far end of the clearing, at one side, breasting the bracken, plunging

196

through it, making her way to the rough path that ran back up to Jacob under the trees. But she tripped and fell, disappearing from sight down in the tall ferns.

A group of brown shapes among the trees. The girl sobbed, rising again, limping. This was no game. When a vicious dog moves towards us, moral concerns, civilization, knowledge of the poets, appreciation of good wine, class, even voice, vanish. You might back away and try to reason, and parry uselessly, but ferocity overcomes civility every time. This is what civility is taught, what ferocity intuitively knows.

Jacob did not go forward. They were not chasing him. He did not phrase it with such vulgar cowardice. He moved behind a screen of leaves.

The brown-uniformed men, three, four of them, ran into the clearing and into the bracken, from the dark wood into the sunlight, like actors entering on a stage. This is the aestheticism of violence; how we distance and make it tolerable. Cathartic. But there is no catharsis when the stage rushes towards you.

The soldiers shouted. The girl stopped, staring terrified about her. She seemed to look straight into the trees where Jacob hid. To be looking straight through him. Her head shot a look back behind her. She started to run forward again – towards him. Go back. Go back. Please God – go back, he prayed in terror. They were gaining quickly on her. The first soldier, an absurdly small man for a soldier, a boy, scampered up behind her. He swung his rifle from the barrel and clubbed her across the back of the legs. She fell with a scream into the bracken. The second soldier to arrive raised his rifle, the short bayonet gleaming on its end, held it poised over where the girl had fallen. The soldier shouted in Russian: Whore. Whore. The bayonet quivered. Then he plunged it straight down. A dull, smacking thud. Jacob sank back, twisting behind the treetrunk. It was as if the weapon had entered his guts with a visceral, slamming shock. He trembled. There were more of the smacking sounds. All the soldiers joined in shouting, Whore. Whore. Shit. Shit. Silence, that seemed to extend time, radiated out from the clearing. Then a gargling, bubbling noise. More sounds; indecipherable, like the scrabblings of animals in a wood at night. The voices were lowered, but still harsh and cursing. Somewhere in the distance a whistle blew. One of the soldiers laughed. One muttered something. A clinking, rustling. Silence.

Jacob's back pushed against the tree as if a great invisible weight pressed on him. The whistle had been blown again, and then again, the thin distant peeps pricking his body like knives. He was too terrified to move. The forest creaked and whispered like a machine in which he was trapped. He knew, he *knew*, despite the fact that he had heard their voices dwindling away, that the soldiers stood in the clearing, watching, waiting for him. Though the thing they had done was minutes, hours, centuries ago, they remained. They leaned on their rifles, lit cigarettes – wasn't that the scrape of a match? – smiled at each other, waiting idly for him to come out . . . Why didn't they call him? There was movement. Through the bracken. In the grass. A dog went hurrying past, its tail between its legs, ears back, a shamed look in its eyes. Jacob's heart stopped, started again, beating ferociously against his ribs. They must hear *that*. A drum. He pressed into the tree, not daring to change position, to relax. The whole world pressed, diminished into this one place.

The birds sang, directly overhead. There were no flurries away. There could be no one there. With a huge effort he made himself move and peer again through the leaves into the clearing. The relief was immense, almost stunning. As he came away from the treetrunk he staggered; one leg was a club with no feeling. He held onto a low branch flexing his knee until he slowly began to be able to rest on the leg. There had been no one there. No one for a long time. The sun now appeared over the tops of the highest pines, barring the ground with long shadows.

The girl? The clearing held her scream, resonated with her presence as he advanced onto it. Was she there, in that trampled hollow in the bracken? Or had they dragged her away? He must look, and dared not. He hobbled forward. A thin branch whipped across his face. Then he was on that stage and a moment later came to the broken patch.

The first things he saw – two bare feet, the suntanned legs

crossed negligently as if someone had fallen asleep in the heat of such a pleasant late-summer day. The white skirt embroidered at the hem with small blue flowers draped demurely just below the knee. A bright red spot; many red spots sprinkled haphazardly on the white. Then great sodden blotches, the material of skirt and blouse rent and almost neatly torn. Tiny black and green movements at these cuts were flies busying themselves. He took another step forward. Dear God have pity, what have they done to her face? She has no eyes. Two bloody sockets. Her cheeks had been slashed open. These things had been done with zest and passion.

He looked down at her with the appalled curiosity of those who have never seen violent death before. They must tear themselves away and they must stay, because all of their past experience, their view of humanity, beauty, the sanctity of life has been thrown down here before them, saying, look, it is nothing but a butcher's shop. All history is a butcher's shop. But you can't look forever. He stepped back, losing the face, then the blotched clothes, then the innocent brown legs and feet. Stepped back until all that could be seen were the broken fronds of bracken bending inwards to what lay there. And as he stepped back, the depression in the bracken patch became at last almost indistinguishable from its surrounding ferns and he ran, hands over his streaming eyes, into the forest.

He was close to the villa. He had come a roundabout route, going very slowly and cautiously, hiding at every sound, every imaginary footfall. That thing in the clearing was far away now, separated from him. He felt numb. Horror is contradicted by reason. What had he witnessed? A murder by soldiers of an occupying army. Two months ago you would have run for the police. But now? Surely something could be – must be – done. He needed badly to see his father. He would know.

He stood among the birch trees that ringed the house and its front yard. He had come up the path that led to the sea. The window of his own room was propped slanting open, reflecting trees and a slash of sky. The front door was open. There was a single, man's shoe on the second top verandah step. All was quiet and still. He walked forward and looked down at the shoe. It lay on its side. There was a horror about it, as if the man wearing it had taken a step down and then taken off, kicking the shoe off, flying up like an angel, snatched from the earth. He halted in the doorway, listening with half-mad intensity. The breeze in the tree-tops, calls of birds, creak of the boards he stood on – from down the hallway between the bedrooms, from the living-room-cum-kitchen, its door almost closed, came the sounds of paper being rustled and a soft humming. *Auprès de ma blonde.* Father?

'Father?' As if released from someone's grip Jacob started forward. He pushed open the door.

On the other side of the table where they took their meals, one hand suspended in mid-air holding a piece of paper, the other taking a cigarette from his lips, eyebrows raised in surprise, stood Max.

For a moment they stared at each other. Max's hand slowly lowered the paper onto the disordered low pile already on the table. His cigarette he held at his mouth. Then he took it away and smiled and smoke came out between his smiling half-closed lips.

'Jacob.'

'Max.' His mouth had become terribly dry. 'What are you doing?' He came nearer and looked down at the table. 'Those are my father's papers. What are you doing with my father's papers? Where are my father and mother?'

'Safe. Safe, Jacob.'

'But where? Where are they?'

'Our Russian friends have taken them into town. Now, now . . .' He came round the table and held Jacob's upper arms with strong hands. He was like a doctor gently but firmly examining a child. 'I tell you genuinely, Jacob – they are safe. There's a general round-up. They have them. A few questions – a couple of days.'

'To the city?'

'Yes.'

'I must go. See them. See if they want anything.'

'Don't attempt that, Jacob.' Max stepped away from him. 'Not if you are wise. And – you can't stop here. Our friends are coming back. They'll arrest you for simply being here. This is an operational area, Jacob. Their area.'

'I don't understand.'

'You must *go*, Jacob. *Now*. You look terrible.' Max looked quickly round. There was a bottle of brandy, half full, on the dresser. He picked up a cup and poured some in.

'They killed a girl. In the woods,' said Jacob. 'They have murdered her. They hunted her.'

'Drink.' Max closed Jacob's hands round the cup.

'They killed her.'

'You must *go*, Jacob.'

But Jacob just held the cup and looked down at the papers on the table again, then back up at Max. 'And you work for them.'

'Listen – now listen, Jacob.' Max bent and peered out of the window. 'These people are hard, very hard sometimes. You do not know them. It's a different way now. Who do you think you are dealing with? Now – be a man. I'm giving you a chance. If they find you here, me talking to you, they'll think – Well, never mind. It will be both of our heads. Get away from here. They'll pick me up any moment now. I don't want you here when they come back. If I can help your father, I will. They want his papers. He is of no importance. He'll be free soon. If you stay I cannot help you. Now go.'

Jacob trembled. He felt reduced, weakened. He should put up some challenge to this man, but he had no firm place to stand. He was of no consequence in the enormous, dreadful events happening about him. History squeezed. Everything was past. Everything was in the past. There was only this awful everlasting Present. And no future. Only the short stubby shadow of the Present. And Max was the Present, contemptuous of the withered past, a man who throve on opportunity, on the moment.

There was the noise of a motor engine coming up the track – the track Jacob had come along so often in his father's car.

'Go,' said Max.

Jacob bolted down the brandy. As the spirit balled hot in his stomach, Max opened the back door, pulled him by the arm and propelled him out, threw him out, between dustbin and waterbutt, and closed the door again, silently.

Standing outside, his body refused to hide; his mind saying absurdly, heroically – well, I will take my chance then – Jacob heard the motor stop on the other side of the small wooden house. Someone got down. A shout in Russian.

'Yes, yes.' Max's answer carried from the front verandah.

That was all. The doors of the truck or whatever it was slammed, it reversed whining back along the track and Jacob was alone.

He moved in the house like a blind man. There was water in the sink and he washed his face and hands. The water felt strange in the dark, like a cold film that touched, wet, and fell from your face. The scratches he had got coming through the woods stung. Ham and cheese in the box, half a loaf in the stone jar.

He had hidden in the woods until it got dark. Now his eyes grew used to the residual light. The papers had gone from the table. He wanted a cigarette. His coat and case lay back in the woods, beside the tree that had been his barricade against the girl's death. He searched the dresser. Blessedly there was a box with half a dozen cigarettes. He found matches. He lit up. The small physical comforts of life manage to distance horror. He leaned on the table and stared out into the night. No moon, but stars lit the great, peaceful forest. The window was propped open. He could hear nothing but the sounds of the forest at night; of small creatures scuttling for fear of larger predators, of the cold wind off the sea soughing through the pines.

He went carefully along the much darker passageway into his old room. He did not want to look in his parents'. Especially now. It was important to keep a grip.

He sat on the made-up bed. There was only one pillow. Of course his mother had not expected him to sleep with Ella. Where was she to go? Where were they now? Angry at himself, at his impotence and self-pity, at his being safe while others suffered, he pushed another cigarette between his lips. He took off his shoes. His feet felt hot and swollen. He padded back to the kitchen, fumbled for the brandy bottle and a glass, and carried them back to his chilly room.

12

He had smoked the last of the cigarettes staring out into the
night until its dark clouded before him in a grey mist of
weariness. But he was so tired and nervous that he could
not sleep even after all the brandy. In the kitchen he found
aspirin and a bottle of wine. He took six of the tablets and
drank some of the wine. He wrapped himself in all the blankets
he could find in the bottom of the wardrobe, and at last slept
fitfully, dozing into and out of dreams in which voices shouted
and bellowed; his father smiled; his mother became the girl in
the woods; the girl became, disgustingly, his lover. He moved
over her and at the moment of entering her, her mouth gaped
and blood trickled from the corner . . .

It was half an hour past dawn when Jacob slipped off the
verandah and hurried into the trees.

He had shaved with his father's razor. He had changed into
a pair of old corduroy trousers, a blue shirt that looked like a
workman's, and an old jacket of his father's, too wide across
the shoulders. There were some sweet biscuits and cheese
wrapped in paper in one pocket. He had checked round
quickly before leaving the back room and saw a slim black
book under the table. He picked it up. It was his father's
diary. He jammed it into the other pocket and left.

In the woods he thought for the first time of Ella. If this
was just some sort of local or country round-up perhaps the
city was untouched. They would hardly dare do these things
in full view. And what could they want with Ella? His father
was a member, an ex-member, of the government and one of
their prime targets presumably. Perhaps what he had seen and
heard in the forest yesterday was only a horrible aberration.
This could not be the normal order of things now, surely?
His head ached, the terrible images of his dreams recurring
whenever he closed his eyes. But the wine and brandy of last

night had not worn off yet and still buoyed him up, soggily. He stopped to eat the biscuits and cheese and felt stronger.

The woods are very beautiful at this time of the day. He came to a break, a grassy field curving upwards. Between grass and fern, spiders had stretched their webs overnight. Shining with dew, they were nets, tents, pavilions of light, each one a tiny exquisite murderous trap.

He came eventually to the last line of trees, and could see the distant city and the road that went to it between the open fields.

He made for the road, reckoning that he would be more conspicuous attempting to make an uncertain way across country than walking straight up the roadside as an early morning worker.

There were no cars, no bicycles about. His shoes slapped on the macadam surface. He was intensely nervous, but he tried to walk with the swing and purposefulness of the workman. Then he heard the first truck coming up behind. He dared not look round. The sound of its engine drummed louder and louder until, suddenly, it was up to him, and thundering past. The soldiers in the back looked down at him without expression. What seemed to be a whole family of farming people huddled in the middle, old men and women, middle-aged, children, they stared back at him, their eyes desperately scared, their faces grey. Three, four more times this happened, the trucks growling up on him, coming upon him like a physical punch, and leaving him, with a contemptuous roar.

Then he was past the last smallholding and into the southern suburbs. There were more trucks outside the big clinic. He got off the main road and a tortuous crab-like progress by way of alleys, side streets, orchards, gardens, brought him on the main way just before the road bridge into the city.

The great river sparkled, smoke rose from chimneys in finely drawn blue filaments, the hatpin steeples gleamed, and at the foot of the bridge a new sentry post had been erected. Half a dozen soldiers and an officer in a cap surveyed the queue of workers, some on foot, some with bicycles, waiting to cross the bridge. Jacob walked slowly towards them. Over the last month the Russians had lost that slightly bewildered and over-awed look and now they stared at people with a blatant arrogance and contempt – occupiers realizing their power. Every now and again the officer would step smartly forward and stop someone, demanding to see their papers, two of his soldiers at his back.

Papers? They lay in the inside pocket of his jacket lost somewhere back in the forest.

The officer examining the papers had a young, tanned face with keen brown eyes – in any other circumstances an engaging face. He opened identity cards briskly, glanced at them and then stared at their owner with a bright, mocking expression. He waved Jacob through without challenging him. Cold with sweat, a drenched puppet, Jacob walked jerkily across the bridge, expecting to be shouted to halt any moment, not daring to look back. But he reached the other end of the bridge safely and there were only two idle militiamen there, looking over the wall into the water.

The workers seemed to dive away into doors and offices. There were few other people in the street. All appeared pale and frightened, glancing at each other as if they feared each as a stranger. He was a foreigner in a strange land, a land no longer his, but transformed by some drab magic. Shops had their blinds down. No one stood at the upper windows. The first café he passed was empty except for one Russian officer breakfasting. Trucks roared through the streets in urgent little convoys. Soldiers clustered on each main street corner. Going past an angled shop window, Jacob instinctively stepped aside to avoid another young man, tall, scruffy, a mark across his face – and realized with a shock that it was himself reflected.

He made for his home – what was still his *home*, his parents' apartment. No one stopped him. The soldiers, their trucks and green Marias went busily about their business, which evidently did not include him at this moment.

He hurried up the stairs of the apartment block. Here and there, on this step, then on another, were objects abandoned in flight or haste: a child's dog with wheels for legs; a book on physics; a bag of sugar; one of those paperweights filled with water, upside down, the snow sunk in a white pool in its dark blue sky. He arrived at the third-floor landing. All the doors were closed. Each little warm separate world – did people press themselves against those doors, trembling, listening to his footsteps, dreading that they would stop? He went on to the end of the corridor. He heard one of the doors open behind him.

'Jacob?'

Mrs Karner, plump, pretty, in her thirties, peered out. She was dressed in her street coat.

'Jacob. You shouldn't be here. There were soldiers looking for you. They knocked on our door and asked where you were. They had a list of names. They've been rounding people up all night. Your parents weren't here, thank God . . .'

'They took them at the sea,' Jacob said flatly.

'Oh no . . . I mean . . .'

'I thought there was a chance they may have been brought back here.'

'No, no. They have brought no one *back*. They've taken others from the flats here.' She gestured down the corridor. 'Number 31, 32, 36 – Old Mrs Vardys and her son even. It's so senseless. They said they were being sent to Russia. To Russia. Why?'

The sound of footsteps came from the stairs at the other end of the corridor.

'Have you a key? A key?' he demanded.

She closed the door, retreating, but returned a moment later and pressed the key into his hand.

Then she drew back, whispering vehemently as she closed her door, 'You must go at once. Please.'

He twisted the key and hurried in.

The apartment was undisturbed. White dust-sheets covered the chairs, the table, the sofa. All else was cleared away into the cupboards. A few gaps on the shelves indicated where books had been taken to the sea. This was the way the apartment was shut up for the summer every year, but he had never seen it like this. He and his mother had always gone to the coast first, Father following a week or two later; when they returned at the end of summer the maid would have cleared all these sheets away, unlocked the ornaments and cutlery, opened the windows.

The blinds were drawn. He felt cold. Had the weather changed? He eased the blind aside. No; the morning sun still shone along the street; a metallic glare that gave no heat back, the rays slanting into the heart of the stone of walls, pavements, road. Along the pavement of the quiet street below, a young couple came hurrying, urgent, strained expressions on their faces as they looked behind them. The young man, brown hair flopping, put out a hand to pull the woman, blonde hair flying, along. His mouth opened and an anguished 'Come on' barely penetrated the window glass. They turned the corner. Here came their pursuers. The small stocky soldiers ran, knees high, rifles held trailing back. They ran dreadfully *steadily*, implacably. Then they too rounded the corner and the street was empty again.

Jacob guided the blind into place with his fingertips so it would not swing and betray him. Everything was capable of betrayal; a friend, a piece of white calico hanging over a window.

The cold, sick feeling lived in him. If Ella had not been taken, would she assume he had been? He must contact her. His legs felt shaky as he went to the telephone, humped under the white sheet of the sideboard. He rolled back the sheet. He dialled his own number. The other end rang and rang; he imagined the monotonous clangour filling the empty room.

Was she at the agency? But she never went there before ten, there was so little to do now with the censorship biting on all the foreign journalists and the telegraph service. Besides, Max might be there . . . and if Max was a traitor? If? Of what sort? These sudden transformations of people you thought you knew were unbelievable, unbearable. It did not occur to Jacob that he himself was being changed, had changed.

He put down the telephone. He lay back in the dust-sheet on the sofa and gave himself up to a gazing, sightless day-dream. Of despair chasing hope, of inertia desiring action; dreaming of rescue, heroics, and convinced only of utter uselessness and impotence.

It was six in the evening when he left. He did not dare to hurry, but he wanted to get to Ella quickly now; to warn, to escape, to take themselves off somewhere, anywhere, to be safe. He had tried to ring her again but the telephone had gone dead when he picked it up once more.

So he had fallen asleep on the sofa, his body taking the sleep denied it in the night. When he forced himself at last to rise he shaved and bathed and dressed in fresh clothes, a dark suit, one of his father's shirts and ties.

Outside, he felt terribly conspicuous again. There were still trucks on the streets, but only one or two now, ambling singly about, tired after their long day's work. None of the NKVD troops on the street corners or the guards at the mouth of each large building stopped him, though he felt the almost physical weight of antipathy and contempt that came from their bearing.

He was glad to be in the side street bordering the Old Town, heading down to the slummy street in which his apartment house stood. There were gulls circling and screeching over the brewery, the conical roofs that looked in silhouette like sails, the gallery on the top of the office like the bridge of a ship. Clouds coming in from the sea. It would be dark before curfew.

He ran up the steps into the apartment house. He didn't know if the Russians had been here too, but, again, all the doors in his corridor were shut. No one here opened up to speak to him. He did not know his neighbours; clerks, dock-workers, shop assistants. But here too he felt the suppressed, fearful thing called life crouching behind each closed door.

The door of the apartment next to his *was* open, wide open. He had often heard their wireless, tuned always to dance music, through the thin wall. Now their room stood empty, somehow reduced, a doll's house room into which a great hand had reached and plucked out Mama and Papa and – what was it? – two, three children? The cheap furniture looked embarrassed.

He turned to his own door. He hunched, listening, close against it. Down the hall, in a room, someone coughed.

His door was unlocked. He went in.

Ella was not here. That was evident from that peculiarly dead calm of empty, rented rooms. There was no sign of a struggle, of anything remotely dramatic. The evening, painted on the window, had gone grey.

In the bedroom he did not at first see what had been left for him. The sheet of paper, stuffed above one of the revolving joints that joined mirror to dressing table, resembled a grey dove trapped, silent, its head and beak repeated in the mirror. He plucked out the crumpled paper.

Jacob,
    I have only a few moments. I must go with the men who have come. Do not worry, I will be quite well. All foreigners are to be moved across the border. I have taken some money from the drawer. I will write further when I reach my destination. Forget me. I am going where I wish and of my own will.
                    Ella.

Well, that was it. The last piece removed. He felt light-headed. And not only that. What? A sense of relief? Lightened of all responsibilities. His world had been cancelled out – an eraser rubbed away parts of the picture and you had to make your way between them. Why did he not feel guilty? He *was* frightened. That had become a permanent state. The world had removed its mask revealing a pitiless blank face. When he had changed his clothes a little while ago he had looked into that diary of his father's. His father had hoped in those neat, blue-inked pages, to be a philosopher of sorts. To catch up on his reading, to *think*, now that he had the leisure. Leisure? Philosophy? What fantastic conceptions. That was all over. No more of that.

He must get out of here. The room had darkened. Outside the window rain had begun to drizzle. Even as he watched it thickened and came faster, falling in a miserable stream down the opposite factory wall from a break in the guttering. He got out his white raincoat from the bedroom wardrobe and belted it tightly. The feel was comforting. Out of the secret drawer in the bureau he took the rest of their money. Ella had taken very little. There were cigarettes in the cabinet on her side of the bed. His hand shook as he lit one but the smoke calmed him. He would go now. To the only place he could think of.

Out on the street the air of abnormality seemed normal; the rain stopping, the clouds parting. The whole city had a silvery, antiquated, daguerrotype appearance in which the soldiers' brown uniforms, the red stars on truck sides and caps glowed as bright colours. Looking back towards the centre of the city, a red flag hanging on a flagpole occasionally flapped out and fell back.

And here, incredibly, bearing the solid Past, crawling on its snail-silver tracks, came a trolley-car from the city, its bell clanging slowly. He ran and swung onto the back platform.

It dropped him on the northern edge of the city. The rain had set in again, it seemed for the night. But the air was still clammily hot and he sweated inside his raincoat as he walked quickly towards the Stillinghurst house. But he was glad to be out of the city, and then off the road and going up the pathway to the house.

Had she gone too? The front door was locked. He didn't dare knock. He walked round the side of the house, treading softly. Leaves glistened on the wet earth. The garden was drear and neglected. He went up the verandah steps. No dog. No light in the back of the house. He peered through the glass panel of the door. Mrs Stillinghurst lay, her face tilted back, slumped in an armchair.

Mrs Stillinghurst was dreaming. A train between Lewes and Newhaven. She was on her way to meet her husband off the Dieppe boat. She was pregnant with Gerald though she did not know that what moved gently within her was Gerald. The future tugged and the train flowed forward. It was an evening in mid-summer. On her left, in the east, the downs rolled and dipped towards the sun. She must tell the driver something. It was most important she tell the driver something. Her compartment, which had held some nondescript people, sitting in shadow, not like her, lit by the sun, by love, and the expectation of love, was empty. The compartment became the telegraph office in the Strand. She wrote a wire to the driver of the train. The landscape dissolved. Gerald, she cried out. Gerald. The door of the office was shut. How could she send her wire? Now it was addressed to Gerald. She tapped and tapped on the door but could not, could not . . .

Tap, tap. She woke. The room was gloomy. Standing in the clear glass panel of the door, somehow thinner, taller, grey in the light behind him, dressed in the splendid white uniform drawn in at the waist, as if he had just walked up the steps from their play-acting in the garden . . . 'Gerald?' she whispered. 'Gerald?'

But Gerald was dead. She knew that. The figure tapped insistently. She felt ashamed at her weakness. This was not part of her dream, she would not allow herself that sentimental fiction. In dreams miracles are permitted. She raised herself in the chair. To let go of her grief so *lightly*. She drew herself up and walked to the door, the warm balm of her dream falling away in the darkening room.

'Who is it?' she demanded of the figure in the glass. 'Who's there?'

V

And when they are tortured, when they are
deliberately broken and killed, it is spring
that is being attacked. It is as if the living
centre of human life was being dirtied and
then smashed. An eyewitness saw a mother and
daughter at the head of a line going into
the gas-chambers at Belzec, and he heard the
child say, 'Mother, it's dark, it's so dark,
and I was being so good.'

Philip Hallie, *Lest Innocent Blood Be Shed*

I

He woke, disoriented. He found himself in a white room, his white pillow pressed against the black enamelled head of a brass bedstead. Then he knew where he was. He rose and dressed with the quietness and circumspection of a guest.

'No, no,' Mrs Stillinghurst protested. She stood beside the table that was laid for breakfast. 'Why have you put your old clothes back on? I have laid out fresh ones for you in the bedroom.'

Upstairs again, he saw a freshly laundered shirt, socks and underclothes stacked neatly on the dresser.

'I do hope they are not too bad a fit. They were Gerald's.'

He sat at the table. She poured him some coffee.

'You did know that Gerald was killed?'

'N . . . no. How . . . ?' He sat in the dead young man's clothes and stammered out the usual redundant commiserations. 'How . . . ?'

'He was killed flying. He was on active service.' She spoke with a sort of intense conviction, as if to say, my own grief is incidental, this thing had to be borne, it is a chance of duty, of honour. 'Please pass me the butter, would you, Mr Balthus? Now, please tell me what has been happening to *you*. I stopped you last night because you needed sleep. If you want to, tell me now.'

He was exchanging a lesser grief for a greater; perversely it made him feel better. He told her of the seizure of his parents, of many hundreds, perhaps thousands, of others. He did not tell her about the girl in the wood. He showed her Ella's letter.

She put on spectacles, read it, and said,

'It is very difficult to know why people behave in this appalling way.'

Who did she mean – Ella? The Russians?

'Your mother, father. This young lady. Your country is not at war. They are innocent civilians. I am so sorry, Mr Balthus. I will pray for their safe and speedy return to you. One wonders what is the point in locking everybody up or sending them away from their own homes.'

He was grateful for her stern kindness. 'Your son . . .' he offered in return.

'My son was in the Forces. On active service. There is a difference. Your coffee is getting cold. Please do not waste it, Mr Balthus. It is very nearly the last we have.'

She had adopted him.

The rules agreed for his survival were these. Each night he must ascend into the attic by means of a rope ladder made by Gerald when he was eleven, with the help of his father – 'That was their den,' said Mrs Stillinghurst. 'When Gerald came home for holidays from his school in England. If there is anything untoward I shall knock twice against the stairpost with my stick.' He might take exercise on the landing in the evening. He could come down to the lower part of the house and eat a meal when she had ensured that all the curtains were fully drawn. 'We will hear them coming for miles,' she said. But with the danger of someone gossiping or informing on him it would be safest for him to keep as much as possible to the attic during the daylight hours too.

'How will you buy the extra food and other things?' asked Jacob. 'I have only a little money but please take it.'

She took the purse gravely and locked it away in a drawer of the huge walnut sideboard.

'Perhaps we will be lucky. The Russians inspected the house only a week ago. Too much space for one person alone, they said. In Russia evidently many families live in one room. I reminded them that I was a British citizen. Sent them away with a flea in their ear.'

Looking at her, Jacob could believe that. She was almost the last of the British left in the country. She said, 'There is only old Mrs Grahame who lives up the coast. I must visit her. She is in her eighties. She will stay. As she said to me, where should she go *to*? And, really, that is true, Mr Balthus. We must make shift to live where the Good Lord puts us and trust in Him.' She sighed and looked out of the window. 'Oh, my poor orchard. We shall have a very scant crop this year, I'm afraid. That terrible winter, you know. Now, have you everything you need? We had better start making you as comfortable as possible.'

The attic ran the length of the house and had one small dusty gable window.

'You must poke around, Mr Balthus. Anything you can find to amuse yourself. Time will pass faster that way. Until we can make better arrangements for you.'

At the very end of summer it was warm and stuffy in the day under the raftered roof. Once or twice, before the weather cooled, the warm air trapped under the roof would not cool and he lay awake, staring into the dark. Around him he could hear the furtive rustles and scratching sounds of birds under the eaves.

In the day he read by the shelving daylight from the small window; at night he blocked it off with a piece of board and lit the storm lantern she had given him.

There were many books. Old, thick, English books. Novels; travellers' tales with pictures of women who looked like Mrs Stillinghurst or young men, moustached, who looked like Gerald, mounted on camels, standing in dhows; before mountains, in deserts; all splendidly incongruous in their heavy European clothing. The Victorian novels involved their characters in lives of great decency and much spiritual torment about 'sin' – though the nature of this sin was always obscured.

> ... It was very still in the house. The sweet and solemn dusk was falling after one of the loveliest of September days, and high above the smoke of town and city the harvest moon . . .

It was getting too dark to read. He put the novel to one side and looked round his universe.

The large, upended travelling trunks with their once brilliant labels, brown leather straps, dull brass buckles and locks. On top of one was a white plaster hand, the fingers pointing upwards, like a mute appeal from someone locked inside.

217

A rocking horse, also white, but white with a dingy blue in it. A child's bicycle. An abacus, with one of its wire rods bent out of the frame; two beads drooped on the end, the others had run off onto the floor. A large framed oil painting of two longhorned cattle standing in heather, before a lurid orange sunset. A wooden watercolour box with stiff Struwelpeter-haired brushes, the colour tablets dried up and curling their edges, each tablet with a darker, muddied depression in its centre. A cricket bat. A pair of field-glasses. The umpteenth game of patience laid out on the floor beside his mattress – Mrs Stillinghurst had shown him some elegant variations; he had invented his own colossal, frustrating, time-wasting versions with two, then three packs of cards. His table, with plate and mug. Behind a Chinese screen, his enormous chamber-pot, so matter-of-factly provided by Mrs Stillinghurst, for use when he could not leave the hiding place. He was too ashamed to use it often. As a boy, he had seen similar pots under the beds at Grandmama Clara's *Schloss*, and regarded them with horror as some gross Teutonic joke. So here, as there, he endured agonies, letting himself down at night to use the lavatory on the ground floor, bringing each time a sharp call from Mrs Stillinghurst's bedroom of 'Who's that? Who is there?'

Things must get better. What was he to do? Mrs Stillinghurst brought the news that many people had fled into the forests rather than face arrest and deportation. Great trainloads of men, women and children had left for the East. He must have looked miserably at her and she said, 'Of course Mr Balthus, you must stay as long as you wish. I am in no particular danger. I have a permit to stay here. With winter coming, perhaps things will die down a little and we can make life more comfortable for you.'

But the next day she told him that he must remain hidden for the next few days. The Russians were going round collecting up all wireless sets. 'But – see – how clever of me.' She opened a cupboard. 'This was Gerald's set. I shall hand in mine. You can wire this one up in the attic. You will be my news-bringer, Mr Balthus, my Mercury.'

So Jacob, after weeks of idleness, found a useful task for himself. He located the wires in the roof that led into Gerald's old room and connected the wireless. He was now able to have an electric table lamp also.

'There are friends of mine who would like regular reports, Mr Balthus. Do you think you could write something?'

In his attic he followed the war. He could listen to German and English bulletins and with the help of the *Times Atlas* in two great volumes he tracked their armies, their ships and planes. From the Germans he learned that massive waves of Luftwaffe bombers surged every day over the south of England. From the British, that every day these were repulsed and broken up. It seemed in September that the invasion of Britain must be inevitable. How could they stand out? Yet Mrs Stillinghurst remained supremely confident. She listened calmly as he read the reports it had become his task to write up for her. What she did with them he did not know. Someone, a man, whose voice he heard murmuring from the room downstairs, called for them every night.

But in all the broadcasts, contrary, threatening, suddenly buoyant, subdued, there was no mention of *his* country and what had overtaken it. Of course, they were not in the war as such, but it seemed they had been abandoned to their fate and were as forgotten as Jacob himself in the gloomy attic.

In such moods of self-pity he was sometimes uneasily aware that British defeat might benefit his country. Would it not, sooner or later, lead Hitler's armies to turn east again? To liberate them from the Reds? Surely even the Nazis would be preferable to living under this tyranny. The old enemy rather than the new. But there seemed at the moment a ghastly complicity between the two great powers that was leading them to carve the world into this mad jigsaw. He was grateful for this Englishwoman's help. But how typical was she? All the other English he had met – well, what were they? Gerald, the businessman Egeus, the dreadful Frank – weren't they in the end, all of them, irretrievably frivolous; conceited in their Empire, their infuriating light-hearted, light-minded air of superiority which seemed to be born in them rather than earned? Lying on his back on the attic mattress, the light outside fading too quickly now, he was by turns comforted and irritated by the thought of that indomitable, grey-haired woman stalking the house below. Indeed, he sometimes thought he must almost hate her. She witnessed his fear, the degradation of that awful chamber-pot when he had to stay up here all day because she had or expected visitors. The stench of his cell. Wasn't he her prisoner too?

A sort of madness came down on him then. He imagined that the world outside, the trees, lawn, far view of the city, clouded and then flowering in the sun, that that world had never changed. The horror in the forest had been an illusion. His father went to the Ministry every morning, returned every night. His mother helped the maid prepare food. That he, Jacob Balthus, shuffled bills of lading, letters of credit, store dockets in the office up the wooden staircase at Schwarzwald's warehouse. That he lay in bed in the mean flat with Ella – then Katerina – and Ella again. And when he thought of those two his flesh was intolerably provoked and he wrestled like a saint with images of love, not daring to give in to their demands.

He got lazy. He knew he must exercise; his only time was walking up and down the landing and his occasional trip downstairs to talk to Mrs Stillinghurst, to drink coffee when they had it – now a peculiarly tasting grey liquid. To play cards. To hear her reminiscences of places he did not know, would never see. The village in Sussex where the Stillinghursts had lived after the last war; the beauty of the countryside; the dim military career of the man in the photographs on the walnut sideboard. In uniform, he aged through promotions, reappearing in civilian clothes just before his disappearance into death. One picture showed Mr Stillinghurst almost shockingly naked in a shortsleeved shirt with Gerald, pretty, five years old, dark curls tumbling over his forehead, on his father's knee on some forever lost beach.

All this, the photographs, the treat of the coffee – such as it was – the sips of whisky from the last bottle, were, he supposed, a reward for his presents of last night's news. The punctilious records of events arriving from far away that he illustrated with little maps traced from the *Times Atlas* – Sidi Barrani, Crete, the North Atlantic . . . There was no way he could record the snatches of dance music, the concerts from

Berlin, the thin sound waxing and waning tantalizingly from the almost completely turned down wireless.

In return Mrs Stillinghurst brought news of the occupation.

The arrests continued, if at a lesser intensity. Most of the *best* people, she said, had gone. They now worked mainly at night; the big daytime round-ups had stopped.

'Everything is absolutely topsy-turvy.' She had been on one of her weekly visits to the city. 'The shops are empty of anything worth having. The factory bosses have been turned out and workers put in their place. Can you imagine!' The Russians' wives and children were coming off ships in the harbour like billy-o. The schools were being 'reformed'. All the books in them had been seized. There were to be no more fairy tales, it seemed. The teachers had been taken away. 'And the most atrocious women – gangs of them – viragos, ransacking the library and the bookshops, taking away all sorts of things. Really, what busybodies they are, Mr Balthus. I don't know how your fellow countrymen put up with them.'

He pressed her. Had she any news of his mother or father?

'No, Mr Balthus. I am trying to find out. It is very difficult.'

At night, his candle pinched out, he looked across through the field-glasses at the house perhaps half a kilometre away. Larger than this one, it had been the house of the Frobishers, Mrs Stillinghurst's English friends. Now it was occupied by Russian officers and their families; the men always in uniform, but sitting about shirt-sleeved, eating, drinking, walking up and down in their rooms; the women laying meals, talking, talking, their mouths opening in silence.

It was late. The attic was cold. There were only two upstairs windows lighted in the Russian house. One of these had the blind down. His field-glasses focused on the other. He couldn't be quite sure what he was seeing at first. The immutable window frame determined what he could view of the man's naked back, its odd plunging and rising motions, the arms flung up around him, a woman's thigh. They were making love. Were they? The shapes of

221

flesh writhed and moved ambiguously in the dark barrels of the field-glasses.

He tore himself away in disgust. Sitting on the edge of his mattress he began to think about Katerina, though he had sworn to himself that he would not. Aroused, he forced himself to the window again. The blind had been drawn. He lowered the glasses. Somehow that small, softly glowing rectangle was more erotically stimulating than the sight of the rutting couple. Ashamed, he masturbated under the window, like a boy again, his eyes on the house opposite, groaning suddenly as he was released into a mechanical ecstasy. He cleaned himself up with his towel and dropped back onto the mattress. He pulled the bedclothes around him, a coldness creeping over his body. It was a long time before he grew warm.

'Mr Balthus. Mr Balthus.'

Mrs Stillinghurst's calm, clear, lowered voice – you could never accuse her of whispering – sounded below his trap. He came awake at once with a jerk. It was difficult to sleep deeply now that the cold of early winter bit into the attic. He skimmed over the surface of sleep as if over water in which his dreams were submerged, beckoning to him as he shyed away, sank again.

He had dozed into the late morning. He stood. Out of the window the far city glittered like a fairy palace and there the Russians ruled and there, in the Frobisher house, they lived. He looked down into the garden. The black apple trees were laced with a little early snow; pale grass showed in footprints which led from the orchard to the house and back again.

He opened the trapdoor.

Her face met him. 'I think you might come down again today, Mr Balthus. There is no one about and I have some news for you. Of your family.' He clambered down, cumbersome and comic in the two pairs of trousers, the three jerseys he wore to sleep under his heap of blankets and clothes.

She regarded him with distaste. 'I shall run you a bath later, Mr Balthus. I shall stand watch. I think that perhaps you need one.'

'You said you had news?'

'Come downstairs. I have closed the shutters.'

Her shopping bag, thinly packed, was on the table.

'As you asked me, some time ago, I went to your parents' apartment house. There are Russians in the flat now. I made an excuse. They banged the door in my face. Most rude. But as I was coming away one of your neighbours – a Mrs Karner? –' He nodded. '– popped mysteriously into the hall and clutched at my sleeve. Gave me the most enormous shock, I can tell you. But, anyway, she gave me this.' From the pocket of her thick, buttoned cardigan she took a grubby brown envelope. She handed it to him.

It was addressed to Mrs Karner. There were violet and blotched black rubber stamps on the envelope.

'A letter from your mother in Russia. She encloses a letter for you. She thought it safer to send it through Mrs Karner than to your old apartment.'

He stood quivering.

'It is not bad news?'

'I would have no way of knowing, Mr Balthus.' Her voice softened. 'Perhaps you would like to sit down here while you read your letter. I will get some food. See, I have brought a small feast back with me. Though most of it is from Mr Lunts, the carter. There is nothing to be had in town but bread and some fish.'

He fingered the letter and gazed at the few things she unpacked on to the table: a tin of peaches – my God – a loaf of black bread, a bottle of beer – the pre-war kind – other things wrapped in paper. Ham, she said. Cheese. She swept them up and went out to the kitchen. He sat and drew out the folded, thin leaves from the envelope. A moment later she came back in carrying an opened bottle of beer and a glass. 'There.' Then she left him. He began to read.

My dear Jacob,

I hope fervently that this finds you well. I have sent it to Mrs Karner because I know she can be trusted. I am in a small village near a town called Karaganda in Eastern Siberia. We are allowed to write and conditions are not so bad.

The journey here was very hard and took weeks it seemed. The day we were taken from the villa was

223

hot and we had no time to take any winter clothing. A lorry drew up outside full of country people and one or two from villas around whom we knew. They were all totally at sea, poor folks, not knowing what was happening. A Russian officer simply came running up the verandah steps, waving his revolver and shouting, You must come. Now. Come on. Papa had not even his shoes on. He started to protest but the Russian pointed his revolver and said that he would shoot if we did not get out immediately. They practically threw us into the back of the lorry. We drove straight to the city, to the back of the railway station.

Already many thousands of people and soldiers were there. The men were separated from the women and children. The last I saw of Papa he was being led away to one of their green vans. Our group had then been waiting for a train for over an hour. He did not see me. It does not seem likely he was put on a train that day. Perhaps the next. The men have had it much harder than us, I think. I have heard a story that one trainload simply reached the end of the line in the middle of a forest, disembarked there, and the men told this is where you must live, you must build your own houses. And nothing there, Jacob. No tools, food, clothes. And endless breaking work all day. It is said many have died. Certainly more will with winter here. Perhaps Papa, with his education and position, will be given easier work. If he can avoid the worst conditions we must give thanks, but they say that all are treated equally harshly and rank does not count.

I share a room with two ladies from our country. So at least I am with my own kind. I have a job in the dispensary and although we have little money we are given vouchers for food from the central store and may work extra to earn more for clothes.

I do not know where all this will end, Jacob. Or when. I just pray that my dear son and husband are well and safe. Please if you can return a letter but if it is not safe do not attempt to do so. We shall be reunited one day. Do not worry about me,

Jacob, I am in good health though there is much sickness here.

I look forward to the day when I can embrace you both once more.

Your loving Mama.

Jacob read this letter daily, keeping it fresh between the pages of his father's diary. It seemed a miracle that it should have made its way over thousands of miles. And from the day that he received it, he began to have fresh hope, to re-order his life. He cleaned the attic, pushing back the detritus of the Stillinghurst family, enlarging his living space. His *Lebensraum*. Cracking the thin ice on the top of the bowl Mrs Stillinghurst left out in Gerald's old room, he made it a duty to wash all over every day, no matter how cold the weather. He must regain control. Time had become discontinuous, a matter of moments. Through his mother's letter he regained a sense of past, and of futurity. There must come an end to things. There must be hope. He took a new pride in his wireless bulletins and his little maps.

Mrs Stillinghurst complimented him on them. She began to produce odd little presents for him; a few cigarettes wrapped in paper, a tin of pressed ham – and once, unbelievably, an orange. It glowed like a sun in the gloomy living-room.

'Where did you get it?' he asked.

'My neighbours are very kind. They drop things in to me.'

'They must think a great deal of you, Mrs Stillinghurst.'

'Yes. Yes – I suppose so.' She turned indecisively about as if looking for something to do. He could see that she was embarrassed, but also pleased. 'I will make tea,' she said. 'Your last report was very good. Our friends were very pleased.'

'Our friends' were the figures in the garden late at night. The door opening and closing softly. The leavers of footprints in the snow. At first he had thought them neighbours of Mrs Stillinghurst. But no – now he realized they were partisans. He was proud. At last he was of use to someone.

So he got through to spring again. But with the unfreezing of the country the outings of the Russians began again. Mrs

Stillinghurst told him that another big deportation was under way. It could not be long, thought Jacob, before they come here. The 'friends' had not collected any of the past week's bulletins. Perhaps they had been taken. One of them would surely betray him. He must run away to the forest. And do what? He was afraid of the woods now. He dreamed of them. Of the girl. The murder grew bloodier in his dreams. He took part – and woke, sweating, the birds calling out dawn.

But nobody came for him. Spring strengthened into summer. He sunbathed in the little square of sunlight as it moved across the floor of the attic. He had become pale and thin.

It was quite by accident that he heard the announcement from Moscow. He had been about to turn off the set when a tired-sounding, faltering voice came on. Jacob's Russian was not so good. Had he misunderstood? The voice announced that the Germans had made a totally unprovoked assault on the Soviet Union. He hurriedly swivelled the dial to the German wavelength. The armies of the Führer were advancing on a front reaching from the Black Sea in the south, to the White Sea in the north. The Bolshevik armies were in chaotic retreat.

'Mrs Stillinghurst. Mrs Stillinghurst!'

'What on earth is it, Mr Balthus?'

'Come up. Come up.'

They had to wait only a few days before they heard that the first German tanks had sneaked through the forests to the south of the city and crossed easily the only half-completed defence trenches the citizens had been forced to dig. There had been air-raids during the day. The German Stukas hung like flies over the city, above and below them the white and red flashes of anti-aircraft shells, the puffed white smoke, then the following crack of their sound. Then the deeper *crump-crump* of the bombs in the city.

Jacob watched the battle for the city for two days. The Stillinghurst house was full of people fleeing from town. The Russians were in total panic, shooting at anyone out on the street. They had withdrawn over the river and failed to blow the bridges before the first Germans reached them. Jacob had left the attic at last and used it only as an observation post, relaying news to the rest of the house.

It was here, on the morning of the second day of the battle, that he focused his field-glasses on the city again. Two green and white flags on two pinnacles were separate for a moment, then coalesced into one image in the adjusted glasses. As Jacob watched, a shell burst over the Lutheran cathedral in a cloud of lilac and grey smoke. The sound was lost in the never-ending rumble. Watching, fascinated, the succession of fireworks, he became aware of the voice calling from below the open trap.

'Mr Balthus. Mr Balthus. You are wanted. Come down.'

He swung down, a free animal, and followed Mrs Stillinghurst down the stairs.

Through the house, the open front door, he saw a crowd of refugees in the driveway waving and cheering.

'What is it?' he turned to her. She was pressing something into his hand. He looked down. It was the purse he had given her, still full.

'No, no – that was for you.'

'Go on, go on, Mr Balthus. You will miss them.' He felt her hand on his back.

Propelled by her goodness, he hurried forward onto the front verandah. The refugees were running towards the lane that ran beside the house to the main road. Above the hedge he saw a halted truck, the heads of young men, the green and white national flag furled on a pole at the rear.

Then he was running towards the lane, pressing between the cowards, the families, those who had not endured the lack of light, the bone-aching, teeth-chattering cold – so he thought, running to the flag, the suntanned heads and arms of the young men who raised their rifles in salute at the people's cheering.

He stood, shaking, at the tailboard.

'I gave the news. Take me with you. I must go.'

They laughed. The thick wrists pulled him up as if he were a child. Then he was in the truck with them. The people were behind him, shouting tinnily as the truck roared forward. Then they were on the road, the flag streaming behind, heading for the city. Back into time.

2

Fires bled in the city. The pall of smoke billowed and drifted in darker and lighter clouds, becoming a secondary sky, a storm anchored to the ground. The truck entered the inner city. To be with these men on this day. To find he was not after all a coward. Jacob stood in the back of the truck, gripping onto the flagpole. A crackling noise came from ahead of them. Something like a bee hummed past his ear, displacing the air. He was astonished and exhilarated to see his companions crouch suddenly below the sideboards. He laughed. Another bee.

'Get down you fool.' He was pulled to the floor, cracking his knee on a bolt. The truck accelerated, rounded a corner and bumped along a cobbled side street. Ahead, another main road was signalled by a red shop sign, lettered in white *Mendelssohn's the Dressmakers*. Jacob crouched, rubbing the pain in his knee away.

The partisans stood up again. Their odd miscellany of pistols and rifles and shotguns were pointed up at the windows.

They turned on to the main thoroughfare and headed for Palace Square. German aircraft flew low across roofs heading to bomb the Russians north of the city. The sun winked off the glass cockpits; Jacob could see the faces of the crews. In their turn the Russians were shelling the city still; the explosions came in groups of three or four, then ceased for perhaps a minute. A whole building collapsed behind them, its facade sliding into the road as if some giant had pulled elegantly on strings at its base. A cloud of dust rushed into the air.

They drew into the side of the square across from the Palace. The huge billboard portraits of Stalin, Lenin and Marx had been pulled down and lay drunkenly; defaced, hacked into splintered lengths of plywood and paper with, here, half a moustache, there, an eye gleaming. A group of captured Russian soldiers were huddled, under guard, at the foot of the Palace steps.

Jacob saw his first German officer coming down the steps. Smiling, suntanned, he handed a map-case to a soldier and began to cross the square. What a beautifully elegant thing war could be, thought Jacob at the sight of this crisply uniformed upright gentleman coming towards them.

'We'll drop you here,' said one of the partisans. 'We're going on.'

But Jacob wanted to go with *them*, to prove himself at last a hero. They did not want him. He climbed down over the tailboard.

The truck moved away, the partisans waving their rifles to people in the apartment houses who had gathered on their balconies to cheer them.

The Russians were being marched away; the curses of their guards floated across the square. And floating across the square too came the German officer. A terrific explosion behind the Palace; it seemed that the edges of the Palace shivered. The German's step did not falter.

More planes over the square.

Jacob's eyes feasted on the liberator. The man put him to shame. He looked down at himself. Gerald's white shirt was torn; Gerald's grey flannel trousers were smeared with dirt.

The prisoners had gone. An armoured troop carrier was disgorging more Germans at the steps. The black cross edged with white on olive-green. The German officer was past the first President's statue. Jacob started forward to greet him.

He heard himself stammering in German.

'Welcome. We . . . we must welcome you. You have freed us.'

The German stopped a yard away. Smiling, he said,

'Your papers please, my good sir.'

They took him to the old Fortress.

He had been here before; his father had taken him round as a boy, to see with all the excitement of a ten-year-old the huge black, obsolescent guns that had never been fired in anger; to scamper up the spiral stone stairs to the top of the lookout tower; to look down on the city below, the steeples' winking scales and needles; the foreshortened tiny men and women, the sea a blue saucer tilting to the horizon; then down, down, down, passing the gun casements once more, descending an iron staircase. Down here, under the guns, steel doors and shutters closed off the ammunition stores and hoists, and the dimly lit corridor curled away in a great circle under the hill and he had shivered and felt frightened.

So he knew where he was. This wedge-shaped shell store-room, damp and cold, was now a cell. There was no window. He had been here for three days, though the only difference between day and night was the rhythm of breakfast of black bread and a bowl of thin greasy soup; supper of dried fish and mashed parsnip; lights-out. Jacob had been brought along the dim, slippery corridor. Though he could hear nothing he had the impression that most of the other cells were occupied. The guards accompanying him behaved with a cheerful brutality. When they opened the cell door and Jacob demanded to see the officer in charge, one of them put a hand on his chest, pushing him back, while the other punched him hard in the stomach.

Two other men were thrown in after the third breakfast. The first, a thin man in a black suit, his white face puffy and lacerated, crawled without a word to the mattress against the end wall, where the ceiling curved down giving the impression of a cave. He lay facing the wall, his body curved like a bony, black foetus.

An hour later the second man was put in. The door banged shut. This one, short, stocky, weasel-faced, dressed like a dock-worker, looked about him quickly, nodding to Jacob, frowning at the back of the black-suited man. Then he sat down on the mattress opposite Jacob and stared across at him. All his movements had a sort of aggrieved jauntiness about them.

'Been here long?'

'Three days now,' Jacob whispered.

'Don't worry. Can't hear you through these bloody great doors.' Again he looked about him. His eyes, cocky and bright, engaged Jacob's once more. 'Name's Karl.' He held out his hand across the stone-flagged floor. The man's great warm paw squeezed.

230

'Jacob.'

'Yeah.'

His contemptuous gaze had summed up the lack of strength in Jacob, the softness, the gentility that was worthless in a place like this. Karl, the gaze said, was top man here now.

'Three days? You missed all the fun up top. All the cheering and bloody waving. The Germans coming in, the Bolos going out. Lovely. Had our own government again. Flag above the Palace. They damn soon put a stop to that. They've hauled all our flags down and put their own up. Well – I suppose they can't be any worse than the other bloody lot. It's his sort are going to cop it now.' He jerked his thumb towards the man at the end of the cell.

'Sh . . .' Jacob whispered involuntarily.

'Don't bother about him. Swine. Lost a couple of teeth, have we?' he shouted. 'Oh dear. Deserves everything he gets,' he said savagely, turning back to Jacob. 'Communist bastard. He'll lose more than his fucking teeth. What are you in for?' He returned to his matter-of-fact tone. He was like a great actor, or a madman, moving easily from one pitch of speech to another.

'No papers. I lost my papers.'

It was plain he had sunk even further in Karl's estimation; that Karl's elevation to lord of the cell was now firmly established. He brought a battered packet of Russian cigarettes out of his trouser pocket and stuck one between his swollen lips without offering the packet to Jacob. Then he patted all his other pockets thoughtfully. He took the cigarette from his lips.

'Got a match?'

Jacob went through a pantomime of going through his own clothes.

'I'm afraid not,' he said.

Karl glared across at the Communist. 'I'm not asking that bastard.'

'I'll go. I'll go.' Jacob got up, wincing at the pain from the bruise under his ribs. He stood over the Communist. Without turning, or lifting his head, the man touched his suit pocket. Jacob inserted his fingers and delicately drew out a matchbox.

'Thank you,' he whispered.

He was rewarded with a cigarette by Karl, who pocketed the matches after lighting them.

'Don't waste your thanks on him.' He glared over at the thin, prone figure, but his voice was lower. 'Small thanks they gave us.'

Karl's ascendancy in the cell gave him a monopoly on the starting and ending of conversations and their content. He filled the afternoon with an Homeric saga of fighting, drinking and whoring – 'Three litres of wine on Sunday, shagging a widow up in the Old Town when the bombing started again, she wants to go down to the shelter while I'm in full flow – you know – mid-stroke, I say hang on you stupid cow I'm only just started and she starts shouting in my ear, well it was a dead loss after that, might as well have been stuffing this mattress.' He thumped it. He couldn't remember rightly how he had been picked up. It had been on Monday; he had got drunk in the evening. 'I must have shouted something. Next thing I know I'm in a fight then they're dragging me off in a carrier and I wind up here. I ask you!'

The dim bulb in its steel cage in the ceiling flickered and died, a red glow fading in the filament.

'Lights-out. Bastards,' said Karl. The world was divided between him and bastards.

Jacob lay on his mattress and pretended to sleep. Through the peephole in the cell door, light fell the size and colour of a small dull-silver coin on the back of the Communist. He did not move.

Karl's cigarette glowed in the dark. He pressed it out in a tiny shower of sparks on the stone floor. Jacob heard his hand brushing at the stone. He was clearing the ash away.

Karl began almost immediately to snore. Evidently he had been in places like this before. In between Karl's long-drawn, shuddering grunts, Jacob could hear nothing from the Communist, not even his breathing.

They fetched the Communist sometime in the night. Jacob was dreaming that he was treading water, cold sea water, and he woke to hear the bolt clang back. The corridor light seemed to follow the large dark figures of two, three soldiers as they went in quick strides to the end of the cell. Almost before Jacob was fully awake they had bent down and seized the man, their huge shadows like one fantastic animal curving up the wall and ceiling. They dragged him out swiftly. A hand grasped in the thick black hair. An arm crooked tightly under the chin. The Communist's feet bobbled on the uneven floor. The third soldier followed them out, tapping the palm of his left hand with a truncheon.

The light narrowed swiftly like a fan snapping to. From the corridor came a shout; a scream like a cat's. The bolt grated into its socket.

The Communist did not come back.

After another few hours of dozing, frightened misery, breakfast came round again.

The docker Karl was called out of the cell shortly after. He had been silent over breakfast. Jacob expected him to exult over what had happened to the Communist, but Karl simply tore at his bread and drank his soup, staring fixedly ahead.

When they opened the door and called his name he got up quickly, straightening the single blanket over his mattress. He marched out in silence, his face pale, as if Jacob did not exist.

Jacob did not know how long he sat alone in the cell. The memory of that scream; of the fear in Karl's face, the silence now; the terrific weight of stone above him . . . The bolt was being worked back. He felt sick. He would disgrace himself. He stood up, adjusting his glasses. The door swung open.

A large figure in a green officer's uniform, shining black boots, shining brown and black leather belt and holster, a huge shining face.

'Balthus? Young Jacob Balthus?' The voice boomed in the corridor. 'What's this trouble you're in now, eh? Don't you recognize me?'

His saviour, Herr Schwarzwald – Major Schwarzwald – led him up iron stairs.

'The Russians are on the run,' said Schwarzwald. 'We are chasing them out of the country. And soon we'll be chasing them over the Urals. Back to Asia where they belong. Animals, young Balthus. Animals.'

Schwarzwald's speech had become crisper, his movements, once rolling and slothful, brisk and commanding. He had lost a little weight from his stomach, unless he was corseted under the uniform, but his face was as round and ruddy as ever.

'Animals – see.' They halted at the window on a wooden landing and looked down into the circular sandy courtyard. A party of shabbily uniformed Russian prisoners were assembled at one side, holding shovels. A corporal was shouting something at them and two other soldiers held machine-pistols on them.

'We're making them work. We think the Russians buried something in the yard. Well, they're going to have to dig it up again. Come on.'

They went up to the next landing and then along a newly whitewashed corridor that led into the heart of the Fortress proper, behind the sea-battery where Jacob's cell had been.

The place was full of soldiers. Emerging smartly and purposefully from doorways and around corridors they saluted Schwarzwald, and looked curiously at Jacob. Schwarzwald had had him kitted out in a rough green shirt that made him itch, a pair of Wehrmacht trousers a little short, thick woollen socks and army boots. 'Every inch the soldier,' Schwarzwald's laugh reverberated around the kit store.

'My office.'

Schwarzwald threw himself into the swivel chair behind the desk and swept the papers on the desk to one side. He motioned to Jacob to sit on the bench facing him.

'Now, young Balthus. Now. You may consider yourself a fortunate man that I happened along, eh? Not that it is entirely just luck. You have a guardian angel. I mean it. Coffee,' he barked at an orderly who had appeared in the doorway. 'Two. Um. Yes, when we moved against the Bolsheviks I at once volunteered for action in this sector. By God, I knew we were good, but I didn't know we were that good. The swine scattered like . . .' His hand clawed the air for the word he wanted. '. . . like swine. Ha.' His laugh rumbled out of him. 'Now our lads will press on to Petersburg. It'll all be over before the leaves fall off the trees. But I'm staying on here. Things need doing, organizing, Balthus. Yes.' He looked dreamily at the map of the capital on the wall. There were many little pins with different coloured heads stuck on it. A thick black line enclosed most of the Old Town. 'We have a brief – well, well . . . We are fast workers, Balthus. Don't let the grass grow. Now, I have a duty to discharge. Guardian angels – your Grandmama, Frau Hugenberg. You know that she has an estate now in Poland? Near Posen, where I have made my home. Well, she asked me to visit her before I left. My God, she knew we were going to move against the Russians before I did. A very shrewd woman, young Balthus, your Grandmama. She has many friends in the highest circles of the Party. Now . . .'

He opened the desk drawer and took out a package wrapped in oilskin.

'She asked me to give you this.' He passed it across the desk.

The coffee arrived. Schwarzwald sipped and grimaced. 'Filthy stuff,' he said, 'but I suppose one must make sacrifices. You know they burned down my warehouses. I suppose I was a sitting duck with a German name painted all over the roofs. They have done a lot of damage retreating. Scorched earth.' All this time he was watching as Jacob undid the parcel. Inside, a letter was tied with blue ribbon to another package wrapped in brown paper.

The letter was short and not noticeably affectionate. It began simply 'Jacob' and went on to observe bitterly that the Bolsheviks had taken her only daughter from her but that the retribution of God and the Führer would surely follow shortly. She was entrusting this money to Herr Schwarzwald – in a reflex Jacob's fingers squeezed the brown paper package. He was to keep himself pure and to serve the greater good. To remember the words of St Paul to Timothy, ' "If we suffer, we shall also reign." Your loving Omama.'

He opened the package. What looked to be several thousand marks in bills of high denomination.

'Count it, count it,' said Schwarzwald, a big grin on his face. 'You are quite the rich man, Jacob – I may call you Jacob, mayn't I? Between ourselves?'

'Frau Hugenberg is a very fine lady,' he went on. 'Here in this country she was the backbone of the Bund. And she hopes to return when the Russian bandits are driven out of

235

the North. Let us hope so, eh? Despite her age, she is a very tough old lady, is she not?'

'My father?' Jacob said; his fingers rested on the banknotes. 'Have you found out anything about my father?'

Schwarzwald spread his hands. 'I would have told you of course, Jacob. In their haste to run away their political police left most of their records behind. We are checking them as fast as we can. I have given orders that any news of your father be brought to me immediately. But, there were many thousands of good people arrested or deported by the swine. There may well be camps we have not reached yet. But –' he slapped the desk with the palms of his hands '– we will find him, Jacob.'

He stood up and looked at the map on the wall, toying with a red-headed pin, his back to Jacob.

'I understand you hid out with the partisans during the Soviets' occupation? Um? Fought with them?' He waited for Jacob's answer.

'N . . . not until the end,' Jacob stammered; the modest warrior. 'An Englishwoman, Mrs Stillinghurst . . . She was most kind. I hope . . .'

'Yes. The Stillinghurst woman.' Schwarzwald turned. 'A difficult position. And the partisans – in that situation perfectly understandable. Do you still have any contact with them?'

'No.'

'Good. They have been disbanded – though there are a few still opposing *us*. Some people are never satisfied, eh? The question is, what are we to do with you? I promised your good Grandmama that I would look after you.'

'I don't know. The warehouse?'

'Oh, the warehouse. Finished, as I said. These things come and go. But there are opportunities in business all the time, Jacob. The National Socialist revolution has given every man his chance if he will seize it. Not a revolution in the absurd Communist sense. I did not choose my word well. A restoration – of the great German nation and race, of all that is noble in our ancient history – all that has been defiled and betrayed by Jews and anarchists and Communists. It is a revolution, Jacob, not to elevate some *class* of people. Not worker. Not aristocrat. It is to elevate the race. This is the revolution of the ignored, Jacob. The ordinary man, struggling not to be *free*,' there was an infinite contempt in his voice at that word, 'but to take *his place*. The State is all; it reveals us. Worker, businessman, soldier – all German, all working together.

'For years, Jacob, your trade unions, your treacherous international cartels, your Yiddish freemasonries, your, your fal-de-dal of modern artists, have sneered at us. Well, I tell you, this is our time. Our revenge. The ordinary man. The man of common sense.' His hands chopped the air. 'This is their hour. I tell you, Jacob, I have seen a lot in Poland. My eyes have been opened. These Slavs, Jews – they live like pigs – they'll die like them.'

He stopped. Had he seen the look of horror that passed across Jacob's face? He sat down again. His voice softened and once again bubbled humorously out.

'Straight talking, eh Jacob? Never hurt anybody. You think the Jews you knew were not so bad, eh? Old Finkelfeffer not such a bad old man? Frau Goldblatt a kindly soul? And we've all had our pretty little Jewesses, um?' Schwarzwald leaned back, winking grossly, slowly.

'Make no mistake – they are all to go. They all go. You understand? Why, if we each spared our favourite Jew, where would we be then? Back in their pretty clutches – and this time they wouldn't let go. So, no excuses this time, Jacob, no prevarications. We are men. We know our duty. We are out to cleanse the world. And who in God's name is there to stop us? The Yids? The Bolsheviks? The British? My God, their boys are not a patch on ours. I saw some of the prisoners we took in France. Pasty-faced, rotten-toothed, round-shouldered. Weakness, Jacob. Weakness. Bad blood.

'Well now. Enough of that.' Schwarzwald looked about his desk top as if impatient for something on which to vent his consuming energy. 'Now. I have to get on. Work to do.' He stood up. Jacob did too; his legs were rather weak.

'Do you think, Herr Schwarzwald – I must go into the city. To visit my parents' apartment. The neighbours may have news . . .'

'Of course, my boy.'

'I need to buy clothes. If my own . . .'

237

Schwarzwald was sweeping him along the white corridors, down more iron stairways. From being a curio, the Old Fortress was being restored to its military purpose. In the open offices, as they passed, men talked loudly into telephones; girls clattered on typewriters; clerks gravely sorted documents; all was bustle and decision. Schwarzwald, diving into one of these offices, took ten minutes to fix him up with a temporary *Ausweis* – 'There you are, your passport back to the world, young Jacob. See you back here at –' he examined the huge, many dialled chronometer on his wrist '– at 16.00 precisely. Later perhaps we may dine together. Good.'

Jacob stepped back into the world through the main gate, under its rusted portcullis, the huge black and red and white swastika flag that hung above that . . .

He came down the winding road that overlooked the Palace grounds, the lake, the rear of the Palace. Above that too the German flag was now flying. The road dipped and the view of the Palace and the city beyond was lost. But the closely packed buildings were gap-toothed where parties of men, stripped to the waist, cleared bomb and shell damaged sites.

The town was full of Germans. As Schwarzwald had said, these men bore no resemblance to the small, undernourished-looking Russians. They walked, swaggered rather, spreading across the pavements in threes or fours, looking into what shops were left. The Jewish shops were shut, their counters bare. Propaganda posters had been stuck over their windows, urging citizens, redundantly, not to buy from Jews. More posters on walls, lamp-posts, curving on the little pillar-like kiosks, showed barely idealized portraits of the young men in the streets. *With Adolf Hitler in The New Europe.*

He wanted to get back to his parents' apartment as soon as possible. Perhaps father would be there. It was hardly possible, but who knew what miracles could happen? He did not want to arrive in these clothes, at any rate. He would go to the big Epstein store in Palace Square.

The store no longer existed; the back floors rose behind a huge heap of rubble like a shallow, jutting stage-set of dereliction. On the Palace front was a giant portrait of Hitler, his rather flabby, disagreeable face retouched and tightened in an expression of mad resolve, the eyes huge and compelling, but with that curious nose that always looked somehow false, like an actor's putty nose, unimproved. Long banners of red, black and white hung down between each bank of windows.

He arrived at the apartment block. At least it was still standing. The whole quiet street was untouched.

He knocked at Mrs Karner's door.

It was opened slowly, on a short chain.

'*Da?*' The face was small, frightened. Was it his quasi-uniform, indistinctly seen in the dark passage, that made her flinch?

'No, no. I am not a soldier,' he assured the woman in his bad Russian. 'Not German.'

She looked even more frightened.

'Open the door please,' he demanded; he might as well make use of his borrowed authority. She undid the chain and stood in the middle of the room.

He could not get much out of her. No, she knew no Mrs Karner. She knew no one. They had all left. All gone.

The next apartment? Was there anyone in the next apartment?

She shook her head. All gone. Everyone has gone.

She was plainly terrified of him. Not personally, but of whatever he was the symbol. What did she think he was? The apartment was shabby; the woman looked hungry and thin. The Russians must have left quite a few behind like this one. Did she think he had come to arrest her?

If he had, it would be no more than she deserved. She had usurped his kindly neighbour and now imagined that it was her turn. She was a coarse, uneducated woman the war had deposited here. She was of no importance. He turned. At the door he looked back. She stood dead still in the same spot, her small white fists clenched. Well, let her stay like that, in the centre of a stolen room, another little piece of memory. Someone else would come for her, or forget her. She would wait for them both. She was of no importance.

The door of his parents' apartment was locked. In his rush to leave Mrs Stillinghurst's with the partisans he had left the key behind. He looked through the keyhole. Carpet, edge

239

of chair. The bookshelves empty. The books and china looted? Sold?

He thought about the books as he came down the stairs. And about the Russian woman standing alone in Mrs Karner's room. The terrible thought that Mrs Karner had been taken by the Russians because of the letter received from his mother in Siberia. It was the ultimate pleasure for the guilty to lure the innocent into implicating the innocent. For the innocent to *destroy* the innocent.

He knocked on the janitor's door. A new janitor, with a night's growth of beard and the sweet-sour smell of liquor curling off his breath. Would it be possible? My parents' old apartment? The sight of the wad of German notes was sufficient. Jacob left with the key.

He could not face going back to the apartment he had shared with Ella. What was the point?

Searching round, he found another store. There was not much to be had, but he bought a half-way decent suit, shirts, socks, new shoes, new underclothes. He changed in the shop. He wished he had bathed and felt curiously unclean in the fresh clothes. The makeshift uniform was made up into a parcel by a smirking assistant and he carried it out under his arm. Not his property after all.

The clock on the Lutheran cathedral showed two. He must get back to Schwarzwald by four. Time for a drink. A sentimental drink at Stieckus's.

On the way he bought a newspaper. Though the masthead and typeface remained the same, the news had undergone an *Alice in Wonderland* transformation. Good Comrade had become Bolshevik Bandit; the collective inspiration of Comrade Stalin had changed to the glorious leadership of our great Führer. On the front page, in a frame of black lines, was a list of – he counted them with his eyes, looking for anyone he knew – thirty names of hostages shot for 'outrages' against the German Reich. That was a step forward in press freedom. The Soviets had not advertised. A poor joke. He knew two of the names.

Stieckus's was loud and crowded. True to Stieckus's catholic tastes there were Germans at a number of tables, three rather tense-faced students, and a gaggle of girls, eyeing the soldiers casually. Loud, jolly music came from the wireless on the bar.

The chess players had gone.

There were no ghosts. The bar was just the same; but everyone who had once been here had been swept away. He was the only ghost, the revenant. If Max had fled, then presumably Katerina had gone with him. There were none he wished back. Except . . . Katerina.

He had two beers and aquavits. The whey-faced girl served him his first meal in freedom; she, like Stieckus, was among the immortals. And Freedom? What was that? He was beginning to get used to the relativity, the elasticity of that word. If the Jews and Communists suffered – so then? Had they not, in innumerable smaller and larger ways, brought it upon themselves? They irritated; they clogged the conscience. He did not want to live forever afraid. He had his own life to lead. 'I have my own life to lead,' he said out loud. The couple at the next table looked across at him. The woman whispered behind her hand to her companion.

Jacob stripped another note off his wad.

'We have no change yet,' said Stieckus at the bar. He had not recognized Jacob.

'Keep it. Keep it,' said Jacob, and strolled out; the man with clean clothes, a little money, a little freedom.

When he showed his *Ausweis* back at the Fortress he was told that Major Schwarzwald had been called away to some urgent business. Please wait.

He was not pleased. He had to sit in the common waiting-room. Behind the grille set in the wall two soldiers were installing a telephone switchboard, testing the lines by putting in plugs, whirring a handle, saying over and over, Excuse me Herr Major, excuse me Colonel, excuse me Captain, we are testing the lines; and then pasting little handwritten roundels above each plughole with the Herr Major's, Colonel's or Captain's name. This was amusing for a time. He tried to ignore the others on the bench. He was after all a gentleman and one who had suffered something for his country. It was insulting to be kept waiting. He was on some terms with this new regime. These people were mere supplicants; the woman in her flowered dress, bent like a question mark, the man who kept twisting his hands in and out of each other as if drying them on an invisible cloth, great red hands that had no business being nervous.

Twice Jacob got up, then sat down again. He wanted to smoke, but there was no ashtray. He took the newspaper from his pocket and read again how the armies of the Reich were driving north. At this rate they would be in Leningrad by the autumn. Perhaps then the Germans would just pull through this country, purging it of the Reds, and his people could resume their lives here, elect their government, live once more as a prosperous, small republic. The prisoners in Russia would be liberated, and his mother and father return.

He had hardly given Ella a thought. He looked down at the not very good new suit. Soon he would have good clothes, a mistress. Be a man of whatever world was coming. Having been through the fire . . .

One of the soldiers was calling to him through the grille.

'Herr Balthus? You are to go up now.'

The other soldier led him back through the confusion of white corridors.

Schwarzwald stood by the map.

'Balthus . . . ah . . .' he cleared his throat. He appeared embarrassed. It was not a condition usually associated with Schwarzwald. 'You know Zech of course.'

Materializing from the corner behind the swung-back door was Herr Zech, of the Resettlement Commission.

'Of course,' said Jacob as they shook hands.

Zech too had been mysteriously transformed by his uniform. He was taller and broader but at the same time his pale freckled face looked astonishingly young. In his other hand he carried a cap with the silvery skull badge of the SS on its peak. He bowed and put on the cap, extinguishing the shortcropped, flame-coloured hair.

'Balthus.' Schwarzwald twisted and turned at the desk, fingering the papers that had arrived there since the morning.

'Your father . . .'

'If you will forgive me, Major,' said Zech. 'Herr Balthus, it is necessary that you assist us. The cells here were empty when we arrived. From information received we have had the Russians digging up the yard.' Zech's eyes gleamed as he spoke, examining Jacob's reactions.

'Some bodies have been found,' said Schwarzwald. 'It is not conclusive, but from the documents found and other evidence . . .'

'Perhaps you will follow me.' Zech held open the door.

They had laid the bodies under sheets on the floor of one of the old gun casemates. There were twenty or more arranged in three rows. The stench was tremendous, mingling with the resinous smell of disinfectant that a sergeant was pouring over them from a jerry can. Jacob struggled to keep from retching. In the second row . . .

'. . . possible it is not,' murmured Schwarzwald.

Zech drew back the sheet.

It was and was not.

The hair was disordered. The first thing you notice is my father's beautiful hair, Jacob thought absurdly. The temples were sunk in and turned to blue-black bruises. The eyes were shut, the lids seeming too big and too round. He had fine eyes. The lower part of the face was hideous, again this black discolouration, earth in the nostrils, the lower jaw drawn impossibly down, so that the mouth gaped in a silent scream.

All the cafés, the trips to the sea, the little glasses of cognac, the books, cigars, flirtations, languages, conversations, loves, evenings, afternoons, harmless vanities, coffee, mended chair, straightened newspaper, lips, tongue, eyes, hair, warm hands; all jokes, words, arguments, philosophy; everything heard, felt, seen was gone from this kind terrible head.

On the white curved wall many small brown flies clung, waiting to descend.

3

In the months that passed after his father's funeral, the shock reverberated with decreasing intensity, surprising him at the oddest moments – shaving, or making coffee, or picking up something fallen to the floor – forcing tears in a sudden flood, reducing him for an hour or more to a core of misery hunched on the sofa in the apartment. Then he began to dream of his father as he had been in life; beautiful, fragrant dreams where the smiling face came close to his, they walked together, talked with an intimacy never known in life. But when he woke he could remember nothing of what they had said. The ghastly sight of his father's body was thrust down, not permitted, even in dreams. He was the only one to have seen it out of all the relatives who gathered in the apartment on the day of the funeral. They paid their respects to a closed coffin. Grandmama Clara, returned for the occasion, raised her black veil and lowered her stern yellow face to kiss the box. Schwarzwald, accompanying her from the station, black band on one arm, swastika band on the other, rubbed black-gloved hands together and gravely accepted a glass of schnapps from the bottle he had brought. His large uniformed frame, the voice lowered to a rumble though it was, the vulgar lightning flash of his armband as he cumbersomely turned to pay his respects, sympathizing with the supremely unsympathetic Clara, made him into a sort of beast, one better extinct, a mastodon in the apartment. It was only when Grandmama Clara signalled her desire to leave, and Schwarzwald flurried about her, easing her passage downstairs to the staff car, only then did the assembly begin to break down into that state of mixed sanctimony and ill-judged humour that divides the survivors at any funeral party. True, they were more distant relatives of his father, or colleagues from the Ministry. It was astonishing how many he had expected to see were absent. He was told of so-and-so imprisoned, of another shot, another deported, letters from Stockholm from those who had fled from the fishing villages up the coast; some hiding there for more than a year, fleeing from the Russians; others, new arrivals, escaped from the Germans. But in the end he wished they would all go. And eventually they did, good people all, backing out of the apartment, low-voiced, apologetic, sympathetic; none of them had visited him since.

Well, perhaps he was not very good company now. He kept the apartment scrupulously clean. It was too large for him, but he felt it his duty to keep it on. With his salary from the Germans and an allowance from Grandmama Clara he was well off. He had a full ration card, a German card; his fellow countrymen got half of that; Jews and Russians half that again. Always orderly and tidy, his ways became the parodically feminine ones of the lone bachelor. The set routines of waking at the same hour; wash, shave, breakfast. If there was a girl she slept on in the bed to be woken just before he left. Paid off, or kissed sentimentally. Either way she would not be there in the evening when he returned.

One could not, he thought, be less than chivalrous. Schwarzwald and the others might visit the brothel, and he look ridiculous and suffer half-veiled jokes to be made about his virility when he demurred from joining them – but one was not a rapist, not a barbarian. How was one to think of women but to fall in love, or think them in love with you? If he was a fool, that was not to be eradicated, was it? Not overnight.

Another quest obsessed him now. A more innocent, honourable one. He felt it his duty to restore the empty shelves in the apartment to as close a state as they had been before. A modern, civilized man is made up partly of the words he reads; he could reconstitute his father in part by restoring his library. There had been two bookshops where the Russians might have sold off the books – if they had not been destroyed. At least he could get duplicates of as many as he could remember, filling the gaps to his own taste. The shop owners, both Jews, had of course gone; one shop was bolted and barred. From the other, with a new German owner, the Germans had taken the pick of the best books, and seized others for destruction. But among the secondhand shelves he found quite a few he thought he recognized as his father's copies, though his father never signed or placed bookplates in his books. Philosophy, Poetry, Science – the censor was uninterested in *them*. The books, their ideas superseded by the holy simplicities of the New Age, were acceptable as beautiful objects. As texts they were redundant; their world, orderly and rational, governed by law and God, a sealed museum.

He bore them home, loaded in bags. He arranged them lovingly on the shelves; as far as possible in the old order. If he read them, perhaps he could discover a sense of his father, of what went on in that *head*. But, as yet, he opened none of them, giving himself the excuse that the library must be complete before it could be used.

Meanwhile there was drink, a little sex and sentimental attachment, music on the wireless. And work.

Jacob left the apartment at eight o'clock each morning, except Sunday. He went by way of the back streets as far as possible, to avoid meeting the lines of Jews and Russian prisoners of war being marched and countermarched across the city, to and from barracks and Ghetto (the thick black line round the Old Town on Schwarzwald's map had been made solid in a high wooden fence topped with barbed wire). Not allowed on the pavements, these processions used the middle of the road. At first they had been jeered at by passers-by; now the people on the pavements hurried on their way as if the ragged lines of workers, harried along by their casually, effortlessly brutal guards, had become invisible.

He slipped through a side door into the old Foreign Ministry. At half-past eight he hung up his hat and coat in the Special Traffic Office. He shared the fairly large room with an SS corporal and many olive green filing cabinets, though some of these were still empty. The frosted glass door at the end led to the Traffic Superintendent's office. Next along the corridor was the typing and signals pool. Then Schwarzwald's new office. On the floor above, the colonel in charge of them all had his father's old room.

Jacob was glad he was never called up there. There was no reason. He was too lowly a functionary for that. He was a part of this machine, and liked to think that he was not a part. Once or twice he saw Mrs Stillinghurst in the city. He always avoided her. Realizing that her small income from England would not be reaching her now that the Germans were here, he sent the money she had looked after back to her. Please regard this as a small 'thank-you'. It was returned with no note. He was offended. Did she consider him as working for the Germans? One had to live. It was not his war.

Details and problems numbed time, made it pass in a neutral flow of abstractions. Could he arrange for a train from Minsk to be received at Poltava to meet the fleet of barges that crossed daily to the new resettlement camp on Goda? The train would be full. He must then send the empty train to Danzig, then onto a transit camp a little way up the coast. Here are the duplicate lists of cargo; a file copy for the Traffic Office, another to be duly stamped and receipted to Berlin. Twelve hundred names on the list; twelve cattle cars. This was a 'special' shipment. Every week there were many such movements into and out of the country, apart from the normal traffic. The number of special shipments had increased dramatically as the number of resettlement camps opening grew at the rate of one or two a week. When Jacob had suggested to Schwarzwald that, in the interests of economy, something could be found to be carried on the empty return trips, Schwarzwald had roared with laughter and hurried away to share the joke with the colonel.

Then there was the fleet of lorries and cars of the special unit led by Captain Zech to be accounted for. They were very busy. On one of his flying visits to the office, Zech had said that two 'technical' vans would be arriving soon through the docks. Would Balthus inform him immediately they were signalled to arrive.

'They'll make our work considerably easier,' he said in his pompous manner.

When Schwarzwald, sometime in the autumn, cajolingly asked him if he would not like something a little better than his present job, 'a little livelier, eh?', Jacob said, 'No thank you, Major Schwarzwald. I am quite happy where I am.' If happy was the word.

From then on Jacob was made to feel that he owed Schwarzwald a favour, an obligation that he had not honoured. Perhaps Schwarzwald was disappointed that Jacob

had shown no signs of ingratiating himself with Grandmama
Clara now that she had moved back to her northern estate;
doubted indeed that Jacob had any influence on her goodwill
at all. It was obvious that Major Schwarzwald was going to
get no help in that quarter from the grandson and he began
to direct jokes and sarcastic remarks at Jacob, gently at first,
then with an increasing malice. 'Slow as your bloody trains,
Balthus.' 'Must get on with it, Balthus. Get on with it.' He used
Jacob's surname now even when they were alone together.

Schwarzwald was not a man to be on the wrong side of.
While feeling inwardly a superior contempt for the man,
outwardly Jacob grew just a little obsequious and eager to
please. This is part of the price we have to pay, each of
us, he thought. Until they go away we have to find ways to
live.

Books. Transports schedules. Drink. A safe job with a bad
boss. A weekly whore. Avoidance of bad sights. He had found
a provisional way to live . . .

A bad sight.
He drank some more wine and found some dance music on
the wireless. But its bumpy, chirpy rhythms sounded empty
and tinnily irritating. He turned the set off.

His nerves were unsteady. He refilled the glass. The gas fire
whispered urgently. The first, the second, the third thing you
realize, he thought, is that you do not get used to bad things. It
was easier to call them *things*. He had no vocabulary to describe
them in any other way.

This morning he had had to go to the Civil Courts. One of
the civilian drivers had collided with a milkcart. A question
of compensation.

A November day. The sun winked bleakly off some high
window in the building across the street. The light flashed
randomly into the courtroom so that the magistrate looked
up irritably from his table and said, 'What is that light? Can
no one stop it? You sir.'

Jacob stood at the window.

'Lower the blind, please,' said the magistrate.

There were five people in the room; Jacob, the magistrate,
the driver, the milk seller and the milk seller's lawyer, a fat man

like an enormous pear who fiddled with his papers, blinking in the flashing light.

As his hand reached up to the ivory pull, Jacob looked down. He had not realized that the courtroom backed onto the Ghetto. The high wooden fence topped with barbed wire ran down the middle of the wide street below. On this side people walked to and fro, heavy in their winter clothes, in their comparative freedom. On the other side of the fence the street was empty, the shops windows boarded over, this morning's light snowfall undisturbed on the pavement. Jacob pulled down the white blind. The light still danced over the wall above the lawyer.

'You must pull the other blind down also,' said the magistrate testily. 'What is that shouting?'

Jacob moved to the next tall window. He looked down into a short side street that ran at right angles into the Ghetto. Soldiers had moved along the main street and blocked this near end. They were setting up a machine-gun on a tripod. Two handlers held the leads of Alsatian dogs, who sat patiently. Other soldiers, large in their winter greatcoats and helmets, like civilized bears, gazed up the street. The noise was coming from soldiers working their way up both sides of the street, beating on doors with their rifle butts, shouting, 'Out! Out!' Women and children and a few men were beginning to file out of the doorways, behind and before the soldiers. They were not all dressed in winter clothes; some had to make do with blankets round their shoulders. They carried bundles and small suitcases.

'Well? Well?' the magistrate called.

'It's a *Razzia*. An *Aktion*.' The driver had joined Jacob at the window. 'They're clearing the bugs out of the Ghetto.'

The street was filling. The dog handlers started forward, one on each side. The dogs strained forward, dog and handler disappearing into, reappearing out of each door. A huge soldier walked from the machine gun, pulling out and uncoiling a whip from his belt. The crowd bunched together in the middle of the roadway. Jacob looked at the driver standing beside him. The driver was smiling, the corners of his eyes creased in intense amusement.

Dogs and handlers dashed in and out of the small houses.

From one door a woman ran. She carried a baby. Soldier and dog pursued her, snapping at her legs. She fell onto her knees, somehow keeping hold of the bundled-up baby. The man with the whip ran up and whipped at her. She struggled to her feet and ran in front of the soldier who applied his whip strenuously, pursuing her until she joined the comparative safety of the crowd that was now being driven on by shouting soldiers, striking randomly with rifle butts and clubs at the slowest. From somewhere out of sight came a rattle of gunfire. The shouting diminished as the column, like a wounded, ragged animal, reached the end of the street, and turned out of sight at the corner. The dogs were still being taken at the run in and out of the remaining doorways, disappearing for a few seconds as the houses were searched, re-emerging, barking with excitement. At this end, the crew picked up their machine-gun and doubled up the street, past the gaping doors. The driver lowered the blind. 'Good work. Neat work,' he said approvingly, and grinned.

'Come, come, gentlemen,' the magistrate called, tapping a small gavel on his desk. 'The show is over. The Law must go on.'

4

He was sick. He had sent the girl who cleaned the apartment to the Ministry with a letter saying that he had influenza. Perhaps he had. He did not care to go out. Terrible things were happening. He did not wish to see them. He could not help seeing from his window when the Synagogue was burned.

The whole sky was a dull orange, blotting out the stars. Yellow and red flames outlined the spires and roofs between the Synagogue and his window. Yellow and red, yellow and grey and red, the flames fell away but the orange lasted in the sky. The Jews had long gone away on the train.

'We are better off without the beasts,' said Frau Hossbach, his new neighbour in the Karners' old apartment, when she came in later in the morning. 'Here – see. I've brought you some broth and some chocolate. Your maid said you were ill.'

'Most kind, most kind,' he murmured.

Perhaps he *did* have influenza. He felt guilty at remaining away from work on a pretext. A small anxiety, a small guilt in this, this . . . They, the Germans, were at war after all. One must expect . . . things. The Jews were transferred – that was German policy. He would not believe in these tales of mass killings in the forest. He had seen a killing, had he not? To imagine that men could do these things on a regular basis was impossible. The new camp on the island of Goda. The Germans could be coarse, brutal. Admittedly. Those scenes in the Ghetto. Unforgivable. But outrages, *excesses*, losses of control were bound to happen in war.

This reasoning was half convincing, it sufficed, and in the apartment he could believe as he liked.

So, perhaps it was influenza. He shivered and shook, felt weak and dizzy, conjured pains in his legs, in his chest. He coughed exploratively. He pampered himself like a child.

At this time of year evening seemed to begin about three in the afternoon. He settled himself on the sofa, a checked blanket covering him. He nestled his head against a cushion on the arm rest. His book was an English one, Hobbes' *Leviathan*. He was almost sure it was his father's copy. At last he had determined to see what interested his father in these philosophical works. To create a sense of order to shore against the world. He twisted slightly on the cushion and opened the book at random.

> . . . as Voyces grow weak, and inarticulate: so also after great distance of time, our imagination of the Past is weak; and wee lose (for example) of Cities we have seen, many particular Streets; and of Actions, many particular Circumstances. This *decaying sense*, when wee would express the thing it self, (I mean *fancy* it selfe,) wee call *Imagination*, as I said before: But when we would express the *decay*, and signifie that the Sense is fading, old, and past, it is called Memory. So that *Imagination* and *Memory* are but one thing . . .

*

There was a soft knocking on the outer door. He started. Frau Hossbach? Schwarzwald? The knocking came again. The blackout curtains were drawn. He had only the reading lamp on. He checked in the mirror; yes, he did look unwell.

He opened the door, on its newly fitted chain.

The woman stood against the light.

'Jacob Balthus?'

It was Anna, from the English Theatre.

'May I come in?' Her voice was as coldly neutral as ever.

He undid the chain.

Her swagger was if anything more pronounced, more purposeful. She swung round to face him, as if he were entering *her* apartment, her hands thrust into her winter coat.

'I cannot stay long. You are the only one who can help me with this.'

No hint of begging or beseeching, she plunged straight into her questions. He had access, did he not, to travel passes for rail travel to restricted areas? My friend Katerina – your friend – no, Katerina had not escaped from the country. She looked at him as if he were a fool to ask. Anna had been tipped off about the *Aktion* in the Ghetto and had gone to the factory where Katerina worked. Anna had taken one of her own coats and a pair of new shoes and Katerina had simply walked out with her. But she could not be hidden in town.

Anna's eyes did not waver from his.

The Germans were all over the place, searching, she said. There were denunciations, betrayals every day. Katerina must get away very soon. Friends had found her a new identity card, of a girl killed in the bombing. With luck that would get her through the city in the dark evening. But they needed a rail pass for the coast without having to go to the office, where the identity card would be properly scrutinized.

But what can she do at the coast?

Friends – always these mysterious, dangerous *friends* – had ways of getting people over to Sweden.

'You must help.'

'I don't see . . .'

'I know you don't like me. That is immaterial,' she said. 'I am asking this for Katerina's sake. You must know what will happen to her?'

'Yes, yes. Of course.' He floundered about the room, picking up a cigarette packet from the table, offering them to her, forgetting to take one himself, then taking one but not lighting it. He could not have said, then or afterwards, what was going on in his mind. We have our own internal censors. The world he had thought he had put away at arm's length, no further perhaps, but safely, had suddenly rushed in here as a black flood.

'This is the name she is using, and the destination for the rail pass.' She held out a folded piece of paper. 'Don't be afraid. I know there is some danger for you. What you have to do is to get a pass stamped and filled in. I will collect it in three days' time, on Friday evening. Then you will not see me again. I can tell her you will help?'

How could he let her say anything else?

Where is she at the moment? Can I see her? Will she know I am her benefactor? Her rescuer? These and a dozen other questions that raced through his mind were by turns foolish, dangerous, or ignoble. But he must help, mustn't he? Why couldn't the world leave him alone? Why had it chosen this one, that one, this room, this city, to enact its terrifying dramas? For this was the only way he could deal with it. To envisage himself, a scared man, attempting to be brave. What after all were they asking for? A little piece of card, nothing more. In books men tricked or browbeat generals and sentries, performed heroically with pistol and knife. But all it was – was just this. Little transactions.

'I can tell her?' Anna insisted.

I don't even like you, he screamed inside. Why can't you find someone else? It won't be so bad. You're over-dramatizing. People can always hide somewhere. After a while, things will die down. And what if Katerina was caught on the train to the coast, with the pass he had got for her? How long would it take to trace it back?

'Yes. I would be glad.' His mouth was dry. He straightened his back. 'Tell her I shall be honoured to help.'

'Thank you.' She did up the top button of her coat. 'I will come back at six o'clock on Friday evening.' She held out her hand and he shook it. Sheathed in a thin silky glove her hand was soft and warm.

'You look bloody dreadful, Balthus,' Schwarzwald boomed. He halted at Jacob's desk. 'The Reich's railway lines have ground to a standstill without you. Absolute chaos.'

He laughed loudly again and went on his way, pausing to lean over the typist's desk outside the Traffic Superintendent's office. She giggled.

Jacob watched him go into the Superintendent's office without knocking and shut the door.

He looked down at the latest sheaf of lists on his desk. So many names. So much reorganization of lives. By the side of each their occupation and date of birth: Salesman; Farm Worker; Publisher; Salesman; Plumber; without; without; without (for housewives and children); Gardener; Farmer; Economist; Tailor; Tailor; Seamstress; Housemaid; without; without; Butcher; all must go; everyone. These were going to a camp in the North; they came from the Netherlands. Others came from Russia, Poland; to the camps; to Goda island. What could he do? Why should he be asked? He had taken a job because you must have a job. He had no uniform. If you had to take a side . . . His father had been murdered. The mutilated head lolled in *his* head. What side was Max on? Katerina? Ella? His father? Was everybody to be drawn in, to be alternatively executioner and victim? His father had been innocent. He himself was innocent. Schwarzwald's laugh came through the frosted-glass door.

He had told Anna he would help because faced with a person, not an abstraction, it was impossible to do otherwise. He split the duplicate copies up, putting each into its own tray. He lifted his eyes to watch the SS corporal across the other side of the office.

The corporal sat in front of the steel cabinet in which the many passes and forms were kept. Each pass had to be issued and numbered by this man and countersigned by the Superintendent or Schwarzwald. The pile of blue-edged rail passes seemed to glow in the depth of the cabinet. It would be a simple thing to cross the room whenever the corporal went out, and to slip one in his pocket. They were not pre-numbered; the corporal stamped them with a hand-machine and entered name and number in a ledger. That was a difficulty. He would have to stamp the number then turn back the machine so there would be no gap in the ledger. That would mean there would be two cards with the same number. But unless a check of some unbelievable thoroughness was run, it would go undetected. And, if it was checked it would be believed perhaps to be a clever forgery. All the same – the danger . . .

'Dreaming?' The corporal was talking to him. 'What's her name?'

Jacob buried himself in his schedules. There was a notification that the first of Zech's 'technical' vans would be arriving at the docks next week. He stamped the lading bill, got up, and walked across to the corporal's desk. At its side was a wooden rack for inter-departmental communications. Jacob fiddled for a moment, pushing the notification into Zech's slot, looking down at the thick black hair of the corporal's head as he bent forward. Then – a miracle – the corporal rose, pushed back his chair and went out of the office without a word.

Within a second, in a dream, Jacob, his fingers fumbling at the stack, had seized one of the blue coastal passes. He transferred it to his inside pocket, feeling his heart bump, walking jerkily back across the office, astonished at this extraordinary piece of daring. He had only just sat down when Schwarzwald came out of the Superintendent's office, the last line of a joke bellowing from his mouth. There was an answering cackle from inside the office.

'Cheer up, Balthus. Don't worry – it may never happen.' In a cloud of his own good humour, Schwarzwald went sailing past Jacob's desk. 'Cheer up, old man,' he boomed. 'May never happen. Ha. Ha.'

The corporal came back and sat down without so much as looking at Jacob. For the rest of the afternoon they worked on in silence. At five the corporal yawned and stretched, his fists balling above his head. 'That's it,' he said. 'You going, Balthus?'

'No. Things to catch up on.' Jacob smiled, blushing.

'Hum?' The corporal was dismissive, disbelieving. He gathered up his papers and began to stow them in the cabinet.

Jacob did not dare to watch. Would he also put away the special numbering stamp? The sound of the cabinet being locked. The corporal left, whistling tunelessly. Jacob raised his eyes. The machine stood by the pen holder.

Five minutes later the Superintendent came out, straightening his peaked cap.

'Still here, Balthus? Tell the sentry when you go.'

His footsteps went away down the corridor.

Heart thumping, Jacob stamped the pass, then turned the machine's wheel back. He applied the rubber stamp with a dotted line for signature below the eagle straddling the swastikaed globe. He could do Schwarzwald's signature quite well. That could be added at the apartment.

Anna did not come back on Friday evening. Not at six as she had promised, nor at seven, eight, nine, nor any hour after. The weekend passed in a misery of waiting; his resolution dissolving with each noise in the street below; each tread in the corridor outside. Hobbes' *Leviathan* was of little use. Or any of the other books he picked up restlessly and almost immediately put down again. What did they say about *this*? Nothing in literature, presided over by the personally comic and personally tragic, had prepared them for this; the feeling of being at the same time impotent and threatened.

On Sunday night he burnt the coastal pass and the piece of paper with Katerina's false name on it. The end of heroism was this endless miserable expectancy. As the pass curled in its own intense life, his own life shrank so that it was small, smaller than the card, the room surrounding him, the huge world outside.

The indelible ink of the stamped number shone black on the shrunken white-grey card. He crushed it into ashes. It was after all only a ghost's. Its ghostly number, breaking up, pressed down, represented no one. No one at all.

5

'Balthus – come in.'

Schwarzwald's face was set in a scowl. Another man, small, dapper, in civilian clothes, stood beside him behind the desk. The man smiled encouragingly. Zech leaned against a filing cabinet.

'This is Herr Dollmann of the SD. He will ask you some questions. Full co-operation is essential.' The words were barked out, with no trace of the usually jovial Schwarzwald in them.

It was Monday morning. The telephone on Jacob's desk had been ringing when he came in at eight-thirty. It was Schwarzwald, ordering him to his office. Now, Balthus. Now. He sat for a moment, stunned. What was the matter? What could Schwarzwald know? Was he going to be arrested? How could anyone know? His hands shook. Question and counter-question, absurd and all-too-sane answer, tumbled in his head as he made his way along the white corridor. My hands are cold. I shall give myself away. I am a coward. What, after all, have I *done*? Why, nothing.

'Good morning, Herr Balthus.' Dollmann's voice was soft and conciliatory after Schwarzwald's. It appeared that he had a professional charm to comfort his clients. Perhaps all the stories about the SD were untrue. Schwarzwald frowned fiercely.

'I wonder . . .' Dollmann began. He opened a small notebook in his left hand and held it balanced in the palm, his right forefinger, daintily wetted at his tongue, turning the leaves at their corners. He stopped at a page. 'Are you acquainted with a woman by the name of Anna Vermehren?' The notebook closed, almost with a little sigh.

'Yes. After a fashion.' Jacob cleared his throat. 'I *did* . . . that is . . . She was a friend of friends . . . you understand. She was never a friend as such. I knew her . . . She was someone

I knew . . .' His words petered out, his voice seeming to come from somewhere outside himself.

Dollmann smiled again. Jacob warmed to that smile. He was aware of Zech studying him. He attempted to smile himself, but the effect appeared ghastly, he knew.

'Could you tell us when you last saw the woman Vermehren?'

The *woman Vermehren*. For the first time he saw his position. He must tell something approaching the truth. They had arrested her. The woman Vermehren.

'She came to see me last week. In the middle of last week.' His voice gained strength.

'How long was it since you had last seen her?'

'A year – more, two years.'

'What did she want – after such a time, if she was not a friend?'

'She wanted me to help her.'

Schwarzwald nodded savagely.

'Did you?' asked Dollmann.

'Did I?'

'Help her?'

'I told her it was outside my power.'

'What did this help entail?'

'She seemed to have some idea I could help her with a rail pass.'

'For her?'

'For friends.'

'Which friends?'

'I don't know. We did not mix in the same circles in that sense.'

'Why should she come to you? Why didn't her friends apply for passes in the normal way?'

'She knew of my job somehow in the Traffic section. She thought I could expedite matters.'

'Could you?'

'No. I have no part in that side of things. That side. My job is to handle rail and dock schedules only.'

'Did it not seem strange to you that this woman – who was not a friend – should seek you out after such a long interval and ask you to act as a sort of travel agent?'

'I suppose so. It was a surprise.'

'Did it not strike you that what she asked was for you to commit an illegal act? That the person or persons she wished to assist must be unable for some reason to legally apply for travel documents?'

'Yes, it did, frankly.' *Frankly*, was a good, ingratiating touch, he felt. 'I told her to apply through the usual channels.'

'You know that there are foolish people who through mistaken notions of "charity" or "friendship" persist in assisting enemies of the Reich. Jews, Communists . . .'

'Trash,' Schwarzwald exploded.

Dollmann went urbanely on. 'That was what the woman Vermehren was engaged in. If you thought her requests irregular why did you not report them?'

'I . . . I simply told her to go away. It did not occur to me . . .'

'No,' said Dollmann thoughtfully. 'No.' He looked steadfastly into Jacob's eyes. Jacob blinked. He felt he had done quite well, as well as he could have hoped.

Dollmann at last dropped his gaze. He examined the page of his notebook again, then closed it with a decisive snap.

'So, what you are saying is this – that Vermehren came to you because she was simply putting out feelers for those who might help in her criminal activities? That you refused her? Correct?'

'Yes.'

The worst was over. He was in the clear. He had been brave; seen it through. It was at that moment that he realized with a sickening sinking of his heart, that while Anna had quite probably exonerated him, he had succeeded only in damning her. This man Dollmann had not actually said anything of any substance, it was quite possible he was just checking on all of Anna's acquaintances; Jacob had volunteered everything. The first treason is always the hardest – they become progressively easier.

There was silence in the room. Schwarzwald and Zech stared unrelentingly at him. Dollmann studied the map that had been spread across the whole surface of the desk. 'There is just one more thing you might help us with,' he said. The tip of his right index finger gently grazed across the forest to the north of the city.

'In these woods and marshes are groups of Bolshevik-Jewish gangsters. Now, Herr Balthus, I understand from Major Schwarzwald that you had quite a lot of contact with the partisans during the Soviet occupation.'

'Well – I did. But things were quite different then.'

'Of course, of course. But it would be of the most *enormous* help to us if you could point out on the map precisely the location of the camp you knew. It is entirely possible the bandit elements are using the same sites. So – please point it out for us.' Dollmann's gesture invited Jacob forward to look down on the map.

'I hardly know . . .'

'Their camp please.'

The map was very detailed, with farms and roads and lanes and paths marked; the forest areas marked by little black fir trees, the marsh areas by tiny spiked shrubs. He could not give them any more. Particularly, he could not give them Mrs Stillinghurst. He did not know where the partisans' camp had been; somewhere, five, six kilometres north of the Stillinghurst house; a distance walkable both ways by the messengers who came from the dark orchard every night. What could he tell them? He began to panic. There was a marsh near the top of the edge of the map, north-east from Mrs Stillinghurst, passed by a single road, a path petering into it. Well away. Near the coast. He pretended to study the map, then his finger uncertainly wavered down. 'There. I think there. Of course it is different seeing a map. I cannot be wholly certain.'

They bent forward, Zech joined them. Jacob stepped back.

They began to discuss its position eagerly.

'See, there is what looks like a bald rise facing south.'

'And only the one road leading in and out.'

'I hope you are right, Balthus,' Schwarzwald glared up at him. 'I hope also you realize your position.'

'Shh.' Dollmann put a finger on his lips, his charming smile behind. 'I'm quite sure Herr Balthus realizes everything about his position. He has been most helpful.'

They turned back to the map, Dollmann seeming indolent, yawning as the other two debated how to take the marsh by surprise; how they could approach by this road *here*, go past north to *there*, strike from this unexpected direction after sealing

260

both ends of the only road, putting men here, here and here among the tiny drawn trees.

At last Schwarzwald said, 'That's it. We'll go, Zech. You don't mind me coming, no?'

Zech bent; even his great long arms had trouble as he battled, grave-faced, to fold the sail-sized sheet.

But it was in Zech's hands now, rustling and crackling, the wild-goose chase Jacob had set in motion.

'M . . . may I go now?'

'You don't want to see the results of our little expedition? But you must. I insist. No, you sit down here, Herr Balthus. Make yourself comfortable.' Dollmann's clever, comfortable smile looked like a shark's. 'Until we return.'

How could he have been so stupid? He had sent off God knows how many of their troops on this fool's errand. *This* fool's errand. He had been sitting here for hours, staring at the walls, his hands, Schwarzwald's empty desk. He had taken these men for ordinary human beings, hoping to fool them like a child fools his parents. Innocent jokes at which the adult smiles, half-amused, half-patronizing. For the first time a sense of his own light, deadly frivolity became apparent to him. Victims or victors – the people in the ghetto, the girl in the forest, his father's battered, corrupted face, Anna, Katerina, Max, Ella, the stupid worker and the Communist intellectual in the cell; Schwarzwald, Zech, Dollmann – they all lived in something called History. They had causes, ambitions, crusades, which moved them, and caused them to move others, as certainly as his invisible trains moved bodies and goods. Though that was not the right word; they were not invisible, were they? Merely out of sight. If you pretended it was all a dream – well, they entered your dream nevertheless. If you moved to escape, they followed. You could throw them off for months in the attic, for hours in the cell, but all the while they erected their great machine, regardless of you. You do not exist until we call you into being, said the machine. You are nothing. The frivolous, fluttering little soul is nothing. No. No. No. He sat hour after hour, waiting for the machine to execute the one small motion he had set going, the one revolution.

*

A soldier came in. He laid a piece of paper on the desk, glanced at Jacob, then turned the paper face down, placing a glass paperweight on it. The snow fell in the glass. The clock on the wall showed six.

The soldier left the door open. From the corridor came the clattering of feet. 'What is that?' he asked, if only to establish contact with someone.

'Party come back,' said the soldier and went out.

He looked up at the electric clock. Its face was set in a hideous bakelite octagon. A minute began to pass, the second hand moving incredibly slowly.

Footsteps in the corridor. A bellowing. Schwarzwald bulled into the office. 'Schnapps, schnapps,' he was shouting to the orderly. He swayed in the doorway. He was drunk. 'Got 'em,' he said. He sat down heavily and a blissful smile halved his large face. The chair swivelled this way and that. 'Not the partisans. They must have done a bunk. Big party of Yids. Men, women, children. Hundreds of 'em, waiting for the bandits to take them up the coast.'

Was this some trick? It was impossible. An absurd, filthy joke of Schwarzwald. There cannot have been anyone there. He had picked the spot at random.

'What do you mean?' he asked with dread.

'What do I mean? What do you think I mean?' And the violence of Schwarzwald's tone made him know that this was not a joke of any sort.

'Wh . . . what will happen to them?' He meant, what will happen to me?

'What do you think will happen, you silly bastard? What do you think?' Schwarzwald's eyes glared across the desk. 'What do you suggest? We give 'em all a ticket to Sweden, eh? Eh?' He laughed.

'I . . . I don't know.'

'No, you don't know much do you, young sir. With your rich Grandmama – who's the only reason you're not in a cell right now – and your refined Papa. Well, I'll tell you, young Balthus – get up. Get up. It's about time you went about in the world a bit, I think. It's about time you saw where your bloody trains and trucks go. Then perhaps you'll realize which side you are on. Come on. Get up. I'll show you, boy. Where people go . . .'

VI

What is the knocking?
What is the knocking at the door in the night?
It is somebody wants to do us harm.

No, no, it is the three strange angels.
Admit them, admit them.

D.H. Lawrence,
Song of a Man Who Has Come Through

I

At last a dreamless sleep, from which he came with a sweet, languorous slowness into a radiant morning. The room, out of focus, was suffused with a hazy yellow light. The strip of wardrobe mirror cast back the bed and their two humped bodies. His head sank back on the pillow. So it was true. He felt immeasurably lightened and youthful. His hands lay on the cool white sheet. The small, unintimate noises of the hotel came to him. The rattle of a trolley's wheels in the corridor. Laundry? Clank of a bucket. A voice talking in a low insistent indecipherable monotone from a radio next door.

The mass of tumbled auburn hair on the pillow beside his did not move. It was almost a shock to see a grey glint on the edge of a hair. He was going to draw her to him, wake her gently, but something held him back, some sudden sense of the ridiculousness of his position, the sense of age creeping back into his body. So he just watched the slight, gentle movements of the bedclothes as she breathed. He felt a cramp begin to ball in the calf of his right leg. The pain grew quickly. In a moment it would be agonizing. He jerked down the bed and worked his foot against the bottom board. She stirred.

It was another day. It was no longer sweet night. He was an old man.

'Julia,' he said. 'Julia . . .'

They had landed at the airport to the north of the city two days before. 'None of this was here years ago,' he had said, looking out. He gripped the arm-rest as if, at the very last, he was unwilling to leave the aircraft.

'Come on,' said Julia Wallace brightly. 'No one's going to eat you.'

She had appointed herself his shepherdess. Her father, Max, would not be flying in until the next day. 'Business. I'm afraid you'll have to put up with me. What a pity Mrs Balthus could not come with you.'

He did not tell Julia that Ella had refused to come with him. 'It is your country, not mine.' She had become morose and impatient with his excitement at returning. 'You go then. Go. But leave me here. I have enough things to do tidying up the house. No, nothing will happen again. I will be safe. Go,' then her voice had softened a little. 'Go. Be careful.'

Seated on the plane beside Julia, he was the distinguished gentleman, the dandy, the man of the world flirting with an attractive woman. The other passengers would think she was his wife, or better still his mistress. It was only when they changed flights at Leningrad and took off again across the Baltic that his anxiety returned.

The smashed-up front room. The shock of meeting Max after all the years. His stammering refusal – which sounded absurd even to himself, even as he uttered it – 'I am afraid I cannot accept your hospitality. In view of all that passed between us . . .' And that refusal swept away by Max's extraordinary charm, his almost feminine solicitude . . . 'Quite understand old chap, what was in the past. But things were not as they seemed at the time. They never are. We have all suffered in time . . .' all delivered in the new rich, rolling English gentleman's accent. 'You must, you must, Ella, Jacob, stay to dinner. I absolutely refuse to let you go . . .' And the charm had propelled them to the dinner table, to take wine. After dinner, Max had poured them brandies, in what 'I grandly call my Library.'

'The complete works of P.G. Wodehouse, Jacob. Almost a complete set of G.A. Henty. Apart from their value – well, you know about that, being in the trade – I like them. I read them. Boy's stories, the Hentys. Uncomplicated. Very English. When I came to England I asked someone to tell me who were the most typically English of writers. From them I chose these two.' He took down a book entitled *With Moore at Corunna*. 'Battles. Heroics. Simplicities in this modern world. I can relax after business with them.'

'Not my field,' Jacob said sourly.

'History, I believe – is that right?'

'Slavonica.'

'Well – if you make a living, what the hell. But history passes, Jacob. These things date. I suppose these books of mine are old-fashioned. But they have *charm*, Jacob. They speak of the old values. Now tell me – this terrible thing Julia has told me about. The attack on your home . . .'

And on and on, with Jacob finding it impossible to hate this man. Max seemed to inhabit this parody of a fruity-voiced English gentleman as surely as he had once the smartly dressed, handsome young journalist of uncertain nationality, of floating values . . .

'Are we going to get off?' Julia was saying. 'You are home again.' She stood in the aisle looking down at him, people squeezing past her towards the door.

'Do I look all right?' he asked nervously, heaving himself up.

'You look fine. Come on.' She began to be pushed along towards the exit.

'Do you know the terrible thing . . .'

She flashed a smile back at him. 'Nothing terrible. Come on.'

He let go of the seat.

Reunited with their luggage after Customs, they stood in the high, cold, glass-walled hall. A young man came hurrying across to them. 'Mr Balthus?' he said, and held out his hand. 'Ruksans. Velta Ruksans.'

Jacob blinked.

'The Committee for Patriotic Democracy. Our letter . . . ?'

'Oh yes, of course.'

Ruksans bowed to Julia. 'Mrs Balthus.'

Julia laughed, and said, no, sorry, Julia Wallace.

Ruksans put his hand to his forehead. 'So sorry. Miss Wallace. Your father . . .'

'He's coming on tomorrow's flight.'

Sprightlier, flattered by Ruksans' mistake, Jacob followed them to the glass doors. Ruksans talked in an excited, bubbling way. How honoured they were that Mr Balthus had come. Friends of his father – those who have survived . . . They cannot stop us this time. Your trouble in London. Oh yes, we heard of it. The KGB. Yes, the KGB. They had been told it was agents of the Soviets. Every now and then they try to roar, but their teeth are rotten.

Then they were all in the taxi and heading towards the city.

'I do not recognize any of this.' Jacob stared at the regimented lines of high blocks of flats that seemed to go on forever.

'The Russians. They have ruined much of this part. This is called the Proletarian district. What you would have known as the Durava.'

So all this was built on the countryside that had stretched between the old northern edge of the city and the patches of orchards and market gardens where Mrs Stillinghurst's house had been. The blocks went on and on. The only trees were new, thin and spindly on mounds of pale green grass.

'There is more traffic than I remember too,' Jacob said disconsolately. He glanced at Julia. She took his hand and squeezed it. A foolish old man.

The city was still recognizable, its needle spires and red and green tiled roofs cheered him. But still the changes irritated. The expected had disappeared, and the new and unexpected had that undistinguished tawdriness that afflicted most cities now. An air of shabbiness, like a damp smell in the air, hung irremovably about the few unaltered, narrow streets. What had been left alone had decayed. The hotel they drew up outside, the Hotel Potemkin, had once been the Imperial. The old name's ghost lingered, the stone marginally paler where the letters had been removed from the pediment above the entrance.

The service was not good. With the help of Ruksans, they had to carry their own bags to the lift. 'Miss Wallace is in 352. You are here, Mr Balthus, in 344.'

Ruksans sat on a straight, gold-painted chair against the wall in 344 and talked excitedly about tomorrow's Congress. Jacob felt tired and said he would rest on the bed.

He must have fallen asleep almost at once. When he woke the room was dark, a neon light from outside flashing red, blue, red, blue on the wall. An eiderdown had been laid over him. Someone was knocking on the door. The handle was tried. But, before he was properly awake, whoever it was gave up. When he opened the door the corridor was empty. Closing the door again he saw that a note had been pushed under it.

> Dear Mr Balthus,
>   Mr Ruksans has told me you are resting. He says that he will pick you up at 10.00 a.m. to take you to the Congress. My father has telephoned to say that he will definitely be here by tomorrow and hopes you will have dinner with us. Have a good night. I will see you for breakfast.
>
> Julia

Their coffee when it came was lukewarm. The waiter, a Russian, listened to Jacob's complaint and then walked away without comment. 'You see what they are like,' said Jacob. Julia smiled and looked round. It was plain that to her this was a great adventure.

Whatever its shortcomings the dining-room was full. A steady hum of conversation came from the other tables. Jacob was disappointed in a way to see other elderly, well-dressed, prosperous-looking men talking energetically to younger people who strained forward, their faces eager and welcoming. 'People have come from all over the world,' said Julia, her eyes shining. 'Refugees like you. From the States. France. Germany. Australia. Oh, all over.' But he felt vaguely let down; his sense of uniqueness, of the value he had put on himself in accepting this invitation cooled. He fingered the wad of papers in his inside pocket – the speech he had prepared for the Congress. All these *others*. How were they all to be fitted in? He had not actually been asked to speak – but the work he had done over the years, his father's reputation . . . Perhaps he had assumed too much. How humiliating if he had mentioned this speech to Ruksans, and then there was no opportunity for him to deliver it. He would keep quiet for now. But surely he *would* be asked?

'Listen,' said Julia. 'I have been trying to learn your language.' She tried out a few commonplace phrases on him, and he smiled, correcting her pronunciation. A pleasant game, it drew them together, was mildly, innocently erotic.

They lingered on in the dining-room, until the four or five waiters and waitresses lined up behind the long table along the wall glared hostilely at them. They moved, Julia giggling, 'They must think . . .', to a small empty lounge whose bar glinted coldly behind a locked grille. But, perhaps because of the bleakness of the room, their conversation died out here, and Jacob was glad when Ruksans came bubbling in.

'Ah there you are. Ready? Ready?' He glanced at his watch. 'I think we'd better go. I have a car outside.'

They moved through the city traffic. Jacob was beginning to feel a little more at home now, pointing out to Julia buildings he had known, bemoaning the recent concrete and glass.

Rain had begun to drizzle down when they arrived at the National Theatre. Two Russian militiamen stood on the steps, glowering at the arrivals. But inside everything was bright and busy. Everywhere on the walls were posters: FREEDOM; INDEPENDENCE. Above the wide open doors into the auditorium hung a huge green and white flag.

Happily harassed, Ruksans guided them through the crowd, introducing them. Mr Jacob Balthus – son of the late Tomas Balthus. May I shake your hand? Your father was . . . Miss Julia Wallace – *her father* is Max Wallace. Mr Balthus. My dear Balthus. Someone asked him to sign a book. 'It is about the sufferings of our nation under the Soviets.' He signed with a splendid flourish. Then they were suddenly free of the crowd and standing on its edge. 'How exciting,' said Julia. 'How good-looking your people are. How vibrant. You feel there is nothing they couldn't do.'

'This way please.' Ruksans had been replaced by another young man. 'Mr Balthus. Mrs Balthus.'

Again Jacob gave a jaunty denial, while managing to suggest that the lady was something *other* than his wife. Fortunately Julia could not understand this much of his language. With a smile she took his arm as the young man led them inside.

The choir of women in long yellow skirts and white, embroidered blouses sang *O, my Country*, the pre-war national anthem. The audience stood, linking hands along the rows of seats, joining in with the choir, their voices rising and falling away in a great joyous sob.

How brave, how brave you all are, he heard Julia saying. She still had hold of his hand. Yes, he thought, how brave we all are. The Congress had been marvellous. And yet. The speech in his pocket remained unspoken. He had not been called.

Honoured guests, as they were called by the chairman of the committee ranged along the table on stage, 'Honoured guests are with us today.' He began to read the names. Professor Ulmanis; Doctor Treschau. Jacob – he stiffened in his seat – Jacob Dauraga; Estvan Kirilian . . . Each bobbed or creaked up from their seats in the audience, bowing or waving tentatively, resettling themselves, surrounded by applause. Jacob Balthus. His name at last. He rose. Hands clapped, heads turned to view him, the applause died. The chairman went resolutely on. He sat down again. Perhaps later.

But it was their Congress. The men on the platform. Words – serfdom, pollution, tyrants, deportation, traitors, murderers, conservatives, democrats, oppressors, freedom, Freedom, Freedom, swirled in the theatre. Cheers, and clapping and stamping feet.

Jacob felt frightened for the men on the stage. This was what he had feared. An excess of freedom. We must proceed carefully, slowly, step by step. Terrible dangers. Must not provoke. Remember. Remember. Phrase by phrase the speech in his pocket crumbled.

'We will not be intimidated . . .' The voice rang from the tall loudspeakers at each side of the stage. These were good, courageous men, thought Jacob, but surely they were courting disaster? He wondered at the survival of their spirit after all these years of the Soviet regime. Perhaps the human spirit must suffer. He had suffered after all, had he not? And he took a little vain pride in the historical precedence of *his* suffering.

The speeches lasted into the early afternoon. The buffet lunch laid on for the foreign delegates was unexpectedly lavish.

'I thought – with all your shortages . . .'

'Miss Wallace's father has been most extraordinarily generous to the movement,' said Ruksans. 'Most of this stuff goes for export normally. He has many good business connections here.'

'Mr Balthus knew my father before the war. Did you know that?' Julia's face glowed.

'No – really? It is amazing how many here have discovered old friends. Relations.'

'Well, well – you are the ones who must take the credit for that,' said Jacob. 'For enabling us to return. I never thought to see this day. For years we spoke about it – but I do not think we ever expected it to come.'

'And do you intend to stay, Mr Balthus?' The question came from a slim, dark-haired young man who had appeared at his side.

'I am only here for three days in the short term, you understand. Naturally I would be glad to return at any time if I could be of service.'

'I'm sure you could.'

'But obviously I have some commitments in England.' An image came into his mind of Miss Vacik seated among the books she was so loath to sell. It seemed to belong to another world.

'And there is your wife to consider of course.' The young man did not say this in English, but smiled at Julia as he spoke. Jacob was again flattered by the assumption that she was his wife.

'I am afraid I cannot claim the great honour that would be.'

Julia had turned away, was being introduced to others by Ruksans. Jacob was surprised by a pang of jealousy. He forced himself to concentrate on the young man. Was the smile he faced now slightly derisory?

'I understand that you lived here all through the first Soviet then the Nazi occupations. You left in '44? It must be quite an experience to come back after all these years?'

Jacob watched the animation of Julia's shoulders, back, hips as she talked enthusiastically to another man.

'I wondered – my name is Berzins, I'm a journalist with the city newspaper – would you consider giving me time for

272

an interview. Of all here I think you could give some unique insights into the early struggles – and indeed your work later in London for the Government-in-Exile.'

'You are very well informed, Mr Berzins. But –' he adopted a slightly disingenuous modesty '– would anyone be interested in all that? So long ago. And you must understand we were not the *official* Government-in-Exile, in so far as there was such a thing. And could you publish it? It must be frank, you know. I could not agree to any form of censorship.'

'Our censors are too busy out looking for other jobs. It will be frank, I can assure you.'

Jacob laughed.

Berzins went on, 'I thought tomorrow morning. At your hotel? Ten o'clock?'

'Certainly. I shall be pleased to see you, Mr Berzins.'

Jacob was pleased to see that the journalist did not stop to speak to anyone else as he made his way out through the crowd. It confirmed the importance of the interview, of himself as interviewee. For the rest of the lunch he was rather grand with people, words falling with a plump portentousness as he spoke of the forthcoming liberation of his country, of freedom, the marvellous past before the war, the excellence of this salmon, this wine. He gave advice. He waited impatiently for others to finish speaking so that he could start again.

'My – you have come out of your shell,' said Julia. 'I do believe you're beginning to enjoy yourself.'

That night he dined with Max, Julia and Ruksans in one of the new privately-owned restaurants that had opened in the city.

'Mmm, excellent. Excellent.' Max was tasting the second bottle of wine. 'Couldn't get anything like this here even last year.' He looked splendid in dinner jacket and bow tie. The violet of his extraordinary eyes had darkened to a purple-brown. Discoloured grapes, thought Jacob. Age. What did he look like to Max? And as Max charmed the waiter, charmed Ruksans, charmed even his own enchanted daughter, Jacob felt the confidence of that afternoon begin to drain away.

Max's eyes gleamed merrily, his voice rumbled with contentment. He had had a good life.

273

'You have had a good life,' Jacob said out loud.

They all looked at him.

'Fortune, Jacob,' said Max. 'Good fortune. I should be grateful to be alive. I am.'

'The last time I saw you . . .'

'Yes. Extraordinary story, Ruksans, Julia. It was at your father's villa by the sea, wasn't it? That's it. I'd travelled out to see Jacob's father – wonderful man, I was honoured to be his friend. That was the first of the Russian round-ups. We all know with what tragic consequences.' Max allowed a moment's silence for tragedy. 'When I got there they'd been taken. There I was, middle of the forest, Russians all around. I remember – yes – I'd lent your father some rather confidential documents. I knew their NKVD people would be back to go over the house so I started to look for them. And who then should turn up but dear old Jacob. I was able to tip him off just in time. Um. Of course, I knew the old rogue,' the corners of Max's eyes wrinkled in amusement, 'was still with us. I'd seen your name, Jacob, in that paper that used to come out – the émigré newssheet thing. Should have looked him up years ago. But, you know what happens, you get busy and selfish. Old friends get lost in history.'

'Indeed,' said Ruksans gravely, too young for history.

The table fell silent again in memory of the lost.

'There were terrible things going on that time,' Max explained to Ruksans and Julia. 'Unbelievable.' He avoided looking at Jacob. It was as if his version of the meeting in the villa was the correct historical line to take; this was how he wished it to be regarded, this was to be the basis for whatever relationship he and Jacob were to have from now on. It was a fencing off of that area of their lives, a little patch only they knew about, now to be left alone. And – this being civilized society, the soft light of candles on the table, the stiff white napkins, the glittering wine-glasses, the broken bread – how could Jacob contradict him? Play the scene often rehearsed in his head after their meeting in England – the scene where he accused Max of treachery, of complicity in murder, torture . . . He could no longer even convince himself of Max's guilt, or decide what guilt was, or how it was to be apportioned.

Now Max was telling how he had escaped in a small boat

to Sweden in '41. His story was at the same time heroic and self-deprecating.

'But Jacob here – he must have had far worse experiences than mine. He stuck it until '44.' Max directed the spotlight back onto his old friend. 'What adventures he must have had.'

What could you talk about of those old days? The girl in the forest? The long isolation at Mrs Stillinghurst's? A ride on the back of the partisans' truck? A prison cell. And as for the terrible things . . .

'No, no.'

'Ah – you are too modest, Jacob,' said Max softly. 'Look here. Tomorrow I have a surprise for you. A little outing.'

Outside the restaurant, Max excused himself. Another appointment. His car, then the night swallowed him up.

Ruksans got a taxi for them all. Julia sat between the two men, her left leg pressing innocently against Jacob. Ruksans stayed on in the taxi when they were dropped off at the hotel.

Inside, the bar was busy. A party of German businessmen were whooping it up with loud, somehow deodorized joviality. It was not inviting, but he did not want to go up to his room alone yet. Will you allow me to buy you a drink? They stood on the threshold of the bar and looked at each other. Perhaps if you would not mind – my room . . . ? If she did not think it would, ah, compromise . . . How glorious, she laughed, and he felt rather hurt that she found his gallantry so amusing.

She seemed bubbly and happy in the lift. He wanted a drink badly and felt a semi-pleasurable, nervous anticipation at being alone with Julia for the first time since the plane.

Apologizing for the odd-sized glasses he poured out two drinks from the bottle of Johnny Walker he had bought at Heathrow. No, no, you have the large one, she insisted. He topped up the drinks with water from a white porcelain jug with blue flowers on its side. Then he perched on the edge of the bed and Julia sat facing him in the single armchair.

The whisky soothed him. He realized he was tired and was surprised to see by his watch that it was only half-past ten. Julia was full of life.

'What extraordinary, marvellous people you all are. The enormous risk . . .' What did she know of risk? She was an Englishwoman. A member of the safe bourgeoisie, Ella would have said in the old days, in love with revolution at a safe distance. A different revolution from the one Ella had admired for a time. You grow out of revolutions. He looked at Julia's long dress, her legs slanted elegantly to one side, the emergence of an ankle, a foot in a blue shoe. His look travelled discreetly up her body, to her face, her mouth talking excitedly. 'How brave you all are,' she said again.

He smiled. 'No, not brave. You would not know, could not know. How old are you, if you do not mind me asking?'

'I'm thirty-eight,' she said, with a faint hint of defiance.

He had thought thirty, perhaps a little more.

Sensing something, some sexual enquiry in him of which he was hardly aware, she said, 'I'm not an old maid or anything, you know. I have been married and all that.'

'I did not mean . . .'

'I took my own name back when the marriage ended.'

'Oh yes – I see. Tell me, my dear – I have a reason to ask – your mother? It would interest me to know who Max married?'

'She died five, five or six years back.' She was now leaning forward. She swirled the whisky gently round, looking down into the glass.

'She . . . she was from this country?'

'No – English. Daddy met her over there.'

A whole other scenario, fantasy – whatever you call these things by which the brain over the years rearranges the past – collapsed in Jacob's mind. It had been some comfort to him to be able to persuade himself that Katerina *might* have escaped with Max. That she was not one of the Jews rounded up in the forests. Not one of the names on endless lists. Her slim, small, dark ghost slipped between forest, train; millions were taken, but she slipped through. And for this day, as for every other, he invented an alternative fate for Katerina. She could not be involved in that horror, could not lie in the trench, the pit with the other white bodies; mouth, sex, full of shadow.

Julia was touching his hand, patting his hand.

'Hey, hey – what is the matter, Jacob? Jacob?'

'No, no, we are not brave.' He became aware that he was crying. 'Do you know . . . what is worse. As we get older we get worse. We become more cowardly, not less. The memories come back, you see. They have never been away. They sharpen.'

She crossed to the bed quickly, changing her glass from one hand to the other, so that she could put her arm across his shoulders.

'*Sharpen.* All these fools with their "Memories fade", their "Time heals", "It was all a long time ago". The past was yesterday. An hour ago. It will be there tomorrow. It surrounds us. Do you understand?' He took off his glasses and drew his sleeve across his eyes. 'It is not an old film. An old black-and-white film. It is *here*.'

'I understand. I understand,' she said. She rested his head against her breasts and stroked his hair. 'I understand.'

2

He washed and shaved in the small, mirror-tiled bathroom, many Jacobs stooping and straightening, bowing to and away from each other like some elderly, absurdly polite Oriental court.

Julia had gone back to her room.

When she woke, sat up and looked at him, he could see the fine lines radiating from the corners of her eyes, the slight puckering of skin and the down above her thin upper lip.

She dressed quickly, her movements jerky and embarrassed. Half-heartedly he tried to persuade her to breakfast in his room. 'No. I'll see you downstairs.' She hesitated as if she were going to say his name. She had left with only a perfunctory smile from the door, hurrying away as if ashamed.

His first, rosy awakening vanished. What after all, he thought bitterly, had she done but comfort him? An act of charity, not love. He had fallen asleep in the act of making love. At least, he could remember no climax. He was an old man. Like all women she would be quite collected in the restaurant over breakfast – they never showed any sign of the night. He decided that he could not go down. Not yet.

He jiggled the cradle of the room telephone up and down for what seemed an eternity before a man's voice answered grumpily. No, the guest could not have breakfast in his room. Reluctantly he supposed that, yes, the guest might have a pot of coffee.

Jacob dressed with more than his usual care. He turned the armchair to the door and sat down to wait for the coffee. After half an hour it still had not come. As he reached out for the telephone again, it rang.

Berzins.

He hoped Mr Balthus had passed a good night. Afraid he could not make it for ten as arranged, but he had heard that Mr Balthus was arranging to visit some of the places that had been most significant to him in the past. Perhaps . . .

'What visits? I do not understand. What are you talking about.'

'Sorry. Have I let the cat out of the bag? I was talking to your friend, Mr Max Wallace, last night. Aimed to surprise you I suppose by taking you round your old haunts in the city, and particularly to your parents' old villa by the sea. Is that correct?'

'I know nothing about all this.'

Berzins rattled on. 'Wonderful opportunity to combine our chat with some photographs. Tell you what, what do you say that we meet at the villa – just north of Poltava? About one? Mr Wallace said that's okay. Okay?'

'Really – I don't know . . .'

'That's fine. One o'clock. The villa. I look forward to it.' Berzins rang off.

He lit his fifth cigarette of the morning. Max appeared to have taken charge of his life once more. The coffee arrived. It made you nervous. Too much coffee. He drank it greedily. He had been born nervous. What else could anyone be? Happy? And all at once the sweetness of Julia's body came back to him and he knew she would be the last. The feel of her body possessed him. Why weren't men content just forever to languish in the embraces, to wake among pillows and hair, to hear the thunderous rocking – like a train running – of the bed's headboard against the wall; the anonymous flap-flap-flap of the hotel bed; the soft jingle-jangle of the brass bed? Because all things decay. What else in God's name is there? The only true forgetfulness.

What was the purpose of this troublesome memory? Memory should be abolished. Or, rather, only a few, selected memories be left. As a photograph album is weeded. Taking out ugly portraits of ourselves; discarded wives; unflattering views of our children, the places we have visited, leaving only those that strangers may admire. Ah, how sweet – what a pretty place! Where is it? Promise you will not tell. He sat and smoked and began to turn Julia's act of charity into a seduction by himself. He eliminated first his tears; he lowered the lights; invented the words he should have said; prolonged his love-making past sleep. There were three loud, confident knocks on the door.

'Come in.' His voice was tiny. He cleared his throat. 'Come in. It is not locked.'

'Jacob. How very elegant you look,' Max boomed in his unnaturally natural English gentleman's voice. He had on a grey suit and a tie that might be mistaken for that of one of the Guards' regiments. 'Glad you're ready. Come to take you out. Understand that reporter chap Berzins told you all about it. Damn fool. He's meeting us at the villa, you know that? With a photographer and all the works.'

'Happy childhood memories?' said Jacob coldly.

'Something like that.' Max's smile seemed buried in his face. 'Ready? I have my car outside.'

'There are other memories I have, Max. And bad dreams. Sometimes you do not know where to sort the dreams from the reality. What some people call the reality. I do . . . I do think you might have consulted me about all this.'

Max held the door open. 'Oh Jacob – I *know*. I do know. Your feelings. But, come – it will mean such a lot to people. When they read of your adventures. These people have invited you, Jacob. You must do your bit. They believe in you. They are the future. Come.'

The car was too large and too warm.

Once inside the forest everything was familiar. It seemed to him for one moment that he had never been away, and then that an abyss opened out in the sunlight outside the car's windows.

Some of the old villas had been freshly painted. Trees had been cleared before them, the front yards tarmaced. As they slowed round a bend a TV flickered in a room. But other houses had slumped into decrepitude; here a roof with tiles missing; there a shattered chimney; one with broken windows and lace curtains fallen down, making what looked like a huge, filthy spider's nest.

The villa must be near. With a sort of horror he recognized a white marker stone set in the verge. He clenched his fists in his lap. He looked down and was shocked by the appearance of his hands, by their age; the almost transparent skin, the brown liver spots on the backs.

They slowed and turned abruptly off the road. Was this the old, bumpy track? It had been re-surfaced; they glided between the trees.

'Are we there?' he asked breathlessly.

It was as it had been, and it was not. The window frames were painted deep green. Telephone wires led from the end gable. The trees had been cut back to make a larger yard. But the essential geometry, the underlying structure of the past persisted.

A big man with a camera hung round his neck and a photographer's black case slung from one shoulder came out on the verandah. He left the door into the house open, and lifted his hand as if giving a signal to someone inside rather than greeting the newcomers in the car. He came down the steps as they stopped.

'I . . . I do not wish you to come in with me, Max. I do not wish that.'

'As you like.' Max's eyebrows arched in surprise, but then the famously charming smile spread slowly across his mouth. 'As you like, old man.' He consulted his watch. 'It's now a little after eleven. I'll pick you up at about one. All right? Then we can have lunch in the city.'

'I don't think that I shall be here for that long.'

'No? I think that Mr Berzins has quite a lot of questions to ask you, Jacob. You'll be surprised how time goes.' Then Max's face for the first time grew serious. 'Just one thing, Jacob – you know these journalist chappies – think before you speak. Things are still very sensitive over here.'

Was Max pleading with him not to betray *his* past?

Berzins had appeared on the verandah now. Jacob got out of the car without replying to Max. The procession of men entered the house; Berzins, Jacob, the big photographer following. Max watched them disappear inside, his finger drumming on the wheel. Then he reversed the car smartly away.

They went straight through to the back room. Both of the old bedroom doors were shut. All the old furniture had gone from the kitchen.

The walls painted white. Steel sink. New, cheap-looking pine cupboards. The window, that window he had loved to sit by at breakfast, the window that slanted outwards held on its notched stick, that window had changed; it was smaller, with a view of the forest through the glass criss-crossed with wire.

A plain pine table. Chair behind. A foolscap box file. Chair in front. Their steps were loud on the wooden tiled floor. Berzins busy, purposeful, sat behind the table. 'Please take the other chair, Mr Balthus.'

But Jacob stood. He felt cold. 'I have changed my mind,' he said. 'I do not think this is a good idea. We must talk somewhere else – if you still wish it. There are too many memories. It is upsetting for me.'

'Would you like a drink? That will perhaps make you feel a little better. A drink for Mr Balthus.'

The big photographer was closing the door. Then he went to the cupboard at the sink and took out a bottle and one glass.

'Whisky? I understand that is what you drink, Mr Balthus. A large one?'

'Well – I will have your drink.' Jacob sat down. 'Then can we go back to town? It is cold in here.'

'A little difficult . . . I'm afraid we have no transport at the moment. Until Mr Wallace arrives.'

'Then how did you get here?'

'Colleagues. They will pick us up later.' Berzins pushed the tumbler of whisky nearer. 'Do have your drink. Perhaps that will warm you a little.'

Jacob took a pull at the whisky. It went down quickly. The photographer leaned over and refilled the glass, leaving the bottle on the table. He went and sat down behind Jacob, by the door.

'I suppose I must make the best of it,' Jacob said crossly. 'I must say, your arrangements are not of the best, Mr Berzins. I thought this was to be in the nature of a sight-seeing tour. It is not especially pleasant for me to be stuck here.'

'Mixed emotions? I understand.'

'I do not think, with all due respect, that you could possibly understand, Mr Berzins.' Jacob drew his overcoat around him and looked again at the room. It seemed smaller and meaner than he remembered, robbed of life. 'Strange. I hadn't thought about it before but I suppose that I must still own this house. Or was it expropriated, like everything else, by the Soviets? Perhaps one day we may persuade them to disgorge every-thing they have stolen. Sooner than they think – what do you say? Who are the so-called owners of this place now?'

'As you say, it is owned by the State.'

'No. I mean, who actually lives here?'

'They are away.'

'They do not mind – us making ourselves at home?'

'They don't mind.'

There was something not right about this whole situation. What was that Ruksans had said? There was no country without traitors. Security. He was an important man now. Self-importantly, he said to Berzins, 'I think that as long as we are stuck here you may as well ask your questions. Take your photographs. But before we begin, I should ask to see your credentials. Do you have something like – I don't know what they call them – a Press card? Something of that sort?'

Berzins smiled and leaned forward, his fingers caressing the edges of the box file. 'Ah, there you have me, Mr Balthus. Time to be honest. To get down to business.'

'What do you mean? Are you a journalist? Or what are you?'

'We thought this more discreet than inviting you to headquarters.'

'What is this charade? I insist upon leaving at once. Please ring for a taxi.'

The photographer had got up from his chair and stood blocking the door.

'This is outrageous.' Jacob got to his feet. 'You have tricked me into coming here. I insist upon leaving.'

'Sit down, Mr Balthus.' Berzins' voice was harder. 'I must remind you that, whatever your friends may say, we are still in the Soviet Union and that we have certain rules and regulations.'

'You are one of their policemen, I suppose.'

'A sort of policeman,' said Berzins sardonically. 'We would like you to help us.'

'You cannot intimidate me.'

'What did you expect – a torture chamber?' Berzins laughed. 'We leave those things to the Chinese and the South Americans now. Every state, I suppose, employs certain types who will do certain things for them. Things that civilized gentlemen like you and I could not bring ourselves to perform. We did not think such treatment appropriate in your case. Another drink?'

'And I suppose that Max – my old friend, Max – is still one of your men? Your agent?'

'Men? Agents? You are too old-fashioned, Mr Balthus. Max Wallace is one of those men the world needs. One of the lubricants that help everything slide along. He would not be of anything like the same value as an *agent*. Invisible ink, dead-letter drops, codes – all that nonsense. No, Max is a merchant. He trades between systems. He can talk to Ministers in London and to Ministers here. He oils the wheels, and his own into the bargain. He is necessary. No, Max Wallace does the sensible thing having a foot in both camps. That is not treachery.'

'If it is not treachery, what is it?'

'Perhaps you can tell me, Mr Balthus. Take Julia, his daughter. There is a real idealist for you. She has had contacts for the last year with the so-called independence and freedom movement. Why, she even regards you as a hero.'

Jacob glared at him, then, his voice thick, said, 'This country, my country is fighting for democracy. True democracy. And there is nothing you can do to stop that.'

'We have no wish to *stop* it, but to *manage* it. True democracy – there's an interesting concept. Don't be so naïve. Every society has its leadership class. Their first duty is to protect themselves – otherwise how can they lead? You think anyone has clean hands? The Christians burned each other for a thousand years. The British Empire stole nations to build its prosperity. The United States was built on the slavery of the Negro and the genocide of the Indian. We have barely started our own revolution in historical terms, and is it all now to be brought to an end? Do you want to see the world reduced to warring tribes again? The Balkan states are already at each others' throats. Do you want the Hungarians at war with the Romanians? A reunited Germany flexing its muscles? A fundamentalist Muslim empire stretching from China to Turkey? The Pamyat fascists to take over in Moscow with their promises of pogroms against the Jews? Do you want such people to have control of our nuclear weapons, for God's sake? Because if any of these scenarios come to pass you will see such blood, Mr Balthus, that you will be down on your knees praying for Stalin to return.' Berzins stopped; he sighed heavily. 'The world may break up, Balthus. It is not a matter of reform but of containment. Things must be managed.'

'And you are to be the managers?'

'We are . . . Do you think we are simple-minded, or something?' Berzins tapped the box in front of him. 'Do you know what I have in here? Would you be interested to know that for all the years of your Government-in-Exile, from 1945 to your own retirement, every single detail of your activities was known to us, followed by us, sometimes indeed controlled by us.'

Jacob felt sick. 'That would be impossible,' he blustered. 'They – we – were all good patriots. Why, all of those men lost someone under your filthy regime. It would be unthinkable.'

'Simply because you never thought of it?'

'Our security was of the highest.'

'Ah, yes – your contacts with the British Secret Service. Your *agents* here . . .'

'We did not tell the British everything.'

'Just as well perhaps. But it made no difference.' Berzins flipped back the top of the box file. 'I'd like you to take a look at these.' He dealt out papers along the table, in front of Jacob.

Jacob remained sitting stiffly upright.

'Look,' said Berzins.

'What are they?'

'Look.'

Photographs of letters, pages of minutes, reports from their agents. All of them would have passed through his hands. The work of thirty years laid out in front of him. Berzins went on dealing the papers out.

'They . . . they must be forgeries,' Jacob stammered. 'Or you have stolen them from my house in my absence here. These are anyway old papers. What use are they to you? You made one attempt on my house in London – if your thugs have returned . . . my wife, Ella. For God's sake – we are old people.'

'The demonstration made in London was aimed not at you, but at your wife.'

'My wife. What has she to do with it?'

'Don't be ridiculous.' Berzins laughed. 'You didn't give so much thought for your wife last night perhaps.'

'How dare you.'

'No matter.' Berzins swept a hand over the papers. 'No, these were all received contemporaneously, very shortly after the dates on them. We kept well in touch, you see.'

Jacob was silent, looking down again at the papers on the desk, the thick pile still in the box.

'You really have no idea, Mr Balthus? Where they came from? Come, use your intelligence. Think.'

Jacob did not want to think. All at once, he *knew*.

'Perhaps this will help.' Berzins made a signal with his hand. The photographer got up and opened his black case. He took out a small cassette player and went over to plug it into one of the points at the side of the sink. He placed a tape in the machine, snapped the lid shut, and looked over to Berzins.

'Play.'

The voice, tinny, distorted through the cheap speaker, was unmistakably Ella's. She spoke in German:

'. . . for instance to supply a list of all editors and journalists throughout the country.'
'To whom?'

The questioner sounded to be a young woman, her voice cool and supercilious.

'I reported to Max Sawallisch. He was my senior at the agency. He introduced himself as my cell leader.'
'What was the purpose of the list?' *
'To identify those who might be useful. To see who was friendly to us.'
'What of those who were not friendly?'

A pause. The tape hissed.

'To indicate those also.'
'Were any other requests made to you?'
'I cannot quite remember.'
'Lists of other categories?'
'Essers.'
'SRs? Social Revolutionaries? Emigrés from the Soviet Union?'
'Yes. Socialists, Trotskyites. Members of all political parties. Catholics. Protestants.'
'All those classed then as counter-revolutionaries?'
'Yes. Then. Things change.'
'Did this include Jacob Balthus?'
'No.'
'Why not?'

286

'He was simply not that important. We were not collecting . . . I think that he may have left the Government service by then.'

'His father, Tomas Balthus?'

'He did not come in my range. It was just gossip. Low-grade intelligence. I was no Mata-Hari.'

'You were told to remain underground. Not to appear as a member of the Party?'

'That was difficult. But there was no reason to suspect me. Most of the people I mixed with were socialists of a sort.'

'Did you realize that the lists you helped compile were later used for arrests and deportations?'

Ella's voice sharpened.

'Please allow me to say this. Those were different, difficult days. Then we – I – wanted to do everything we possibly could to help the Revolution, to assist the Soviet Union. Things were different then.'

'You had no doubts.'

'Not until the Nazi-Soviet Pact. That shook us all. Max explained it as an act of expediency. To win time in the war against Fascism.'

'Did you believe this?'

'I'm not sure . . .'

'You lived at this time with Balthus? How did you meet him?'

'Socially.'

'You were not instructed to make his acquaintance by Max Sawallisch because Balthus's father was in the Foreign Service?'

'No . . . it may have been. At the start.'

'You went to live with him even though he was not a comrade?'

'After the Pact I was not so interested in who was a comrade.'

'You liked him?'

'Yes.'

'Did you report on him?'

'No . . . I may have passed on gossip I heard.'

'After the Soviet Union absorbed the Baltic republics – you were asked to carry on your work?'

'Yes.'

Ella's voice sank to a whisper.

'You became an informer for the NKVD?'

'You do not understand the situation then . . . I was not a professional . . . I was reprimanded. Threats were made . . .'

There was no response from the questioner.

'Evidently I was insufficiently zealous. I was not reporting enough. Every other person seemed to be an informer – most of them unwilling. When the first big deportation happened they came for Jacob. They swept me up. I was almost grateful.

'You were deported to the Soviet Union?'

'To a camp for Poles. It was very hard.'

'You were there till '44?'

'They let the Poles go then.'

'The NKVD approached you before you left?'

'I was told to keep my mouth shut. The man reminded me that my family was still in Poland and that they would soon be liberated by the Red Army.'

'They asked nothing more of you?'

'I thought *that* was at an end. I wound up in a DP camp in Germany.'

'There you met Balthus again?'

'Yes . . . We were exhausted . . . all of us. Any survivor was a friend. I wanted to get to England – those places were no holiday camps. He had contacts.'

'So you went with him to England? Married him?'

'Yes.'

'Did you carry on your work for the Party?'

Pause.